Of EMPIRE
AND ILLUSION

or the manuscript as it sat August 27, 1987

BOOK ONE

JR HAZARD

PAGE PUBLISHING, INC.
Conneaut Lake, PA

First originally published by Page Publishing 2021

ISBN 978-1-6624-2089-4 (pbk)
ISBN 978-1-6624-2090-0 (digital)

Printed in the United States of America

"To Mom—
This truly was our thing"

Introduction

My thoughts may be of little consequence, but I feel obligated to advance my own sentiment regarding the words that follow.

People are often judged in glimpses. Moments. Scenes. The truth is unknowable. And still we guess. And guess.

I hope you're horrified by this work, yet still able to contextualize the arcs of those involved. Actions are the endpoint. The answer, but not the formula. The destination without the trip. The entirety is relevant, not as an excuse, but as an experiment. An attempt to answer "Why?" for the rest of us, a wretched tribute to the victims.

I have tried to understand these individuals, truly understand, but please know the depictions are imperfect. Despite the commitment, I have heard only snippets of their lives often scored by those with various axes to grind, legitimate or not. What I have found are sporadic, far flung breadcrumbs and I apologize they are not the precise clues and confident conclusions of other storytellers. In truth, I'd say I have no indisputable answers at all. Just a picture, drawn in the prose of a flawed man and his flawed knowledge. It is as accurate as I could ever hope to be.

My belief in the story, in its essence, is sincere. I have looked many of these men in the eye. Some I deemed villains, liars, and beasts. Others, more trustworthy than clergy. A binary discussion, assigning simply black or white, is a stunted reading of these individuals, the death of "Why?". The color black is an unintelligible void, and white, an incoherent scream, each lacking the constructive facets shrouded in the other. Only through shades of each is there an understanding of reality, any conception of an image. And so, I've sought them, these violent shades of gray.

JR Hazard

Giordano Family, circa 1973

Leadership

Alphonse "Mr. Al" Giordano: Born 1908 in Capaci, Sicily. Boss of the Giordano Crime Family.

Phil "Buffalo Books" Scozzari: Born 1923 in Buffalo, NY. Underboss to Don Giordano.

Vincenzo "Papa Vic" Palmieri: Born 1900 in Castellammare del Golfo, Sicily. Longtime *caporegime*.

Nicodemo "Nicky Six" Pisani: Born 1930 in Brooklyn, NY. Enforcer, *caporegime*.

Pietro "Petey Fingers" Caltagirone: Born 1921 in the Bronx, NY. Racketeer, *caporegime*.

Giacomo "Joey Jugs" Poletti: Born 1921 in the Bronx, NY. Racketeer, *caporegime*.

Soldiers

Anthony "Tony Special" Maceo: Born 1942 in Brooklyn, NY. Soldier in Vic Palmieri's crew.

Vito "Stripes" Maceo: Born 1941 in Brooklyn, NY. Soldier in Vic Palmieri's crew.

John "Trigger" Giordano: Born 1941 in Brooklyn, NY. Soldier in Nick Pisani's crew, son of Alphonse.

Paulo "Paulie" Panzavechia: Born 1930 in Queens, NY. Soldier in Nick Pisani's crew.

Vincenzo "Vinnie" Damiani: Born 1922 in the Bronx, NY. Soldier in Petey Caltagirone's crew.

Nicodemo "Nico" Catalanotte: Born 1923 in Jersey City, NJ. Soldier in Petey Caltagirone's crew.

Ricardo "Ricky One" Caruso Sr.: Born 1922 in Brooklyn, NY. Soldier, serving time for assault, racketeering.

Sammuzo "Sammie" Palmisano: Born 1930 in the Bronx, NY. Soldier in Petey Caltagirone's crew.

Associates

Benedetto "Benjie" Maceo: Born 1952 in Brooklyn, NY. Associate reporting to Vic Palmieri.

Ricardo "Ricky Two" Caruso Jr.: Born 1946 in Brooklyn, NY. Associate reporting to Petey Caltagirone.

Adam Landau: Born 1926 in Brooklyn, NY. Former lawyer, current board member of Clearwater Investments.

Calcedonio "California Phil" Roselli: Born 1925 in the Bronx, NY. Associate reporting to Phil Scozzari.

Gerlando "Jerry" Turnino: Born 1910 in Tusa, Sicily. Owns Jerry's Place in Brooklyn, a Giordano hangout.

Giacomo "Joe-Joe" Tessaro: Born 1953 in Brooklyn, NY. Associate reporting to Johnny Giordano.

Jimmy the Driver: Born 1948 in Philadelphia, PA. Drives privately for Don Giordano and Adam Landau.

Angelo Butero: Born 1940 in Queens, NY. Associate reporting to Joe Poletti.

Ernie "Millions" Nocellaro: Born 1931 in Staten Island, NY. Associate, owns the Onyx in Queens.

Marc "Markie" Darrieux: Born 1964 in Brooklyn, NY. Nephew of Petey Caltagirone, runner for Ricky Caruso Jr.

Relations

Kiara "Carrie" Giordano: Born 1945 in Brooklyn, NY. Daughter of Alphonse, fiancée of Bobby Guiffrida.

Cristiana "Cris" Giordano: Born 1916 in Palermo, Sicily. Wife of Alphonse.

Gina "Jennie" Giordano: Born 1950 in Brooklyn, NY. Daughter of Alphonse.

Ariana "Ana" Maceo: Born 1946 in Burlington, VT. Wife of Tony, mother of Carmine.

Carmine Maceo: Born 1965 in Brooklyn, NY. Son of Ana and Tony Maceo.

Sonia Pisani: Born 1941 in Queens, NY. Wife of Nick Pisani.

Oscar Giordano: Born 1924 in Capaci, Sicily. Brother of Alphonse.

Regina Andreotti: Born 1949 in Dunkirk, NY. Girlfriend of Johnny Giordano.

Marietta "Mary" Caruso: Born 1921 in Sciacca, Sicily. Mother of Ricky Caruso Jr., wife of Rick Sr.

The Others

Frank "Frankie Changes" Capello: Born 1918 in Brooklyn, NY. Boss of Capello Family.

Charles "Charlie" Guiffrida: Born 1917 in Montelepre, Sicily. Underboss to Capello, father of Bobby.

Bruno "Bobby" Guiffrida: Born 1945 in Little Falls, NY. Soldier in the Capello Family, fiancé of Carrie.

Joe "The Lever" Pisciotto: Born 1920 in Naples, Italy. Boss of the Pisciotto Family.

Cesare "The Emperor" Provenzano: Born 1892 in Pozzillo, Sicily. Boss of the Provenzano Family.

Salvatore "Sally Boy" Lucania: Born 1912 in Lercara Friddi, Sicily. Boss of Lucania Family, jail from 1965.

Samuzzo "Sammie" Calabrese: Born 1946 in Brooklyn, NY. Capello associate reporting to Charlie Guiffrida.

Det. Andrew Clayburgh: Born 1931 in Ithaca, NY. Police since 1951; Homicide, 19th Precinct.

Det. Brady Murdock: Born 1941 in Brooklyn, NY. Police since 1963; Homicide, 19th Precinct.

Capt. Braden Quinn: Born 1925 in Staten Island, NY. Police since 1945; Captain, 19th Precinct.

Henry Dalton: Born 1906 in Harrisburg, PA. President Manhattan First, board member Clearwater Investments.

Sean Whelan: Born 1945 in Queens, NY. Bartender at The Blue Raven.

Kay Dedrick: Born 1947 in the Bronx, NY. Service manager at The Blue Raven.

Patricia "Patty" Uhlhousen: Born 1930 in Madison, WI. Office manager, 19th Precinct.

"Gloves": Hitman.

Frank Ramsey: Born 1945 in Brooklyn, NY. Reports to Neil Burke, enforcer.

Neil Burke: Born 1931 in Brooklyn, NY. Leads Brooklyn gang the Irish 48s, close with the families.

August 12, 1983, at 10:15 a.m.
Sing Sing Prison in Ossining, NY
"The whole lifestyle works on you, every day like raindrops..."

His nametag said he was the Corrections Administrator. The rest of the prison staff were wearing brown-on-darker-brown uniforms, but the Administrator was wearing a blue suit cut close around his hips with a red tie. He read from his clipboard, "Mr. Usenko". A squat man with broad glasses, a briefcase, and a pair of well-worn tennis shoes jumped to answer him. The Administrator smiled politely. "This way, sir."

The two stopped short of a metallic door patinaed by its years, and the Administrator called out for an invisible doorman, "Open! Visitation!" There was a slight pause before a buzzer sounded and the lock clicked free. Mr. Usenko's well-dressed escort pushed through the door, his heel clicks proceeding them down the hall.

"I know what you're doing," the Administrator said as they walked, "but I don't know what you're looking for. There's nothing worth learning about this man, his friends. They are just black hearts with sob stories. And you're going to help them spread their message."

"What is their message?" Usenko asked, nearly jogging to keep up with his escort's strides.

"Hate and violence. It's all they know."

Usenko smiled. "I will note your objection."

The pair continued farther until they faced a gray door with red numerals and a small window. Usenko peered through at an angle to remain mostly hidden from anyone on the other side. He recognized his subject waiting quietly.

The Administrator's lip curled unpleasantly, and he motioned toward the door. "He's waiting for you," he teased.

"I know," Usenko said, waiting still another moment. The steel handle burnt cold to his touch, but he forced his fingers to curl, tensed them, tugged the door free. The room was so white and the lights so bright he needed several seconds before the inmate came into focus and he could take his seat.

"It's good to finally meet you," Usenko said over a handshake.

"Cigarettes?" the inmate asked, his voice little more than a hoarse grumble.

Usenko edged his chair closer to the table. "Um…yes, I did. They told me you smoke Marlboro Red." He pulled two packs and a lighter from his briefcase.

"Much obliged." The inmate lit a cigarette and leaned his chair back on two legs. The chains on his wrists were fastened to the table, but they were long enough; he still enjoyed a good deal of movement. "What do your friends call you?" he asked. "I want to be your friend."

Usenko pushed his glasses up the bridge of his nose. "My closest friends just call me V."

The inmate found the name amusing. "Interesting…in your letters, V, you said you're writing a book?"

"Yes. I want to tell your story." V reached into his briefcase again, this time for a tape recorder. He set it on the table.

The inmate glanced at the recorder and then back to his visitor. "So, it's about me?"

V struggled to read the subject's mood, his eyes were too dark and calm. *I have come too far to be shy.* He snapped the record button down and watched the tape begin to spin through the plastic window on top. "I think," V said, "it will be about the impact you and men like you have had on New York."

The inmate sat forward, shoulders now over the table. "So, you think we've had an impact?"

"A great deal. And the more stories I hear, the more I know that to be true."

The inmate examined his cigarette, the smoke pluming from its orange tip. "I'm not the first person you've talked to then?"

"No. You are the fourth." V passed him a scrap of paper with the names of the others scribbled in pencil.

"Did you record them?" the inmate asked as he read.

"Yes."

He tossed the scrap on the table for V to retrieve. "Not what I would call star witnesses."

"Are you my star witness?"

The inmate smiled. "Depends on your questions, V."

"Well, first, if possible, I'd like to establish a few basic facts and your relationship to them. Can you tell me about *the Mafia itself?* The history of the organization?"

"It's *La Cosa Nostra,* not mafia. The word 'mafia'," the inmate said, pointing at the bare white walls, "has been perverted, demonized, used to justify centuries of racist bullshit. I don't use that word."

"Sorry," V said, hands surrendering. "What did *Cosa Nostra* look like when you first became involved?"

"Powerful."

"Who was powerful?"

The inmate hesitated, his eyes on the wall as he settled into his chair. "The Families. Originally five of them in New York, but by the time I became involved, there was basically four." He talked with his hands and the names allowed for a lot of activity. "Pisciotto, Provenzano, Giordano, and Capello Families, named by the Feds, eventually anyway, for the men who led them, the Bosses. Lucania was in jail when I came up, and the other Families distrusted his guys, so they were never around with us then. Those four Families, though, they had real power and they seemed to get stronger with each passin' day. Everythin' they wrote in the papers, it was mostly true. We ran shit."

"Can you describe what that looked like? *Running shit?*"

The inmate's hair was mostly gray, but you could see resilient splashes of color clinging to the sides. Even his arms, dark and muscular and tan, were besotted by splotches right up to the sleeves of his jumpsuit. "We ran shit like martial law. Don't pay us? We hurt you. We come to your house, sit in your family room, sell your car, bust your jaw, extort your employer, threaten your friends, all until we got what we needed. Politicians, judges, unions, cops. The FBI wouldn't even admit our organizations existed because they couldn't beat us. The FBI kept tellin' everybody they was making us up, even when we were bigger than US Steel. We controlled billions in that fuckin' city."

"With the threat of violence?"

The inmate laughed. "Yeah, with the threat of violence. That's the only way anybody controls shit."

"I just want to make sure I understand."

"You can ask me as many questions as you want. You're not gonna understand." The words came out more aggressively than the inmate intended. He apologized. "I'm not trying to be difficult anymore."

"I can only promise to *try* to understand," V said. His subject was becoming more comfortable. It was the same with the others. They wanted to talk about it.

The inmate distracted himself with the front of his jumpsuit, flicking at imaginary spits of ash on the black numbers across his chest. "When you grow up as poor as we were, there's only a few ways to make it out," he said, waving the ember of his cigarette like a sparkler, "and I mean really fuckin' make it out. I'm not talkin' about you're a fuckin' manager at the McDonald's two counties over. I mean really make it. With the big house and the hot wife and the expensive car." He hit the cigarette and coughed into his hand. "You either do it by startin' a company or learnin' finances, years of school whatever…or you *take it*. You just up and take it. You become a gangster, and if you're Italian, that's a *mafioso*." He held his two hands in front of him as though comparing their weight. "When you're thirteen and you're bigger than the other kids, bein' a *mafioso* seems easier. And the whole lifestyle works on you, every day like raindrops, until one day you start payin' attention and by then you're all wet. You wake up with the shit," he counted on his fingers, "you eat with it, you go to sleep with it, you kiss your wife with it…it works on you. *Cosa Nostra*…and I had it for a long time. *That feeling*," he said with a flourish that ashed his cigarette. "It's crazy to look back and realize that. But when it's finally missing, you can see where it was. Even in the old pictures we had around the house. I can see it was always there."

V scribbled a few hurried notes on a legal pad. He probably wouldn't be able to read them later. "What were your parents like? You said you were poor growing up?"

"Yeah, but no more than the other kids. My ma had a job for most of it at least, which not everybody could say. She was worried at first when I started runnin' around, probably the whole time actually, but I never was. Everyone I hung around thought the same way I did. None of us wanted to be crumbs, civilians, saps. Where's the freedom in that?"

"And you were involved with Alphonse Giordano?"

"I first met him when I was still in elementary school. He was beloved in our neighborhood."

"But he ordered murders?" V could not make eye contact for the answer, but instead focused on the tip of his pencil, hovering an inch above the paper.

"Yeah, he did."

V's hand set the pencil to motion. "And you carried these out?"

"Some of them. Yeah."

"And you were involved with the apartments? The ones on Park Avenue?"

"Yeah. I was involved."

V tried to smile. "Not poor after those I guess?"

The inmate matched V while he searched the lines of the man's face. "I made millions, right? Just ask the prosecutor, he'll tell you."

V accepted the diversion. "Did you enjoy working for Don Giordano?"

The inmate paused, hit his cigarette, and coughed again. "We had rough times like anyone, but it was better than schleppin' my ass to some bullshit job forty hours a week. I didn't love it *all*," he said, letting the final word drag out, "but I loved being a gangster for a long time. Right up till the end."

"And when, do you think, you really became a gangster?" V asked, the curiosity now beyond his control.

Something flashed across the other man's face, but he stifled it before V could get a sense of what the first reaction might have been. Gathering himself, the inmate slowly brought his eyes level with V's. They were as calm as before but seemed to radiate heat, simmering in the white lights. "One of the old men used to tell us," the inmate began, his hoarse tone filling the room, "he'd say, 'Kid, a gangster is just a fella who tries to get money and power from those who already have it.' By that definition, we were born gangsters."

PART ONE

...AND THE PURSUIT OF MONEY

One morning in May of 1973
Manhattan First Banking Group in Manhattan, NY
"It was either him or the mayor. It depended
on what you wanted done."

Adam Landau sat in the waiting room outside Henry Dalton's office and marveled at its pretentious design. He wondered if Henry inherited it from some past bank president or if he had been involved directly. He wondered what hubris might boil beneath the banker's shell. *Or maybe I don't.*

The ceiling of the room felt unnaturally high, close to twenty feet, and was ornamented by a sparkling crystal chandelier. A rounded black desk hid the fit build and attractive dress of the secretary but not her necklace with the diamond centerpiece. Adam guessed the diamond was a product of an off-hours friendship with Mr. Dalton. *No matter though, this is not the time.* The office itself was located behind two heavy wood doors stained dark brown and accented with red leather and golden studs. Dalton's nameplate and title were displayed across their face and twinkled against the issue of the chandelier. The whole of it was enough to put Adam in a disagreeable mood.

Inside was no less of a spectacle. Dalton's office windows were eight feet high and bathed the entire room in natural light despite clouds shadowing the city here and there throughout the morning. His desk (dark, dense, and ornamented) held the center of the room, adorned by antique lamps with yellow bulbs. Henry sat behind it when Adam entered, the man's jacket slung over his chair and his tie falling loose from an unbuttoned collar.

"I was pleasantly surprised to see you on my schedule today," Henry said, standing to pour two snifters of brandy. "It's good to see each other outside the boardroom for a change. It can be such a serious atmosphere in there."

"I call us 'the peacocks' to my wife," Adam said, accepting the drink and a chair. "We treat our pocket squares like plumage."

Dalton chuckled. "We are a sensitive group of birds though, aren't we?"

"We are. And at our best when we find common cause."

"I agree, I totally agree." Dalton paused and drank. "Forgive me though, Adam. I feel like you're about to tell me about a problem."

"Nothing serious I don't think," Adam said as airily as he could manage. "A small issue I think the two of us can rectify, if not take advantage of."

"Let's hear it," Dalton said, his face relaxed and pleasant. "I'm happy to help if I can."

Adam was a less expressive man but did his best to summon a positive energy. "It's about the apartments on Park Avenue. The Board's apartment project."

"Ah, of course. Your baby."

"Yes, my baby. We're making great progress. The architect will send a written briefing to all of us next week. We finalized the lobby décor yesterday, the floor and wall swatches anyway. It looks fantastic."

"I'm sure, I'm sure," Dalton said. "The problem though?"

"Yes," Adam said, proceeding cautiously. He had rehearsed his pitch in the mirror this morning, even scribbling a few notes in the margin of the *Times*. "The site is being managed by Roselli Construction. I have known Cal Roselli for quite some time. He is great at these things—"

"You have a nose for those builders—"

"And still, his effectiveness be damned, he was forced to liquidate his former business a few years ago. Cal Roselli is a down-to-earth construction man, a blue-collar guy, a lifer in the industry like you just don't see these days, but he was taken advantage of. His accountant fleeced him. The business was quickly in the red and overleveraged. The bank eventually took control and seized his assets, and this new iteration of his business, the Roselli Construction employed by Clearwater Investments today, does not have a credit history to speak of, and with his unfortunate record, Cal is struggling to get financing even though the loan itself is a simple one, short-term. It's a loan to purchase the materials necessary to break ground. It's essentially a loan to Clearwater despite the Roselli signature on the bottom line. Seeing as we've worked together before, Cal asked me to help him find a bank willing to offer him some credit and reasonable terms—"

"And you thought of me?" Henry said, his blue eyes thinning above a smile. Adam sensed he did not find the idea flattering.

"I did," Adam said, composing his own features. "No one is going to have a better sense of this project than you. The first payments to Roselli from the Clearwater Board will repay much of the loan, and Roselli will only make money after he repays your bank, he knows that. He's just a guy who needs some help at the beginning."

"How much help?"

"It's not pennies," Adam said, hoping to brace the banker for his punchline. "Five million dollars."

Dalton did not seem surprised. "That's not pennies at all."

"I know. Cal is aware of the magnitude of this request. As am I."

Henry Dalton leaned forward and steepled his fingers. Adam had lost him, and he could see it everywhere. And when he spoke, Dalton's icy tone confirmed it. "I'll be honest with you, Adam. I don't see why I…sorry, *we*, the Clearwater Board, however you want to categorize us…I don't see why we need Mr. Roselli on this project. Credit problems? And now he's managing a project of that size? C'mon."

Adam slouched slightly and crossed his legs. "I think at this point we are too far along to change. He has been involved since day one. And he's more than capable."

"No ditches have been dug, no posts planted. Am I right?"

"Yes," Adam agreed, "but the blueprints have been a collaborative effort. This architect, Abrams, will not like a change this far along. That is why this loan is so necessary, Henry. We need Roselli as much as we need Abrams at this point, unless you want to restart the site preparations from scratch. And Roselli needs this loan. That means you and I need this loan." He was determined to swim upstream if only to say he tried.

"Abrams is an idiot," Dalton snapped. "You have said as much yourself. I am asking why we cannot find another construction company that can find financing independent of my bank. Surely that is possible. I have given enough to the project already."

"Of course, it's *possible*…but it is an unnecessary risk. Cal is an asset for us, there's no doubt about it."

"We have known each other a few years now, Adam," Dalton said, pausing after for an aggressive drink. "You joined the Clearwater Board almost five years ago. We were acquaintances even earlier, when you were still practicing law…"

"Yes."

"Have I ever seemed unprepared to you?"

"No."

"So, would you think I would have allowed you to join our Board without knowing exactly who you are?"

Adam knew he had no choice but to indulge the man. Still, his stomach tightened, hot, as the upcoming defeat settled on him. "I would not think so."

"Your name is Adam Efrem Landau," Dalton said with a theatricality that nearly made Adam roll his eyes. He held himself in check. "You are a Jew from Park Slope, Brooklyn. You graduated from Penn and then from Yale Law. By 1955, you were successfully representing major unions in suits against their members, and in 1968 you walked away from that to pursue what you have called 'business ventures,' but let's be honest, huh? You facilitate a cadre of goons," Dalton's volume began to build as he continued, "in the city of New York and elsewhere as their primary unaffiliated emissary to legitimate sectors of American business. And you have the audacity, Mr. Landau, to come into my office and tell me about the troubles of your hand-picked man, Cal Roselli? The man cannot get a loan because he is an indecent hack set about to rob any project he sets his hands to. Now I have allowed this connection, *your* connection, to continue because I realize there are certain financial benefits for our Board incumbent upon the services you provide, but if you think that means I will provide someone like Cal Roselli with five million dollars from my bank as a favor, you are sorely mistaken. And furthermore, I think another construction company would be beneficial for the legal integrity of this project anyway. Surely your Bosses would not lose motivation if such a change was made?"

Adam kept his voice soft to contrast the banker's. "You mistake me, Henry."

"You are what you are, Mr. Landau. You are helpful in your own way, but this does not entitle you to favors from me or a disregard for what I know is the truth of the matter. I am not some two-bit hood to be taken advantage of. Explain that to your wop Bosses."

Adam could have clapped, but only smiled. "I will notify the individuals I think relevant."

"Don't throw veiled bullshit at me," Dalton said, lowering his voice back to normal. "I don't want our relationship to become contentious, but I want you to know, unequivocally, that I know what you are doing, and I will not endanger myself or my business by entangling myself with your shady partners any more than is absolutely necessary. Keep them away from me and I'll allow them to go about their own business in peace…or what passes for it in their line of work."

"I apologize for wasting your time. Honestly, I was rather confident this meeting would be a success. I was wrong." Adam rose, set his snifter on Dalton's desk, and took a few steps toward the door before stopping to look back at the banker behind his desk. "You know, this meeting reminds me of a quote. 'Knowledge is largely a collection of the perceptions we've seen proven wrong.' Funny idea, I think. Have a good day, Henry."

* * *

Adam Landau stepped through the front doors of Manhattan First, briefcase in hand, and descended the ten or so steps to street level where a blue-on-cream Chrysler Imperial was waiting for him. Inside sat three men. The driver Adam knew only as Jimmy the Driver, a local kid who chauffeured for a select clientele including Mr. Landau and his associates. The passenger was a balding man with glasses over a round face in a muted suit, Phil Scozzari. Phil was a familiar figure, a friend if they exist in business, and trustworthy to most. The man in the back seat, a stout man with graying hair, large ears, and a bony beak of a nose, held a black fedora in his lap and a silver-pommeled cane between his legs. He was well groomed and, despite the paling wisps of hair, affected a handsome profile with light-brown eyes, which danced when he was in good mood. They were just enough to soften his gravelly Sicilian accent.

As Adam took his seat behind shotgun and closed the door, this man spoke first. "Jimmy, let's get lunch. The Hamilton."

"Yes sir, Mr. Giordano."

As the car pulled into traffic, Don Alphonse Giordano tilted to face Mr. Landau directly. "So...how did it go?" he asked, smiling as he did when he sensed Adam had experienced something unpleasant in his name. He found it amusing.

"Just be glad you weren't there," Adam said. He greeted Phil with a polite tap on the shoulder, before tugging a pack of cigarettes from his pocket and searching for a matchbook.

Don Giordano waved the cigarettes away. "Adam, not in the car. Any additional expenses?"

Adam replaced the cigarettes. "He said no."

Al swiftly checked Phil's eyes in the rearview mirror. "Go on then."

Adam shrugged. "He told me to go fuck myself." Al and Phil were silent, expectant. "He wants Roselli off the project. And no loan."

"Why?"

"He gave me some shit about a 'cadre of goons,' which is apparently what he calls you two," Adam said, pointing. "Told me to take Roselli off to add 'integrity' to the project. If he thinks there's still a chance at integrity here, he doesn't know how we got this rolling in the first place. I guess we can count that as a small victory. Henry believes he is omniscient."

"Remind me why we want this loan again?"

"Roselli's company is a shell. They don't have any real money. We need rebar, machinery, concrete...the company has no credit, especially with Cal's history of...innovative accounting practices."

"Have one of the real companies front the money," Al said. "Some subcontractor or something."

Adam anticipated this suggestion and dove into his rebuttal. "It's all about isolating the payment diversion. It will be much easier to divert funds to and from Roselli if it's a direct line back to them. If we strong-arm one of these outsiders, it's going to get complicated, I promise. The way we planned this is to collect a *very* large chunk of money from the job as middlemen for these building supplies—for sourcing them essentially—if anybody decides to ask that question. Those are simple transactions, and we can make the invoices read whatever we want and call it a finder's fee. Simplicity is what we're looking for. And simple means, as few people as possible."

"In the old days, we would've elbowed a few of those outsiders and been done with it," Al said, shaking his head. He was not angry though. He understood the need to adapt.

"This is an issue with appearances," Adam continued. "Permitting, inspections, that all means government officials asking people questions. I know it's not ideal, but I'm trying to minimize the long-term headaches here. Simple, simple, simple. Worst-case scenario, our contractors price gouged an investment firm."

"How much did you ask for?" Phil asked, each word carrying his own Sicilian twang higher.

"Five million dollars."

Phil turned completely in his seat. "Jesus Christ."

Alphonse ran a finger across his forehead, tracing a line or two. "You have anything to add, Phil?"

"I wouldn't loan Cal five dollars, much less five million."

"That's what the shit costs." Adam pushed back into the seat and turned to Al, hoping his eyes conveyed exasperation to the man. "While we're having this conversation, we may as well discuss another problem we all have. The concrete union, more specifically their president, is not willing to work with us. He has declined our labor terms rather emphatically."

Al instinctually sensed Phil's participation. He checked him in the rearview mirror with momentary disappointment. "How 'not willing' is he? A man can be many types of 'not willing.'"

Adam saw no point avoiding the truth, as deep in this mire as he was now. "Pretty fucking not willing, as I understand it. It's possible he just wants a better offer, but to be honest, we are stretched thin on the project already. I don't think he's worth one penny, this guy, this Al Benfield guy."

"He won't fix the non-union jobs?"

"No, he says he won't do that," Adam said.

Phil nodded his silent agreement from the front seat. "He is dead set—this is my understanding anyway. I sent someone to talk with him already."

Al used the rearview mirror again. "Who?"

"Roselli," Phil answered, his register even higher than normal. "I figured it made more sense sending someone with some legitimacy than any knee-breakers. Might as well use them guys where we can. This concrete guy makes no sense anyways. He acts like his union is gettin' the short end, but it's Clearwater bitin' that bullet. And even *they* aren't gettin' the short end 'cause the locals are droppin' tax breaks on the back end. So, I don't know what newspaper this guy's been reading, but he doesn't make any sense to me, Al."

Al spun the point of his cane into the car floor as he did when discussing serious matters. "What did he say specifically?"

"Cal says it's a lost cause," Phil said simply. The words stayed for a minute as Al twirled his cane and Adam watched the people milling about on the sidewalk, oblivious of the men in the Chrysler.

Al shrugged. "All right. I'll take care of the union thing. I'll take care of this loan for Cal. And the two of you shouldn't remind me how much money you make anytime soon."

One afternoon in early May 1973
Casey's Discount Laundromat in Brooklyn, NY
"He was a good man once. A Man of Honor."

Tony Maceo's bulky form frowned over the makeshift counter at the man kneeling on the other side. "Benjie, hit him." Benjie hit the man. "What's it take to get real answers around here?"

"I don't know, Ton," Benjie said as their captive wiped a trickle of blood from his lips. "He seems to be thinkin' too hard about what he's gonna say next. What's to think about?"

"Hit him again then." Benjie hit the man again and tried to shake the pain it caused from his hand. Tony slid around the counter, agile for his frame, and knelt next to Martino Caselotti on the floor.

"C'mon, Marty, seriously. What the fuck am I doin' here? I like you. I don't want to do this shit. How'z this help me? And after all we do for you…"

"I don't have it," Caselotti said, his eyes on the floor, on the droplets of his rosy spit. "I told you I don't have it yet."

"Yeah I heard," Tony said. He turned to another man whose bloated torso lay casually against a row of Caselotti's coin-operated dryers. "You hear him, Vito?"

"Yeah, unfortunately," Vito said, smirking through his words. "It's a sad thing to see a grown man skip out on his responsibilities. You just can't trust anybody to be an adult nowadays."

"Hit him again, Benj."

Benjie swung again, the pain in his hand knife-sharp and enough to make Tony laugh at his little brother's stifled growl. "How hard is this motherfucker's head? You're actin' like a little schoolboy."

Benjie straightened Caselotti by his collar. "He's bony in the cheeks."

Tony smiled. "Hit him again."

Benjie did and Tony put his arm around Caselotti as he recovered. "Any new thoughts before my brother starts cryin' and I sub in?"

Caselotti ran another swipe over his bleeding lip. "I told you, Tony. I don't have it."

Vito tapped a fist against the coin slot of the dryer next to him. "A shame he don't have any money left over after chargin' these motherfuckers $0.75 for some warm air. Gotta think there'd be some profit in there for our friend."

Tony moved across the room to Vito, poking the tip of his own finger into the coin slot. "How do we get these things open?"

"Baseball bat?"

"C'mon. If we destroy these things, Marty will never get back on his feet…eh, maybe we smash just a few…count until we hit our number—"

"There's a key," Caselotti said, head bent low. "It's behind the counter on a ring—" But Benjie interrupted with another fist against the bony cheekbones. Tony heard the crack and spun, incredulous.

"You serious, Benj? First useful thing he says all day and all the sudden your hand is made of fuckin' steel?"

"I don't know." Benjie shrugged. "He had already told you the important part."

"Save the rest of your thinkin' for another time. Check behind the counter."

Benjie released his grip on Caselotti's collar to quickly follow the command, tugging drawers and shuffling paperwork. He found a small nail holding a set of keys on the wall.

"It's the black one," Caselotti said, answering the metallic jangle. "It's a master for the whole row. The other rows are green, red, yellow."

Vito chuckled and it threw his large stomach into heaves. "Listen to him now. This is the very spirit of Italian brotherhood we've been waitin' for, Marty. If you had taken this approach a few minutes ago, you wouldn't be as ugly as you are now."

Benjie tossed the keys to Tony, who moved to the keyhole and turned. Down the row, the metallic covers dropped in unison, revealing square boxes filled to varying degrees with coins. Tony inspected the exposed boxes, his brothers' eyes following him as he went down the line. "What are we gonna carry all these fuckin' coins around with?"

"That's all I have here. The coins and the register. There's nothin' else."

Tony turned to Vito. "How much does $700 weigh? In quarters or whatever else these are?"

"How would anybody know that?"

"I don't know, you count stuff sometimes, don't you? Benjie, find somethin' to put all these coins in."

Benjie scanned the room, a straight-edged and poorly lit pattern of washers and dryers from the wide front window to the hard-worn office door on the back wall. "What about one of the dryers? We could dump the coins inside and carry it out."

Tony hesitated between laugh and reprimand. "Are you shittin' me? *You* drove us here in the Cadillac. What am I gonna do with a dryer, strap it to the roof?"

"I'm givin' you ideas, Ton."

"Stop, never mind, turn your brain off forever. Marty, you tell me. How the fuck am I gonna get my money into my car?"

Marty brainstormed desperately, sensing the discussion would end with the right word. "Garbage can? Mop bucket? My soap comes in these brown boxes, maybe you could fill them. Take whatever you need."

"Fine," Tony said. "Benjie, fill that garbage can and we'll dump it in the trunk." He knelt again next to Mr. Caselotti, his words now carrying a harsher edge, his dark eyes narrow. "I'm takin' all of it and I'm gonna count it. Anything over $700 is ours for the mental anguish you've caused me and Vito over these past few months. Anything under and I swear, Marty, I will come back here and beat the front of your skull"—Tony paused to put a soft finger to Mr. Caselotti's forehead—"straight out the back of it."

Benjie went to work collecting the coins from their slots, a noisy process of scooping the metal coins into an equally metal trash can and then dragging it over the floor and down each row. Vito and Tony left the owner of Casey's Bargain Laundromat to clean himself up and waited by the car until Benjie pulled the now heavy garbage can over the threshold, across the sidewalk to the curb, and the three men poured the mini-mountain of silver into the trunk of the Cadillac.

Vito stuck his hand in the pile, spreading the little circles around. "It looks like $700, but who knows? I may come back for his vending machine either way."

Tony clapped the oldest brother's shoulder. "Vito, we gotta ease off ole Marty. At least until we know for sure this pile is short." He turned to his other brother, who was massaging his swollen knuckles. "How's the hand?"

"It hurts, Ton, but it's not the end of the world."

"You gotta keep punchin'. That's all I can tell ya for it. Those bones, they grow tougher every time they get a bruise. You gotta bruise 'em whenever you get a chance."

"You've told me."

Tony grabbed Benjie's hand to check it. The knuckles were red and cut and bleeding slightly from their peaks. They would be purple in the morning. "We're gonna go see Papa Vic before we try and count these, Benj'," Tony said as he released the injured hand. "You want us to drop you back at Ma's?"

"Hell no. She's prolly already passed out. What time is it?"

"Eh, you might be right. Sun's almost down."

"And the only reason the kid has any money is for drivin' us around," Vito said. "We gotta make sure he does it enough to get him out of that fuckin' house. If it takes eighty hours a week, it's worth it."

"Fair point. Let's check in with the skipper. Hopefully, he knows somebody who likes to count fuckin' quarters."

* * *

Jerry's Place was a Bensonhurst neighborhood restaurant owned by the Turnino brothers, Jerry and his younger brother Joey, since before the Second World War. The brothers survived by serving mediocre Italian dishes to a plurality of "connected" regulars who considered the place an alcove of security and anonymity. Vincenzo "Papa Vic" Palmieri was the most prominent and perpetual of these men, a *caporegime* in Alphonse Giordano's organization and the Don's trusted friend since well before his gangland coronation. Vic's crew, which included Tony and Vito Maceo, was a murky web of criminal enterprises, most of which were unaware of the others and reported directly to Vic, often at his favorite table in the front corner of Jerry's dining room.

After Benjie parked in the restaurant's private lot, he and his brothers entered as they always did, through an unnaturally skinny side door near the dumpster on the southside of the building. The restaurant was always dark because the only light was either filtered through burgundy curtains or flickered from tableside oil lanterns. Tony guessed this was Jerry's attempt to achieve some form of romanticism. If so, he had failed, instead finding a shadowy pitch that prevented his guests from seeing the cheap prints of Roman generals, emperors, and Renaissance art hanging from the walls. Jerry used this as an excuse to repaint the pictures verbally for his guests. Benjie never asked Tony or Jerry or anyone else for the tour because Vic had told him once, he may have been seven or eight years old, that since the Maceos originated in Milazzo and not Rome, they would have resented the authority of the Romans on the walls around him. The idea permanently dampened his interest.

Each Maceo brother waved to Frank the Bartender manning his post and made their way through the main dining room to Papa Vic's table, where the little old man sat with his pale-gray eyes buzzing and a plate doused in red sauce in front of him. He was surrounded by four or five other men, but as the brothers approached, Vic shooed his guests away.

"You finally come back to see me?" Vic said, smiling through a crooked set of teeth. "I thought maybe they accidentally published my fuckin' obituary." He hugged each brother in turn. "Benjie, go get us a drink, kiddo."

"We wanted to check in," Tony said as Benjie stalked off. "I need some volunteers to count coins from our favorite money-borrowing detergent salesman."

Vic waved them off. "Get a drink, wait for the drink, will ya? You hungry?"

"No, Paps, we're fine."

Vic yelled over to the bartender or waitress or whoever else might have been listening, "Two bowls of *caponata*. And have Joey make 'em. Get Jerry out here."

Tony let a protest die in his throat. "Okay, all right. But I do need some guys to count these fuckin' coins. Think on it if you have to."

"Stop acceptin' payment in coins, problem solved. You're too soft on that motherfucker."

"Eh, he couldn't find his checkbook. I was tellin' Vito how forgetful this guy must be, always losin' our money like this."

Benjie returned with three glasses of wine. Vic thanked him, hugged him another time for good measure, and then sent him back to a barstool across from Frank the Bartender. When Vic sat back down and Benjie was settled out of earshot, Vito asked, "So, what else we got goin' on around this place besides a coin-countin' competition?"

Vic sipped his wine, whatever type Frank decided on, and rubbed a warped finger around the lip of the glass. His suit, charcoal gray with a flat blue tie, was perfectly manicured, but he habitually neglected the rest of his appearance. The white hair he had managed to retain stuck out at all angles, his teeth were yellowed by years of cigars, he carried a musty smell, not unpleasant but of note and imbued into his clothing. He tilted his head as he talked. "Most of 'em are the same problems, you know the problems. Money always, women always. The new guys can't collect like you boys. And here I gotta buy Nick and Sonia somethin' for the anniversary. Sammie Calebrese, he's like my own nephew, is about to be married. And here I might as well be broke with half the idiots I got workin' for me."

"Nick likes those models. Like the little models you can build with the numbered parts. Cars and planes and shit."

"That won't help Sonia much."

"Some couples are hard to buy for. It's not your fault anyway. He can buy his own models. He earns."

Vic drank again and paused. His eyes were light for the company of these men. They fell on Tony. "You and Ana are hard to buy for. All that blessed shit you keep around the house."

"Just buy Carmine toys," Vito said. "I don't buy Tony or Ana anything anymore."

"We noticed."

"Quit invitin' me then. I see too much of you as it is."

Jerry Turnino was a man fond of his own cooking; and the three men, along with several tables nearby, took notice as he approached with the bowls of *caponata*. "You were just sayin'," he said when he was close, "that these two screwballs don't come here no more, and look...your misdirected prayers have been answered."

"Sit down a minute, Jerry," Vic said, waving to an open chair. "They were just tellin' me a story about a Laundromat and a lost checkbook. You'll love it."

Jerry's chin wobbled when he shook his head. "Too much of that goin' around these days. It's an infection. That other one too,

32

that Hartel kid you were tellin' me about. Says he can't find his anywhere."

"Fuckin' Stanley is in trouble again?" Tony asked. "That guy…"

Vic dug a crooked digit into his forehead. "Yeah, that motherfucker. He thinks his money only works on cars and dishwashers. I sent somebody over there to look in on him, and he says Hartel's got a brand-new Dodge Monaco out front of his momma's house. Then Stanley tells me he don't have two dimes to rub together."

"He doesn't have two brain cells is his real problem. He owes Joe Poletti money too," Tony said. He tended to exaggerate his accent around the older guys. Jerry and Vic at a table was always enough to push that button. "Every time I see Stanley, he's got creases in his khakis, that accountant-lookin' motherfucker."

"These guys," Vic said to the boys, "Hartel and Marty, these guys have no problem incurrin' debts to people, people with children and mortgages, and then they just don't care. They've only got cares for themselves. I mean, tell me if I'm wrong here, but I'm thinkin' they're some selfish pricks and don't care how anyone else makes a livin' around here."

Tony and Vito agreed. "Send us for a visit then," Vito said. "I don't mind sendin' Hartel on vacation. If anyone's had chances, it's that little shit."

Vic shook his head. "Eh, I gotta talk to Joe P. …and then," Vic hesitated before tugging his ear to signal a specific individual to the other men, "before any of that. Nothin' yet out of you," he said, wagging a finger between the brothers. "I'll see what Joe P. thinks…see if he has an opinion on the whole thing. I'll have news by Friday or so. Until then, we all love accountants."

One evening in May of 1973
Home of Mary Caruso in the Bronx, NY
"He never understood them. He knew it was frowned upon, but
he didn't understand they held that creed in their bones."

Ricky Caruso's parents had lived in the same Victorian-style brownstone his entire life. It was at the end of a block and had one circular turret on the corner, a graffiti-ridden castle tower with two windows like eyeballs to oversee the Bronx. Ricky suspected they could anyway; he had never seen the view himself. The brownstone was subdivided into four units, and his parents lived on the left side of the bottom floor. Of the units, they once preferred this section for its lack of stairs, until the landlord moved the unit entrance to the alleyway where no entrance had ever been conceived of before. Now their visitors were forced to brave the poor drainage of this cramped and dingy cut.

Ricky kicked a cluster of discarded dolls and a stained teddy bear from his path as he approached this entrance dotted on its door by small muddy handprints. Serena, the seven-year-old, must have seen him pull up or heard his approach, because the door opened before he could touch the handle. "Mamawz mad at you!" she yelled as she hugged herself into his legs. He patted her bony shoulder and scanned the area inside. "Yeah, I'm used to that. Where's your sisters?"

"Timeout!" she yelled again with a cockeyed smile. Her hands marked her guilty for the muddy prints with another slew on her shirt. She grabbed her stuffed duck from the floor and held it to her chest while leading Ricky to the couch by his finger. "They broke Mamawz plate when she was making them sandwiches."

"Both of them broke it?"

"Marisa was trying to take it away from Aly, but Aly didn't wanna give it to her," Serena reported, wriggling up onto the cushions while battling to keep the joy of not being in trouble off her face.

Ricky smiled as her internal conflict played out so blatantly before him. "Well, I guess I don't like when people take my plates either," he said.

"I was good though. I promise. I just ate my sandwich."

Ricky mussed her light-brown curls and found mud there as well. "Where's Mamaw?"

"I don't know, prolly still yellin' at Marisa. She *made* me play outside with her before the plate broke too, and Mamaw got mad we was dirty."

"That's 'cause you kids act up when Mommy's not here, isn't it?" Ricky inspected the little girl's arms. They were covered with scratches.

"I wasn't actin' up. I was good."

Ricky found another clump of muddy hair and crushed it gently between his fingers. "Sure, kiddo." He kissed the little girl on the forehead and chased his mother's voice down the hall to find her scolding the twelve-year-old, Marissa, in the bathroom. "You're not in charge of her," his mother said, the cross tone so familiar to this ear, "and you broke my plate because of it."

"I'm sorry!" Marisa was yelling. She was not crying though. The oldest girl never cried. "Aly would've broken it anyway! That's what I was *stopp*—" She went silent when she saw Ricky in the doorway. His mother turned for a second too before coming back to the girl. "Fine. You're not in timeout anymore. I don't care what you do."

"I'm sorry!"

"Marisa, help clean Serena up," Ricky said, although she needed as much cleaning herself. She ran past him and back to the living room. "Ma, what are you teachin' these kids? Fuckin' mud wrestling?"

"Shut your mouth," she said, welcoming him with a brusque peck on the cheek. "Your sister's late again."

"Why?"

"Hell if I know."

"She call?"

"Said she had to work late." His mother's eyes narrowed. "She's full of shit."

"How late?"

"She said she'll be here around nine."

"Fuck," Ricky said, shaking his head. "Sorry, Ma."

She brushed the sweaty gray fringe from her eyes. "Just another day pickin' up your sister's goddamn slack."

"Where's Teresa?"

"She's with Paul's family till Monday."

Ricky could not remember who Paul was. "That her boyfriend?"

"Yeah. You won't like him. He's older."

"How old?"

"Midtwenties. I don't know. I said four words to the guy."

"Fuck that."

"If I said he was eighteen, you wouldn't like him either."

Ricky did not answer. His mother pointed toward a door across the hall. "Aly's in there if you want to see her."

The girls slept in Ricky's old room when they stayed at their Mamaw's. It was decorated by the same carpet, paint, and most of the same toys, but it now held a twin bed for Marisa and Serena and a small wooden crib Ricky had bought for baby Aly two years ago. The chubby, helpless ball was lying on her back, looking up at her mobile when Ricky leaned his head over the side. She smiled up at him, dimples pressing into her cheeks, as he flicked the mobile to spin the stuffed elephant, lion, hippo, and giraffe in circles. "Up!" she demanded.

Ricky's nose flinched over the rail, and he sniffed the chubby ball with caution. "Did you shit yourself, little girl? Ugh, yeah, you did." He carried her at arm's length to the living room where his mother had taken a spot on the couch with a cigarette in her mouth, and the two other sisters were splashing water from the sink onto their faces and hands. Streams of mud ran to form puddles by their feet. His mother looked so tired, her eyes so bloodshot, her shoulders so slumped, the corners of her mouth so slack, as to earn his sympathy. "This one shit herself," he said, but when his mother did not move, he continued, "I'll change her," and lay the little one on the floor. Aly started crying as soon as he put her down, but he soldiered on, wiping the smears from her backside and replacing the diaper with a clean one.

"I went to see Dad," Ricky said as he shoved Aly off to splash in the dirty kitchen puddles with her sisters. "Barely even talked. He just yelled the whole time."

"Prison does that to men. You'll see someday if you keep up," his mother said calmly. She hit her cigarette and tapped it against the tray. "How is he otherwise?"

"He's still a piece of shit."

"Don't you judge him. You two are fuckin' twins only separated by a goddamn time machine."

Ricky lit his own cigarette as he fell back into the couch. There was a hole in the fabric next to his hand, burrowed out some years ago through one of the couch springs, and he ashed through it onto the floor below. "He didn't read the fuckin' letter."

"What letter?"

"Teresa's letter."

"How do you know?"

"I mailed it for her, Ma…he didn't read the fuckin' thing."

His mother nodded. "He ask about me?"

"Yeah, he asked. He looks like shit without you around, if that makes you feel better."

She laughed. "His hair?"

"It was fuckin' terrible." Ricky rubbed his hand over the stubble on his chin. "I told him about me and Petey too. He got real preachy after that. Turns out, I'm wastin' my education, you believe that?"

"Told him about your Chicken Ranch?"

"Our bar. Our nightclub."

"You're just like him. Your father, not Petey. Not yet anyway. If you ever get like Petey, I'm gonna ask you to stay away from me."

"I'm not like either." Ricky lay his head back and blew a plume of smoke into the ceiling, staring at it for an extra moment. "What are you gonna do with these kids for another couple hours?"

"This bath should last a minute. Plans are pointless with these ones."

They do seem to be enjoying themselves. Aly was "sneaking" close to Serena before her sister would put her finger over the spout to send a jet of water after her, and the little one would laugh hysterically and waddle away as fast as her little legs would take her. Her white T-shirt was already soaked, and the new diaper would be soon. "Why don't you go get dinner or something. Just run up the street. I'll watch 'em for a little bit."

"I can do that, I guess. They need to eat, and I don't want to cook." Mary Caruso did not leave right away, but finished her cigarette, scrubbed a few haphazard stains from her dress, and combed her hair back to respectability. She was a tough Sicilian whose years had earned her a few proud grays, but she maintained a streak of pleasant vanity despite her husband's absence. Before she finally left, she gathered her girls around her, still sopping wet and dripping on the floor. "All right, girls," she said, her voice back to its less frenetic center, "I'm going to go get dinner. And when I come back, this floor should be clean." She kissed them each on the forehead. "Marisa and Serena, you're my big girls. Watch Aly for Uncle Ricky." Then his mother was off and out the door.

The girls were definitely cleaner than when they started, although the floor was not. Ricky let them continue whatever procedure existed in their minds, turned on the TV, and tuned its antenna to a suitable station. One appeared eventually, although crisscrossed by dotted lines of white and gray. Ricky fell back into the couch for another cigarette just as the girls streaked full speed across the living room.

"Listen! Serena, get over here and sit on the couch." Ricky was surprised when she listened. Marisa crawled up next to her with Aly traipsing behind and jumping toward, but unable to climb up on, the couch. Ricky gave up a clear TV signal and set the little girl on his lap. Something in his movements must've fixed the faulty antenna, and when Ricky turned back around he saw a man appear on the screen with neatly parted hair, a wide smile, and garish red suit standing before some unidentified downtown building with a local news reporter at his side. Ricky clenched his jaw instinctually, and blood rushed to color his cheeks as he watched, intent to hear every word.

Newscaster: Here he is, community organizer Joe Pisciotto, who has really put together quite an event for us coming up at the end of June, haven't ya, Joe?

Joe Pisciotto: Yes, Mary, we're putting together an event to demonstrate for the city of New York the true nature of the Italian people, not the stereotypes pushed on the public. We're a happy, law-abiding people, we're a loving people, and we're happiest when we're enjoying our great food with friends and neighbors. And that's all this event is about.

Newscaster: So, you were telling us off-screen how to get involved?

Joe Pisciotto: Yeah, if you wanna get involved as a volunteer, you can head over to our storefront in Queens. It's just a little shop, you know, we're a small organization, but we'll get you on staff in the food trucks or maybe at the games or somewheres down there and you can help us out that way. Or, if you own or work for an Italian organization, either a singer or a restaurant owner or if you just wanna be a sponsor and be a part of this great event, let us know. You can call us, PE 6-5000, if you wanna get involved that way, ya' know, as a vendor or sponsor.

Newscaster: And it's June 30, is that right? So, they have, oh, about six weeks to figure everything out?

Joe Pisciotto: Yeah, and it's gonna be a great day for Italians all over the city, and we hope to help a few non-Italians along the way. Maybe teach 'em to make a perfect lasagna or something.

Newscaster: Well, it sure sounds like a great time. Again, that's the Italian Heritage Festival in Columbus Circle Manhattan and that'll be on June 30. I know Joe will put on a good show and he'll be ready to greet you all down there. We can't wait.

Serena pointed to Pisciotto as he waved at them through the screen. "Who is that? Is he famous?"

"Yeah, he's famous."

"He looks like an actor."

"Don't actors play real people? How do you look like an actor?"

Serena shrugged. "He looks like he's in the movies."

"If he's an actor, he's a villain," Ricky said, wrangling the two-year-old into a better position. "You don't ever wanna be around that man there. Remember his face, girls. It's not smart to talk on the news like he's doin'."

"So, he's like Captain Hook?"

"Somethin' like that. He's real selfish. Just like you are sometimes."

"I ain't selfish!" Serena said. Marisa laughed and told her she was. "No, I'm not! And you broke Mamawz plate!"

"Serena, calm down and respect your sister." Ricky hit his cigarette while Aly pulled his fingers apart to a painful distance. "Your grandpa had friends like him," he said when Pisciotto was no longer on the screen. "That's why he's in jail like some schmuck and can't see his grandbabies."

"'Cause of that man?" Marisa asked. She always wanted to talk about her grandpa.

"Men like him. Men with no Honor," Ricky said, an edge steal-ing into his voice. "Men who can't quit talkin' to people that ain't their friends." Ricky kissed Aly on her forehead, stood her back on the ground, and watched her waddle back over to their indoor water-park. "Marisa, dry your sister off. Serena, mop the water up in the kitchen. Both give me a kiss first though." The two girls moved to obey, but he stopped them and put his hands on their shoulders. "Your Uncle Ricky loves you. You know that?" The girls nodded. "Your mamaw loves you and your mommy loves you. You ever have any problems, you come to us, right? You gotta trust us, your family. No one else. That's why we have families, for tough times when we can't trust no one else in the world."

A morning in the spring of 1973
Home of Bobby Guiffrida in Brooklyn, NY
"Carrie loved Bobby the way men love Corvettes."

Carrie enjoyed smoking cigarettes. *Fuck health warnings.* They relaxed her and the repetition gave her thoughts a rhythm, a flow. Her thoughts needed rhythm.

So, she lay there in the early morning as the sun rose through the sea of rooftops, smoking a cigarette in bed. She was naked under a thin sheet with Bobby lying next to her, his chest lying bare above the covers to rise and fall as she watched. His mind was likely clouded from the night before, effected by a mix of spirits and sexual fatigue, and altogether reluctant to face the impending reality. *Let him enjoy it while he can.* She hit her cigarette. Lucky Strikes were always her favorite, but she'd begun trying others; this one was a Pall Mall. She grabbed the pack from her nightstand, felt the movements of the few left inside. The label was simple, gold and white, with a special advertisement attached. *Mildness you can measure.* She wasn't sure she wanted "mildness," but she liked this cigarette and hit it again.

When Bobby stirred next to her, she used the opportunity to sit all the way up. She brushed flakes of ash from their sheets, watch-ing them float slowly to the floor. She remembered Bobby ordering an expensive wine the night before, a dry red wine, but could not remember the name. It had been a fantastic choice, even her mother said so. She knew it was special before her first taste because the sommelier had elbowed their waiter out of the way to make the pours himself. He made an awkward performance of it, staring intently as her father tried the first sip even though it was Bobby who ordered and paid. They ordered another and then another and must have drank a bottle each by the end of dinner, but she did not feel hungover now. Soon the wine would wear off and she would crash, but not yet. And the cigarette had resurrected her buzz.

Her makeup had left splotches on her pillowcase during the night, and that roused her from bed to finish the job with hot water from the bathroom sink. Carrie was an attractive woman. She was slim and athletic with high cheeks, short blondish hair, and barely olive skin, but in the mirror, still drunk and naked, she pinched her sides with stubborn disappointment. *The wedding, the wedding.*

When she came back to bed, Bobby was awake and leaning against the headboard with his own cigarette dangling from his lips. "You're gonna be tired, Car," he said. "You're up too early."

"I'm more worried about how my head's gonna feel." She expected the hangover to begin any minute now without another cigarette. "What was that wine you ordered last night?"

"I don't remember. Some Cabernet."

"I wish you remembered."

"We could call and ask…Silvio will probably remember." Silvio was the waiter who had been elbowed aside. "Or your mother. She pays attention to that stuff."

Bobby adjusted his position, and Carrie could see his stomach muscles stir as he moved and felt a brief pang of guilt. She laid her head across Bobby's lap so he would play with her hair. "Anything important happening this week?" she asked him.

Bobby thought for a minute, his eyes pointed at the ceiling, fingers aimlessly combing. "You know Pete Liesewicz?"

"No."

"Well, he exists," Bobby said through a drag, "and he's trying to move some cars. Probably towards the end of the week."

"What type of cars?"

41

"Volkswagens, I think."

"Ugh…keep 'em."

Bobby laughed and grabbed her chin to pull it toward him. "Money's still green."

"I know." She brushed his cheek and then his chest with her fingers. He was lean and warm with brown skin and hair, dark eyes and a jawline that grew stubble in mere hours. She kissed him. The dry smoke of his cigarette sat on his lips, and she wet them with her tongue. "I'm going to shower," she said and kissed him again before getting up and walking to the bathroom, her body on full display.

"C'mon. Back to bed."

"Sorry. I have to meet my father. It's Wednesday."

"You were with him ten hours ago."

Carrie smiled. "We have things we can't discuss around you and mother. Father-daughter things."

"How to get rid of me?" he asked, but Carrie had already disappeared behind the bathroom door. He finished his cigarette thinking about the wine and the dinner. He liked his soon-to-be father-in-law, whatever his own father thought. The man was predictable to a cynical mind, but *dependable* was probably a better word. And he was not overbearing. He gave the couple their space. Even still, Bobby felt a cloud, a relentless pressure, in marrying the daughter of Alphonse Giordano.

* * *

Carrie Giordano was the only person in the world who could cuss at her father with impunity. She loved to do it in Sicilian because the blasphemy of his mother's tongue made him squeamish, and so few things made him squeamish. She knew it was exhilarating for him to hear his children speak their ancestors' words, a Western dialect of Sicilian called *Palermitano* by whoever names such things, no matter what they discussed. Alphonse told his daughter their lunches were *"a verbal thread to what we've lost."*

Al had picked a restaurant in Manhattan for their date, which was rare, but the place had a clean patio, handsome staff, and a fish special. He wore a full suit, as he always did, and the hot afternoon had reddened him already. Carrie watched as sweat collected around his eyebrows and ran, slowly but inevitably, over his spider-veined cheeks to fall on the table. She shook her head. "*Papa, you are sweating,*" she said with energy in the Old Language. "*Come here.*" She dabbed at his forehead with her napkin as he waved it away politely.

"*This place was pretty good, no?*" he said, scanning the other tables on the patio. The sky was perfectly blue, and he leaned his head back slightly to bask. "*It was recommended by one of the cooks who interviewed at The Hamilton. He said they had these specials.*"

"*You spend too much time there, Papa. Too many people know about it.*" They had discussed breaking his routines many times; his trips to The Hamilton were his most careless of all.

Al shook his head and chewed the last of his meal. "*You are too cautious. I would not give up a good restaurant for something as small as that.*"

His defenses, by now rote fits of syllables, were nearly impenetrable. She would have to be more subtle. "*Did you hear about your friend? The Napoletano?*"

"*I did,*" Al said, unable to stifle a grin, "*but go ahead. What advice do you have for me, Kiara?*"

"*He is loud. Loud men are dangerous. You have told me this too many times to count.*"

"*Very true,*" Al chuckled. "*He wore a red suit, I hear. Who wears a red suit?*"

"*You didn't watch the interview then?*"

"*They told me about it…the man is foolish. No doubt about that. He says he is working for 'our people.' He lies. No one has asked for his help. The need is only present in his imagination, and he disguises his theft with charity. I know this. Ask Phil, ask Nick, ask Vincenzo, ask Petey. Even Adam. I tell them the same things.*"

Carrie's eyes tightened. "*He said 'mafia,' Papa.*" Her father's eyes rose to meet hers and hardened. He simply nodded. "*And rats wear red.*"

Al took a drink of his iced tea. He preferred more carefree conversation, but Carrie tended to chase dark topics. "*I heard he's buying*" *a place on Long Island too,"* he said. *"And I've heard he and Mr. Fiata are taking their families to the Amazon this winter. Can you imagine a trip like that on his reported income? They're going to get him for the taxes before long. He may as well have a sign on his door."*

"Johnny doesn't have any business with them, does he?" Carrie could never keep up with her brother's schemes.

Al stirred the lemon wedge in his remaining ice. *"Some dock-related stuff, same as everyone else. That port has kept them alive for decades, going back before Garbinia, before Camilleri."* He shrugged. *"Johnny will be fine, don't worry yourself about it...and how is your soon-to-be-husband doing?"*

"He's fine. He's been quieter than usual. His father has him running all over, so now Bobby gets to say he's busy whenever I need something." Carrie paused; it was her turn to grin. *"Maybe he's running around on me."*

Al nearly choked on his ice cubes then shook his head with hypothetical indignation. *"I'd kill him."*

"I would kill him," Carrie laughed. She took a bite, a chance to pause. *"Do you think they are giving him more work because of our relationship...a show of respect for you? He is getting more opportunities than he ever has."*

Al answered no. *"His father is the reason, I'm sure. Charles Guiffrida is not a man to be trifled with. And Frank Capello is a man who rewards loyalty. Bobby has both going for him."*

"I like his father, despite whatever stories people may tell."

"Good. We all have to like him right now."

Carrie understood the comment as a veiled directive. *"He's all over the Park Avenue project, isn't he?"*

"Everyone will be all over it."

"That's going to be very good for us."

Al nodded. *"Adam has handled all of that very well."* Carrie did not respond. *"It has been running very smooth."*

Carrie finished the last bites of her lunch and waved down their ruffle-haired waitress for the check. *"It all sounds good, Papa. You should be proud of where we are today."*

"How are you and your Mother doing with the wedding plans? Of course, I have to ask before we go."

Carrie groaned and shook her head, as Al expected. He knew this was, in fact, the true purpose of their lunch dates: for Carrie to vent about her mother. *"She embarrasses me with these planners, Papa,"* she said while inspecting her nails for defects. *"Nothing they do is good enough for her, and back and forth they go. The florist made a sample bouquet, and she spent twenty minutes dissecting it with him. She kept telling him it was too fucking purple! And then she didn't like the napkins or the goddamn chair covers, and we'd already paid for both of them. She sent them all back. She has to control everything. I don't care about it enough to fight her, but it's embarrassing when she does it in public. Did she do this for your wedding?"*

Al remembered that wonderful day and the long months beforehand. *"We had her dress altered eight times."*

"It's like that now. The excruciating detail of it is exhausting. I can't deal with it. Nothing is good enough for her...and it's my wedding!"

Al answered with a calm tone. *"You did not finish that sentence correctly. Kiara, the problem is, nothing is good enough for her...daughter."* They were the same, his wife and eldest daughter, and yet they would not understand for the world. *"You are the first of her children to get married. This is her day too."*

"I just want her to relax. Give me some control."

"I will mention my concern. I am quite accomplished at translating your anger for her."

Carrie changed the subject. *"Is someone picking you up, or are we getting a cab back to your house?"*

"Cab, I think."

"I'll flag one while you pay." Carrie straightened her blouse and jacket before collecting her purse and moving quickly from the patio to an open area along the curb. She raised her hand, and just a moment later, a grimy yellow cab appeared, ready to take her on her way. "Hold on," she said to the cabbie as she took her seat in the back, "my Father is coming. Just a minute."

He responded in broken English, some unknown accent, almost so she could not understand him. "Da time...miss...how long for him?"

"Calm down." She peeked at the patio; her father was still talking to the waitress and in no hurry. "You see him?" she asked, pointing. "That is Alphonse Giordano, and he doesn't care about your little time clock. Here," she shoveled a crinkled twenty-dollar bill into the driver's lap, "I will make it worth your while."

The man raised the twenty dollars and nodded his head several times. "Yeh, miss, that'z fine, miss."

Carrie leaned through the window so her father could see her. "Daddy!" she called in English now. He saw her and waved away her impatience, instead casually laughing at whatever secret words the waitress was telling now. Carrie grabbed her compact to fix her hair and lipstick before they set off. "He'll get here when he gets here," she told the cabbie. "Do not mention that fuckin' time clock to him. Or the twenty dollars."

An afternoon in early May of 1973
Home of Tony Maceo in Brooklyn, NY

There was only one picture of the entire Maceo family, the nuclear family headed by Sandra and Raoul Maceo, in existence, and Tony kept it stored in a lock box in his bedroom. The years had furnished it with a translucent film that distorted their details and two thumbprints of faded, near-white ink pressed into its edges. Someone had originally scrawled "December 21st, 1952" on the back with a dull pencil, and Tony had retraced it rather poorly with a blue pen when it started to smudge. He remembered the day it was taken. His father liked to tinker with old cameras. Sandy had gone on about how pointless the tinkering was, but after seeing Raoul's excitement when he finally got one of his favorites to work, she conceded, "He should at least use the damn thing.". Vito and Tony were displayed in their church clothes, Benjie was swaddled in a plain white sheet, Sandy and Raoul stood on either side with their eyes staring into the flash. Tony remembered Christmas too. His aunt Nikkie had come over with her children for dinner, and Tony got a little red convertible from her. And Raoul was gone by New Year's.

Tony had his own hobbies, some he would not admit to, and one was tending the small garden at the back of his house. He had been skeptical when his wife, Airiana, purchased a wooden box garden, about six feet by six feet, and set it just underneath their kitchen window, but she had been right about it. Tomatoes were the first things they planted. Ana loved to cook, and like any traditional Italian woman, it was important to control her own ingredients. So first it was four or five tomato plants. Then, after a serious consultation with her mother, she planted eggplants and thyme before eventually squeezing red onions, bell peppers, and basil into the garden box. But often it was Tony, not Ana, on the patio pulling weeds and watering the seedling plants. *See a weed, pull a weed.*

"Tony!" Ana's voice called to him from the back door. She must have been getting a head start on dinner because her apron was askew and spattered by red sauce. "Phone's for you."

Tony tossed his burgeoning pile of weeds in a trash can and brushed the concrete dust and dirt from his knees as he followed her inside. The phone in the kitchen was off the hook. "Hello?"

Papa Vic's voice fed from the other end of the line. "Hey, Ton, I talked to our friend Joey, and I need you and Vito to get down here. There's a discussion to be had."

Tony had heard this summons enough to read between the lines. "Okay, no problem. What about the kid?"

"What fuckin' kid?"

"Benjie."

"There's some work to be done here, Ton. You want him involved in that?"

"Yeah, if it's the right thing here…don't you?"

"I just want you to think carefully on it…bringin' him all the way in, especially when your mama's only got you three boys. It's not a black-and-white situation."

Tony stared at the earpiece before putting it back to his ear. "What do you mean by *that*, Vic? How could this Thing be good enough for me and you and then it's not good enough for him?

What're we sayin' then? If we say that to him, we're just sayin' this Thing ain't no good in the end." Vic was silent on the other end, and Tony softened his air. "Paps, if I've gotta tell Benjie to stay away, next I gotta ask…what the hell is this Thing?"

Vic sighed like old men sigh at youth. "Fine then. Bring the fuckin' kid, you idiot. Two hours. Be at Jerry's."

Tony hung up the phone, kissed Ana on the forehead, and went to get dressed.

* * *

Home of Sandra Maceo in the Bronx, NY

Benjie woke in a panic, sweat cooling the sheets all around him. He spun quickly for his watch, the silver banded one his brothers had given him. It was not on his nightstand. He rolled to the ground, and a glob of empty beer cans clamored wildly across the floor. It was not under his bed, his dresser. He grabbed his clothes, some dirty and some clean, from wherever they had been thrown last: bed, night-stand, floor, chair, TV, windowsill, doorway. He kicked the plates of nearly finished pizza and sandwiches he'd stored by his bed, nothing. "Shit!" He tipped the TV forward, knocking a broken chunk of its plastic shell to the floor. He stepped for the bathroom in the hall; his knee screamed, swollen and mad, and he stumbled then recovered. He hobbled through the door, his head bobbing back and forth… and snatched the band at last, sparkling on the sink. *4:52 p.m. Thank God.*

The water from the bathroom sink helped stir Benjie's senses, although he had to cup and splash with his off-hand, because of the muffled shards of pain that lingered in the other. It might've been broken, Benjie didn't know, but it was definitely colored purple and gray-green from his pinkie to middle finger. Tony said the bones would knit together, but for now, they stabbed at the slightest touch.

He splashed water into his hair, grabbed pants from his floor, and pulled them on as he walked down the hall and to the kitchen. His mother, a spindly woman of fifty-two with thin brown hair, was leaning against the stove as a pair of eggs sizzled, a cigarette held loose between her lips.

"Good mornin', son," Sandy Maceo said, scanning him.

Benjie grunted a greeting at her and reached for the final dregs of a milk carton in the refrigerator. It might have been spoiled, but he finished it and threw the jug away.

"Are you gonna do any work today?" his mother barbed.

"Yeah, Tony and Vito are pickin' me up soon."

"Good," was all she said, stirring the eggs while her ashes fell on them.

Benjie continued perusing the fridge. "I've been goin' with them almost every day for ten months. Don't act like I've just been sittin' here, Ma. They don't let me do everythin' yet."

"You have put forth a poor effort, I think. You should be doin' more for them. They're the only breadwinners me and you got. Hand me the milk."

"I just finished it."

She shook her head and eyed him. "You can see I'm makin' fuckin' eggs over here."

Benjie ignored her. "I do what they ask of me. I'm ten years younger than either of them. No shit they make more money than me." He grabbed a few pieces of ham from the butcher's paper and ate them plain.

"Bullshit. You can do more. Ask Vito what else you can do."

Benjie gulped water from the tap and sat down at their table. Gari settled across his feet, and he snuck the dog a piece of ham while Sandy worked her ill-temper into the preparation of her eggs. If muttering under her breath and shaking her head weren't enough, she finished by tossing the spatula on the counter and hammering the pan with salt and pepper. Benjie scanned the counter for her vodka. It was three-fourths gone when he saw it.

He dodged her stares and escaped back to the bathroom for a cool shower. He diluted a squeeze of shampoo and rubbed it on his underarms, splashed his chest, and combed the stream of water through his hair which grew thick and was longer than he wanted, shagging over his ears in dark-brown bumps and down past his eyebrows when he didn't brush it constantly to one side. Stubble had still never shadowed his face, but he "shaved" every day in hopes some attention might draw it out. His frame was toned, quite like his brothers before they let themselves go, if still adolescent by comparison. That frame was enough to fill the blue slacks and cream button-down he wore each day, despite the fact neither concealed a gun if you were looking for one.

Benjie monitored his window as the time came closer but still missed his brothers' arrival until they were already talking in the kitchen with their mother. "Vito, the boy is lazy," his mother reported as loud as she could, "and he needs more work from you guys. He's afraid to ask for himself." She heard Benjie enter and flipped her focus to him. "Aren't ya, Benjie?"

"No, I'm not fuckin' *afraid* to ask."

Sandy's eyes went back to Vito, wide with false astonishment. "You hear this? You hear the mouth on this fuckin' kid!"

Vito grabbed her hands as they moved wildly in front of her. "Ma, leave him alone. He's comin' with us today. There's nothin' more we can do than that. Calm down already."

"Yeah, Ma, we all know you're insane," Tony teased. He was the best at calming her outbursts. "You don't need to play concerned mother for us. Save it for the judge or the psychiatrist, whichever we call first."

"I just want him to grow up to be respectable," Sandy said, forming tears on cue. "He's softer than you two. I have to worry about him all the time."

"I'm not soft, Ma. Fuckin' hell." This criticism was one of her favorites, maddening Benjie to no end given his brothers' literally soft bodies that mounded over their belts and sunk from their frames.

"Again, with the fuckin' mouth! You hear this?"

"Don't worry, Ma. We'll wash it out with soap. Just like Daddy taught us," Tony said as the brothers backed their way out the front door. "Run along now. Find your bottle, woman." They closed the front door with their mother still talking inside.

"Jesus Christ, Benjie," Tony said, walking for the car. "You need to get out of that nuthouse."

"I want to. And I do want more work. She's right about that part."

"The ball will find you, Benjie boy, don't worry. Today is your first day at the ballpark, and you're startin' for the fuckin' Yankees."

* * *

Once again, Benjie guided the Cadillac into the rear parking lot of Jerry's restaurant, and the three Maceo brothers entered through the narrow side door behind the dumpster. They waved again to Frank the Bartender and wound their way through the Friday night patrons to find Papa Vic seated at his circular table, this time alone. His suit, a light blue with a patterned gray and white pocket square, was pressed smooth and his hair wildly unkempt, as always. He stood to greet them, hugging each man with soft taps on the back of their necks.

"Benjie, get us some drinks, will ya?" Vic said, and Benjie traced steps to the bar to order them.

Vic sat down and motioned for Vito and Tony to do the same. "So, I talked to Joey and he says he's done with accountants and we're both ready to resolve this issue *tonight*. Now, when you meet with this accountant, your first priority," Vic said, aiming his gaze down his knotted fingers, "is to get *my* fuckin' money. Your second priority is to get Joey *his* fuckin' money." He glanced around the bustling room, but the noise was such that no one else could hear him. "Now at the same time you're checking this accountant's bank statements, Joey wants your help with another problem he's become aware of. Joey's got this guy that's been goin' with him, this guy named Angelo Butera. He's been around for a while, but he's not a Friend of Ours,[1] not yet. Joey hears this guy's been holding some money back. Some

---

[1]   Vic uses the phrase "not a friend of ours" here to mean the man has not yet "made his bones" or been officially accepted into an organized crime family. This was used as a shorthand way of letting other members know a stranger's status. If "he's a friend of ours," it means he's a made member. Conversely, they could also use the phrase "he's a friend of mine" to convey he is my friend, but not a made member.

of his jobs are a little too light, Joey says. Good leads, should've been real money, and then Angelo says, 'Oh, sorry, Joey, not as much there as we thought,' that type of shit. So, tonight Angelo's gonna go with you as a way to 'represent Joey's interests,' and we want you to keep an eye on him. If you see anything you don't like, you're gonna let me know. I'll relay it to Joey and then we do whatever it is we gotta do. You never know with these things until you get out there…guy might be a choir boy. I don't know, but we're gonna kick his tires and see what comes crawlin' out."

"It's hard to find trustworthy guys like us these days, huh, Vic?" Vito said, smirking as Benjie returned holding three glasses of red wine and placed one in front of each man before turning to take his usual seat at the bar. Vic stopped him. "Kid," he said, "don't you drink? Get a drink and sit down. I want to talk to you."

Benjie's face ran a brief gamut of emotions before settling into a subtle grin. Vic called to Frank the Bartender, "Hey, Frank, pour another one for the kid, will ya?" Benjie hustled there and back again as a flurry of nerves poked at his stomach.

Vic spoke seriously, deliberate with each word. "Kid, now I know you've been drivin' your brothers around for a while, and it's a bit of a thankless job," he said, Benjie nodding his agreement to every word, "but, recently, your brothers have vouched for you to me. I've known you for a long time and, obviously, I love you like my own, but this is a very serious thing they've done for you. *On their Honor*, they tell me I can trust you to do the right things for us. They tell me you are Loyal, Trustworthy, and worthy of my Respect. They tell me you are a *man of action* who would protect his Friends before himself in the face of enemies. Is this true, kid?"

"Yes, sir." Benjie's nerves were gaining momentum. What had his brothers taught him? *Look all men in the eyes, especially those you respect.* He sat, twitchy but transfixed until the periphery blurred and the words were all he heard. Vic had never spoken this way to him. Before it was all smiles and innocent jokes, but now his tenor had changed and each word evoked a stronger purpose than before. Vic leaned forward, his brow furrowed, his eyes sharp. Benjie's hands sweat as he clasped one in the other. His throat tightened.

"Do you know what it is your brothers do for me?"

Benjie tried to gauge his brothers' reactions. They were sitting forward, hands together, with silent eyes on him. "I believe so, sir," he managed to answer.

Vic took a drink of wine, letting the question and answer hang, suspended in the air. "Are you aware your brothers have chosen a new Family for themselves? Not that they are not members of the Maceo family like yourself, but another Family?"

"I am, sir." Benjie wanted to gulp his wine. He was too afraid to actually do it.

"Do you know who they work for?"

"I believe, sir, they work first for you and then for Mr. Alphonse Giordano." Benjie glanced again at his brothers for affirmation. He received none.

Vic nodded before taking another drink of wine. "Son, and listen closely to me here," Vic pointed a finger at Benjie this time, "if you were called upon, do you think you could take a man's life to protect your Friends? To protect your Brothers?"

Benjie felt as if he did not need to answer at all; he wanted Vic to *see* the answer. The question was not entirely new; he had thought about it before. As early as five years old when he heard stories of the wise guys on his block and since he was twelve and heard his brothers' friends talking late into the night. He had thought about it since Vito had given him that snub-nose .38. "Yes, sir, I think I could."

Vic paused for another drink. "Benjie, I want to make sure you understand. If you want this life, *Cosa Nostra*, the Life your brothers have chosen, you must give up your old one. I will become your Family—Al Giordano will become your Family. If your mother is dying and I call, you will leave her and come to me. If I tell you to take a life, whether it be a stranger or your best friend, you will do it without question. There is no room in this life for hesitation, for second-guessing. You leave this Life in a box, one way or another. There is no retirement community, you do not ride off into the sunset. Do you understand the magnitude of this commitment?"

Benjie looked to his brothers, both still without expression. "Yes, sir," he said. "There is nothing for me to give up. My brothers are in both my Families now."

Papa Vic leaned back from the table slightly. "All right. I believe in ya, Benj," he said, patting the kid's hand. "First rule of the club, you are no longer permitted to speak the Boss's name. If you need to reference him, you just tug your ear," he demonstrated, "and anybody that should be knowing who he is will know exactly what you mean. You do not say his name out loud to anyone, ever. You understand? Second, tonight, you will go with Tony and Vito and you will do everything they say, absolutely everything, to the letter. And then tomorrow you will meet me here at ten a.m. and you will wear a suit. From now on, every time you are with me, you will wear a suit. And you will never be late."

"Yes, sir." Benjie took a drink of his wine and smiled.

One evening in early May 1973
The future Blue Raven Social Club in the Bronx, NY
"Nothin' looks all that promising when you're stuck at the beginning."

Pietro "Petey Fingers" Caltagirone was a titanic man in every sense of the word. By the spring of 1973, he had been tall, fat, wealthy, and important for over twenty years. His height and weight were hereditary blessings from his father and mother, respectively. Wealth and importance, he earned administering a lucrative black-market network centered on sports, women, and loan sharking for the benefit of the Giordano Crime Family. Petey didn't have any redeeming qualities per se, but he did have two unique traits among his peers. First, he preferred young guys on his crews. Any work was seen as a favor by these men, but it was not born from the goodness of Petey's assuredly ill-functioning heart. His guys worked hard and cheap for whatever stray opportunities he found for them. The second was his tight lips, even in the most exclusive circles. And if you worked for him, the expectation was the same. You made money with your mouth shut. Always money first.

Ricky Caruso was one of his hardworking men receiving stray opportunities, although with a sideways eye some had called it nepotism. Petey had known Ricky Sr. since they were children and Ricky Two since he was scurrying between his father's legs at cookouts. With the father behind bars, a nagging sense of neighborhood responsibility seemed to give him a soft spot for Ricky. So, after Petey acquired the property destined to become The Blue Raven Social Club, Ricky carried an eight-pound takeout order to the half-finished skeleton of a club to discuss the future.

Petey described his vision in between puffs of his cigar. "And there's no disco shit in here, kid. I'll take the fuckin' hippie money if it comes, but I'm not dealin' with this disco shit. I'm gonna get you a guy, a music guy that can get some popular acts in here. The one's who think their dreams are 'right around the corner' type shit. And I want you to hire girls this week. Bring 'em in, learn about 'em, and then narrow it down. I don't know how many you need, that's all your shit, but you're gonna end up firin' half the first lot anyway, so don't fall in love. And I don't want any junkies and I don't want single mothers. Those broads have other priorities, and they're fuckin' unreliable. And if you hire the mothers, you can never fire 'em because they'll cry to you about the fuckin' kid and it'll be a whole big thing, the other girls will cry, all that shit. So, we're not gonna start off in the hole with that. And I'm takin' care of the fuckin' painters...and I got a chair guy that owes me a favor...what colors you think for the trim and shit?"

"Uh..." Ricky followed the trim with his eyes. There were only a few working lights, so the room was dark despite a few rays of sun shining through the windows. "Is there gonna be a piano?" His mother had a picture of his father in an old club with a white piano.

Petey answered with a slice of prosciutto in his mouth. "Fuckin' piano? Yeah, there's a piano. I'm talkin' colors for the fuckin' trim."

"White then," Ricky said.

"There ya go. White trim." Petey scribbled in a notebook. "What about the bar bein' there? You like that?"

The main bar was small and circular and located in the middle of the main seating area. "What do you think," Ricky said, "about buildin' a new bar near the cardroom? That way our guys in the card-room have a closer option if they need to go to the bar. Less visible, don't have to fight traffic."

"Two bars. Fine." Petey made a few more notes. "Look at outfits for the girls this week. You don't need to ask me for approval, but show the tits off, all right, or what are we doin' here? There's some bartenders comin' in for interviews next Thursday. You gotta hire Leo Cerrone 'cause he's Ray Ray's cousin, but other than that, I could give a fuck. And if Leo don't work out, I could give a fuck about that too. Keep that in mind. This place ain't a charity. Nico and Vinnie are gonna run the cardroom for us, did I tell you that? You just pro-tect them from any curious motherfuckers. They're plenty capable of the other stuff. How many suits you got?"

"Three."

Petey pulled a stack of money from his pocket and counted from the wad. "Here," he said, tossing money on the table, "go get some new suits. Tailored fuckin' suits. Every time I see you in this building from now until the place burns to the fuckin' ground, you're wearin' a tailored suit. You gotta command respect from these motherfuckers."

Ricky had to stifle a laugh. Petey's suits, when he wore them, were wrinkled and too tight for him to button.

"Customers, girls," Petey continued, poking the air with each word, "bartenders, these motherfuckin' singers, wise guys, it don't matter. They all gotta respect you and know you're the motherfuckin' boss in here."

"I get it. New suits." Ricky stashed the money in his jacket. He didn't mind wearing suits, especially when they were bought with Petey's money.

"And get a fuckin' notebook. You see this thing?" He waved his notebook in the air. "I carry it with me everywhere. Get a fuckin' notebook so when I teach you this fuckin' stuff, you don't forget."

"I'll get a notebook," Ricky said, ignoring the lie. Petey didn't carry a notebook with him everywhere. Ricky had seen that note-book three or four times in the previous decade.

"And not Family stuff," Petey continued, "that stuff's private. In the notebook is club shit. I don't want you to leave it sittin' on the counter and then some asshole has the keys to the kingdom." He tossed his notebook back on the table, scooped a cold bite of pasta, and looked purposefully around the unfurnished room. The surfaces were dusty from months of disuse, and wires hung from the ceiling where the previous owner abandoned his renovations. Even for a club, the main room was large with a high flat ceiling, exposed rafters, and shades of antique brick covering the walls. The disorder masked its potential.

Petey scooped a final bite through the red gravy crusting his lips then brought his eyes to Ricky's. "You wanna be like your father?"

Ricky scoffed. "No, I don't wanna be like him. He's in a cage."

"Before the cage." Petey's tone held weight. Ricky felt it. "You wanna be what he was before the cage, or you wanna run a nightclub?"

"I wanna be better than what he was before."

Petey opened a fresh tin and speared a ravioli. "That's about what I thought you'd say. What if I reminded you that the Bronx is half burned to the ground, Brooklyn's in shambles, wars are going on around the world, mail bombs, cults, hippies, homosexuals, terrorism? It's fuckin' chaos out there," he gulped the oozing pasta, "but this club is a recession-proof business. Poor men won't eat for days so they can come get drunk and eye pretty girls. You could run the club, and that's it. If that's what you wanted to do."

"I want more than that. My father made mistakes, but at least he wasn't some crumb, scrubbin' tables and shit. There's more out there for me than this club. I would never be able to stay away from the rest, hidin' in some office."

Petey dabbed his chins with a spare towel covered in drywall dust. "Then we've got work to do. I've got faith but we've gotta get to work. Nobody comes full blown into his world," Petey said, tugging his ear. "You gotta earn it."

Ricky nodded. Pete went on, "All right, kid. Hearin' that answer from ya, tomorrow I need you to help me with somethin' of a more peculiar sort. Not club related. 'The rest' related."

"What's that?"

Petey waved a hand dismissively. "There's this Provenzano shit-head named Vinny Cacase," he said. "Nico didn't know any better, and he beat the shit out of this shopkeeper that apparently was under Vinny's protection. I didn't know that, Nico didn't know that, but whatever. So, I don't want Nico around, and Cacase wants to have a sit-down about it. I need you to pick me up from my house at 2:00 p.m. tomorrow and we'll run over there and see what this guy has to say."

"Just me and you?"

"Yeah, prolly just me and you. Vinny's a little arrogant punk. Nobody gives a fuck about his little shopkeeper. The guy is actin' like I'm trying to muscle in on his fuckin' doughnut shop."

May 1973
Hartel residence in Brooklyn, NY
"Hartel had a nose for money…"

The Maceo brothers and their guest Angelo Butero were parked three blocks from Stanley's small gray house and the hideous yellow Monaco parked out front amidst a hard, dense rain. Tony used Janis Joplin to fight pounding clamor as the men planned their entrance into the house.

Angelo, an obese thirty-five-year-old with curly brown hair, was a fast and frequent talker. "What's this guy's name again?"

"Stanley Hartel."

"And he's an accountant?"

"I don't think he really is," Vito said. "He just looks like he would be an accountant. Fuckin' shifty like that. So, we started callin' him the Accountant, so we could make accountant jokes."

Angelo finished loading and stowed his pocket pistol. For a man of his girth, the weapon was underwhelming to the point of distraction. "Joey tells me Hartel owes him over $1,800."

"He owes Vic $2,000."

"And you think he has that much in the house?"

"The motherfucker has a new car on the street," Tony said, stuffing a much less underwhelming .45 caliber in his jacket, "and he's tellin' us he's strapped for cash. He wasn't bein' straight with us. I know that much."

Angelo paused but seemed too disturbed by his own silence to let it stand. "So, we just knock the fuckin' door down or what?"

"I say Benjie and Vito head to the back in case this guy gets spooked and tries to run. Me and you head straight to the front door."

Angelo tugged at the sleeves of his track suit. Tony could almost see the price tags hanging from the velour cuffs. "And then we tie him down and have a chat?" Angelo asked.

"We can figure that out inside, but yeah, we'll need to keep him stationary if we have to search the place in case he's got a safe or somethin'. Kitchen chair, find some rope. Whatever he's got lyin' around."

"You didn't bring any rope?"

"No, we didn't bring any rope." Tony knew Angelo without having to spend any more time with him. *He just wants to wear the jewelry.*

"We could still go get some," Angelo said stupidly.

Tony said no. "We don't know how long he's gonna be alone. His ma is playin' cards with a bunch of old ladies, and nobody knows when her bedtime is. We need to move now."

"I think we at least have time to run up to a hardware store and grab some rope."

Vito laughed, but he could see Tony's frustration building, so he said decisively, "Angelo, you're outvoted. We're not goin' to any hardware stores. Benjie, get us closer."

Benjie crept down the street toward the gray house and the Monaco, stopping less than a block away. He pulled the keys and looked to Vito for directions, who simply said, "Here we go, Benj." Vito remembered the nerves of his first "official" errands. *He's not crying, that's a good start.*

The four stepped into the sheet of night rain and ran with purpose toward the warm-yellow windows of Stanley's house. Each man was drenched by the time they got there, and the cool drops pulled Benjie's shirt snug against his chest and shook from his hair as he moved. He and Vito broke from the other two as instructed and moved to where two separate windows glowed on the backside of the house. Vito was taller and stood on his tiptoes to peer through the first, mouthing *kitchen* to his brother and shaking his head. Stanley was not in there. They sloshed forward through a puddle and up to the other window some ten feet farther along. Again, Vito looked inside. This time he turned, smiled at Benjie, mouthing the words *living room* as the rain dripped from the gutters and onto his back. Stanley was home. The pair moved to either side of the back door and crouched out of sight.

They heard knocks from the front and then Stanley's steps across the floor to answer. Vito moved to peek through a window but, before he could position himself, Stanley's slow walk turned into an unmistakable sprint toward the back of the house. Vito squared himself to the door, and when it swung open, he launched himself into Stanley Hartel's stomach, carrying him backward into the house and onto the floor. Benjie jumped in after them and pinned Stanley's arms, allowing Vito to maneuver and control Stanley's legs. Stanley tried to yell, but Benjie let one arm go long enough to throw his swollen right hand at Stanley's jaw as Tony and Angelo shouldered through the front door.

Tony ordered Angelo, "Find some rope," while he helped Benjie control the upper half of Stanley's desperate extremities. Angelo scrambled through kitchen drawer after kitchen drawer, throwing silverware, pots, pans, knives, dish towels, plates, and cups all over the floor. Tony and Benjie took their opportunities to land swings on the Accountant until blood covered his teeth and leaked from the bridge of his nose. His thrashing slung the grim color all around him.

"Look for sheets or something!" Vito yelled.

Angelo promptly waddled down the hallway. Tony and Benjie continued to land a punch or two at a time, but the smaller man was proving tough to control. Vito, who was dealing with the brunt of the labor, yelled for Angelo again. "Come on, motherfucker! Take 'em off the fuckin' beds!" Benjie wasn't sure if this is what Angelo did, but he emerged shortly after holding two white sheets and a pillowcase. Tony and Benjie, still doing their best to control the arms, forced Stanley up and onto a kitchen chair. Tony pulled Stanley's arms behind the backrest, and Angelo tried to tie his hands with one of the white sheets he found.

"It's too thick! I can't get it to hold!" Angelo said, desperately working his clumsy hands.

Vito's face was red, straining to hold Stanley's legs as the little man used every muscle fiber to buck him off. "If you don't tie that fucking knot—"

"Hold on! I saw some scissors over here!" Angelo ran back to the drawers (Tony: "Are you fuckin' serious?!") he had just ransacked and again began dumping a second round of kitchen utensils. Stanley got his right leg free and kicked Vito square in the nose.

"Motherfucker!" Vito yelled, blocking several additional kicks in quick succession with his palm. Red trickled from his nose, but he managed to get Stanley's free leg back under control while purple veins curled over his neck and forehead.

"I got 'em!" Angelo said, holding up a pair of scissors and going to work on the sheets. Stanley paused his struggle to peek at the progress. Tony used the moment to crack him twice more across the face. From either the punches or exhaustion, Stanley was limp when Angelo came back with a manageable piece of fabric and tied knots to hold Stanley's arms behind his back, his legs to the chair, and finally covered his face with a pillowcase. Stanley tried to speak from underneath, but Vito's fist stopped him before much sound could escape.

Vito, furious at the exertion Stanley required, followed the first punch with five or six additional more. He then spun to Angelo. "Way to take your time, you stupid fat fuck." Vito's nose was dripping onto his shirt and his lungs were desperate for air. "You payin' for this?" he asked Angelo, tugging at his shirt and pacing the area to catch his breath.

While they couldn't see the underlying damage, the front of the pillowcase was bloodied and Stanley seemed much less inclined to make noise. The floor was littered with spoons and pans, and Stanley had marked the floor with the black soles of his shoes and the red spray of his blood. Vito regained his composure enough to chuckle and wipe the blood from his own nose and chin. "All right, Stanley. We calm now? We just want to talk." Stanley stayed silent under his pillowcase.

Tony punched the white that represented Stanley's face again, right across his unseen cheekbone. "My brother asked you a question, Stanley. Are you calm now?" The bloody pillowcase nodded slowly. "All right, I'm gonna take the pillowcase off. If you make a sound, I will pistol whip the fuck out of you. Do you understand me?" Stanley nodded again and Tony removed the pillowcase.

The lower half of Stanley's face was crimson from his broken nose. He attempted to spit what had collected in his mouth onto the floor, but it just dribbled weakly to his shirt and chin. Tony continued, "Okay now, Stan. You owe some people some money, is that correct?" Stanley looked up at Tony, his right eye near swollen shut. "And you have the money in this house, is that correct?" Stanley shook his head no. This time Vito punched Stanley, a straight right into his upper lip. Tony spoke in a playful, childish voice. "I don't believe you, Stanley. You recently bought a terrible-lookin' Dodge Monaco, which is parked right outside this fuckin' house. How did you do that?"

Stanley tried to keep his head up but struggled, and it bobbled back and forth. He managed one word and it was barely audible to the four men. "Mother."

"Are you saying your mother bought the Monaco?" Stanley grunted. "On a pension? That doesn't seem likely to me. Does that seem likely to you, Benj?"

Benjie was caught off guard but was able to parrot back, "It doesn't seem likely, Ton."

"No, it doesn't seem likely. Now, Stanley, I'm gonna ask you again. Do you have any money in this house?" Stanley again shook his head no. Tony seemed to take the answer calmly, putting his hand to his chin as if deep in thought, walking slowly around Stanley's chair. Then, quickly, he snatched one of the discarded pans and smashed Stanley square in the back of the head. The clang reverberated painfully off the walls of the small house.

Tony walked over the streaks of Stanley's blood now radiating from the chair. "*I do not like these answers,*" he said. He stopped in front of Stanley and crouched to his eye level. "Where is the money in this house? Any money at all?" Stanley made no immediate movement, and the hesitation was enough. Tony yanked the chair's front legs upward, throwing Stanley on his back and dropping the full weight of his body onto his hands, bound behind him. Stanley groaned in pain from a broken hand and lay there, nearly unconscious for the second time in ten minutes and bleeding from everywhere above his collar. A gash had developed above his right eye, and blood, which had previously been running into his eyes, was now running down the side of his head and into his hair.

Tony decided their attempts with Stanley were enough for now. He turned to Angelo and Benjie. "Search the house. Especially the desks and closets."

Obediently, the two walked down the hallway off the kitchen to the rest of the house. Benjie went to the master bedroom first. In the closet, he found ankle-length dresses, high heels, shawls, and sweaters embroidered with colorful flowers. He ran his hand across the top shelf and found an empty shoe box, photo albums, Stanley's high school diploma, and an empty pink hat box. Across the room, he pulled the dresser drawers from their tracks and dumped the clothes on the floor. Nothing of interest. A carved wooden jewelry box sat next to the bed with a few gold pieces inside. Benjie pocketed them in case they found nothing else. Between the bedrooms, he rifled through a linen closet with old towels and extra blankets.

Benjie found Stanley's bedroom. It was decorated with pictures of Jim Clark, Graham Hill, and a host of other drivers, cars, and tracks. Benjie searched the closet just as thoroughly for any sign of wealth and found none. Stanley had an oak dresser stenciled with leaves beneath a window with the shades pulled open. The rain had slowed and the streetlights sparkled against the ground to give Benjie a clear view of the world outside. The view unnerved him. He shut the shades and opened the first dresser drawer. Mostly it contained socks and underwear, but in the back-left corner, his fingers tipped something metallic. He pulled the object out. It was a lock box about twelve by eight inches.

"Tony!" he called back down the hall. A moment later his brother was in the room, saw the box, and beamed. He took it and led Benjie back into the kitchen where Stanley lay, still bloodied and beaten on the floor.

"What is this, Stanley?" Tony asked in the same playful tone as before. Stanley was so bruised and his eyes so swollen Benjie was not sure he could see what Tony meant, even three inches from his face. "Angelo, find me a screwdriver or a hammer or something."

Angelo jogged off and reappeared with both tools, as if intimately aware of the Hartel's belongings by now. Tony smashed the lock with a few well-placed strikes, and the lid rattled free. With the other men over his shoulder, he opened the lid. "Jackpot," Vito said as they saw what was inside: a wad of cash a few inches thick and a black leather-bound book with gold trim on the binding.

Tony grabbed the cash first. "What sort of operation are you running down here, Stanley? I may have underestimated you." He handed the wad to Vito. "Count this, will ya?"

Vito sat at the table to count and Tony flipped through the book himself while Benjie and Angelo stood over Stanley, guarding against any recovery of his fighting spirit. After a few minutes, Vito said, "He's got $5,200 here."

Angelo improvised some quick math on his fingers. "That's perfect. We give Papa Vic his $2,000 plus a bonus $100, Joey gets his $1,800 plus a bonus $100, and we chop up the extra $1,200."

Benjie wasn't sure he should mention the jewelry with Angelo there, so he kept his mouth shut and waited for Tony and Vito to make a ruling.

Vito checked Angelo's math in his head (this took longer than one would hope) and shrugged. "My thoughts exactly. Ton? Is that what you're thinking?"

Tony did not answer. He was staring at the leather-bound book, his finger lightly scrolling its page. "We're gonna make a lot more than a couple hundred. Vito, look at this." He handed the book to his older brother, who began to read. "These are shipments," he said eventually.

Tony nodded, a subtle smile on his lips. "Yes, they are."

"What is this, a clothing company?" Vito read a little more.

"Are these imported clothes and shit?" Tony inspected the book again while the others caught up. "This goes three months out. The little accountant is worth more than we thought. Five thousand dollars is nothing compared to this." Tony leaned down to Stanley again, who had hardly moved in fifteen minutes. "Stanley. Hey." He poked him in the shoulder. "Who knows about these shipments?"

Stanley used what looked to be the last of his energy to say, "Pisciotto." The name was met with silence.

Tony flipped again through the pages. The ledger was meticulous, listing not only brand names and vessel information but the sizes, colors, and styles of the inventory as well. The shipments were valued anywhere from $4,000 to $20,000 according to the ledger, spaced every few weeks, and this ledger went back years, recording sixty-two transactions. A credit in, a deduction out, for each and every shipment. And the date for both entries was the same—

Tony shut the ledger. "Do the Pisciottos collect on these shipments at the docks or when they're delivered to the store?"

Again, Stanley had to build himself up to answer. "Fees from the boats. Fees from the trucking companies."

"Do they track the shipments to the door?"

Stanley shook his head no.

Tony turned to Vito. "They pay Pisciotto's men at the docks to look the other way, and after that he doesn't give a damn about this stuff. It just gets delivered to the stores. The trucks could be jacked on route, occasionally at least, if not all the time." He went back to Stanley, "Is that what you're telling us?"

Stanley's bloodied face simply nodded.

Tony patted Stanley's leg and turned to the other men. His eyes went first to Angelo, the outsider, then back to the crisp pages of Stanley's ledger. "This stays between the four of us," he said, lightly feeling the indented penmanship on the page. "We came here and did what we were supposed to do and more. Vic and Joey will be happy. They've got their money. But these shipments are for us. Everybody okay with that?"

The four men looked each other over, each hoping someone else would say it first. Finally, Angelo quit fiddling with the front of his tracksuit long enough to speak. "You've got me, Tony. Their money is their money. These shipments are ours."

* * *

Tony moved without hurry up the steps to the front door of his house. The night air still smelled like the rain, and he liked the cool touch of it on his face. He stopped at the door and looked back to the street, even turning completely around to stare down the block in both directions. Lampposts hit the street every ten yards or so with pale glimmers, their edges misted by the precipitating dew. The moonlight showed the cuts on his hands as he opened the door, and he could sense the impending bruises in the stiff flex of his knuckles. He kicked his shoes at their usual place and shuffled toward his bedroom. The door to his son Carmine's room was cracked, and Tony nudged it just enough to see him fast asleep. He pooled enough courage to enter, tensed as he moved by each faint wooden creak of the floor. Carmine's face was cast in a purple-blue shadow, and Tony combed his dark bangs with a finger as he knelt by the bed. He was wearing pajamas, Ana must have bought them, with racecars and trucks, and his little hand was curled against his bottom lip. Tony kissed the boy and lingered before finally tiptoeing to his bedroom, where Ana was under the covers and asleep. Tony went to the bathroom to wash the dried blood from his hands.

Tony could see in the mirror he had blood on his dress shirt, and when he removed his jacket, he saw more of it splattered across his chest and sides. He undressed to his boxers before turning on the water at the sink. He let the water warm itself as he rubbed his hands beneath the flow. When the water wet the caked blood, it turned red and rusted and swirled down the drain. A bar of soap lay unused in the soap dish, and he brought it to lather with both hands, scrubbing the cuts Stanley's face had left on him with a washcloth.

"Hey, baby," said Ana's voice from the doorway. She was in her nightgown, a purple thing that vaguely showed her body underneath. "You're home late," she said, moving behind him and resting her chin on his shoulder. He blew a kiss into the mirror for her, and she wrapped her arms tightly around his midsection as he cleaned his hands.

"Yeah, I know, baby. Sorry I had to leave so quick." Tony did his best to rinse the soap thoroughly before half-turning to kiss her properly.

"There's leftovers downstairs if you're hungry."

"I had to eat at Jerry's. I knew there was a chance I would have to work late." Tony flung the excess water into the sink and found a towel to dry them. When he was able to face her fully, he pulled her close and kissed her again, longer this time. "I feel good tonight," he said to her. "How do you feel?" He cupped her cheek in his hand and smiled into her brown eyes.

She loved his moods like this. "How should I feel?" she asked with a playful smile. Tony lifted her off the bathroom floor, and she wrapped her legs around him.

"Give me a few minutes," he said, rubbing her thighs as he did, "and I think you will feel as good as I do." She laughed and kissed him again as he carried her to bed. He pressed his face into hers, quick and aggressively, and she responded in kind. They were practiced with each other. Tony's hand was already under her nightshirt and pulling it over her head to expose her full breasts to the same purple-blue shadow of the moon. She filled his palm, and he pushed her up and around, kissing her still more aggressively on her lips and neck as she unbuttoned his pants. He stiffened with her touch, and his blood rose, hot into his arms and face. His wrists cramped as he pushed against the bed, but she pulled him inside and adrenaline numbed his discomfort. Her nails scratched his back as they fell against each other, moaning together. He fell to one side, continuing to move in unison with her, the air now present on the exposed sections of him in metronomic rhythm. Airiana pushed him to his back and adjusted herself above him. He steered her as she bounced and tightened above him. He tapped and rubbed her, watching her eyes dance as he did, his arms and hands full to bursting with excitement, heat, and passion. And they fell against each other. Again and again and hugged each other as they drifted off to sleep.

* * *

"Hey, get up."

Tony's face was pressed into a particularly soft bit of pillow. "Why?"

"'Cause I've got to change the sheets."

"What? Why the fuck do you need to change the sheets right now?"

"Don't use that language. Carmine is up. Your hands are bleeding. It's everywhere."

One night in May of 1973
The Dalton family residence
"He didn't understand the rules, poor guy."

Headlights shone through the front windows to briefly illuminate a hodge-podge of finery in the Dalton family living room. Al Giordano turned to face Mrs. Dalton. "Is that him?"

"Yes." She was sitting, shaking more accurately, in her crimson night gown and fluffy white slippers. Three men—trusted Giordano family *Capo* and enforcer Nick Pisani, the Don himself, and his son Johnny—stood before her and she could not help but flit her eyes back and forth between them. The lights in the home were off, but the moonlight was enough for her to see their guns.

Nick pulled their curtains back for a better look. "Which door is he gonna come in?"

Mrs. Dalton struggled to control her breathing, her tears. "I don't know for sure."

Nick snapped to face her, but his voice remained soft and even. "Well, normally then? Believe me, Mrs. D., this works out best if the three of us don't get surprised." He tapped his revolver, a .38, with his off-hand. "This thing has a hair trigger."

"The garage," she said, her words muffled by sobs.

Nick moved quickly to cover an entrance from the garage. Mrs. Dalton squealed, short and loud, prompting Al to gently touch her shoulder. "Now, now, Mrs. Dalton. We don't plan to hurt your husband." Her back heaved with each new second, but she managed to weep quietly.

The car engine stopped. One beat, then two, and shoe clacks could be heard. Nick positioned himself where he would not be visible from the doorway and leveled his revolver at head height. Al turned the light on to his left, ensuring he would have the man's attention first. Johnny stood to his father's right and back a step, his face hidden in shadow, his gun drawn, his finger light on the trigger. The hinges twisted with a creak as the door swung and Henry Dalton filled its frame, briefcase in hand. His eyes were down for a split second, but when he caught Al Giordano's figure, a gasp caught in his throat. He ran back toward his car before ever stepping across the threshold.

"Motherfucker!" Nick yelled, running after him with Johnny just behind. The two men reached the banker, and the sounds of their struggle could be heard back in the house. Mrs. Dalton had stopped her breathing, eyes up and red. Al peeked at her crumpled, fearful figure and shook his head. "Not an impressive start," he said. She put her head back down, and the sobs returned.

The banking tycoon was led by his tie to the couch in his own living room and shoved into the cushions next to his wife. "Mr. Dalton," Al began in his rough Sicilian timbre, "my first question was supposed to be if you know who I am. I think we've established that you do." Dalton stared at the ground, hesitant to make eye contact with these men. Al did not like that. "Mr. Dalton, I am speaking to you. Eye contact is polite when people are speaking to you."

Dalton's eyes responded with fiery resentment, first for the men who wrestled him inside and then for the Don and his silver-pommeled cane. "Thank you," Al said as if they were sharing a sun-covered park bench. "Do you know why we are here?"

"The loan. You're here about the fuckin' loan. The construction loan."

Al nodded. "An important bit of business, Mr. Dalton. For you and us."

"A loan that will strap my bank of cash and which you may never repay. You could shutter Roselli Construction and never pay it back for all I know."

Al laughed. "A very good idea, Mr. Dalton. It's a wonder no one mentioned it to me." Dalton, perhaps gaining confidence, set his features aggressively and glared up at the Don. "But no," Al continued, tapping his cane against the hardwood beneath his feet, "at this moment, I have every intention of repaying the loan, despite your rather offensive suspicions."

"Our bank does not have the cash," Dalton said. "I simply cannot do it. The bank trustees will roast me. I will not be able to defend it. It's too reckless."

"Get creative," Nick said, gesturing casually with his gun.

Dalton's face reddened, and a vein sprouted from his forehead. He was unaccustomed to directions. "The trustees will *take my job*."

Al sat on the coffee table, eye level with Dalton's bulging vein, and spoke as if to a child. "You're the Boss of your bank, Mr. Dalton. I am also a Boss. What's the thing about Bosses, Nick? You remember the thing about Bosses?"

Nick chuckled. "The Boss is the Boss…is the Boss," he said, his cadence rhythmic.

"That's not how it works in the real world," Dalton said, begging now as if he sensed finality in the phrase. "They will take my job for a reckless, asinine loan like this. Roselli's company has existed for what? Three months? It won't work."

"Oh," Al said, "it'll work, Mr. Dalton. I promise you it will work." He pulled a small packet of paper from his jacket and laid it open on Dalton's lap. Al held out a pen. "Here's our contract, Mr. Dalton. Don't make me splash your brains on it."

Mrs. Dalton reacted with a fresh howl and more tears. Nick pressed his gun into the tightly cut, blond-brown hair on the back of Mr. Dalton's head. The Bank President reached for the pen slowly, reluctantly. Don Giordano gave it to him, stood up, and watched Henry Dalton scrawl his name on the bottom line.

One morning in May 1973
Jerry's Place in Brooklyn, NY
"A high stakes life means high stakes lessons."

The suit was too big for Benjie. They were the same height, but he was too skinny to fill a suit meant for Vito's gut, and the jacket sagged almost to his knees and the sleeves reached his fingers. Vito had given him shoes as well, but they were worn and flopped against the floor when he walked. He had to slide his feet to the toe and curl them into the sole with each step to keep them from falling off. It was a sorry image, and that morning the corroded mirror in the bathroom of Jerry's Restaurant was brutally honest in the light of a single dying bulb. At least his hair was tame; that was one part of the ensemble he could control. He shaved his face (no one could tell the difference) and greased his hair with scraps from a forgotten tin. As underwhelming as it was, he had wasted enough time. A deep breath, a few head shakes, and he plunged forward into Jerry's dining room and its gallery of cheap reproductions.

Benjie waved meekly to Frank the Bartender as he passed the bar and found Papa Vic sitting with two other men at his circular table. Vic rose to meet him as he always did, this time laughing hysterically as he hugged him.

"My god, son, who gave you that suit? Willis Reed? Jesus Christ."

The two other men laughed along with Vic, and Benjie felt his face grow hot. "Sorry," he said, "I've never owned a suit before. I had to borrow this one from Vito."

"We'll get you somethin' else, kid. I can't have you looking like that if you're gonna work for me. People will say I don't pay you fuckers enough. But sit down for now, sit down," Vic said, waving off Benjie's concerns and pointing to an empty chair. "I want you to meet these guys. This one here"—he pointed at the tan man with cropped hair in a black pinstripe suit—"is Sammie Calabrese, if you haven't met each other. He's an up-and-comer, some might say. He runs around with another crew of guys, but he comes to slum it with us every now and then."

Benjie shook Sammie's hand. He recognized him, as anyone who ever met him probably would. Underneath his suit, Sammie's arms and chest threatened to rip the fragile seams, and he was a head taller than anyone else in the room. "And this so-called gentleman," Vic waved to the smaller of the two, "is Nick Pisani. Nicky Six, some call him. You don't mind that name, do ya, Nick? He's a friend of mine and your brothers. A good friend I have to say after all these years."

Nick was about five feet, six inches (all the smaller next to Sammie) with a crooked nose, sharp features, and precisely trimmed brown hair combed back from his forehead. His teeth were precise as well, straight and clean and inviting as he shook Benjie's hand. He wore a starched blue jacket but no tie, a gold watch, and several rings that glimmered even in the dim restaurant. Benjie had seen Nick more than Sammie, a vague presence who always seemed to be shaking people's hands and accepting their well-wishes since Benjie was a kid.

"Anyway," Vic said as everyone resettled from their greetings, "to business. How's our favorite accountant doin' today?" Benjie hesitated, eyes skirting between the two visitors. Vic motioned for him to go ahead with it. "Don't worry about these two. Speak freely, kid."

"Well, first," Benjie reached into his jacket for the $2,100 Tony counted out the night before, "this is your money, plus an extra $100 we found that the Accountant had been hiding from us."

Vic slid the money into his pocket without a second glance. "And is he still active?"

It took Benjie a second to understand, but he got there. "Yes," he said. "Although I'm sure this mornin' was rough."

The other men snickered, although Benjie was only half joking; Stanley's eyes were swollen shut and dark purple when they left, with blood caked around his mouth and hair. Benjie hesitated again, still not sure how much Sammie and Nick should know. Vic sensed this. "Go on, kid. No edits."

"We found that money in a lock box in his bedroom...even a little extra. But that wasn't all. Tony found a book Stanley had been keepin' for a fashion house. A log of imports that Tony thinks we can make some money off, with some help. Tony said for me to tell you, 'Joey's friend knows about the ledger book.' Tony told all of us right then—me, Vito, Angelo—about the book and the imports. But at the time...when we were still in the house...Tony told Angelo that we would keep it a secret and do the truck jobs under the table, without Joey or you knowing what was goin' on."

Nick and Sammie looked curious and turned to Vic for a reaction. He just laughed. "Tony baited him?"

"Yeah, that's right. He said you'd get why."

"Beautiful," Vic said, still laughing. "Tony's always had a good head on his shoulders. I'll let Joey know, and from there, hey, we do what we gotta do." Vic stood and yelled to Frank the Bartender, "Frank, for these two," he pointed to Sammie and Nick, "whatever they want. You should know that by now. Sorry to run, gentlemen, but I've gotta help this kid buy a fuckin' suit before my whole reputation goes to shit."

* * *

Papa Vic directed Benjie through the heart of Manhattan and into a small parking garage on the east side of the borough. The streets were wet from the night before, and puddles lined their walk to street level and then across an intersection, down one block and into a men's store called *The Murphy House*. Four mannequins displayed their goods proudly in the windows, and inside the walls were lined with coats, vests, slacks, dress shirts, ties, and socks of every color and pattern. Benjie trooped several steps behind Vic, acutely aware of his outfit and clambering gait. Even Vic's disheveled profile was salvaged in Benjie's eyes by the crisp lines and iron flat expression of his suit.

Vic introduced a bent-over figure as the Murphy House tailor Antonello Carrisi but only called him "The Old Man" after that. The name fit the white hair growing from his ears and eyebrows, his rhinophymatic nose, the thin folds on his arms, and their clusters of brown moles. He stored a pencil behind his ear and kept a length of tape measure over his shoulders that he tugged spuriously as he worked. When Vic explained they were there to buy for Benjie, Carrisi showed a set of chipped gray teeth and nudged the kid onto a wooden platform in front of three mirrors. Vic pulled up a chair to dictate and observe.

"What types of suits?" the Old Man asked, tilting his head back to look up at Benjie's face.

"Uh…I'd like a gray one, I think," Benjie said before checking with Vic, who nodded.

"Double breasted?"

Again, Benjie checked with Vic and relayed the yes to the Old Man. "Do you like any colors? Maybe light blue or red?"

Vic shook his head for Benjie.

"Good answer," Carrisi growled, "bright colors are for insecure men."

The Old Man measured Benjie's legs from knee to groin and wrapped his withered forearms around the kid's midsection before pulling modeling suits picked from here and there in the racks. He felt their fabric, cool and smooth against his skin, and swelled to fill them in the mirror. Vic watched patiently while reading a newspaper he found on the floor nearby.

"How does that one feel?" the Old Man asked, several styles along.

"Good," Benjie said. He was unsure of what feedback to provide although neither Vic nor the Old Man said he was doing it wrong.

"And around the thigh?"

"It feels fine to me," Benjie said. Still, the Old Man leaned to inspect the area further. He grabbed the pant leg between his fingers and pulled it to its extent before marking it with a small piece of white chalk.

"And here?" he asked, pulling the fabric to a peak behind Benjie and off his backside.

"It feels fine."

Carrisi shuffled to scribble another note before inspecting the area again. He pulled the zipper down and wriggled his fingers inside, stretching the fabric forward and measuring, before shuffling to his notes and back again. He tugged the pantleg firmly into Benjie's groin and held it long enough to rest the tape across him more than once, each with a minor adjustment and another note. Benjie stared into the mirror and onto the top of the Old Man's spotted baldness, then at Vic's distracted reading, then down the rack of suits just to his right.

"I've got the measurements," the Old Man said finally. "How many suits you want for him?"

"Make five of 'em." Vic looked up from his paper. "Normal colors. Two gray, two black, and a blue or something like that. Simple patterns. I don't wanna be walkin' around here with fuckin' Liberace."

"I'll bring you some patterns. Give me a few minutes." The Old Man scuttled off toward the back. Vic set his paper down and clapped a hand into Benjie's back as he put his original clothes back on. "You ready for some clothes that fit?" he asked, smiling.

"Yeah. Long time coming. Tony teases me about my clothes all the time. And still living at home."

"We'll need to fix that too." Vic paused. "Did I see him touch you?"

Benjie was startled and could feel his face reddening for the second time in just a few minutes. "What do you mean?"

"Did he touch you, ya know…the wrong way?"

"He was just takin' measurements."

"You don't need to touch anyone's dick to make a suit."

Benjie did not know what to say. He just kept looking into Vic's pale eyes. "Did it make you feel uncomfortable?" Vic asked.

"Yeah…I mean I didn't like it, but I just thought he was takin' measurements." The words were stupid and clumsy when he heard them.

"Why didn't you say anything?" Vic did not seem angry, but his tone was sharper than the words. "You didn't have to slug him, but why didn't you tell him to stop?"

"I just wanted him to finish. I didn't know how it was supposed to work."

"That's fear. You were afraid of me, afraid of him, afraid of what we'd say. Fear. You can't be afraid in my world. You'll get killed or worse."

75

"S-sorry, Vic. I would've said somethin' if I knew it's what you wanted."

Vic's face muscles twitched. "*I* didn't want it. *You* wanted it. You just said so. 'I just wanted him to finish,' you said. 'I didn't like it.'"

Benjie tried a smile. "Sorry. I'll know next time. That's why I'm here, right? To learn?"

Vic nodded, his eyes searching Benjie's features. "You are," he said.

Benjie did not know what he hoped to find, but he wished Vito would have brought him here or Tony. They would've told the Old Man off and gone about their business. But Vic did not. Instead, he reached his hand inside his jacket and drew a pistol from its folds. It was small, black, and shining beneath the store lights. And then Vic was pulling a short cylinder from another pocket and attaching it slowly, metal scratching metal, to the end of the barrel before dropping the gun into Benjie's open hand. It was heavy and cold. The kid curled his fingers through the guard and over the trigger and let it hang loose at his side as he brushed against the racks of perfumed suits all the way to the back of the store. There was a curtain pulled closed to his right, and Benjie parted it just enough to peer in. *Silent now.* Carrisi was standing about ten feet away with his back to the entrance, flipping quickly through a binder of swatches. Benjie could hear him humming softly to himself, swaying back and forth. *No need to get closer.* Benjie raised his hand, his arm, the gun, through the curtains and held it even with the Old Man's back. *Pull it quick,* he heard Tony say, *pull it sharp and don't lose control when you feel the shot.*

"That's enough," Vic whispered in Benjie's ear, pulling the gun gently from its mark. "Lesson over."

May 1973
Petey Caltagirone's house in Brooklyn, NY
"We're all born stupid and most of us never change."

Petey lived in a plain house with red brick and small front windows. It had a gray porch covered by wrought iron furniture, where he would often sit with a newspaper in his hand and yell after cars traveling too fast for his liking. The front was well tended by his wife, Muriel, a German woman who was introverted enough to live happily as his glorified cook and gardener. Ricky found her shrill voice excruciating and avoided her when he could.

He could hear Pete hollering at his dogs before he answered the front door. "Come on in," the Fat Man said, extending an arm above his belly.

Pete typically received guests from his orange recliner, but when Ricky entered, the chair was already occupied by a young kid with mousy brown hair, an Allman Brothers T-shirt, and blue jeans. Petey frowned, as if disappointed the kid had not had the courtesy to disappear. "Ricky," he said through his cigar, "this is my cousin Claudia's firstborn son, Markie. He is a bum…but I've agreed to let him work at the club on account of his frog-eating father who can't hold a job for more than a couple months and is near starvin' my blood relatives because of it. He works directly *for you*," he said, pointing a thick finger at Ricky's chest. "I don't want Nico and Vinnie around him. He's family, or so I'm led to believe." Petey turned back to the kid. "Now, Markie," he said, "this is a job without hours, so I'm sure your lazy ass is gonna hate it, but who knows? Maybe you'll have a talent for it. We've eliminated so many other possibilities, we're bound to find somethin' soon. From now on, whatever you gotta say to me goes through Ricky. And anything he asks you to do, you do with fuckin' bells on. Understand? If I'm talkin' to you other than 'Hey, how ya doin, shithead?' somethin' went wrong in the whole process of our communication."

The kid stood up with a weak smile and extended a hand to Ricky without a retort. Petey was parading his new footman. Ricky knew how that felt. He shook Markie's hand.

"All right," Petey continued, "you're best friends now. Let's go meet this asshole. Markie, drive my car."

Petey outlined the situation as they drove. They would meet Vinny in the backroom of a haberdashery in Schuylerville Ricky had never heard of, but Pete assured him they should feel comfortable. He explained his "longstanding financial interest" in the market where Vinny ran competing protection, but Petey believed the whole area was quickly going under. "This Vinny is a small-time hothead, but he's made his bones with Don P., and we fucked up or, more specifically, Nico fucked up…eh…a little bit. Truth be told, I shouldn't be in that market anyway. Fuckin' slum these days."

When Petey's musings died out, Ricky allowed a courteous pause before changing the subject. "There's some girls comin' in Monday," he said. "I put some notices in the paper and another few on the radio. You knew about both of those ideas by the way, if anybody from down there comes askin' after favors…who's our music guy? You got that figured out yet?"

"Yeah…uh…" Petey said, searching for the name in his addled brain, "what's his fuckin' name…Buddy something. I got it at the house. When we get back, I'll get it for ya."

"I'm askin' 'cause I don't know too much about the music part. I was gonna put together a list of acts or somethin', and I have no idea where to start. I was gonna ask your guy a few questions and see where his head's at." After their planning sessions, Ricky had scribbled down a bunch of well-intentioned lists.

"I told you about the bartenders, right? Ray Ray's fuckin' cousin? Lenny? Lucas? Leavitt?" Petey squinted more with each guess as if the name was coming into focus.

"I'm ready for the bartenders. Thursday."

As they got close to the haberdashery, Pete turned his attention back to Markie, his T-shirt, and jeans. "Markie, you're gonna come in with us, even though you're dressed like one of those hippie fuckheads who've never met a barber, and you're gonna stand in the corner and not make any noise. And, Rick," Pete turned as far sideways as his gut would allow, "if it somehow comes up, we're gonna call him Markie *Aiello*, because that's my sweet cousin Claudia's maiden name. If these guys know he dresses like a shithead *and* is half Frenchie, I'd have to kill myself from embarrassment. And from now on, Markie, wherever you're at, wear a fuckin' collared shirt. Pretend you're undercover as someone with a promising future." He counted out a couple hundred for Markie as he had for Ricky. "Here,

OF EMPIRE AND ILLUSION

kid. And, Ricky, pick 'em out for this idiot. He'll end up comin' back with a fuckin' tuxedo."

"Uncle Pete," Markie said, almost whispering and wary of more attention from his uncle, "I should be getting close here. Do you know which one it is?"

"Up here on the left. Blue awning. Get close so I don't have to walk anywhere."

The store was completely empty of customers and the air was stagnant, the displays needed dusting. A man with a top hat (Ricky assumed he was the store owner) walked them to the backroom where three others were waiting for them. The first introduced himself as Vinny Cacase, the principal plaintiff. He seemed to have dressed up for the meeting and grimaced to see Petey's wrinkled suit and loose tie-less collar. They shook hands and traded nods. Ricky recognized the second man as Rudy "Red Face" Bordanarro, a Provenzano Family man who had frequented a body shop Pete and Ricky's father had owned. He remembered his father telling him, "This man gets what he wants here, no questions," when Bordanarro joked about Ricky Sr.'s quote for an oil change. He was a thin man with narrow eyes, and he greeted Pete and Ricky with a hug and pecks on either cheek. Bordanarro was almost certainly the choice to mediate because of his pleasant history with Pete and his relationship to Vinny's benefactor, Don Provenzano. The last man, a plump little observer called Archie by the others, nodded nervously from his post in the corner. Ricky's eyes ran over the man's soft frame with indifference.

Vinny and Pete took their seats at an unsteady table with circular brown stains and a hole punched through the middle. Petey slid an ashtray to his right-hand side and used it extensively as they talked. The fiery cigar stock slowly set a smog upon the room and gave it an acrid smell. Markie joined Ricky on the opposite wall where they lit cigarettes, leaned on the windowsill, and listened closely to the flow of conversation.

Rudy found his own chair, cigar, and ashtray. "Okay," he said. "So, Vinny has a shop owner. What's his name, Vin?"

"Zimmerman." Vinny had black hair that he slicked to the side and was leaning back with his arms crossed, trying to stare daggers across the table at Petey. The Fat Man, in contrast, looked entirely untroubled, as if they were discussing where to have dinner.

Rudy continued, "All right then, so Mr. Zimmerman is under Vinny's protection at the market. He runs this nice little doughnut shop down there. Now, what happened, Petey? Nico get carried away or what?"

"Nico thought I had rights to it," Petey said. "I've been in that market for almost twenty-five years and Nico goes down there, on my behalf, and collects for me. He wasn't trying to make anything complicated, I promise. The doughnut stall is new on the block, and my guy was just tryin' to do his job. Honestly though, I didn't know the guy was connected with anybody, and Nico says he didn't either. I think you gotta take him at his word on that."

Vinny uncrossed his arms and leaned forward. "Zimm says he told Nico he was with me." Ricky thought the tone betrayed him— Vinny could not believe his name hadn't sent Nico running. That was his real gripe. *Petey is gonna chew this dumbass up.*

Petey answered through more puffs of his cigar. "Nico didn't believe him. He thought the guy was bullshittin'. There's no reason to complicate this. It was a mistake. Nico thought he was using you as cover to get outtav a debt."

"He wasn't. I got him the license for that stall. That should be my action."

"And I'd agree with ya on that under the typical circumstances," Petey said, "but, in my opinion, it's all too confusing down there. Our Thing is better off with only one guy runnin' protection in that market. So, in the interest of our own peace and prosperity, Vinny, I'm gonna ask to buy you out of that market and we can put this confusion behind us. How much you want?"

Vinny's narrow eyes widened. "I don't wanna sell. That's not the point of this."

"C'mon…how much?" A smile tugged the corners of Petey's lips. "We won't ever have to worry about this shit again. It's simpler."

"I don't wanna sell."

Petey hesitated as if generating another argument behind his rosy forehead. "Then this sort of confusion is bound to happen again.

I can't be there all the time, and I've got a bunch of different guys collectin' for me. What if I send my cousin's punk kid down there? He can't tell his head from a hole in the wall. Let me buy you out. For the license money and a year lost earnings? Lump sum. There's better headaches than protection on that market."

Ricky saw Vinny's own gears began to whir. "How many stalls you got down there?" he asked.

Pete let a wide smile win out. "Vinny, I've been running that market for almost twenty-five years. I shouldn't be the one that has to sell. What's your price?"

"I'm just curious," Vinny said, his tone softening. "How many stalls and how much you bringin' in?"

Petey shot a deliberate glance at Ricky. To the rest, it looked as if he was looking for assurance from his second, but Ricky knew it was a subtle brag. Petey was going to get everything he wanted and knew it. "I've got eighteen stalls. Some of those guys down there are old friends that I've known for a long time. I'm sentimental like that."

"How much you chargin' 'em?" Vinny asked. Ricky was curious himself.

"Depends, like I says, some are old friends."

"What about in a month? How much? Total?" Vinny was growing more adamant as the conversation wore on. He could smell what he thought was victory; Ricky knew it was defeat. It was a dangerous point of confusion.

Pete took a deep breath and looked at the ceiling. "Somewhere around $10,000. Per month."

"I'll give you $60,000."

Pete laughed, deep and loud, and his chins quivered. "Don't insult me." He turned to Bordanarro. "Twenty-five years in that market. Twenty-five years. You think I'm gonna toss that for six months allowance?"

"Rudy, what do you think about it?" Vinny asked.

Bordanarro shrugged. "Petey, are you willin' to sell? We're not here to force you. We don't want to force you."

"Not for anywhere near $60,000. Suggest a number, Rudy, and I'll consider it."

Bordanarro thought for a moment, running numbers in his head. "$10,000 a month…$85,000 for the stalls."

Petey didn't answer but simply looked at Vinny and waited, puffing his cigar. Vinny was hooked. "Eighty-five thousand dollars," he said, extending his hand.

Petey let the offer hang there. "I've got some friends I don't want hassled," he said. "Just two. There's this Jew named Krakowski that makes a fantastic latke with my favorite peppers in it. My wife invites him over every year around one of their holidays, and it'd break my heart to see him poor or injured on account of my financial interests. And there's another guy, Birkhelder. He sells sausages the size of my thigh, and I always bring them to my sister for breakfast the day of her birthday. It's a whole thing with my brother-in-law…they're loyal guys. I want you to honor my arrangements with those two and protect them."

Vinny re-extended his hand. "Done." They shook on it. Plump Archie brought in a bottle of chianti, and they each had a glass to celebrate. Vinny looked especially pleased with himself and almost fell over thanking Pete and Bordanarro for their help when they left.

As Ricky, Petey, and Markie left the desolate haberdashery, the Fat Man grabbed his young cousin by the neck and whispered, "Remember that face, Markie…Vinny's face. That's what idiots look like when they're all grown-up."

One evening in May 1973
Jerry's Place in Brooklyn, NY
"We've got a story like any other religion."

Nick Pisani and Vic Palmieri were an odd couple. Nick was three decades younger, and his skin was brown, coarse-haired, and firm. He wore a shimmering set of gold rings and necklaces, his jackets were worn, and his shirts were always unbuttoned, sometimes two buttons past normal. Vic's skin was papery, pale, and plain of any jewelry; his suits were pristine, pressed, and tailored to his every whim. Still the most startling difference was their eyes. Nick's were dark brown and settled back into his face, Vic's were hollow and gray-blue.

When Benjie arrived for work, the pair was seated at Vic's favorite table. Vic greeted Benjie as he always did, with a firm hug, kiss, and a smile, but it surprised Benjie when Nick did the same, finishing with a touch of his rings to the kid's cheek.

"You want somethin' to eat, Benj?" Vic asked as they sat down. "Jerry said he's got some red prawns back there today that I'm gonna try. Hey, Frank!" Frank the Bartender stuck his head out in answer. "Bring some red wine over, whatever you got back there." Vic went back to his menu. "The special is *sarde a beccafico* today. Nick, you always was into them little fish, weren't you?"

Benjie scrunched his nose. "What's *sarde a beccafico*?" Vic seemed happiest with him when Benjie asked questions, so he had started asking. Unfortunately, his retention was proving imperfect.

"Stuffed sardines," Vic said. "You gotta be careful with that though. Jerry's not afraid to extend an expiration date around here. That's why I'm gettin' the prawns. He told me yesterday they was gettin' some in today."

Nick turned skeptically to his senior. "And what do you know about the restaurant business? What if they clear out the fridge when the new ones come in and give you some of the old prawns?"

"Nah, they don't do that to me in here. What you say that for? You're gonna hurt our friend Jerry's feelings, you say something mean-spirited like that."

"That's what I'd be doin' 'cause of all the extra work you put 'em through around here," Nick said, his Sicilian accentuations heavy.

"You misunderstand, son. I keep this place in business. I keep all these motherfuckers employed. Don't I, Frank?"

Frank the Bartender set a wine bottle on the table. "I have no idea what you're talkin' about, Vic."

"See...they love me here." Vic went again to his menu while Nick poured a glass for each of them. Benjie smelled the glass like he'd seen others do, although he couldn't tell it from grape juice until he drank it, so he did. It was warm and made him smack his lips—

"Benjie pointed a gun at a man yesterday," Vic said. The words dropped nerves into Benjie's stomach.

Nick chuckled but did not look up. "Oh, yeah? What'd you have Old Man Carrisi feel him up?"

"Yeah, I did," Vic said pointedly, "'cause it's a good fuckin' lesson—"

"Does that man know you've been havin' trigger-happy kids point guns at him for a quarter century? If he's such a bad guy, he should be gone already. Get it over with."

"That's the whole point if you'd pay more attention. He's not a bad guy. But he does shit that should get his dumb ass killed. I've taken pity on him, and what can I say? He cuts a nice suit. Still, I'm gonna use the resources I have to teach the lessons that need to be taught."

"How's that make you feel then, Benj? Vic is willin' to sacrifice your dick to some old man just so he can make his speech about holdin' your gun straight."

"Actually," Vic said, his crooked finger in the air, "I hadn't got to the gun part yet..."

"Well, carry on then. Don't let me stop your fuckin' lesson."

Vic sipped his wine. "Is that the first time you've pointed a gun at someone, Benj?"

"No. Once or twice I took it out when I was drivin' for my brothers. I cracked a guy across the head with a .38 once and about knocked him out."

"First time you thought you were gonna use it?"

"Yeah."

"It's an unsettling feeling. Your hands shake, your eyes twitch, your heart flutters, your mind gets involved. And yet, that moment is a pure test of your values. It is the most important moment to do your duty, to fulfill your obligations, 'cause if a man escapes that moment...he leaves with every intention of killin' you and your friends." Vic took another sip of his wine, and the liquid sat in droplets on his lips. "That's the life you've asked for. Do you understand that?"

"I know. *It's the responsibility I owe*," Benjie quoted Tony, his voice humble.

Vic sat forward and let a smile tug again at his mouth. "You weren't much of a history student, were ya, Benj'?"

"No, I guess I wasn't."

Vic shrugged. "That's not the worst thing. A lot of those school-books would be better off with more pictures."

"Me either, kid," Nick said, offering support. "I don't remember how long quarters were in school, but I'd get my ass beat at the end of every single one like clockwork."

"I'll make sure you get the important stuff, the bullet points of existence. You're Sicilian to start. Do you know anything about Sicily?"

"Yeah, it's an island."

Both men laughed. Vic said through head shakes, "In its most basic sense, yeah, it's an island in the Mediterranean Sea, a strategic island for Navies and their Armies to use as they traveled to Europe, to Africa, the Middle East, wherever on that sea. Our People were the masters of this little island. We were the underdogs with Rome above and Egypt below and the Ottoman's east, each with eyes on controlling us." He turned to Nick. "You still remember the list of invaders I had you memorize?"

"Most of 'em prolly." Nick hesitated and Vic held his gaze. "Jesus, really? Fine…definitely the goddamn Greeks," Nick said, counting them off, "Romans, Muslims, frog-eaters, Spanish, Germans, Vikings…I don't know. A *series of invaders* we can call it and the kid will still get it."

"Them all and the Phoenicians, Etruscans, and Byzantines. And the fucker with the elephants. And all of these invaders came onto our island with larger armies, better weapons, more disciplined troops, etc., and we was just villages of humble fishermen, unable to defend ourself. Our women were raped, our towns put to the torch, our governments put under whoever's thumb…bad shit to every side. A lot worse than the flower power fuckers have endured of late. And the rural communities in Sicily came together in small groups to protect themselves, groups called *cosche*, run by *padrinos*, and they were called *mafia*. The *'protectors against the powerful'*—"

"I don't remember you buildin' this story up like a Greek myth to me," Nick quipped. "Al did that, I always thought you were, shall we say, less respectful."

"I'm plenty goddamn respectful…and don't undermine me. This is the real history of Our Thing that the kid needs to know. He needs to know what we're workin' for here, our origins in the sands of time and shit."

"Wow, those are definitely Al's words—I know, sorry, sorry. Continue."

"With your permission…" Vic bowed with playful defiance. "These *cosche*," he said to Benjie, "had defined principles. The first of these is *omerta*."

Benjie nodded. "I've known *omerta* my whole life, from Tony." And he had. His brothers spoke about it with reverence whenever the conversation allowed.

"He's a good soldier, your brother. *Omerta* is honor at its most pure, basic responsibility. You conduct yourself like a man, like your brothers, sometimes even like my idiot friend Nick here. *Omerta* is born from the invasions. Don't run to others, especially the incompetent-until-they're-corrupt politicians and police, to solve *your* problems. You solve your shit for yourself or otherwise those politicians start lookin' at your family with their hands outstretched. They start trying to take what's yours, what you earned, what you made, and we've got about ten centuries of evidence for anybody that says they wouldn't do that. They made our men beggars and our children an uneducated rabble."

Nick leaned away from the table. "Let me know when you get to the part of this story that's in color," he said, smirking. "The kid doesn't have the patience for all this, Vic."

Vic ignored him physically but spoke with even more intensity as he went on, his eyes still fixed on Benjie's. "And then we had the last invasion, from our supposed brothers to the north. Mussolini and his Fascist army came in the 1920s and started cracking down on our *cosche* and putting them in prison, no trials, no evidence. He was making a point of how he treated the south…that no matter how 'unified' Italy was, Sicilians were a second class. And a lot of our men, *Men of Honor*, came to America to join relatives and found less Fascists than at home. But the situation was the same. We lived in ghettos with corruption around us. Politicians made our men serve votes for food and shelter, Irish cops beat our boys for stealing a scrap, vigilantes arrested and lynched us, and employers shunned us so we did what we always did. *Cosche* came together and fought for our community. We started sellin' alcohol and runnin' whores and takin' bets because the government made it so easy and we could live better outside the law than within it. We worked with the Irish and Jews to build a wall for the poor to play behind. We brought our children up with tradition, tough and disciplined and ready to fight if we need to. And is it any different today? Look out there, on these 'modern' streets. Number one murder rate in America here in our city, the workin' stiffs are broke, inflations and exposures all around us. But the men in Our Thing, we keep movin' on and movin' up. That's what the real tradition is all about. *Cosa Nostra*, the Brotherhood you've joined." Vic let the words hang as he took another drink of his wine. Even in the middle of the day, the lighting was poor and with Vic's back to the window, his face was cast in shadow but for the nonromantic flames reflected in each eye. Benjie was nervous to speak and more nervous to turn away.

Nick broke the silence for him. "This shit is important, kid," he said, his brow furrowed for the first time. "No way around it. The principle of Honor is a principle we must all understand and live by. You admit, by acceptin' this life, the safety of the group is superior to your own. And this follows you everywhere. It's rare, but treachery happens. I just had one of my young men put his needs before Ours in the face of danger. Now, his girlfriend is cut off, his lawyers will leave, his protection in the joint is gone, his assets will be redistributed. We cut the chord," he whistled and snapped his fingers, "and now this kid is on his own, no friends, no Family. All because he forfeited his Honor, his pact."

Vic shook his head. "It was the drugs, wasn't it?"

"Yeah, usually is."

87

"Shame. That's the fuckin' kryptonite." Vic took another drink. "Which brings me to another principle. The *padrinos* called it *vendetta*. What's done to the Family is done to you. And you got rights when you're connected. You have people behind you, equality within the Life. And if you get fucked with, we're there to do some fuckin' back."

"No soldier gets left behind."

"That's the gist of it."

Benjie listened, more intently than he ever had in school, acutely aware of the respect Vic expected this conversation to demand. "I'm ready, Vic. My brothers have done what they can for me, but I'm ready now. I'm ready to start this for real."

"I hope so, kid. I hope so." Vic finished the last of wine, his mouth curling with newfound distaste. "Frank! Take this swill outside and burn it. What was this shit?"

Frank the Bartender answered from his post. "Tell Jerry. You know I don't pick that stuff."

"You should," Vic said, chuckling to himself. Making fun of Frank and the other staff members was one of his favorite pastimes. "Take the rest of these outside and"—he whispered then to Nick— "What's that fighter plane I like?"

"The F-86s?"

Vic turned back to Frank. "And shoot some F-86 style missiles into all of it! Blow the whole case of that shit sky-goddamn-high. Where is this from? California? A shame that half of the country is useless. We can't do everything here in New York."

Nick looked at Benjie, smiling. "Good luck workin' for this guy, kid. It'll be a wonder if you see Christmas."

One evening in the spring of 1973
A cabin in Little Falls, NY
"That kind of money, serious fucking money, makes
everyone think they're smarter than they are."

Alphonse was never comfortable before big meetings. Not big as in important meetings, big as in meetings with too many people.

He knew, whenever reprobates gathered in numbers, their paranoia would soon after stain the wallpaper, dust the floor, glow through the light fixtures, and hang bitter in the air. In his more lucid moments, Al did not blame them for this. These men were survivors of their system, and the flaw was congenital to the system itself, a catch-22. Wrong and paranoid sustained men longer than wrong and comfortable.

Al enjoyed the scenery of upstate New York. In the city, every-thing was placed at right angles. The buildings were squares or rect-angles, the roads crossed at perpendiculars or didn't at parallels, like comfortable, agreed-upon urban uniforms. Designs in the country were more spontaneous. The edge of the woods was not parallel to the road. It approached the road, maybe slowly, maybe quickly, then retreated from it to try again further on. Any one tree was the con-sequence of the specific wind on a specific day. Even the road itself, man-made as it was, could incorporate a hill or a curve to avoid this obstacle or that.—

But Al rarely left the city. "Have you ever been to Charlie's house?"

Adam did not look up from his newspaper. "No, I haven't."

"It's a beautiful place, green everywhere," Al said, looking out the window of his Chrysler, "except in the fall. It's even more beauti-ful in the fall with the orange and red leaves."

Adam folded his newspaper into his lap so as not to have a dis-tracted conversation with the Don. "I've never been out here much. If you have your own place, I bet it's nice, but I wouldn't want to stay in someone else's cabin out here or anything like that."

"Ya know," Al said, his gravelly Sicilian accent adding to the flat English words, "I grew up in Brooklyn, and I don't think I left the city until I was twenty-six years old. I mean, when I came over on the boat, I was out of the city, but I was six when we landed, so I didn't remember anything about the ocean or the boat or the cap-tain...I thought the whole world was paved...just everywhere was this dull black pavement and noise and lights. And then, when I was twenty-five or twenty-six, my father took me and my brother out to meet one of the old-country *mafiosos* who had a place out here. I don't remember where, somewhere up north. This old guy was named Spernanzoni, and he was maybe eighty at the time. He only spoke Sicilian, no English, and he hung around with a crew in Buffalo. As far as I could tell, he didn't do any work for them, but they showed him respect and gave him this cabin to live in and visited him once in a while...and so my Pops drives us out there and we get to Spernanzoni's place and you can't even see his neighbors he has so much land around this run-down little cabin. We pull up and he's got this little pond on his land a few hundred yards away from the cabin, near all these pine trees. And he's sittin' on this dead log with a stick and some string attached to it. I'm not even sure I knew exactly what he was doing, but as we were walkin' up, he pulls this big," Al stretched his hands out wider than his shoulders, "fuckin' fish outta the water." Both Al and Adam chuckled. "And this Old Man, in the middle of nowhere, in some country he's only known for a few years, was fuckin' grinnin' like he just hit 75-1 at the track. So, he's laughin' and carryin' on in Sicilian, and he kept holdin' the fish up, '*Furtuna, furtuna!*' We ate the fish that night, and I never forgot...this crazy old *mafioso* in the middle of the New York wilderness with a stick and a string, as happy as I've ever been in my life."

Phil Scozzari, who had been listening quietly from the passenger seat, gave the tale a moment to settle and said, "It's quiet out here, I'll give you and Charlie's cabin that. Sometimes it's a nice change. But if you got dragged out here all the time, you're gonna have to find all the suckers again. In the city, there's a nice concentrated population of suckers. Out here, you'd have to search 'em out all over again."

Al appreciated Phil's ability to distill an issue. "Yeah, Our Thing doesn't have much of a retirement community."

"Oh, we've got retirement communities. They call 'em cemeteries."

Jimmy the Driver gave Phil a sideways glance and a gawky smile of such transparent misgivings that all three men doubled over in laughter. Phil smacked Jimmy a few times on the cheek. "You can retire, Jim, just not us."

"Fuck that," Al said. "I'll give you a fortune before I ride with a city cabbie."

When the car was calm again, Adam's fastidious instincts gnawed at his mind. He had more meaningful subjects to broach with the Don and his underboss. "Al, I didn't want to plague you with too much of this beforehand, but I think we need to organize our thoughts. Simple stuff, I just want us to have a unified message in the room or whatever."

Al twirled his cane, trying to read the younger man's eyes. They were small below black hair and above a mouth set in near-constant pink neutrality. Al smiled calmly. "Okay then. What should we say in there?"

"First, our simple numbers," Adam rattled off his notes without checking them, "the 55 and 15s split of the construction costs, the subsequent 10 of 10 cut, the timetable, the expectations we have of their union leaders—"

"What do you want me to say about it?"

"Well, nothing really," Adam said before regretting the words. "Well, I don't want you to say 'nothing.' I just…I just want us to be on the same page. It would look bad if one of us says something the others don't like and then we end up backtracking. We'd look fucking stupid."

Al patted Adam's knee. "I can guarantee we backtrack. The 55 and 15s, they won't accept that."

"What? Why?"

"Their guys are gonna be there," Phil explained over his shoulder. "They won't accept the first terms no matter what."

Adam furrowed his brow. He had to slow his words so as not to sound impolite. "Then we start higher and settle on 55 and 15s."

"No," Al said.

Adam coped with a nervous chuckle. "I assume you have your own strategy then?"

"55 and 15s is a fair cut. 10 of 10 is a fair cut. We offer them that."

"Can I ask why we would do that when you expect they'll refuse us?"

"Ya know, Al," Phil said in his nasal tones, "if you think about it, we know Don C. is with us. He's gonna bring the iron and steel workers to the jobsite, no complicated questions asked, on account of the close relationship of our Families. We, meanin' me and you, are gonna figure out the concrete union here over the next few weeks and *we'll* bring them to the jobsite. Now the Old Man and his lap-dog, they're gonna control the carpenters, electricians, and plumbers when we need them. Now, I'm no calendar, but I don't see us needing them at the same time we need iron, steel, and concrete on the job. Correct me if I'm wrong, Adam, but we could draw a hard line at this meeting, on whatever numbers Al thinks appropriate, and then fuck with a compromise later. It'll make for an awkward dinner conversation, but we've all been there before, no big deal. I'm just saying, if that's the route we wanna go, we could play our hand like that..."

Adam watched Alphonse as Phil talked and the Don gave nothing away. "I could second that," Adam said. "Their unions won't comprise the majority of the jobsite until, I don't know, maybe next summer. Maybe later than that. Keep them at arm's length and they'll have to come crawling to you once the checks roll in."

Al twirled his cane, and Adam and Phil let the music, something pre-Elvis, takeover as he did. Even Jimmy checked his mirror with quick, intrigued glances. "No," the Don said minutes later. "No hard lines. We start with what we think are fair terms. And, Adam, I'll explain why before you start. First, 55 and 15s is fair. Don C. will see that and appreciate it. The other two will refuse, or at least we think they will, and make a counteroffer. Their offer and the conversation after will teach us somethin'. I don't know what it will teach us, but I want to hear that conversation take place. Second, if those two miss profits early, they will feel cheated for eternity. No matter how much they eventually make and no matter what we bring to them, it won't be enough to wash that taste from their mouth. They will use it as an excuse to undermine this project from then on. It's better we start level and judge them later. Let them prove their own guilt to us."

Phil flashed a thumbs-up. "That's why he's the Boss."

"It's my yoke until the day I fuckin' die."

* * *

Jimmy the Driver brought Al's blue Chrysler to rest on the gravel driveway of Charlie Guiffrida's cabin retreat in the only place he could, at the very end and barely off the road. Alphonse, Adam, and Phil left Jimmy in the car and began crunching gravel toward the wilderness cabin in front of them. There were cars of all makes, ranging from Crosley Station Wagons to a Rolls-Royce Silver Shadow.

"These guys think they're movie stars," Al said as they walked. "One even thinks he should drive a Rolls-Royce and visit the Amazon."

The cabin itself was red cedar with a wraparound porch skirted by limestone and shale behind a well-tended garden. Al noted the fresh brown mulch when they got close, breathed the aroma of it. *How much is a gardener for a place like this?* The three men assembled before the door, Phil knocked. They heard footsteps and conversation before Maddie Guiffrida, Charlie's handsome wife, opened the door, smiling ear to ear. "Oh, welcome! Phil, so good to see you," she said with respectful pecks on his cheeks, "and Alphonse of course," who received the same, "and of course, Mr. Landau. Welcome all. Please, please, make yourselves at home. We're just finishing up some *antipasti*, and we'll be serving dinner in a few hours. After everyone gets a chance to talk, of course…"

Charlie Guiffrida, Underboss of the Capello Family, noticed their arrival. "Alphonse! We are so happy," the pecks again, "to host you." His eyes moved down the line. "And of course, Phil and Mr. Landau as well. Wine? Scotch?"

"Scotch," Al answered for them all.

"On the way then. Please grab some *antipasti*." Charlie indicated a wooden table covered with food and cluttered by dark and hungry suits. "We'll end up in the dining room eventually." As Charlie moved to pour the drinks, Al held his hand firmly. "Thanks again for being our host today. We have a lot to discuss. All good news." Charlie smiled, but his eyes briefly checked the men nearest them. Since the engagement of their children, they had searched for the right tone to strike in view of the public. They were still searching.

Others came up to them with warm greetings and polite handshakes while they waited. Alphonse embraced the heads of the other three New York Families first, as was expected: Frank Capello, Cesare Provenzano, and Joe Pisciotto.

Frank Capello had known Al since they were tough wannabes beating protection money out of fish vendors on the waterfront. He wasn't quite an 'Old Man' (Frank was in his fifties), but he looked younger than his age. He had retained the color and expression of his hair with a corresponding tan from his Miami beach vacations. Frank had been ruthless as a younger man, the badge of all authoritarians, but with an eye for the loyal inner circle he cultivated. He was considered traditional, as far as the Bosses went. He shied (publicly at least) from the drug business, enforced *omerta* with intractable anger, and expected his soldiers to be creative advocates of the Families' bottom line.

Cesare Provenzano was the oldest Boss at eighty-one years. It was quite a number considering the trajectory of his career. He struck the image of a deathbed patient, emaciated and bent by struggle, while maintaining a reputation for merciless retribution among the crews he controlled. One parable claimed a young soldier working for Provenzano informed the Don when another soldier in his crew was withholding money from the Family till. Provenzano had the thieving soldier killed, and he was found weeks later with his jaw ripped from his face by a cable winch and $5,000 forced down his throat. Still, the real lesson for Provenzano's men came later, when he ordered the younger soldier killed (virtually decapitated by a baseball bat and dumped in front of his childhood home) for the crime of ratting out his friend. "If you allow rats to persist, you will be consumed by them," he reportedly told the men he assigned the job. Al had been weary of the Old Man once, but there were rumors Provenzano had lost control of his men. Reports of rampant drug use, secret incomes, and loose lips among his men were hurting his reputation.

Joe Pisciotto was the youngest Boss and newest to his post, assuming control in 1969. He represented, or at least he purported to, a new kind of Boss. The opinions on his opinions were mixed. The Giordano and Capello Families were known to refer to him by the derogatory nicknames Napoletano and Red, for his non-Sicilian ancestry and flashy suits, respectively. There were rumors about his activities in the papers, but rather than shun the public, he gave interviews, held parades, and consulted on books and movies. Further, and perhaps the biggest affront, he was not shy about his drug smuggling or the ensuing distribution by the Black and Irish gangs. He claimed to enforce strict sobriety among his crews, but long prison sentences and Federal attention were a fact, whether the dealers were users or not.

Al greeted his attending Caporegime's as well: Papa Vic Palmieri—his reliable old friend—Ernie Nocellaro, Joey Jugs Poletti, Petey Caltagirone, and Joey Bellomo. And those men greeted their counterparts from other Families like Provenzano Underboss Attilio Guzzo, Capello Family Capo Tommy Carluccio, Pisciotto Underboss Carmine Fiata, Don Provenzano's son Michael, and so on and around it went. Among these men, respect was currency. It was earned on the streets and collected upon at these meetings.

The next half hour saw a slow migration from the appetizers to the dining room until the last of the gentry found seats. Don Capello stood to address the members, raised his glass, and said, "First, on behalf of Charlie, his beautiful wife Maddalena, and their lovely children, I want to thank you all for joining us here today. I was thinkin' earlier, there are probably more felons per square foot in this room than any Federal penitentiary in the country," the men chuckled politely, "but we're a little light on law enforcement, so it shouldn't be a problem." The punchline got a laugh, and Capello paused to accept it. "Seriously though, I appreciate everyone comin' out. Every so often, one of these meetings becomes necessary to coordinate our efforts both within the borders of New York City and without, and to plan a path forward under ever-changin' circumstances. A path that we hope leads to as much money and as little conflict as possible." He gulped from his glass, and those around the table reciprocated. Don Capello finished, "The floor is open," and he sat down.

Don Provenzano, his suit sagging from his frame, stood first. "Don Giordano," he said, "could you give us an update on the apartments in Manhattan? No point in fucking around. That's why we're all here."

"We are moving quickly toward a groundbreaking, Don Provenzano," Al said, "but I am sure Mr. Landau can explain better than I."

Adam stepped forward from a post against the wall. "To this point, Gentlemen, everything is on schedule, and we expect to officially break ground in a few weeks. The architect has been communicating with our man Cal Roselli, whose construction company will be organizing and awarding the bids to your contractors. We wish, or wish to present to you today, a split of the available contracts as such: 55 percent to Giordano-run companies, specifically Cal Roselli, and 15 percent to each of the other three families." Adam scanned the room, but there were no visible reactions. "Cal and myself will inform your men, and how we do that is up to you, as to what prices to bid in order to ensure this distribution is achieved. We expect total expenditures on this project to end up somewhere around $100 million all told, so, and I think this is clear, there is *plenty* of meat on this bone for everyone. After the project has been completed, the Giordano cut will be around 10 percent of the annual revenue from rents, sales, and other applications with the rest paid out to the financiers at Clearwater Investments. Of Don Giordano's cut, we are willing to kick back 10 percent to each of the other three Families. The risk is exceptionally low for a job with this potential, and we have every expectation that this will establish a financial bell cow for each Family to build on as long as we keep the labor peace and get this thing built as quickly as possible."

A number of the seated gentlemen leaned into huddles to whisper. Don Provenzano said, "I would ask, Don Giordano, what labor unions will you contribute to this project? Certainly, the garment workers are of little use?"

Adam began to explain, "We have made arrange—" when Provenzano cut him off with surprising vigor for an old man. "I did not ask you, Mr. Landau. I have heard Don Giordano speak before, and I want to hear him now."

Alphonse calmly let Provenzano's words settle. "I believe we will control the concrete and cement union by the time this job commences. As I am the only one with access to the Clearwater

Investments Board, I believe those two factors warrant the 55 percent cut I have proposed."

Don Pisciotto spoke next, his voice full of a certain distaste. "But as we sit here, Don Giordano, you do not control the concrete and cement unions and your Jew," he nodded in Adam's direction, "is the one who is actually on the Clearwater Board. Your offer is entirely too low. You want my labor unions? The carpenters and electricians from the 902 you'll need? 30 percent of the contracts go to my men and 20 percent of your cut goes to us when the building is complete. With respect, you are asking for more than you bring to this table, Don Giordano."

Adam began to respond, but this time it was Pisciotto who shouted him down while looking directly at Don Giordano. "Send him out! He said what he has to say. This is *Cosa Nostra* business. In the future, memorize your own facts, and leave your Jew in the city!"

Al stifled a physical response. When he spoke, it was with an untroubled tone. "You do not trust my men, Don Pisciotto?"

"This is not about trust. This is *Cosa Nostra*." Pisciotto emphasized his Italian accent on the last two words. Al found it childish. "We heard his numbers," the Don continued, "and at that price, you will not have my unions. Either way, I want him out of the room for this discussion!" Pisciotto made an emphatic motion toward the doors.

"An unfortunate circumstance, Don Pisciotto," Alphonse replied. He turned in his chair to face the men seated around him. "Vincenzo," he said, addressing Papa Vic, "do you think Mr. Roselli's men have ever made a cabinet before?"

Papa Vic answered with a wry smile. "Most of them. If I can find a tape measurer, I'll do it myself."

Pisciotto bristled in his chair. "I want the Jew out of the room," he said, more under control than before, "before we discuss this any further."

This time Alphonse did not hesitate. "Adam, go eat some bruschetta." There was no point forcing the issue, not here and not publicly. The traditional sentiment would be on Pisciotto's side for once.

There was nothing Adam could do, but still he stared menacingly at the two disrespectful Dons. He imagined consequences for them, imagined regret etched over anger on their faces. For all his influence, his loyalty and success, he was powerless. He walked obediently to the doors, pushed them open, and shut them quietly. A brief silence fell over the room, and some nervous glances were exchanged.

Don Provenzano broke the silence with a much friendlier tone. "Seriously, Alphonse, not only do you bring the Jew into this room, but you allow him to dictate terms to us? What were you thinking?"

"Have you never heard of Meyer Lansky? Arnold Rothstein? Bugsy Siegel?"

"I don't know that you want those comparisons, Don Giordano."

Al shrugged. "Those are still my terms, Cesare. I'm not sure why the messenger mattered. Don Pisciotto, if you expect 30 percent of these contracts for delivering the carpenters union, we can end this discussion now. Cesare, what do you think of this? Do you think the Pisciotto Family should receive more than yours?"

Al knew Provenzano was leery of Pisciotto's aggressiveness, especially as a guest of another family. "No, but 55 percent is too much. Give us another offer."

Al's patience was evaporating. "I create a job out of thin air worth $100 million, come here, and offer you 15 percent of my own accord, and you berate my men and act as if *you* are insulted? This is not a cut of the traditional underground skims, it's real estate. What opportunities have you brought for my family today?"

"Don Capello," Pisciotto said cautiously, "what do you think of this? Will his new building need your labor? Or should we leave him to attempt this venture on his own?"

Al settled back into his chair. He expected a friendly voice from Don Capello. An arrangement of this magnitude was not supposed to be quibbled over in pursuit of a few percentages. "Gentlemen," Capello said, "I think the conversation today has become more hostile than it needs to be. Don Giordano has come here in good faith, to a house where my Family has promised him reasonable discussion, as I have promised all of you today. And yet look at us here. Are we not all *onerato societa*? You, Don Pisciotto, have known Mr. Landau for years and yet you expelled him from this room. Why? There is no need for this bickering. What Don Giordano has brought to us will be very good for *Cosa Nostra*, I have no doubt. But only if there is peace and trust among our Families. We must remember that."

Don Capello's words carried weight, but more practically, Pisciotto and Provenzano recognized the developing stalemate. "Of course, you are right about that," Provenzano agreed. "More important than anything, we must keep the peace between our Families."

"Yes, peace first and foremost. I apologize for my frustration, Don Giordano," Pisciotto said, putting his hands together as if praying for forgiveness. "But I must insist on a counteroffer. I cannot go back to my men with only 15 percent of these contracts."

Al spun his cane lightly into the hardwood floor. "I understand, Don Pisciotto, and in the interest of peace, my companies will accept 40 percent of the contracts on 234 Park Avenue with 20 percent each to the other three Families and 12 percent of my future earnings."

"An honorable counteroffer, Don Giordano," Capello said, smiling at Al, before moving his focus to Pisciotto and Provenzano. "In the spirit of this arrangement," he continued, "the Capello family will cede 2 percent of our contracts to the Giordano Family once Alphonse has secured the concrete and cement union. I know this move will involve considerable risk for you and your Family, but I agree, it is absolutely necessary. We wish to encourage this transition for the good of *Cosa Nostra*."

Don Pisciotto nodded in agreement. "Thank you, Don Giordano. We accept your offer. We will do anything else we can to help you with this concrete problem. Men, politicians, whatever you need."

"To my Friends at the table," Provenzano said, "we are lucky to be around such men as these. I accept Don Giordano's offer, and as Don Pisciotto says, I will do everything I can to help the project moving forward."

Don Capello stood and the rest at the table followed suit. He raised his glass. "*Uomini d'onore e integrità.*" The men drank the dark liquors, and the Bosses walked slowly to the head of the table, around

Don Capello. They each hugged and kissed the others, shaking their hands and demonstrating respect for one another in front of their men. Despite the tense conversation that proceeded, the men in the room felt the atmosphere change. Phil Scozzari watched his Boss, celebrating and congratulating the other men as he was, and he knew a short-term peace was preserved. But deep down, he felt a sickness, a fragility in these relationships that was not always there.

An afternoon in the spring of 1973
A department store in Manhattan, NY
"...the kind of different you know better than you know yourself."

Carrie could not remember learning her father was in the Mafia. It was a familiar if not precise idea held together by instinct in the back of her mind. She'd seen the suspicious reverence in men's eyes when they heard her last name or observed their eyes flit skittishly when he stood behind her. She'd seen it in line at the movies, opening a bank account, sitting at a restaurant, in teachers, cashiers, neighbors, and boyfriends. She'd seen it when Bobby first learned her name and a version of the same when others heard his. The negative aspects were manifest around both men as well. Unexplained cuts, whispered conversations, police cars, money, anger, frustration, absences—all were understood relative to their unseen disorder.

While Carrie could not pinpoint the day for herself, she knew the day her sister had learned the truth about their father. Jennie was nine, Carrie was fourteen. Jennie ran into the house crying about a boy who lived down the street, a blond-haired eleven-year-old named Will. He had pushed her down the steps, concrete steps, to scare her away from the newly minted clubhouse he had formed with his friends. Jennie's wrist was broken. It was obvious from the second their mother saw them and she drove the sisters to the hospital while their father stayed behind, his eyes like Carrie had never seen them. By the time Jennie's cast was set, Will's father had fallen down the very same stairs, unfortunately shattering both arms, his right leg, and jaw. Soon after, Will's family had moved to Colorado in pursuit of a previously dormant passion for rock climbing. Jennie, ever sensitive to losing something she wanted, suspected her father immediately, and the house of cards he hid behind fell quickly after that. Jennie separated friends from her family after Will and any complaints were never voiced in her father's hearing. Carrie respected the decision. It was for the best.

"Do you like this one? Or the blue one?" Carrie asked, holding an orange knee-length dress up for her sister to examine.

Jennie glanced up from the display she was shuffling through. "Blue," she said. "You look like shit in orange. You look like one of those sixty-year-old women from Florida who lay out on the beach all day. The ones that spend their whole life trying to become a leather handbag."

"Fuck you." Carrie put the orange dress back and threw the blue one over her shoulder.

"What about this one?" Jennie asked on her turn. The dress was short, figure hugging, and white with navy trim around the collar. Her tanned skin and hair made the white appear all the more striking against her.

Carrie plucked the low-cut neckline with her fingernail. "I'm guessing you're not wearing that one to church?"

"I've got a backlog of Jesus dresses. I need more options for when I go out."

"You have a boy you want to see you in that dress then?"

Jennie threw the white dress into her shopping buggy. "I have a *man* I want to see me in that dress."

Carrie laughed. "Who is this man?"

"He is a man who went to school with me…"

"How old is he?" Carrie asked and then regretted it. *Too parental sounding.*

"Seeing as I'm an adult," Jennie said, "that is not relevant. So don't worry about it."

"Fine. But don't expect me to cover for anything unless I get to meet him."

"You will…eventually…"

Carrie remembered what cryptic answers like these meant when she was nineteen and then prayed they meant something different. "Is he Italian?" This time Carrie winced as the words left her mouth.

Jennie's face tightened. She recognized the script. "Half Italian, but Protestant might be the harder part."

"Well, I wish you good luck." Carrie hoped her well-wishes were enough for Jennie to forget this exchange. "That will be a challenging one to push through."

"They'll get over it," Jennie said. "We can't all find a Mafia prince."

Carrie flushed red and spun in anger. "Watch it, Jennie. Dead fuckin' serious." Her sister knew better than to say something so blatant in public.

Jennie failed to suppress a triumphant smile. "I know, sorry, shutting up." They both went back to the displays and mannequins.

Neither of them envied the patterns popular with their peers, but shopping at these boutiques was much safer with a partner. They called it therapy when anyone asked. And who could tell them it wasn't? Perhaps their inclination to purchase a hexagon obsessed, red and yellow dashiki was born from some subconscious need for attention. Or rebellion. Or warm weather. In any case, either sister's criticism was warranted, free, and less judgmental than most. Their paths were so similar and distinctive they found the advice of others hopelessly immaterial.

"What about this one for Ma?" Jennie asked, holding up a dark dress of thin material.

"She would never wear it." Carrie felt the fabric between her fingers. "Too short…and too thin."

"She'd wear a thin dress," Jennie said, re-examining the choice at arm's length. It had an attractive, airy feel. Jennie convinced herself it was especially appropriate for the summer months and threw it in the buggy. "Are you going over there for dinner tomorrow?"

Carrie rolled her eyes. "Yeah."

"You don't sound enthusiastic about it."

"Bobby can't go." Because her parents were still getting used to Bobby, they were friendlier when he was there. She hated their dinners without him.

"Why not?"

"*Business*," Carrie said, mocking Bobby's deep drone. "I thought about inviting his parents without him to freak him out."

Jennie cackled. "That would freak him out."

Carrie flipped another blue dress, this one cut more conservatively, into the buggy. "He seems to have a lot of conveniently scheduled errands, is all I'm saying. You're goin' though, aren't you?"

"Nope, sorry." Jennie pointed at the white and navy dress. "Guy from school."

"You're kidding me. He got any friends? I need some better excuses to get rid of Ma."

"I wouldn't use adultery. She'd have a lot to say about that one."

"Yeah, but maybe after she'd disown me," Carrie said hopefully. They both giggled at the thought.

One evening in the spring of 1973
Charles Guiffrida's cabin in Little Falls, NY
"Afterwards, everyone was suspicious of everyone
else…I was suspicious of them."

Adam stood on the back deck of Charles Guiffrida's cabin with his arms and jacket slung over the railing. The air was still and warm enough for him to roll his shirtsleeves to the elbow, and the moon had just popped over the trees, a shining hole in the purple-black sky. He wanted to leave. He had seen enough of this place.

The back door opened behind him, and a few noisy *mafioso* spilled onto the deck to interrupt his brooding. Phil was among them, carrying an extra drink for Adam. To their relief, the others kept walking to the far end of the deck and left the two members of the Giordano Family brain trust alone.

"If we weren't where we are, I'd be talkin' shit about those two pompous dickheads," Phil said under his breath.

"Fuck them. I don't give a shit. Let's just make our money and be done with the whole lot of them."

Phil knew Adam was hurt even if he said all the humble things he was expected to say in public. "Al doesn't forget things like that," Phil promised. "He'll say what he has to say to them, but he does not forget. He does not forget what is done to his *friends*."

"I'm not going to tell you I haven't been thinking about some responses." Adam could not help but clench his fists. "Fuckin' loud-mouthed pricks."

"With all the TV appearances he's doin', he's going to be in the penitentiary soon. Cops don't like mouthy criminals."

Adam had heard Al say something similar once. He wondered if Phil had heard it from him or the other way around. "I'd prefer something worse than that," Adam whispered. They laughed and drank for a moment with taboo thoughts in their heads.

Phil turned to look back at the cabin itself. Through the windows, the rooms were bright and the men all seemed to be smiling and laughing, unconcerned to all the world. Charlie's wife and daughters were hustling back and forth, doing their best to keep everyone satisfied with soppressata, brushetta, guanciale, and every kind of wine and liquor. Charlie and Bobby Guiffrida were talking with Don Giordano, Carmine Fiata, and Papa Vic in front of a stone fireplace with a wood mantel decorated with pictures of the Guiffridas on vacation, at graduations, baptisms, and confirmations. The house looked cheery through the windows, like a Christmas card missing only the fresh snow piling up the door. Everyone had fresh drinks and handsome features that sparkled in the electric light. They were telling witty jokes and laughing in their huddles, but Phil's eyes were drawn past all of it to Don Provenzano sitting in an armchair and Pisciotto standing just a few feet behind him. "He guards that fucking Old Man," Phil said. "I bet he has people sitting on his house."

"He knows that Old Man is all he's got," Adam said, skittishly aware of the other men on the deck. "Big picture, the only leverage he's got is that Old Man's vote and soldiers. His rackets are in the streets, and he only inherited them only because he whacked Garbinia and convinced everyone he didn't. No long-term plan, no white rackets like us. And he acts like he's some genius. *Modern*, he says. And Al's right about the public image he puts out. It's gonna catch up to *him* and that heat is gonna come back on all of *us*. We're gonna get roasted by it."

Phil pointed to his temple. "I don't think the Old Man's got it all anymore. That's the only explanation for what that fuckhead gets away with right under his nose."

"It makes you wonder what he knows…" Adam said, letting the words hang to emphasize the next phrase, "*and what he thinks he knows*. Confusion, if that's what it really is, is a dangerous thing to have around our business. The Old Man has a brother and kids and grandkids. What if he gets put in a spot where he's gotta flip to save one? Life in prison ain't but a couple years to him. What if the government threatens his kids though? What would he do?"

"I don't know." Phil shifted his focus so as not to stare at the frail man inside. "He's a tough motherfucker. He's a lifer. That means something to a Sicilian. You can bang us for a lot of things, but we're a stubborn bunch of authority-hatin' motherfuckers. Cops are enough to make my mother shut up."

Adam shrugged. "Either way, they're untouchable, so we're both just pissin' in the wind."

"Yeah. For all we got out of this life, we've still got a Boss and we've still got rules. Familiar authority seems to get a pass."

May 1973
Tony Maceo's house in Brooklyn, NY
"It was a problem to us. Here's a problem, go fix the fuckin' problem."

Ana's voice rang through the house, "Tony! Phone!" and up the stairs to where Tony was enjoying a warm bath and Frank Sinatra on the record player. He slumped his head and splashed his face with water before getting out. He wrapped a towel around himself and walked to the bedroom for the phone. "This is Tony."

It was Vic's voice, curt and forceful. "Ton. We don't want the greedy fat man at any more meetings. This is me tellin' you we're gonna miss him. You'll bring the kid with you." *Click.*

Tony stood there a moment with the phone still up to his ear. He rubbed his forehead, set the phone back on the receiver, and walked back into the bathroom before the song was over.

May 1973
The Blue Raven in the Bronx, NY
"It was a time for optimism. A time for daydreams."

Ricky pulled into the parking spot nearest the club's back entrance where Markie stood waiting for him, as instructed. His gangly limbs poked out from underneath his new suit, but it was a marked improvement from his T-shirt and jeans. He jogged to the driver-side door before Ricky could get out of the car. "Mr. Caruso," he said, the words flowing quickly and running together, "Kay, uh, Kay Dedrick, I think, is here with a group of the girls for some kind of training—"

Ricky shut his car door. "Markie, how old are you?"

Markie stiffened, pushing his chest out. "Nineteen, sir."

Ricky held the young man by the biceps. "First, I'm gonna call you Mark because Markie sounds like you're twelve. Second, don't call me sir. Rick or Ricky. Three, you're not my secretary. Show up on time and be a fuckin' man. If I need you to do something, I'll ask. Understand?"

Markie's eyes skirted Ricky's. "Yes."

"Now, I told Ms. Dedrick to do exactly what she's doing. That's a good thing. For now, I just want you to follow me and keep your mouth shut."

Markie worked to compose himself as they entered the club and walked toward what would become the front section of booths. Hammers, drills, and saws clouded the room with noise and dust and men, contractors, walking purposefully back and forth from their unfinished projects.

"Fuck, it's loud in here. Where is everybody?"

"Uncle Petey is comin' with the music guy. He should be here any minute. Vinnie is in the cardroom over there." Ricky made a beeline for the room and found Vinnie kneeling beneath a green felt table with a screwdriver in his hand.

Ricky laughed. "That's not somethin' you see every day."

Vinnie crawled out, a tan, well-groomed man in his early 50s, with a huge smile on his face. "Kid, *come here.*" The two hugged. "Back together at last, Ricky and Uncle Vinnie. Give me another."

"I was happy to hear you were workin' the tables," Ricky said, the smile of the greeting still on his face. "I didn't want some kids tryin' to make a name for themselves in here. We want the veterans, don't we?"

"Fuck yeah," Vinnie said, nodding. "I already love this place. The Blue Raven. I love that name."

"Petey gets that credit. I get credit for the broads though. You'll see 'em runnin' around here. I just hired…what, Mark? Fifteen of 'em? We had them strut the stage naked with him takin' notes."

"A good system, I would think."

Ricky ran his fingers over the felt surface, soft and green and rimmed by black leather. "It was good enough," he said.

Vinnie traced his own path on the felt. "Nothin' like the feel of a card table, huh? It makes you wanna touch it. It's got a smell too. I've seen guys smell it from the bar and get their wallets out."

Ricky turned to Markie. "Get us some drinks, will ya?" he said and watched until the door shut behind the kid. "Say, Vin, you don't know anythin' about this Buddy Roehner guy, do you? Petey is on his way to introduce us. He's some music talent scout or somethin'."

Vinnie chuckled. "I know he can't be that good if he's stuck workin' for Petey."

"My thoughts exactly. But whatever. I guess he'll know more about that shit than me."

Vinnie scanned the cardroom, littered with two-by-fours and rolls of uninstalled carpet. "Nico was around here earlier. As you can see, he didn't get anythin' done. I don't know where he ran off to."

"I've seen him enough. He's prolly cost me five years off my life, to be honest."

"I'd hate to know how much that means I've lost."

"You're gonna tip over any minute."

"For a dozen reasons." Vinnie took a seat at the table, lounging with his back curved and his hands in his pockets. "Your mother told me about your visit to your pops. She said you two had a good yellin' match up there."

"He didn't read Teresa's letter," Ricky said, shaking his head. "Piece of shit."

"I'd have thought you'd've known that before you left the house."

Ricky pulled up his own seat. "I suspected."

"So, what really made you mad like that?"

"He gives a lot of unsolicited advice, Vin."

"About money? This place?"

"He thinks Petey's gonna sell me out."

"That's far from the dumbest shit your father's said."

"Fuck him. What's he know? He got beat and now he's whipped in that fuckin' cage up there. My ma's back to takin' on three kids a day by herself with almost nothin' but government money. I think he's holdin' out shit on her."

"He's not. He's not doin' that. He couldn't keep a dime alive. He spent all that shit."

"Yeah, and fuck us, I guess. Fuck his grandkids now. They don't know no better than the shit life they're stuck with."

"I don't know what to tell you about that. He rarely found any money, could never keep it when he did. Your ma's a tough woman though. She'll get 'em through on willpower alone."

"He's a piece of shit." Ricky looked back at the door. "Where'd Markie go for these drinks? Fuckin' Mars?"

Vinnie sat up straight, meeting Ricky's eyes when he turned back to him. "Rick, I'm not gonna tell you what decisions you should be makin'. I'm not your pops, and I ain't you. But I'll say this 'cause you gotta know. Petey ain't your fairy godmother. You gotta figure this out for yourself. This club can help, it really can, and I don't think it's a bad start, but you gotta keep your head on a swivel down here. There's motherfuckers around this Life who just wanna kill people, and they don't care who. There's motherfuckers that'll back-stab you and throw you to the wolves for fifty bucks. There's dumb motherfuckers who'll do whatever you say but can't keep a secret from the postman. This ain't no nine-to-five office. Your pops is right about that. If you step to the plate here and can't hit a curveball…you don't get to go back to the dugout and joke around with your friends. They'll bury your ass under home plate, know that."

"I know all that."

"I hope so. I hope so."

When Markie did come back with the drinks, it was obvious what kept him. The Fat Man was right behind him with two strangers and a moist cigar hanging from his mouth. He waddled to the table, and both Vinnie and Ricky gave him respectful hugs while he eyed the stalled progress around them.

"I can see it comin' together, boys," he said. "We'll be pushin' scrubs through this room like nobody's business in a few weeks. Every gambler likes to try his luck at a new honey hole."

"I'm movin' my big game in here for the opener to give the guys a shot at breakin' it in," Vinnie said. "Should have around $30K on the table."

"Good, good. Rick, I hear you hired some girls? And some bartenders?"

"Yeah, we're all squared away on staff, Pete."

"I assume they're hot enough. Markie was nervous just talkin' about them."

"Oh yeah," Ricky said, a slow smile growing. "Don't worry about that angle. We're covered there."

Petey turned to the strangers, pushing them forward to close the circle with Rick and Vinnie. "This," he said, tapping one on the shoulder, "is Buddy Roehner. He's the music man I told you about." Buddy's attire indicated success: expensive suit, expensive glasses, expensive shoes, and a polished gold watch although he was still not much to look at. He was short and overweight with thinning, gray-brown hair above the square frames of his glasses, an effeminate voice and a perpetual forward and back rhythm on the balls of his feet. As he shook their hands, he took over the conversation from Petey, giving the men a rundown of bands he'd hired at other clubs, the kids he'd pushed forward to success. Ricky exchanged amused glances with Vinnie.

The other man, who Petey introduced as Wayne Foster, was cut from the same body mold as Buddy. He was short, with thin red hair and getting on in years, but where Buddy had a fluidity about him, Wayne was consumed by bursts of energy. His eyes darted and his hands jumped in front of him as he talked despite a quiet voice. Wayne was the front man (read Fall Guy) for the club, and even though Petey was the *de facto* owner, the liquor license, property title, and The Blue Raven business entity were all in Wayne's name. Ricky wondered what leverage Pete had on Wayne to get him to agree to such an arrangement. It could be useful if he ever needed things done independently.

"So here it is," Petey said as the conversation slowed. "The dream team, here to make The Blue Raven a success. I love that name."

"I was just tellin' Rick that. Great name."

"It's all gonna come down to teamwork," Petey said to Buddy and Wayne. "Vinnie and Ricky should have no problem. They've got a long history of solvin' problems together. They're the captains in here. And I'm just the team owner, happy to have my box to watch it all."

Vinnie chuckled. "You're too restless for that."

"I'm turnin' over a new leaf with this place," Petey said through drags on his cigar. "All goes well, we should be singin' Kumbaya soon enough. Even Wayne here, you twitchy bastard."

Wayne shifted on his feet but smiled to satisfy the Fat Man, who turned to Markie. "Hey, shithead, how many of us are standin' here? There's five, that's right. How come you only got two drinks? Go" The others laughed as Markie nearly fell in his sprint for the door.

Petey used the distraction. He leaned to Ricky and said, "Before I forget, I've got a job for you. It might actually be fun ..."

One evening in May of 1973
Giordano family house in Brooklyn, NY
"We were always together. Vacations, holidays,
baptisms, graduations…it didn't matter."

Cristiana Giordano loved to host dinner parties. She would often ask Alphonse to stay home on weekends at the expense of business to host their friends and drink wine late into the night. When he said yes, which wasn't rare, she would agonize for days over the ingredients, the presentation, the entertainment, her wardrobe, the cleaning. She kept a record of who attended, what they ate, and the conversations they had, no matter how many times they had visited before.

She loved when the wives and girlfriends arrived early to help her cook. They whispered as they worked. Who was seen with who, how the children were doing in school and in sports, which boys were getting in trouble, which girls were promiscuous…a familial dialogue.

And Cris had an inner circle, developed over decades. She always invited Oscar, Al's brother, and his wife Marisa. She invited Nick Pisani and his lovely wife Sonia to parade their relative youth before the older couples. And her children…she invited her children to everything now that they were gone from her nest. And Phil, a sweet man and the protector of her husband, and his wife Liv.

Cris surveyed her current team of Italian women, those of her closest circle, each as boisterous as the others, each wearing an ankle-length flower pattern and the pendant of a saint. "Regina," she called to her son's dark-eyed girlfriend, "can you cut those onions there? Not finely diced, just chopped, and I'll throw it in the pan." She knew she must manage the beautiful young girl's kitchen responsibilities. "Liv," the matriarch said, "this chicken is about ready. How's your mix look?"

"Just about ready, hon," Liv answered as Cris peeked for herself. "I'll need anchovies in a minute." Cris dropped a pair of chicken breasts into sizzling hot oil, waited a moment, and dropped the temperature a touch.

"Ten cloves?" Marisa asked her sister-in-law. Cris nodded, simpatico. "Regina, pour a little olive oil in there and then put the chopped onions in there," she pointed, "and when Marisa gets done with these cloves, we'll drop them on top, so the garlic doesn't burn in the pan. But make sure the cloves are on top." The doorbell rang and Cris smiled. She knew it was Nick, always the last to arrive. "Johnny, get the door!"

Cris watched Liv add her mix of anchovies, olives, and chili peppers to the chicken oil and Regina mixed olive oil and onions in the other. The smells were floating with the sizzles and crackling in the air, the excitement in the room climbing with them. Marisa passed her cloves to Regina. "Right on top there, *mimmo*." Cris could hear Johnny at the front door and Nick and Sonia greeting him in the entryway. She could hear Al making his slow walk to join them. She heard a joke from Nick, her son's deep chuckle, her husband's mumbles trail off. Sonia led Nick to the kitchen, smiling widely, her hand in his. "Crissy, *my amore!*" he said. "It smells wonderful in here." Cris moved past her kitchen staff to give the couple more kisses and hugs.

Nick was an eager help in the kitchen, gaining favor with these women by needling their men in the other room. "How can we help, Crissy? Give me something to do so I don't have to sit in there with those *idiots!*" he teased. He made the same joke every time, punctuated by a soft chuckle at the end.

"Sonia, can you help Regina with those red bell peppers? Nick, can you dice those tomatoes over there?" Cris answered, nudging him to his task.

"Yes, Mrs. G., of course," Nick said. "But this kitchen needs some music. Is the radio in here?" He disappeared into the sitting room without waiting for a response and reappeared a minute later, wheeling the old wood radio forward and turning the dial. Nick was an animated man, oozed energy. Cris appreciated him, one of the few men not afraid to interact with Alphonse Giordano's wife and daughters. So many of the others kept an awkward distance, exaggerating, she thought, the stakes. Even more reasons for the dinners, her love for her circle.

Nick feigned fervor from the first note of the old radio. He threw his head back to sing, raised his arms toward the ceiling. His hips swung, moved in a poor Elvis imitation. He pulled Sonia into his dance against her will. He held her close and put his head on her shoulder while his singing went on. "Oh, Sonia, my sweet love child," he crooned in her ear so the others could hear him. The pair twirled, and Sonia pretended to be frustrated with him, hitting his chest with her fist. The others laughed. Nick went on as best he could, smiling as he did. *"I only live for your love and your kiss, / It's paradise to be near you like this, / Because of you my life is now worthwhile, / And I can smile because of you!"* Nick knew only those lines and so capped his performance with a dramatic dip and kiss for his wife. Sonia, as he intended, was blushing bright red when he pulled her up.

The others kept on laughing as they finished. "So romantic, Nick! How could anyone keep their hands off of him?"

Sonia hit Nick playfully one more time. "Every time he hears Tony Bennet. He only does it to annoy me now. With or without an audience."

"An *amore* worthy of this music!"

"Tony is such a wonderful singer," Regina said as the music continued, "but that stage name is such a shame. He tries to forget he's an Italian, so me and Johnny only call him Tony. The name Bennet sounds so boring."

"*Anthony Benedetto*," Marisa said. "A beautiful name. The Americans probably think he's some Brit."

"They shame our people," Nick said, waving a dismissive hand, "these performers who hide their heritage. Dean Martin, Tony Bennet. Sinatra knew. He left it alone. Too Sicilian to care, Frank was…we adding tomato paste to these, Crissy?"

"I have some jarred in the pantry."

Nick pulled it from the shelf and added to the diced chunks already in the bowl. "Regina," he whispered to her, covertly drawing her attention to his work, "if you're gonna add tomato paste, you want to make sure you cover the goodies evenly before the pan. Otherwise, you could end up with burnt paste."

Regina giggled. "I know not to burn stuff, Nick. And how to mix things."

"There's more. You'll see," he said, winking. He turned to Cris again. "How much salt you want on these onions?"

"Just a pinch," she answered, distracted by her bubbling chicken.

Nick frowned. "I think we need three pinches here, Crissy." She had not heard him and went about her tasks. "Trust me," Nick said, more to Regina than Cris, "and after, you tell me what you think. Three pinches. Boom." He grabbed a pinch and peeked down the line before swiftly adding two more. He turned back to everyone's favorite protégé. "Regina, I promise, one pinch of salt is never enough. The salt releases all the flavor," he motioned to simulate the taste release mechanism, "of the garlic and the onions into the sauce."

"You should be able to add the red sauce to the pan of onions and garlic down there!" Cris called out to the Regina/Nick section of the line. Regina went for the bowl Nick had been mixing, but he softly stopped her arm and put his finger to her lips. He eyed Cris again as he scuttled to the spice rack, found his target, and returned to dash shakes of cayenne pepper into the bowl, doubling Regina with barely stifled laughter.

Cris called to them again. "And that's going to need to simmer for a few minutes before we add it to the chicken!"

Nick was still grinning, his eyes thin, as he rinsed tomato paste from his hands. "Cris, you got these women under control? I can hear your husband talking about me in the other room."

"Nick, I had this under control before you got here. I'm sure you've found a way to make it worse already," Cris said, her own smile tugging at the corners. "Go play with the boys."

Nick dried his hands, gave his wife a peck on the cheek, and headed into the living room where Phil and the Giordanos, Al, Oscar, Johnny, and Carrie were sitting around the TV. He sat next to Al, patted the man's leg, and settled in to listen vaguely to news reports about microprocessors.

One night in May of 1973
Giordano family house in Brooklyn, NY
"When a decision like that was made, it was fuckin' made.
No maybe this, maybe that. That shit was over."

Alphonse grabbed a bottle of wine (a sweet, wet red) from the table and dumped the remainder in his wife's glass. She was too caught up in their card game to notice. Al rarely participated in the games, preferring to watch his wife and her happy guests from a distance, even daring to sit on the floor with his back against the couch. He loved to watch his wife the most. The years grayed streaks of her hair and wrinkled the corners of her mouth and eyes, but underneath Cris was the same woman he married thirty-seven years ago. Same as always, they were in a room of people she brought together with happiness on their ears. Whatever warmth was in him, he knew was of her design.

He found his brother Oscar worthy of observation as well. Marisa, Oscar's wife, leaned against his chest as they played, the two of them shamelessly swapping cards and hints in full view of the others and laughing as heartily as anyone else. Al envied them. Oscar had been a humble child. Al had called it weakness then. The early returns were obvious, Al had thought, as he left school to make his way. Al sold his aggression in the early days and made more than their father, who laid bricks on the whims of other men. Before long though, he watched the transactions change. They became about jealousy, frustration, fear, and hate more than money. He saw clearly now; his money was borrowed and he was paying interest now.

A loud round of laughter snapped Alphonse from his musings. Cris leaned her head against his chest. "I won again!" she said, kissing him with drunken clumsiness. The others dropped their cards and reached for whatever alcohol was close by.

Al hugged his wife's head snug against his chest and kissed her hair. He used the moment to get Nick's attention. "How about a cigar, Nick?"

"Perfect timin', Boss," he said from his own wife's arms. "Let me refill my drink here."

Nick poured the drink and followed Al onto the front porch. The night air was cool and humid, and they both fell back into a porch swing where Al lit a cigar for himself and passed Nick his own. The porch was painted light blue against the austere house of red brick Al had bought many years before, just barely a father then. Where the Don placed his feet was worn away, and the knotted brown pine pushed through. He puffed deep on his cigar, allowing the smoke to fill his mouth and nose. He took his time with cigars.

The two men relaxed in the swing, prodding the seat slowly back and forth. It was peaceful. Brooklyn was never quiet, but when you sit on a porch and smoke cigars, it could be peaceful.

"So, I told you I was goin' into the country to meet with the other New York guys," Al said finally. "This happened Monday. It was an interesting meeting, maybe even productive." The front door creaked open and Phil joined them with his own cigar.

Nick and Al went on without a word. "You get the money whacked up?" Nick asked between puffs.

Al remembered Adam's exit with a reflexive wince. "The Old Man and the other guy were resistant to our terms."

"Not surprising."

Phil leaned against the railing as he listened and cocked his head toward the stars, blowing smoke straight up like a chimney. "Don C. guilted them into a little compromise. I think it's fine for now."

"Good...good."

"Assumin' they have really moved on," Al continued, "we have other issues to deal with. One is this cement and concrete union. We need them on board to move on with the build and make a little extra on the bids."

Nick tapped his cigar against the swing's armrest. "Who runs that union?"

"Some guy named Benfield. We've worked on him in the past, but I don't think we're interested in goin' that route again." Al often hid orders behind a trigger word, *interested* was a favorite. Nick understood.

"No problem. I'll take care of it."

"You can farm it out," Al said. "We could test Nunzio or Vinnie's little brother on this one."

Nick hesitated. Nunzio and Tano were young. "I understand why you're sayin' that, I really do, but I'm not comfortable with them around that construction job. It sends a bad message puttin' youth on it when there's older guys with their hands in their pockets... What about Paulie?"

Phil looked away from the stars to make eye contact with Al, but he ended up staring at the orange tip of his cigar, twirling it in the light from the window. "However, you gotta do it," Al said. "I don't want to know, just do it."

"And then who do we put in place?"

Phil turned to face the others and their swing. "Joey's got that. We're gonna put the treasurer in charge, and Joey's gonna handle him, ya know, movin' forward."

"Not much fuss," Al said into the smoke. "Better it's just over with."

"Done. I'll tell Paulie tomorrow. We'll work it out. It's over."

Al nodded. "I know you will."

Phil refocused on the stars. The three men stayed there for a while longer smoking their cigars in the cool, humid air.

An evening in the winter of 1984
Residence of Vyacheslav Usenko

In one swift motion, V stepped through the front door, tossed his coat on a wall peg, patted his wife's tricolor beagle, and shoveled a pair of books to the top shelf of the closet. Despite his efficiency, raindrops fell from his jacket and pooled around him, so he smeared the puddles more evenly across the floor. *Surface area, evaporation, whatever.*

He squeaked to his office, flinging more droplets on his desk as he click-popped his briefcase open. The day's work produced four new tapes, and these he labeled and filed in his drawer with the others, locking it afterward. The key itself fit snug in the bottom of an old snow globe he stored on a bookshelf across the room. He replaced both the key and globe before squeaking back into the main of the house.

The living room was V's primary domain. He had a color television set aimed at his green La-Z Boy and a well-stocked mini fridge beside that. He grabbed a cold beer from inside and fell into the recliner as he opened it. The respite was welcome, the first drink after a productive day. His head lay back into the cushion, and his eyes closed, his breathing slowed and his mind…he took another drink, an icy bite against his throat, and let himself recline a little further, the padding soft around him…

But his moment could not last, and when he heard Helen's footsteps in the kitchen, he roused himself to look for the remote. He knew her next stop, and his best play was to put something disinteresting on the TV. He was all the way to pulling off couch cushions when she walked in.

"What are you doing to the couch?" she asked him from the doorway. She was already wearing her nightgown, and her hair was pulled up into an untidy ponytail. *She will be brief,* he thought.

"I'm looking for the remote. That is the one reason humans pull off couch cushions."

"I haven't watched TV in here today."

V ignored her to continue his prodding at the back of the couch, where springs hide remotes in their recesses. "Did you look behind the TV?" Helen asked while moving to check for herself.

"I did."

"And your chair?"

"Yes."

"What about under the mini-fridge?"

V stopped prodding the couch. "No…I did not check under the mini fridge. Is that even possible? How could it get under the mini fridge?" He examined his appliance. It was nearly flush with the floor, but the lighting was bad, so he tilted it to give his wife a look. She shook her head no. V resumed his search. Helen distracted herself with pictures on their mantel.

"Have you talked to Brandon?" she asked.

"Not since New Year's. Does he still live in the goddamn jungle?"

Helen brushed dust from the nearest frame. "He's going to visit us in September." A smile grew slowly on her lips until she could not control it anymore. She would turn this into months and months of conversation filler, V knew. The itinerary would be updated daily. "Eight days, seven nights. He'll probably just stay right up the road near that little Sixth Street shopping area. And obviously he'll have to bring Luzi to take care of the little one."

"It will be good to see him. Did he find our granddaughter a suitable witch doctor yet? I saw some talented ones in *National Geographic*."

Helen gently nudged two of her frames into proper alignment. "Did you take it with you to the kitchen?"

"I don't think so."

"But you didn't check?"

V knew to control his tone. "I haven't gotten that far yet."

"I'll check," she said and walked out. V regrouped to assess his search before eyeing himself in the black TV screen and grabbing another beer. He checked himself again. 1978, he thought, a distant memory. '78 had been the year of his recliner, the house, his color TV, his mini fridge, the first conception of his gut, the year of *The Conciliators*, the praise. It was the year Brandon left Tokyo for a tent in the jungle. *The remote is not in the kitchen. I will bet my life.*

V conceded defeat. He abandoned his search and tuned the TV with the knob before falling back into his La-Z Boy. He pulled his glasses off and rubbed them cleaner with the bottom of his shirt. The news anchor was finishing his introduction when Helen returned, casually tossing the remote into his chest. She said "Garage" softly to him before turning to leave him in peace.

"Thank you, Helen," he said.

* * *

V woke with his face pressed into the soft wood grains of his desk. He knew them by their cool touch, their subtle up and down rhythm. His mouth was dry and stiff and searched for relief until he opened his eyes. He saw just a blur and then refocused. The blur was thick glass at the end of his nose, the snow globe. He shut his eyes again.

His head was dull and shined with sweat as he lay there. A few minutes more, a few more, until he could not excuse it any longer and peeled his cheek free. A folder lay in front of him, its paper contents spilled across the surface. He pulled the folder to him for a closer look, but he knew it already by the curled brown edges, browner than the manila they had been. He tossed it back. He picked a sheet and read the transcription.

> JULY 1, 1973. (*Could he recite it by heart? He was not sure.*)
>
> UNKNOWN MALE: GLOVES. I'VE TOLD YOU, EVERY MAN NEEDS HIS GLOVES. (*The letters were stamped into the paper, and their ridges brushed his fingers. He backed them off, afraid to smudge the words.*)
>
> BURKE: DOESN'T MATTER TO ME, WHATEVER. THAT'S WHAT I'LL TELL FRANK THEN. (*Frank Ramsey, V knew. Neil Burke meant Frank Ramsey. He had to.*)
>
> UNKNOWN MALE: WHAT IF HE NEEDS TO RETIRE TOO? AFTER THIS? (*So obvious, V thought, so casual.*)
>
> BURKE: FRANK? HE WON'T NEED THAT. BUT I WOULDN'T STRESS OVER IT IF THAT'S HOW IT GOES. THERE'S TOO MUCH ELSE TO BE STRESSED ABOUT. (*Friends for years, Frank and Neil. They first met in 1952.*)
>
> UNKNOWN MALE: AS LONG AS YOU KNOW. SOLDIERS HOLD THE SHIELD, KINGS LIVE ON.
>
> BURKE, *laughing*: HE SAY SHIT LIKE THAT?
>
> UNKNOWN MALE: KINGS SAY SHIT LIKE THAT. AND ME AND YOU ARE GONNA BE KINGS, NEIL.

V flipped the transcript back among the other papers and lay back into his chair, his eyes on the ceiling. It was cold enough outside for the warmth of his office to fog the windows past all seeing. It was cold enough for snow to fall, and he hoped it would.

PART TWO

A BLUE NOOSE OR GREEN?

The morning of May 19, 1973
Nick Pisani's house in Brooklyn
"The only person as crazy as Nick was Sonia."

Nick leaned against the front wall of his shower and let the hot water run down his back and over his face. His head was dull and foggy, but the shock of water sped his recovery. He closed his eyes and raised them to the spray.

The mirror was fogged when he dried himself, and he rubbed it clear with his palm before combing his hair, as flat and polished as he could. It had been days since he shaved, but Sonia liked a few days' whiskers. He would leave them for her today.

His rings were on the dresser. He put them on first, then his necklaces (one a cross and the other a pendant of Saint Adrian), and stood naked otherwise before his closet and his many suits. None of them were flashy, Al had opinions about those things, but Nick added touches of color with his pocket squares. Reds and greens were his favorite, so Sonia would buy him new ones for his birthday and Christmas every year. He picked a gray suit with worn elbows.

"Breakfast," Sonia said, entering with a smile and a tray of food. "And a newspaper."

"Thanks, baby." Nick pulled a pair of boxers on and kissed her forehead as she set the tray lightly on the bed.

"It's Saturday," she said. "Can we go somewhere tonight? Maybe Johnny and Regina want to see a show. Or Carrie and Bobby."

Nick shoveled bites into his mouth. "Al's making me work. He just told me last night."

Sonia huffed. She knew the script. "Of course. I can forget about us ever goin' out."

"It's important work," Nick said, chewing his bacon. "I am not sure how long it will take." He felt compelled to explain further. "Al does not trust these things to other people."

"I know you can't control him, but I'm sick of sittin' here. I'm going out with *my* friends then, if you're not gonna be here."

"Who?"

"I don't know yet. Don't worry, you're busy."

Nick crunched more bacon. "Fine." He stepped into his gray slacks, and as he searched the closet for his belt, Sonia stepped behind him. She ran her fingers over a pale scar halfway up the left side of his ribs. "Did this one hurt the most?" she asked.

Nick put his hand over hers. "For many reasons, yes. That must be why I work so hard. We both need clothes to cover our scars."

"I like yours. They're pretty things."

Nick turned to face her. "Which is your favorite then?"

She smiled and pointed to a red triangle-shaped indention on his chest, just under his collarbone.

"Of course," he said. "Did you almost get your wish?"

"It's perfect," she said, her lips an inch away. He could feel her breath against it. "A perfect triangle."

"Stressful couple hours."

"Worth it," she said, playing with the hair on the back of his head, mussing it for him to recomb. "You *have* to work?"

"I would be with you if I could. But I'm here now..." He pulled her flush against his body and pressed his lips to hers. They didn't have many clothes to remove. The breakfast tray capsized to the ground, eggs sliding in all directions.

May 19, 1973, at "roughly 5:00 p.m."

Nick and Paulie Panzavechia watched from a few hundred yards away as Mrs. Benfield got in her four-door sedan alone, pulled from the space in front of their townhome, and drove off in the opposite direction.

Nick opened his door. "Let's go." He moved so quickly Paulie was jogging every few steps and still trailing him as they climbed the front steps. At the door, they hesitated, bouncing on their toes like boxers about to enter the ring. Paulie stepped forward to rap the Benfield door, and the pair listened for some sign of life on the other side.

Footsteps came a moment later, tapping a confident pace toward the door. Nick pulled his gun from the gray suit coat and clasped both hands behind his back. The piece was drawn, but concealed.

When the door moved, it was slow, peeling away to reveal an older man with wispy white hair, a loose jaw, and mottled complexion under slacks and a bright-blue sweater.

Nick spoke first. "Mr. Benfield?"

"Why yes, I—" the man began but Nick had not hesitated. He fired twice before any more words could materialize, hitting Benfield above each knee. He fell to the ground screaming in rage and agony, veins bulging from his head and neck. "My GOD!" he cried, staring at his legs in disbelief. Blood was already pouring from the wounds to form red pools beneath them. Mr. Benfield kept howling as Nicky stepped over him and into the house.

Paulie turned back to the street. He could not see anyone watching, although it would have been impossible to tell. The houses were stacked close together and each had several windows. He stepped inside, grabbed the bleeding old man under the armpits, and dragged him farther into the house. Nick shut the door behind them.

"Jesus Christ," Paulie said, dropping Benfield a few paces inside. The old man held his legs and writhed against the floor, smearing his blood in streaks. "Everybody in the whole fuckin' neighborhood heard that."

Nick shook his head and went about casually examining the china in a hallway cabinet. "They're not gonna do anythin' we don't want them to," he said, holding a porcelain tea pot under a light to examine its shine. "Drag him into the kitchen."

"Did Al call for something special?" Paulie asked. It'd be easier to rob the house if the homeowner(s) were dead. "Why don't we just kill him right fuckin' now if you want that stuff?"

The comment stoked Mr. Benfield's terror. "Please," he said, crying as he squirmed, "I have money. Please, anything, you can *have anything*! What do you want? Don't kill me, I have CHILDREN! JUST TELL ME WHAT YOU WANT, please." His breaths had become short and sharp, especially the inhales, as he entered a state of shock.

Nick ignored the bleeding man's pleas, instead walking aimlessly around the bottom floor of the home, occasionally inspecting a trinket, drawer, or picture frame. Paulie stayed near Benfield with a gun leveled at his chest to make sure he did not grab a weapon and complicate the situation more. He called after Nick, "What are you looking for? Just ask him where it is." Paulie looked at the man who was by now a fetal-shaped heap on the floor. "He seems cooperative."

"Yes, I'll give you anything you want. Anything AT ALL!" Mr. Benfield recovered enough to resume his crying and twisting on the ground, his face a dark mixture of red and purple. "Just tell me what you want. Please." Mr. Benfield began speaking directly to Paulie. "Just tell me why you're here," he whispered. "You won't have to kill me." Blood had soaked Benfield's pants down to his ankles. Paulie knew he would be gone in a few minutes no matter what anyone wanted.

"Nick, what the fuck are you looking for?" Paulie's heart rate increased with each second of delay. *If the neighbors call the police, how long would it take to get here?* "Let's go, Nick! Fuckin' Christ!" Paulie heard a door open somewhere on the other side of the house. *Where is he going now?* But Paulie knew his role and manned his post until he heard the door open again, this time accompanied by hysterical laughter.

Nick reappeared in the kitchen carrying a large bag, and when Paulie realized what it was, his mouth went slack, words choked in his throat. "Think they'll make this connection?" Nick asked. Paulie was still, observing the inevitable scene in his mind. Nick held an eighty-pound bag of concrete mix in his hands. He set it on the kitchen table and kneeled on the ground, facing Mr. Benfield, whose face was now ivory white. Liters of blood lay in a trail from his front doorway to the base of the kitchen table.

"Now, Mr. Benfield," Nick said, "is there any money in the house? Any expensive jewelry you bought for the wife?"

Paulie was still distracted by the concrete, but he saw Benfield shake his head no.

"Eh, never mind, Mr. Benfield, I don't feel like findin' it."

Benfield was fading fast. Paulie touched Nick on the shoulder. "Come on, Nick," he pleaded. "Let's go. We gotta go."

Benfield tried to roll over, but he couldn't make it. His lips were moving, but neither man could hear the words. Nick leaned closer, and somehow Benfield, mustering the last of his strength, said quite audibly, "Fuck you." Nick smiled, amused. Most guys went out weak and incompetent and covered in shit. Benfield at least had recovered his resolve before the last. Whatever his sentiments though, Nick's face turned serious as he stood up. His dark eyes deepened as he grabbed the bag of ready-mix, raised it over his head, and slammed it onto Mr. Benfield's head with a nauseating crunch. The blood spewed in all directions, including onto Nick's shoes and pants below the knee. He gave his shoes a shake, but the blood clung stubbornly until he used Benfield's blue sweater to wipe them. He frowned at the mess before touching Paulie on the shoulder. "All right," he said. "Now we can go."

Paulie followed Nick out the door, and the two walked calmly to the car.

May 19, 1973, at 6:00 p.m.

Johnny Giordano was a tall man, but Joe-Joe Tessaro was one of the few people who was unequivocally taller than him. He resented it. "It's this one here," Johnny said, parking his 1970 red-on-black Chevy Chevelle SS 454 before a simple house with a blue door and painted cream brick. The pair walked side by side to the front door, souring Johnny's mood. He knocked rather aggressively and said, "I'll do the talking, Joe. Stand at the bottom there."

An older woman opened the door and frowned at the two young men on her stoop without a word. Johnny smiled and spoke politely. "Hello, ma'am. We're looking for Mr. Newman?"

She was losing a battle to gray hair, but the vestiges of her youth were still there to see. Her former beauty most likely cultivated the confidence in her voice. "That's my husband," she said with obvious suspicion. "Who're the two of you?"

Johnny answered officiously, "We are representatives from the local election board and wanted to ask your husband a few questions regarding the position of the cement union. Your husband is involved with the union, correct?"

"Yes, he is." She eyed them critically but conceded. "I'll get him for you," she said and disappeared back inside the house. A few moments later a man who was older, shorter, and less confident than Mrs. Newman appeared. Even as he stood a step up from Johnny, he was inches shorter than the two men.

"Mr. Newman?" Johnny asked.

"Yes."

A smirk was building on Johnny's face. "As in the vice president of the Concrete and Cement Workers Union?"

"Yes. My wife says you have come to discuss the local election? You should really discuss the union positions with our president, Al Benfield," Mr. Newman said. He shifted his feet and moved to shut the door, but Johnny stopped him with a powerful hand.

"We would prefer to discuss them with you, sir," Johnny said, his smirk still growing. "Do you get the newspaper, Mr. Newman?"

"Yes." Newman glanced from Johnny's hand to Joe-Joe's chest and arms, and back to Johnny. "Why does that matter?"

"Please read it tomorrow, Mr. Newman," Johnny said. "It may have a lasting impact on your career." He stared at the man for an uncomfortably long moment.

"What is that supposed to mean?" Newman's brow furrowed half in confusion, half in worry.

"Retirement suits you, sir. Have a nice night." With that the two large men gave Mr. Newman a shallow bow, stepped down from his stoop, and left a flustered individual in their wake.

Evening of May 19, 1973
The Onyx Social Club in Queens, NY

Nick draped himself over Ernie "Millions" Nocellaro, who was sitting on a barstool counting crinkled stacks of money between finger licks. The lights of Ernie's club reflected off the pearly black bar top almost well enough to see your face in the surface.

"Ernie, you know what we're here for," Nick said, kissing Ernie on both cheeks. Paulie followed suit. "We're ready to fuckin' unwind."

"Back room," Ernie said without looking up. Nick and Paulie knew what to do and made for the door. "Help yourselves to anything you can find back there, except my wife."

"You got a phone in there?" Nick asked. "I've gotta make a call real quick."

"Yeah, on the desk. Don't be usin' the long distance."

Nick and Paulie pushed through a red door labeled Management with bedazzled silver letters and into the backroom, a makeshift office with two couches. Nick went to a phone on the desk and spun the dial.

"Hey, Liv, is Phil there? … Yeah, thanks, hon. … Hey, Phil. Everything worked out. … Yeah…so we're on to the other guy? … What Johnny say? … All right, well, we're at Ernie's for the night if you need us. … Yeah, all right, all right. Sounds good. Well, you can join us if you want. … All right, I get it. … All right, bye, Phil." Nick hung up and turned to Paulie. He gave his charge a quick hug and held him at arm's length, smiling as wide as his face would let him. "All the work is done, buddy. Time for some play. I need a drink." He poured two glasses of scotch, handed Paulie his, and walked back to the door, squeezing it open and yelling for Ernie, "Hey, E, send some girls in! And join us, you fuckin' prick!" Ernie must have answered because Nick loosed a few extra buttons of his shirt and fell into the couch with Paulie. Nick sat up seconds later, and Paulie watched his friend, his boss, drum a fast rhythm on the glass between gulps. Nick was a twitching bundle of hasty nerve, even as he slouched again into the cushions with his shirt unbuttoned to his sternum. "God, isn't this the life?" he said when he poured a second drink and kicked his shoes off. Benfield's blood had already leached into their brown leather.

"It's great when it works out," Paulie said.

Two of Ernie's girls joined them, one blond and the other blonder, wearing short skirts and low-cut tops pulled snug around their breasts. Nick greeted them first, grabbing them by the hips and pulling them in for a kiss each. Paulie waited a few steps back until one girl broke away from Nick to focus on his second, kissing Paulie's neck and rubbing his crotch with both hands until he was hard. She straddled him, her pale skin and thick thighs radiating warmth through his slacks, while Paulie pressed his face into hers and gave her his tongue, moving his hands to her backside as he did. She pulled her top down, and Paulie made the most of it before sneaking a glance at Nick, who was in much the same position on the other side of the room.

"Booze and women," Nick said in the midst of his entertainment, "is all any of us should ever have to know." The girls giggled politely whenever he spoke.

Paulie's blond stepped back from him and pulled her skirt off, ditching it with a kick before backing onto his lap and reclining against his chest. "What about our friend today? What did he know?" Paulie asked, his confidence and testosterone perhaps muddled in his mind.

Nick faced him briefly. "You think too much, Paulie. That guy knew enough so as to not have to know things anymore." Nick pinched the pink nipples of his companion with his teeth and smiled at her when they stiffened against his lips.

"Ah…I was just askin' if you knew," Paulie said with contrition. "I don't need to know."

"You start askin' questions and you might start gettin' answers, my friend. And that's the worst thing that can happen to you."

Paulie considered that a moment. "I trust you, never mind. Stupid question."

"It's not a stupid question. Stupid's got nothin' to do with it. The problem is, a lot of times anyway, stupid will make you happy, and you wanna be happy, don't ya? We don't have to concern ourselves with the grander plan, because trust is more important in this Thing than what you know. You gotta trust it. Focus on the women and the booze. They'll get ya where you wanna go."

Paulie fell back into his blond, and they began to sweat under the lights of the management office as they rubbed their cheeks and necks and arms against each other. He heard Nick open the red door again and call for Ernie, "Hey, E, two more broads, huh? And join us, you prick!"

May 19, 1973, at 9:15 p.m.
The Benfield home in Manhattan, NY
"It was a Jackson Pollock on hardwood."

Detective Andrew Clayburgh knelt in the entryway, examining the two dried puddles of blood by the front door and tracing their streaks down the hall. He curled his flat cap in one hand and rubbed his bald crown with the other, frowning. The man's body had been removed, but his outline remained in stark white chalk.

He rose to his feet with an ear for Detective Brady Murdock's questions of the new widow, just out of sight of her husband's outline. "Mrs. Benfield, I know this conversation is gut-wrenching," Murdock said, "but please bear with us. Are you aware of any recent work problems? Financial stresses? Personal disputes involving the union?"

Mrs. Benfield's eyes were spidered red and her cheeks wet and flushed, but she kept her voice even and clear. "None. He never brought any of that stuff home with him. I don't know if those things happened or not, but he never involved me or the children in it. He had no enemies. We were quiet people with a few close friends. He's a good man, my husband. A damn good man. Anyone will tell you that, exactly that, if you ask them." Her eyes began to tear again.

Murdock resisted the reflexive pat of her arm or the promise everything would be all right.

Clayburgh faced her from his position in the hallway. "Anything we can do, we will, Mrs. Benfield. I promise you that."

Murdock continued, "And you left the house close to when we believe this all happened?"

"That's what the officers told me. I went to the store just before five and then to my sister's house to help her cook dinner. He was going to meet us over there. Around six thirty I called him. He was thirty minutes late, which was unusual, but he didn't answer. Around seven, I came back…and found him."

"Did you notice any cars on the street? Maybe that looked out of place either when you were leaving or when you were coming back?"

She shook her head. "I didn't notice anything. It's not rare for every space to be filled on this street though. There could have been cars I should've noticed, I guess, I don't know."

"We understand. Officers will be canvassing the area to see if your neighbors may have noticed anything unusual."

"And your children, where are they?"

"We have four. All but one moved away." Mrs. Benfield pulled a picture down from a nearby shelf and handed it to Murdock. "We have a daughter that still lives in the Bronx," she said, pointing to her in the frame.

Murdock studied the picture. It could not have been less than ten years old, judging by Mrs. Benfield's appearance. The family was standing on a pier with a lighthouse in the background and a group of boulders to hold back the waves. "You have a beautiful family," he said finally. "Your daughter, will she be here later? We'd like for someone to stay with you."

"She is going to take me to a hotel for a few days."

Clayburgh nodded. "That's for the best, Mrs. Benfield." Her absence at the house would give them extra time to process the scene without interruption. He returned to the blood-spatter before something caught his eye. Against the wall, an oak cabinet stocked with porcelain wares and paneled into sections by windowpanes and two doors with small brass knobs. The china seemed to emit its own light behind the glass, but the cabinet itself had not been wiped clean in some time. Clayburgh spotted an exception beneath the right-side door, which had been opened since the last cleaning, and scraped away the dust below it. He leaned toward the knob itself, peering through the windows for more marks in the dust. "When was the last time you served a meal on this china?" he asked, calling back for Mrs. Benfield.

"Years…that was my great-grandmother's. I don't know if I've used it since she died."

"Pardo," Clayburgh said quietly to Officer Pardo a few feet away, "make sure this cabinet and its contents are checked for fingerprints, especially this knob. I believe the perpetrator may have touched it."

"Yes, sir," Pardo said.

"Mrs. Benfield, we will have follow-up questions after we have worked our way through the scene and spoken with your neighbors," Clayburgh said. "Please leave a number with one of the officers before leaving with your daughter."

Mrs. Benfield nodded and walked to her couch, slumping with exhaustion into the cushions. Murdock grabbed a spare officer and motioned him to attend her at the next burst of sobs. It was often when the questioning was over, when the shock wears off, that the permanence of the situation hit the victims and any warm body was better than nothing.

Clayburgh waited on the front porch for his partner to join him. "It's not the family," he said when Murdock stepped outside. "It's not any of them."

"I don't expect *she* could shoulder press an eighty-pound bag," Murdock said, still scribbling thoughts on his notepad, "but you're over the son too?"

Clayburgh thought about the streaks, the initial wounds. "The family would have no need to shoot him at the door. She didn't mention family trouble. Any of them could've walked in and taken most of the noise out of the equation. Someone shot him right at the door. There's spray inside the door track. It was still open. Why? To take immediate control and incapacitate him."

"How do you spell 'incapacitate'? I'm writing all this in pen..."

Clayburgh rarely commented on his partner's jokes because he understood. Homicide was grisly work. "Those shots would have been really loud, door open or closed. Do we know what caliber those were? One of these neighbors has to be nosy enough to have seen something after."

"I bet one of these households calls us overnight. Patty will end up with something for us in the morning."

Clayburgh nodded with a distraction that bristled his mustache. He left Murdock on the porch to re-enter the house and walk alongside the blood trail to the kitchen. Tiny pieces of Mr. Benfield's skull were still lying on the ground wherever they had fallen, and blood spatter radiated away from the chalk outline of his head except in two places. Clayburgh stopped there, his shoes filling the bloodless voids.

Morning of May 20, 1973
Nick Pisani's home Brooklyn, NY
"I never saw a damn thing to suggest that was goin' on."

Nick staggered up the steps to his front door, fumbling with his keys. He tried to collect himself in the doorway, but it was of little use. His head was swimming, and he had to lean against the door-frame to find his aim and enter. He failed to do so gracefully, almost crashing face-first on the floor and stomping about as he caught himself. He steadied enough to sway toward the kitchen with his hands outstretched to block whatever rays of sunlight he could manage, because those he could not pestered the backs of his eyes with glare. He poured a cup of stale coffee and let his aches crumple him into a chair. He felt for a newspaper on the table, but there wasn't one. His eyelids shut and he slouched there, battling the self-inflicted disruptions in his body chemistry, before steps rang down from the bedroom to the entryway. They were angry stomps he recognized and hated. The noise rumbled to the kitchen doorway where it stopped. "All fuckin' night, Nick? You piece of shit."

Nick's hands covered his eyes. "I was working. Jesus Christ. You want this house? You want your goddamn dresses and your fuckin' car and all the worthless shit you fuckin' buy?"

"Don't give me that shit," Sonia snapped, her nostrils flaring with each phrase. "I know what you do. Even with all the bullshit you feed me, I know they don't pay you to drink with whores."

He moved his hands away from his face. She must have just gotten out of bed because she was only wearing one of his T-shirts. Her eyes were wide and faintly red, her features distorted by a weary rage. "I wasn't drinking with whores." She was perfectly aware of what he had been doing, but she would need pictures for him to budge. "Our business was at the club. I had to be there."

"And if I was to ask Alphonse, that's what he would say? 'I told Nick to *stand* at the fucking *bar* all night?!' That's what the Boss needed done—"

"DON'T USE HIS NAME LIKE THAT!" Nick yelled. Sonia flinched. "I'm warning you to shut your mouth. I'm not doing this." His face had changed. Sonia saw it and did not care. She had loved him yesterday.

"Fuck you. I have to sit here all fuckin' night worried about *you*, you fuckin' piece of shit. Why do I even care?" She paused, stifling fresh tears. No sadness, only anger. "Every week I watch you stumble in this house like a common drunk. Fuck you and you're fuckin' gang."

Nick remained seated, but his voice got louder, his tone searing each word. "Sonia, shut your goddamn mouth. I'm not listening to it."

"I know you're not fuckin' listening. You don't have to remind me of that shit. Do they listen, Nick? Is that why you visit them?"

Nick stood and pointed at her with the coffee mug still in his hand. "I'm serious. Shut your fuckin' mouth."

Sonia grabbed an iron skillet from the sink and held it like a baseball bat. Nick looked at it and then back at her. "Put that fuckin' thing down."

She stood her ground. "You selfish fuck. You think I'll just be here whenever you show up, forever and ever?"

"Don't act like you're going to leave me, Sonia. We both know that will never happen."

"Fuckin' watch me, you SELFISH PIECE OF SHIT! Or maybe I won't fuckin' have to leave—"

Nick threw the mug into her stomach. Coffee went spraying in all directions. Sonia's body doubled over, but only for a second and she recovered. Nick slid around the table, and she stretched the skillet in front of her body.

"You gonna beat me, Nick?" she said, a smile pulling on her lips. "Is that how fuckin' tough you are?" She knew he was too far gone. She knew what was going to happen the minute she heard his clumsy steps come through the door.

Nick stepped forward. Sonia swung at him with the pan. He grabbed her arm to stop it and pushed her to the ground. "Is THIS WHAT YOU WANT?!" He controlled her arms. He knocked the skillet out of her hand. He punched her ribs three, four, five times. "You stupid bitch. You think you can FUCKIN' LEAVE? You wouldn't get ten minutes from this house without a bullet in you." Nick hit her ribs again, her thighs.

Fresh tears came again, and she quit fighting him, just curling to protect herself. He grabbed the skillet—it was just a foot or so away—and straightened up above her. She thought it was done. She was sure this time. But it wasn't. He slammed the skillet into the floor a few inches from her head, leaned in, and whispered, "If I *ever* have to do this again, you'll go out that door in a bag." He threw the pan across the room, into the wall where it left a hole. He fell back on his haunches, looking up at the ceiling and allowing Sonia to cry a few more tears, her chest heaving with each new breath.

"I am going to bed. I have had a long night and a rough morning. We can talk when I get up." He stood, stripped down to his boxers right there in the kitchen, and left his suit on the back of his chair. "I need you to take these to the dry cleaner," he said. "The pants are dirty. There's paint on them."

Afternoon of May 20, 1973
Nick Pisani's house in Brooklyn, NY

Nick's mouth was dry with the stench of whiskey and his sheets were dampened by sweat, but he lay there, a glutton. Faint sounds floated down the hall, and he knew his wife was making them. Shame and indignation returned quickly, but it took every ounce of his energy to roll over and read the clock. Time to get up.

He sat on the edge of the bed and ran both hands through his oily hair. The hot, stagnant air was making everything inside his head worse, and the only relief were the fresh beads of sweat forming and rolling over his chest and stomach. He grabbed the pendant of St. Adrian from his nightstand and brought it to his mouth before swinging its gold chain over his head and wobbling bare-assed to the bathroom. The shower took a minute to warm. He let it run until the mirror was covered with steam before sitting knees-to-chest in the tub. The sweats came easier under the water, and the air was less stagnant. He knew it was a meek and fetal pose, but he stayed there while his mind and ire cleared. Sonia was still in the kitchen when he finished brushing his teeth, dressing himself, and mentally preparing to bring her back from anger. He resented these apologies, but it was best to get it done.

When he reached the kitchen, Sonia was in front of the fridge with the door open and her face fixed in a determined frown. She did not look as he approached, instead staring into the refrigerator and waiting for him to speak first. Other men were critical of their women, no matter how young, how beautiful, but even now, with her face set in disappointment, there was nothing for him to disparage. He stopped with a faint smile on his lips. She'd changed into a knee-length floral dress and pulled her black hair back into a smooth, tight ponytail. Nick kissed her lightly on the side of her head. She allowed it briefly but pulled away. He lightly touched her ribs. "Do they hurt?"

She closed the refrigerator and faced him. "I don't need your help," she said, her dark eyes blazing into his.

"I should've called. You should be mad."

"No shit."

"I didn't know it was gonna be all night."

"Me neither."

"C'mon, Sonia. I know you're mad but don't blow this out of proportion."

That got a reaction. Her lips drew taught, and the latent fury bled over her words. "Fuck mad. This isn't *mad*. This is fuckin' *scared*. I didn't know if you were *dead*."

"I know, I know. It's gettin' better though." Nick tugged his ear before remembering where he was... "Al said he's pullin' me offa this stuff and givin' more to the young guys. That's good for us."

"I just want you to tell me when you're not goin' to be here." She shoved him, paced down the hall, and slammed the bedroom door. Nick chased her. It was part of their routine.

"Sonia," he called. "Stop. Wait." When he opened the door, she was waiting, facing him with her hand on her hip and her lip between her teeth. Nick moved forward until they were chest to chest, eye to eye. He grabbed her by the waist and pulled her closer, but she turned her nose from his. "C'mon, baby," he said.

Sonia answered as coldly as she could. "You shouldn't have to stay out all night like that."

"Baby, I know. It was a *job*. That club is disorganized without me or Paulie there. They would burn it to the ground." He stroked her arms lightly with his fingers, and she let him kiss her forehead. He touched her ribs again. "Does it hurt?"

Her eyes burned with tears but not from her ribs. She put her hands on his shoulders and kissed his cheek. "I'm fine, Nick. Really. I just love you." He kissed her on the mouth and she let him. He picked her up and spun, still kissing as they did.

"Let's go out for dinner. I don't want you to have to cook. Anywhere you wanna go."

Sonia smiled, tears still burning in her eyes. "Manhattan," she said.

He nodded. "Manhattan then."

An afternoon in May of 1973
The Giordano house in Brooklyn, NY
"Nothin' scares mobsters like headlines."

The window above the sink in the Giordano kitchen looked out on two dogwood trees that Alphonse had planted years ago. He'd bought them from a florist, a small Italian man born in the north of Italy, on his way home from the grocer. The florist would stand in a soiled apron watering his display at the front of his store, always some collection of white chrysanthemums and rose orchids, some assortment of peonies, lavender, and white and red roses, and often those were enough for Al to stop and watch. And one day the man noticed and asked, "You have a young wife in your home?" Al nodded. The man grabbed Al's arm and led him through the store and into an alleyway where two little trees were beginning to sprout in separate black pots. "For family," the little florist said, but Al told him no and explained he didn't have anywhere to plant the trees. The man persisted. "For family," he said, pulling Al closer to the pots. Al lifted his grocery bags to show he had no way to carry them even if he wanted to, but at this the man grinned, hopping back inside the shop while Al protested. He was back quickly with a rickety wooden cart, pushing the sproutlings up and down the alley to demonstrate. Al rolled his eyes, annoyed now with the pitch, and the man retreated again, this time returning with a worn image of a woman standing in front of two trees with white leaves. He pointed from the picture to the sproutlings to the woman and again. "All right," Al said. "All right, how much? *Costoso?*" but the florist shook his head. "No money," he said. Driven by a mix of confusion and frustration, Al pushed the wobbly wooden cart all the way home. Cristiana had loved them and cared for them, and after his children were born, he put a bench beneath the trees and read to them in the shade.

Now, as he stood at the sink washing dishes, he thought about the trees again. He thought about his daughters, Carrie and Jennie. He thought about his son, Johnny. He introduced the boy to a world of violence and mayhem, a world he was now honor bound to serve. When Johnny was born, Al was still a young man making his way in the world, carving his path with the weapons he knew. The failure, he admitted to himself, was later. His son traveled a well-cut and tended path, Al leading him down a well-remembered trail. Johnny had no need for his own tools, his own weapons. His actions were a tracing of his father's purpose, found in the context of another time and place. And Al knew the path had affected Carrie as well. It was no accident she was set to marry the son of an underboss, a man who was a *mafioso* himself. Al knew that was his doing. He taught them, as he had been taught, to mistrust those unlike yourself. To scrap and claw and harm. He was convinced of it all once, his tribal angst was powerful, the only horizon his eyes could see. But now, the apex found, it did occur to him he might have risked more than his aged cause was worth. The conceit of experience: he could not know until he knew. And now for Jennie. He feared for her the most.

The water ran hot over his hands as his picked at fragments of dried lasagna and red sauce on his dishes. The water in the sink was now too dirty to do any further good, so he wiped a final plate and pulled the stopper. The brown water swirled, growing more intense as it got lower, until the last of it was slurped away and out of sight. He looked back out at the dogwoods, beautiful in the spring sunshine, and saw half his reflection in the window. He was, quite simply, an old man.

As he stood there, lost in his own thoughts, a knock came from the front door. He heard Cris begin her automatic walk to answer it, but he quickly dried his hands and called to let her know he would get it. It made no difference. Her curiosity would never let him answer the door alone. Alphonse checked the visitor through the window, Phil Scozzari. He turned the knob and opened the door.

"Phil," he said. "Come on in."

Cris smiled down at them from halfway up the staircase. "Phil, what're you doin' here?" She came down and hugged him tightly. "Are you hungry? We have some lasagna, risotto—" she said, counting off the leftover dishes in their fridge.

"Thank you, Cris," Phil said. "I just ate. I'm fine. I just came to talk with Al for a minute."

Cris waved her hand at him. "I'll make you a sandwich," she said and disappeared into the kitchen.

"Thanks, Cris."

Alphonse held his hand out toward the living room. "In here?"

Phil shook his head no. "Somewhere private, Al."

Al could see a lot of worry through Phil's lenses. He spun the other way. "My office?"

"Yeah. That'd be good I think."

Al led Phil into the room, a large room with thick doors. Rather than take a seat behind his desk, Al leaned against its front and crossed his arms. Phil closed the doors behind them before facing Al directly and taking a few more steps into the room.

"You read the newspaper today?" Phil asked. He could not make eye contact for long, just enough to be polite.

"Yes," Al said. He was sure he knew where this conversation was going to go.

Phil began cautiously. "Our problem has been handled, it would seem. And we're ready to move forward."

"That's the gist of what I read," Al said evenly.

Phil paused. He had thought at length about how best to present his concerns. "It was a loud solution to the problem, Al."

"Loud enough for other Families to hear, some might argue. We can skip the memo I would've had to send."

"That may be," Phil conceded. That was missing the point, he thought, but he stuck to his plan. "Or you could say it was loud enough to wake guys up that was previously sleepin'."

Al didn't answer but walked over to his bottle of scotch and poured both men a drink. Phil spoke again as Al handed him his glass. "You know that wasn't Paulie doin' that."

Alphonse nodded. "I know."

Phil was getting ahead of himself, but he couldn't help it. "You told him not to go and he did it anyway," he said, louder than he wanted. He covered his mouth after with a drink of scotch.

Alphonse's face was stolid. "I told him he *should* farm it out. I suggested some names. He said Paulie himself and neither of us said another word about it."

"It was unnecessary and reckless." Phil's face was betraying the level of concern he really had. He hoped it did not betray his irritation with the Don as well.

Al's tone changed precipitously and stole some heat from the room, but he didn't raise his voice. "What do you want me to say here, Phil? I told him, 'Do this job,' and it got fuckin' done, just like every other time we ask somethin' of him. Big? Small? Doesn't matter with him. Am I thrilled it's on the front page? No, but I'm hearin' complaints when a problem has been solved. Do you wanna start solvin' those problems?"

"I'm just sayin'," Phil said, pulling back and lightening his tone, "I'm sick of dealin' with things that are harder than they need to be." He took another drink and continued, slowly. "It coulda been, BOOM," Phil shot an invisible gun into the side of his head, "open some drawers, throw some shit on the ground, and he's another fuckin' statistic. Instead, they're actin' like Jack the Ripper come back."

"What's your answer then? What are your orders? I'm sure you've thought about that responsibility."

"Jesus, God forbid, Al…I'm just sayin'." Phil rubbed his bare forehead in thought and frustration. "I don't have the answers. I just don't want unnecessary heat on us." He paused and neither said anything for a few moments. "I just wanted you to hear me out, now you have. I'd be a shitty friend if I never told you what I was thinkin'—"

Cris knocked on the door. "Al," she called from the other side, "I've got Phil's sandwich here."

Al motioned for Phil to open the door. "Thank you very much, Mrs. G. You know I love your sandwiches." Phil came back in and took a seat with the plate on his lap.

Al knew, somewhere in this, Phil had a point. "This isn't high school, Phil. I can't suspend him, and I wouldn't anyway. And it did send a message. A loud message sure, but messages are…messages."

Phil spoke through his first bite of the sandwich. "If you want a suggestion, I say we take the work elsewhere for now. We use…less newsworthy representatives."

"Fine. If somethin' comes up, we go with somebody else. For now."

"I'm not tryin' to win here," Phil said as bits of lettuce fell from his mouth and onto his slacks. "I'm just lookin' ahead."

"I know. I get it."

Phil continued to chew his sandwich, peeling back the breading for a better look. "What is this, Al? Capicola? She's been making some great sandwiches lately."

The evening of May 20, 1973
The Phoenix Steakhouse in Manhattan, NY

Don Giordano had brought Nick to The Phoenix Steakhouse in Manhattan the same night he took the oath in the basement of St. Anthony's Cathedral in 1960. The Don had watched intently as Nick held a burning portrait of St. Michael in his palms, as he recited the Sicilian words, "If I betray my friends and our Family, I and my soul should burn like this saint, forever in hell." The ash was orange when he brushed it away and soot by the time it hit the floor. A group of *Caporegimes* and *mafioso* followed them to the restaurant, and Nick had never been so proud or felt so respected as when he walked past the main tables to their private room with the Don's men patting his back and speaking about brotherhood. He felt untouchable then, sitting in the glint of chandeliers and smiles, with those men drinking toasts in his honor.

The décor was still much as it had been on that day. Shades of red and gold controlled the floor patterns and the felt accents on their chestnut-colored walls. The chandeliers shone bright although perhaps a shade yellower than before. Black-tie waiters still weaved in and out of tables where white cloth covered the tops and chairs. The room was busy for a Sunday, and the other patrons seemed to be enjoying themselves; the conversations were loud, the diamonds bright, the laughs perpetual. Sonia looked enticing in her new dress, a dark green number cut low and taut against her curves with pearl earrings and a yellow-garnet necklace Nick had bought for her.

"I love when we come here," she said, softly running her nails across the tablecloth. "I love this place. It always makes me feel warm inside."

"Good memories," Nick said. They had their share themselves, but she did not know all he meant. He ordered wine and scanned the menu. "What are you gonna get?"

"Filet mignon." Sonia talked fast when she was excited, and Nick liked to watch her when she did. Her smiles grew bigger then, gleaming like few others beneath the crystal coated bulbs. "It's just *so good* here. I can't help it."

"Filet mignon is good everywhere." Then Nick remembered the dinner was an apology. "I'm the same with the strip. You have to expect the best steakhouse in New York will have the best New York Strip in the world, right?"

"Let's get something different then, if we always get the same things. I don't want us to be boring."

"Get what then?"

"I don't know. Just get something you don't like."

Nick laughed. "Why would I get somethin' I don't like?"

Sonia rolled her eyes and pressed her lips together. "You know what I mean. Something you like but not the strip because you always get it. Get the pork chop or something."

Nick read about the pork chop. "Not the pork chop, but I'll play along." He scanned other sections. "Is it weird if I get lasagna here?"

Sonia laughed into her wine glass as she drank. "Yes, it's weird if you get a fifty-dollar lasagna. But do it. You only live once. And what's fifty dollars to somebody like you, huh?" Her laugh was a smirk when she set the glass on the table.

"Or what about the primavera?"

"Does everything with you have to be Italian? Phoenix isn't an Italian word. Why do we gotta be Italian right now?"

"Italians named all the foods. During the empire they were just goin' around namin' stuff."

"Filet mignon is French." Sonia turned the page. "Who eats salmon? Indians?"

"Everyone eats salmon and we conquered the French, just like every other army with more than six people since the dawn of time. They distorted our beautiful language and ended up with one thousand words for a bagel."

"What is that supposed to mean?"

"Filet mignon is ours too, that's what it means."

Sonia shook her head. "There's no French people here, so your lesson is lost on them."

"Vic says the ballet dancers used to work here when they weren't in session or whatever you call it. They're prolly French. They might make more here than dancin' with the prices on this fuckin' menu..." Nick said, his words trailing away until he set his menu down, wrapped his fingers over his wife's hand and squeezed. "Hey," he said. Sonia looked up. "Are you happy with me?"

Her eyes narrowed, wary of such a question during their dinner date. "Of course, I'm happy. Why would you ask that *now*?"

"'Cause it's important to me that you're happy with me. Or otherwise, what am I doin' this shit for?"

"Nick, I'm happy..." Her eyes lingered on his before she refocused on her menu. "They have lobster if you feel like seafood."

"I don't like lobster," he said into his chest. "Are you gonna be mad if I just get the strip?"

"No, I was being silly. Go ahead."

May 21, 1973
The Pisani house in Brooklyn, NY
"The only person as crazy as Sonia was Nick."

Nick was never awake before Sonia. They had been together for twelve years, and he thought honestly it was less than five times total, but it happened the morning after they ate dinner at The Phoenix Steakhouse in May of 1973. He made her breakfast but let the eggs and bacon get cold as he debated whether to wake her up to enjoy them or not. He decided to let her sleep. When he finally ventured back into their room, he found Sonia awake, naked on top of the covers with one leg spread and the other bent.

"Mornin'," he said.

"My head is gonna hurt, Nicky," she said, pouting her lip. He could tell she was still drunk; her eyes were glossy and distant.

He leaned onto the bed and kissed her, making a passionate show of it, a reminder of how they felt a few hours before. "I would imagine so. We got away from ourselves last night."

"It was so much fun. Thank you, Nicky."

"Yeah, it was a good time." Nick adjusted himself to sit on his side of the bed, and Sonia laid her head across his lap. "We're goin' to have a good month," he said softly, brushing her hair with the tips of his fingers. "We've got big projects in the works."

"How good?" He rarely talked about money with her, so she tried to play it cool.

"Good...just big and good is all you need to know."

"Good." She rolled to face him and unbuttoned his shirt enough to run her fingers across his stomach. "Can we keep celebrating then? We had so much fun last night, and I don't want to be hungover yet. Let's get some champagne or go to lunch or something."

"Not today. I gotta check in. I've gotta do it in person." She kept tickling his stomach while each of them followed their own silent thoughts until she sat up, ruffled his hair, and kissed him, pressing her bare chest into his as he lay on his back. "I'm so proud of you," she said, grabbing him and feeling him harden in her hand. Soon, they were in each other again, hard and frenzied. Her nails dug into him, red seeping through the scratches on his back. She traced the three-inch slice of white on his ribs, the triangle under his collarbone, the burn on his left bicep and the other on his thigh, the pink-red mottle on his lower back…and he brushed her ribs and they screamed but she bit her lip and held his hand tighter against them, falling against his bare chest and then past him and into the sheets.

She got up after and went into the bathroom, closing the door behind her. Her ribs were deep shades of purple on both sides, and she lightly prodded them to watch them yellow and then turn purple again. She stood there, posing in front of her mirror and tossing her hair. She was thirty-two, she thought, and had everything she wanted.

An afternoon in May 1973
19th Precinct in Manhattan, NY
"He didn't know much, honestly."

Detective Andrew Clayburgh was a short man with a paunch belly, a bald head, and a face pockmarked by childhood acne, and mitigating these insecurities was the primary intention of his conscious mind. He distracted from the pockmarks with his wide, bushy mustache, and he rarely removed his flat cap in public to protect his bare scalp from judgment. When a chunk of funds became available following the annual NYPD softball game, he petitioned Administrators in secret for darker dress uniforms to more effectively conceal his midriff. These anxieties seemed to serve him well though. By most accounts, he was intelligent, disagreeable, determined, and sincere.

His desk in the bullpen of the 19th Precinct was covered by collections of papers and folders and photographs stacked in haphazard piles. Many of these were coated in a thin layer of dust, but still he kept them close, hoarded them even, blaming the disorderly heap on an underlying sense of optimism whenever Patty scolded him for it. The truth was less heroic: the storage room boxes bore mold and spewed dust, which caused his allergies to flare for days after each visit.

Detective Brady Murdock's persona was tidier than his partner's, and their desks butted up to each other like a before and after organization tutorial. Brady's face was handsome, angular, and framed by blond hair, parted neatly to one side. He was taller than Clayburgh by half a foot, well-framed, and athletic when necessary. The two played up this dualism in the field. Murdock was more often the polite, disarming gentleman, and Clayburgh an aggressive, prodding bulldog. They cleared enough cases to pass this technique off as "successful," so they did.

Murdock rattled a coffee mug against his desk and picked up his copy of the case file Clayburgh was reading across from him. Patty had made hurried red notes on the inside of the folder. Homicide, male in his sixties, discovered by his wife, shot twice in the leg... and the ink was wet enough to smear while they read. "Thirty-eight caliber then?"

"Yeah," Clayburgh said. "Bone fucked those bullets up pretty good, but they've pulled good info off worse—" the words cut off as the voice of Captain Braden Quinn rang out into the bullpen. "Room 3, Clayburgh! Murdock!"

The two detectives popped up like prairie dogs. "Who is it?"

"A witness. The neighbor of your cement victim," Quinn said, his voice booming through the room even as he turned down the hall toward Interrogation Room 3. Clayburgh and Murdock gathered notebooks and hustled after him.

"What'd he say?" Clayburgh asked when they caught up.

"He didn't say shit yet. For some reason, I thought I should get you two, the lead detectives, before we asked him any questions. I can see that being a mistake now that I've actually gone and done it."

The Captain made a sharp right and elbowed his way into the room adjacent Interrogation Room 3, "behind the glass" as it were, with the detectives right behind. A well-dressed man sat in the IR itself, his hands tapping a soft rhythm on the table. He was not as old as Mr. Benfield, maybe in his late forties with light hair, a three-piece suit, and a watch that sparkled against the concrete-laden room.

Captain Quinn pointed through the glass. "He told one of our canvasing officers, whose name I refuse to learn, that he has information that will help us solve Mr. Benfield's murder. I would like for that to happen quickly. Anything involving a union is newsworthy, and I don't want this problem to linger."

"What's his name?" Murdock asked.

Captain Quinn pulled his reader glasses down for an angle at a small notecard. "Christopher Berdan. He's a banker of some kind. If you have any other questions, gentlemen, please ask him yourselves."

Murdock and Clayburgh entered the interrogation room with a nod and a handshake for the man seated before them. "Mr. Berdan," Clayburgh said, "this is Detective Murdock, and I am Detective Clayburgh. We are the lead detectives in the death of your neighbor, Mr. Benfield. We understand you have some information to share with us?"

"Yes, I believe so," the visitor said, loudly and with more than a suggestion of his own importance.

"Please," Murdock said, "tell us what you know, and we may ask a few questions afterward. Anything you may have seen could be helpful."

Mr. Berdan leaned forward slightly, interlocking his hands on the table. "At roughly 5:00 p.m., I was in the living room of my home, across the street and one down from the Benfields'. I heard a car leaving from that direction, although I can't be sure it was their car, I suppose, and shortly after I heard two loud noises back to back. I certainly took notice, but I did not get up to investigate right away. It did not cross my mind they could have been gunshots until later when I heard what had happened. However, I did, shortly after the noises, get up and walk to the kitchen, and from my kitchen I could see out into the street where I noticed a *blue sedan* was parked a few yards down the road from the Benfields'. I noticed the car because it was rather run-down with a little exposed rust on the runners, and I know most of the cars on our block. They do not have rust. I walked to the window for a better look, and as I did, I saw two White men in suits walking from the direction of Mr. Benfield's house. The two men got into the blue sedan and drove away."

Clayburgh jotted Berdan's orientation to the crime scene in his notepad along with "two shots," "White males," and "blue sedan." "Did you see their faces?"

"One better than the other. I could not really see the driver's face. He was looking toward the car, away from me."

"How tall were they?"

"The passenger was rather short, the other man average," Berdan answered while making useless measurements of relative height above the table.

"Hair color?"

"The passenger had a dark complexion, definitely brown hair, and I think I saw jewelry on his hands. I could be wrong about the jewelry though. The passenger also had brown hair. I couldn't tell any more, not from the angle I was at, just the hair, the jewelry, the car."

Clayburgh thought a moment about other distinguishing features these hit men might have. "Their suits, did they have any distinguishing patterns? Their shoes? Hats?"

"The suits were not particularly expensive. Just ordinary, everyday get-ups. Both were simple and a rather dull gray color."

"Did you notice any weapons?"

"No. Their hands were free enough to open the doors and start the car. I didn't see a gun."

Murdock swirled his pen in search of ink and shook it at his notepad when none came. He asked, "I assume if you had the license plate, you would have led with that?"

"It all occurred rather fast, Detective, and I am unaccustomed to writing down license plate numbers."

"We understand. Would you mind taking a look at our book of mugshots? Maybe you will recognize the passenger."

"Anything I can do to help."

"I will bring the book in for you. We appreciate your cooperation. We certainly hope to achieve some justice for Mr. Benfield." The detectives rose, shook Mr. Berdan's hand, and excused themselves. Captain Quinn was waiting for them as they left. "So, we're looking for a man with brown hair and a gray suit. Good luck, gentlemen." He left without discussing the matter further.

* * *

Mr. Berdan reappeared in the bullpen thirty minutes later carrying the book of mugshots. Clayburgh rose to meet him at the edge of the hallway. "Any luck?"

"Sorry, Detective," Berdan said, and Clayburgh could see he was genuinely disappointed. The prospect of his potential importance seemed to excite him. "I did not see the passenger in that book. I wish I could be of more help." He handed the book over to Clayburgh. "If you think you find these guys, I'd be happy to come back. I always liked Mr. Benfield, and it would be a shame to see it end this way, without a real resolution."

"We will do our best to prevent that," Clayburgh said. Mr. Berdan began to exit when another officer came jogging down the hall. "Mr. Berdan! You forgot your briefcase, sir."

"Oh, thank you. I came here straight from the office, and that would have been a tough one to explain tomorrow. Thank you." With that, Christopher Berdan bowed his head to Detective Clayburgh, collected his briefcase, and walked out of the 19th Precinct and onto the streets below.

An evening in May 1973
The Giordano family house in Brooklyn, NY
"She never really left the island."

Cristiana did not enjoy cleaning. She had grown up poor in a Palermo fishing village where the floor was always covered by sand and dust and she padded barefoot over it all without a second thought until her father moved them to America. She missed the winds in Sicily. If you walked far enough away from the fish markets, the air hugged you, warm and crisp and inviting as the beach shifted between your toes. She'd walk into the ocean with fish scales clinging to her hands as the waves nudged her back and forth, back and forth, and then trace the shoreline for miles in a thin dress and nothing else. Alphonse had been too young when he left that place, only a boy, or they would have talked about it. The sun, the wind, the smell of fish and lemons, and the beach whenever the memories ached inside her. Sometimes, in the summer months especially, a cracked window or a sun-warmed spot on the floor would take her back, back to her beaches and their dusty house. But then an obnoxious car would honk, or a siren wail, and she'd be yanked from the island. No beaches, no warm, crisp, lemon-wind.

In Brooklyn, she was expected to maintain a clean house, and so she ran the vacuum in their living room. She pressed a grid into the carpet with the machine, improvising only to collect debris of an odd sort. Al sat in his favorite chair just a few feet away, staring blankly at the TV set. The newsman's mouth was moving, but he was forced to imagine the words because of the noise of her diligence.

"Do you want me to pick up anything special from the grocer tomorrow?" Cristiana asked as she finished her rounds and packed up her vacuum. "I'm going to make some sardines like my mother made us with the lemons. Do you want some of the little oranges he sells?"

"Whatever you think," Al said from his chair. "I like the little oranges."

Cris stowed the vacuum and came to sit on Alphonse's lap, pulling his chin up to smile down on him. "I want to go on a trip," she said.

Alphonse leaned back slightly. Her cheeks were checked by age, but he could see the girl when she smiled. "To where?"

"Home."

Al raised his eyebrows. "Italy?"

She kissed him before she answered, "Sicily."

"When would we go?"

"Soon. No work. You have to put Nick and Phil and Vic in charge of everything. They're not even allowed to call you, no matter what."

Al gave a hoarse chuckle and pushed her hair back from her eyes. "After the construction gets going, we can probably make some time. I'll take you there for two whole weeks if you want."

"Soon, it has to be soon. We are old now. Soon is all we have." She kissed him again. Her makeup smeared, and she wiped it from his lips with her thumb. "Promise me."

"Soon," he said, and she slumped into his chest, resting her head on his shoulder and passively observing the newsman on their TV. They lay there in their daydreams until there was a knock at the door.

"For you I'm sure," Cris said, kissing him one last time as they both got up.

Al strode quickly to the door and looked back to his wife. "It's Johnny." His son looked unsettled as Alphonse invited him inside. "What's the matter with you?"

"We've gotta talk for a minute, Pops."

Cris searched Johnny's features for clues to his nerves. "Where is Regina? Is she all right?"

"She didn't need to come, Ma. She's at the house. Don't worry, I just need to talk to Pop for a few minutes and I'll get outtav your hair." He tried to reassure her, but his smile was so strained Cris only worried more.

"In my office then, c'mon." For the second time in as many days, Al found himself taking an unannounced meeting with an anxious Family member. Johnny closed the door behind them.

"I got a disturbin' call a few hours ago," Johnny said. "Our old friend, the one who just left us. His neighbor saw two men leaving right after. He says he got a good look at the passenger."

"But he couldn't find anyone in the book, right? They're not in there anymore?"

"Nah, neither of them is in the book."

"All right," Al said with a shrug. "Not the end of the world. Nothing rash. Just get the name."

"Berdan. He's some pretentious banker, some kind of executive or something. He works in Midtown. Obviously, he lives next to the other guy, which means...we can find him, if need be."

Alphonse had not forgotten his conversation with Phil. If anything, the intervening hours had fortified its logic in his mind. "Sit on it for now. Figure out which house he is. Not Nicky or Paulie, you and Joe-Joe. And don't park there. Some cop might visit or something, and you don't want to be connected even in the vaguest sense. Don't get your license plates run around there or any of that shit."

"All right." Johnny ran a hand through his hair. "This is bad heat, Pops. Union, newspaper, shock value, rich fellas. That's bound to motivate some people."

Al ignored the last comments. "And I'll tell Phil about this. Nobody else needs to know what you're doing or why. Just tell Nick and Paulie to lay low for a few days. That's from me, not anybody else."

"All right. I'll figure it out tonight."

"Go visit with your mother first. Don't just leave without spending time with your family. You went and made her all nervous. Now you gotta act like it was all a big misunderstanding with Cal or somethin' down there. Go laugh a little with her."

After midnight on May 23, 1973
The Falconhead Gentlemen's Club in Brooklyn, NY

The Falconhead was a hangout in the southern half of Brooklyn's Carroll Gardens neighborhood run by Provenzano Family soldiers and their associates since the 1920s. Tradition was enough to keep it profitable, but the Prohibition Era vibe had proved difficult to scrub. Antique fixtures distorted the electricity into dull orange orbs of almost candlelight and threw hazy shadows on the well-worn flooring. The main connection in 1973 was Raffaele "Rabbit" Costanzo, a slight mousy-haired man with a mole on his left cheek and too many gold bracelets. Vito Maceo made a point to visit the Falconhead at least once a month with a small group of others, a token of the friendship he and Rabbit had forged behind the steel bars of the state.

Tony enjoyed their visits for the women more than Rabbit's surly company. One vestige of the club they had managed to modernize were the outfits, now hardly more than lingerie and enough to get Tony and Benjie to visit without their brother on occasion.

"Ginger, baby, can I get another scotch over here?" Tony called to one of the waitresses for their table. He turned to Benjie. "You need another?"

Benjie simply held his rocks glass in the air for Ginger to see, and she padded away with her short skirt bouncing behind her and leaving little to Benjie's imagination. His eyes stayed on her as she moved through the crowd and up to the bar. "She's fuckin' gorgeous," Tony said, tracking his brother's eyes. "I'm not usually into the red-heads 'cause you end up with too many Mick brothers and cousins on your ass, but that one's put together well enough to get over it." Benjie imagined himself getting over it.

Vito had not joined them, but their table was still full of drunk men, empty glasses, and a pair of Rabbit's girls. Sammie Calabrese (Tony called him Gorilla Man) and another man with the ghost of a broken nose and sunken circles for eyes named Ray Ray were demanding the girls' attention. Papa Vic was just a few feet away, drink in hand, talking (among other things) with a middle-aged blond dancer. His typically perfect suit was growing to resemble his hair, unkempt and wet with sweat and alcohol.

Benjie was alive in the moment as they sat there, his normal hesitations long gone. He had been drunk before, even shitfaced, but this felt different. He did not feel dulled. He was conscious of detail and confident and observant, happy, and enlivened. He saw the women around him, expected they were aroused and enthralled like he was. He felt a sense of mastery. He'd chosen one of the "flash-ier" suits Vic had bought him, a blue-checkered white paired with a black tie, and gone to the barber for a fresh cut and sharp part. Still, he feared the breakup of his group was imminent, the end of his mastery, and a desperation to hold the moment longer grew in him.

Benjie watched Ginger navigating deftly through the small cir-cles of weekday socialites with several drinks balanced on her tray. He touched Tony on the arm and whispered, "Any reason I couldn't take the waitress back with us?"

Tony laughed. "Are you asking me if you can fuck her? Yes, my horny friend, you can have sex with women, if they'll have your ugly ass."

Benjie finished the last of his drink as Ginger approached their table, the dream of her approval clouding his mind. He touched her arm as she set his drink down. "Hey, Ginger, why don't you sit with us for a minute?" Her skin was smooth, pale, and lightly freckled between his fingers.

She smiled and flicked her eyes over the others at the table. "I don't want my boss to get mad at me. I haven't worked here very long." She did not pull away.

"Your boss ain't gonna say anything to us, baby," Benjie said, motioning back and forth between Tony and himself. "We're his friends." Benjie saw Tony shoot him a sideways reproach, but he seemed unwilling to shut his brother down so coldly and stayed quiet as Ginger settled next to them. She was trim with athletic legs and green eyes below her flame-red hair; her uniform was low cut and enough to draw Benjie's attention downward, a symptom of his genuine bend. He laid his arm behind her, reaching only with his hand to touch her shoulder. "You're beautiful, Ginger, you know that? Every girl in here: dancer, waitress, the girlfriends with these other guys. I told my brother, he's right there," he pointed towards Tony, "you ask him. I said 'She beats them all. Like a piece of fine art, that Ginger,' I said. An absolutely beautiful woman."

She smiled and moved subtly to him, pressing softly against his arm. "You know my name's not Ginger. My boss gave me that name because of my red hair. My real name's Nora."

Energy balled in Benjie's chest. He leaned close by her ear. "Even more beautiful. *Nora, my amore.* How late they make you work here, Nora?" He rubbed her shoulder, and she allowed it, even abandoning her nervous scans.

"I should be off in about an hour. Around 1:00 a.m. is when they usually let me go." She met his eyes, and Benjie leaned in close to her to whisper, "You should come with me after, maybe for an after party with just a couple of us—"

"Tony! Benjie! Get the fuck up!" came the commanding voice of Papa Vic over any of the club's ambient noise.

Tony rose and immediately hopped the backside of their booth. Benjie's face must have betrayed his shock and frustration because Vic focused directly on him when he yelled, "Fuckin' now!" Benjie, as much as the alcohol might have slowed his brain function, began to move. He turned to Nora or Ginger or whoever she was. "Sorry, baby, I gotta go. This is a business thing." She looked more shocked than Benjie. He kissed her lips before looking her up and down once last time. "God damnit, Ginger, I'm really sorry about this." He climbed after his brother and trailed Vic through the crowd and into a back room marked Management in bright silver letters.

Vic wasted no time, and his voice came loud and fast. "I just got a call from Joey's little brother Addie. He says the greedy man just left a bar over in Ridgewood and he's drunk as fuck. His house is only a few minutes from there, so he should get there first, but this happens tonight. Right fuckin' now."

Tony did not miss a beat. "Do you have an address?"

"Yeah, I wrote it down." Vic shuffled through some scraps in his pocket, eventually handing Tony a piece of torn notebook paper. Benjie shoved a fist into his eyes, trying to remove the blur.

"Is Addie sure he's goin' home?" Tony asked, recalling questions to his veteran mind. "He's not going to pick up a hooker or somethin'?"

Vic shrugged. "You can never know for sure, right? But he left by himself so we're gonna make a giant leap here and say nobody else is gonna be with him. Addie says he definitely lives by himself, so his mother shouldn't be peekin' out at ya or nothin'."

"Joey want anything special done?" Greedy men were often made examples.

Vic chuckled and shook his head. "As a matter of fact, he does. He's a vindictive guy, Joey. He wants a $100 bill nailed to his chest or some such idea."

"Nailed? He wants me to 'nail' it to his chest?"

"Yeah. Apparently, he stole a lot of money from Joey. Joey's more mad about that than the secret fashion imports. I don't know, he said bust him with a nail and a c note."

Tony lips moved soundlessly for a moment, trying to calculate how much force it would take to pierce a chest with a nail. "What do I gotta go buy a fuckin' hammer and shit?"

Vic laughed again. "I know, Ton. That's why I tell you guys not to fuck with Joey. He's a weird guy. Addie says the greedy man likes to work on cars, so he probably has a hammer at the house. Or step on it or somethin', I don't know."

"Vic, I went through the scavenger hunt with the fuckin' accountant. I told you about that, with the goddamn rope? Every job now, I've gotta complete a fuckin' scavenger hunt beforehand. Whatever the fuck happened to blastin' these motherfuckers and driving home? Jesus Christ."

"I know, Ton," Vic said. The alcohol made him more sympathetic than usual. "After this, I'll give you some time off. Any more work and I'll farm out to some other guys. I just need you here because you're standin' in front of me. And it's easy work for the kid's first time. Pop his fuckin' cherry and then we can all move on."

"Jesus Christ. I get it, I guess. I get it." There was no saying no anyway. Benjie needed to learn these decisions were final. "Benj, you ready?"

Benjie was more drunk than he realized and had been working to compose himself with limited success since Vic had first pulled them from the table. His walk to the backroom had been wobbly, and he was struggling to follow Tony and Vic's conversation. Hearing his name snapped him to attention. "Yeah, I'm ready. I just...I didn't bring my gun. It's at home." Before the words left his mouth, he knew how stupid they would sound. The other two men were completely silent for what felt like minutes. Finally, Vic spoke, incredulous. "Uh...what?"

"Sorry, Vic," Benjie said, trying to control the slur rounding his words. "I just thought we were goin' to have some drinks. I left my gun at home." Benjie looked to Tony for help, but his brother crumpled into a chair and put his hands over his face.

Vic turned to Tony, a bemused smile tugging at his lips. "How many times did your parents drop this kid, Ton? 'Cause he thinks like they were playin' basketball with his fuckin' head."

"I'm sorry, Vic," Benjie said. "I can run home real quick, twenty minutes, thirty tops."

"These kids are gonna kill me," Vic said, now turning to face Benjie. "I'm an old man, kid, and the stress of your stupidity is gonna give me a fuckin' heart attack." He shook his head, walking slowly behind the desk. He felt for a hidden set of keys, opened the top drawer, and pulled out a Colt Model 1903 Pocket Hammerless. He held it out for Benjie. "Use this tonight," he said, "If you don't have a criminal record, you carry a gun, dumbass. Period. If you ever come around me without a gun again, I'm gonna beat you to death with my bare fuckin' hands. Now get the fuck out of here."

After midnight on May 23, 1973
Butero's apartment in Queens, NY
"That was a mistake."

Tony pointed up the street a few doorways. "That's his address right there." The street was lined with cars and plain brown buildings, although Butero's unit had a distinctive awning shielding its numbers. Benjie recognized Angelo's car, a red-on-white 1962 Ford Galaxie with aftermarket liners over the headrests, parked just outside and a couple paces down.

The weight of Vic's commands had tapered his drunkenness, and Benjie was beginning to understand what he and Tony were tasked with. Nothing in his field of vision should have been alarming, just a series of streetlights pointed at the ground, but he felt sick to his stomach and was not sure how much was fear, how much nerves, and how much an impending hangover. "How are we going to get in?" he asked.

"It would probably be stupid not to try the front door first." Tony had been working the same problem through in his head. "You figure, he's drunk, stumblin' into the house like the fat slob he is. He may not've locked it." Tony did not say go, but quietly opening his door had the same effect. Benjie patted the Colt in his suit pocket, and the brothers hit the pavement in unison. Tony surveilled Benjie's slack-drunk features in the porch light before wrapping his fingers around the knob. To their relief, it turned easily and they crossed the threshold, a long moment before their eyes adjusted to the darkness on the other side.

The place was a mess. Benjie had expected stairs or other units along an inside hall, but there were none, just a studio-sized apartment with a stove in the living room and a bathroom in one wall. Food littered the floor, clothes lay on every surface, and the smell of socks and neglected leftovers permeated the entire place. They heard Angelo before they saw him, snoring boorishly on his couch/bed. Tony tapped his brother on the arm, motioning like a hammer and then pointing his fingers like a gun at Angelo. Benjie nodded, pointing his Colt at the greedy man, while Tony looked for tools.

When his eyes fully acclimated, Benjie saw Butero had not even bothered to undress. He lay there in a full suit and tie, one leg on and one leg off his couch. His chest rose and fell with each loud, obnoxious snoring breath. The small gun felt clean in Benjie's hand, and he could feel its oil mingling with the sweat on his hands. His finger touched the trigger, but he did not let it tense, just hang lightly against its edge and ready in the middle of his print.

Tony pulled what looked to be a shoebox from the closet, placed it on the ground, and began to rummage through it. Benjie kept the gun on Angelo but braved a few steps forward to see if by some miracle his brother had found a hammer. He had not, but eventually he found a wrench and shrugged his shoulders. *This will work.* The two men moved slowly toward the greedy man until they were standing directly over his unconscious form. Benjie saw Butero's chest move up and down, heard his loud snores echo into the walls. Tony reached a hand toward Butero's face, gently smacking him three and then four times. He did not wake up. Harder this time, Tony smacked him with an open palm, three, four, five times, and whispered, "Angelo. Wake up," while poking him in his spongy stomach. The greedy man simply shook his head and adjusted himself on the couch. Finally, with a sharp curse, Tony slapped him across the face as hard as he could, and Butero tumbled to the floor. This was enough to at least reactivate his brain. Butero grunted, confused, but the boorish snoring stopped. He pushed himself up to his hands and knees and saw the two pair of shoes in front of him, following their lines upward to see the brothers before him. His eyes were open, but his mind was in a fatal fog. Benjie made a determined move forward, put the gun to Butero's forehead, and said, "Sorry and goodbye," before pulling the trigger, 1-2 in rapid succession. Angelo went limp and flopped to the ground, dead, and voiding his bowels into his slacks. Tony and Benjie flipped him to his back, used the wrench and nails to attach a $100 bill to his chest, and walked back out the front door.

They reached the car doors at the same time, slid into their seats, and sat there. Tony did not immediately start the car but made to study his brother's face in the poor light of the street. He found little there and so sparked the motor to a roar. Benjie turned the music up, and the two Maceo brothers drove away.

Just after noon on May 25, 1973
The home of Richard Newman in Queens, NY

Richard Newman's living room was rather dingy despite their bright orange couch and the homemaker's aggressive penchant for fruit patterns. Detectives Clayburgh and Murdock fell into adjacent cushions across from Mr. Newman. Mrs. Newman emerged only briefly, with two mugs of coffee, before retreating to the back of the house.

"Mr. Newman," Clayburgh said over his steaming cup, "we are sorry to disturb you, sir, but I'm sure you expected a visit after what happened, no?"

Mr. Newman ran a hand through his tufts of graying hair. "Yes, obviously I know about what happened to Mr. Benfield. He was a good man. And a good leader for many years."

Clayburgh asked, "Could you tell us, Mr. Newman, how is the union getting along at the moment? Financially speaking first, and then, if you don't mind, your thoughts on the members' feelings generally about the incident and the path forward."

"It's well-off. You always have ups and downs, but money has not been a problem for us. Membership is strong, no unrest from the rank and file. Pensions are as safe as they ever are. Our membership should really be pleased with where Mr. Benfield has taken us. He was good at his job."

"Are you aware of any conflicts between Mr. Benfield and any union members? Or officers?"

"No."

Murdock was put off by the answer's simplicity. "Just 'no'?" Mr. Newman shook his head and Murdock pushed the point forward. "Has he ever had a conflict with another union member?"

Newman thought a moment, tapping a stubby finger on his chin as he did. "A few years ago, we had a series of strikes and Mr. Benfield was a little more willing to compromise than others, but I seriously doubt any members would have been mad enough to kill him, or if they were, it doesn't seem likely they would wait half a decade to do so."

"And how long was he union president?"

"Since right after the war, 1946."

"And just one strike during that time?"

"One actualized strike, yes."

"Mr. Newman, no offense," Clayburgh said, his mustache flitting beneath his nose, "but if you guys have one strike every twenty-seven years, what exactly do the union officers do all day?" Murdock chuckled; Newman did not. Clayburgh let it drop. "And how many union officers are there today?"

"Six including Mr. Benfield and myself."

"And now you become president, or is there an election?" Murdock asked over his scribbles.

"Technically, I am the acting president for the time being. But there will be an election among the union members."

"And do you expect to be elected?"

"No." Mr. Newman paused. "I am retiring immediately after the election. My name is not in contention."

The two detectives looked at each other, surprised. The news hung there for a moment before Murdock broke the silence. "You are retiring?" he asked with doltish clarity.

Mr. Newman responded with emphasis. "Yes, Detectives."

Clayburgh eyed Newman with some mix of indecision and suspicion. He could only smooth his mustache for a moment. "Did you decide this before or after Mr. Benfield was murdered?"

"It has been on my mind for several weeks. Unfortunately, my decision was practically simultaneous with the incident. A coincidence."

Clayburgh, making notes and trying to stifle his own emotions, questioned, "So, on the night of May 19 you decided to retire?"

"Yes, Detective." Defiance was growing in Mr. Newman's voice now. "After a long discussion with my wife, we decided it was time for me to step away."

"And what did you think the next morning," Murdock asked, aggressively, "when you read about Mr. Benfield?"

Newman bowed his head. "I grieved for my dear friend."

"I'm sorry," Murdock said, "but you must see why this confuses us. You can see how this would seem more than a coincidence from our perspective?"

"Yes, I can. But I cannot let that have undue influence on my life and what's best for my family, Detectives. I hope you can understand that."

"And who do you think will be elected president in your absence?"

"There are a number of fine officers who have the experience and temperament for it. The union will have no shortage of leadership, I assure you."

"Handicap it for us then, Mr. Newman. Who's the favorite and who's the longshot?"

Newman sighed, but answered: "The most experienced man is David Ehlert. He has been involved at the local level for many years and was close to Mr. Benfield these last few. He knows the local politicians who would help our causes. The longshot? Eh…maybe Harvey Kandel? He was a section rep for a few years and had a good deal of support after the strikes. The populist choice you might say. Both capable men. Both men who've had callouses on their hands." Mr. Newman then stared into the room's fruit-covered wallpaper as the detectives scribbled.

"And what will you do now, Mr. Newman?" Murdock asked, curious as the surprise wore off. "You are not a very old man. Your Social Security is still out of reach, right? What will your life be from here?"

Newman sat up a little straighter. "I have a brother in Arizona who owns a sporting goods store. I plan to help him run it with the help of my wife."

"Any children?"

"Two sons. Both in the city."

"How old?"

"Eighteen and twenty-three."

"And they will remain here?"

"For the time being. I hope they will join us eventually."

Murdock closed his notebook and leaned forward, placing his elbows on his knees. "I have a wife, Mr. Newman. I have a daughter. If I told my wife, that we were moving so I could run a sporting goods store half a continent away from her child, Detective Clayburgh would be investigating my murder by 9:00 a.m. the next day. Mrs. Newman is fine with this? Because of a discussion you had two days ago? And all this decision making happened six minutes before your boss blocked an eighty-pound bag of ready-mix with his forehead? It's a big ask, Mr. Newman. It's a big ask to think we're gonna accept that explanation of yours and go home."

Agitation swirled on Mr. Newman's face as he answered. "Detective, my wife understands the stress this job has placed on me and our family. I ask that you respect our privacy and do not make comments about my wife or my children. She loves her children as much as any mother, and she knows this is the right thing to do." He stood and motioned toward the door. "I believe I have answered enough questions. Thank you."

Clayburgh took a final drink of his coffee and stood. "Thank you, Mr. Newman. We appreciate the hospitality."

Mr. Newman ushered them politely out the door, shutting it behind them.

"What the fuck was that?" Murdock asked.

"I'm not sure…" Clayburgh said as they descended the front steps, replaying the events in their heads, until a sharp voice startled them. "Detectives!" Mrs. Newman said, stepping forward from her hedges with pruning shears in her hands. Both men saw the blades were clean and dry. "Yes, ma'am?"

She checked for her husband at the front windows to make sure her husband was not watching before taking a breath to steady herself. "I do not know what is going on exactly, but I want you to know that that night, the nineteenth, two men came to our house from the election board. They asked to speak to my husband, and they did. Only for a few moments. After that, he was 100 percent convinced we needed to move and immediately called his brother. No discussion before that. No mention of moving or retirement. Never. It was absolutely those two men. They must've had something to do with Mr. Benfield, the retirement, I know it." She chopped the pruning shears twice for emphasis.

"You saw these men yourself?" Murdock asked.

"Yes. Both were tall, brown hair, tan skin. They wore suits. I'm pretty sure they were Italian because one had a bit of an accent on certain words. He did all the talking, the shorter one, but both were tall."

"How old?"

"One in his early twenties, just a kid. The talker might have been in his thirties."

"And you had never seen these men before?"

"Never."

"Would you recognize them?"

"I think I would," she said, glancing back at the empty windows. "My husband would not like it though. He made me promise never to talk about it. But after what happened to Mr. Benfield, I had to say something."

"We would need you to look at a few mugshots for us. We could meet you somewhere if we have to."

"My husband cannot know I told you," Mrs. Newman said. "Nothing while he is here at the house."

"We understand, Mrs. Newman. We are going to leave now, but we will be in touch, don't worry." And they turned and finished the short walk down the block to their car. It was hot out and the car was stuffy, but the detectives just sat there for a moment, thinking over the interview and Mrs. Newman's last-minute contribution. "What do you think?" Murdock finally asked.

Clayburgh thought for a minute longer, not sure his theory was ready to press forward, but he did. "This crossed my mind at the Benfield house, and the two visitors lend support to my hunch. I don't think it's much of a leap to say the Italian Mafia is very interested in who runs the cement union."

A Sunday morning in the spring of 1973
St. Anthony's Parish in Brooklyn, NY
"I always used to itch in church. That should tell you somethin'."

St. Anthony's was an old church. Al knew it predated him by a couple of decades because he remembered celebrating its twenty-fifth anniversary when he was attending school there. That year, on the day of St. Anthony's feast, the students performed a short play about his life from the altar in the nave. Alphonse had played Old Anthony in a dull brown robe, gave a speech to the mummer pope, and then was carried around on a stretcher for the last few scenes. His mother kept him and Oscar afterward to help Father Bennie and the altar boys clean up trash bags worth of decorations, hymnals, prayer cards, candles, and balloons well into the night. Al remembered Father Bennie and his mother had not helped for long.

Fifty years later, Jimmy the Driver cruised into the Giordano parking space, and St. Anthony's looked much the same. The bricks were beige and sharp and built themselves into an eighty-foot steeple with a bell concealed behind a ten-foot clock face. Stairs approached from shallow angles on both sides to meet before an arched doorway blocked by red-brown doors with black iron handles. Parishioners were always congregating there, shaking hands with Father Bennie (a second Father Bennie, the first was long dead) and catching the others up on their recent piety. If not for his wife, Al might never set foot in the place again.

"Jimmy," Al said as his door was opened, "are you comin' in today?"

"No, Mr. Giordano," Jimmy said, smiling as he always was beneath his hat and a row of shaggy bangs. "I'm going this afternoon with my girlfriend's family. They go to St. Martin's in Red Hook."

Jimmy had mentioned his girlfriend before. Al could not remember her name. "So, what're you gonna do? Just sit here in the car?"

"I can grab a newspaper, Mr. Giordano. Don't worry about me, I prefer it."

Al clapped his driver on the back. "That's fine as long as it's not my fault," he said. "I invited you in. That's all the Lord asks of me."

Cris and Jennie slid through the car door after Al and fed their arms through his on either side. Carrie and her fiancé Bobby joined them as Al finished teasing the young driver; Nick, Sonia, Johnny, and Regina arrived from the far side of the building and waited for the rest on the front steps, each dressed to Cris Giordano's church standards.

"*Leave him alone,*" Carrie said in crisp Sicilian. She hit Bobby impatiently on his arm. "Give Jimmy some money for the paper."

Bobby tossed Jimmy a few coins, ("Thank you, Ms. Carrie"), and they walked up the steps and through the red-brown doors. The floor of the vestibule was marbled and white and ran under another set of doorways and the holy water font on the other side. Al dipped his fingers, made the sign of the cross, and strode down the middle aisle, giving waves to the church's sinners. The nave was tall with stained-glass windows filtering the sunlight into colors and throwing them over parishioners and saintly statuettes alike. They sat beneath the second station of the cross.

"Whose Gospel is today?" Alphonse asked his youngest daughter when they were comfortably seated.

Jennie scrolled her finger across the page. "Luke."

"Of course it is. The longest one. He had a lot to say."

Jennie repressed her smile. "Daddy, don't talk like that in here."

"I said it was long. I'd say that to Jesus's face if I had to."

"Don't talk like that. It makes Ma nervous for you."

Cris leaned forward to face her daughter. "I'm not nervous. Your Father will have to deal with the Lord on his own. I'm leaving that up to the two of them."

Al held his wife's hand lightly in his own. "Don't worry, Cris. With the way his priests are actin', he might be lookin' for guys like me."

Cris hit Al playfully on his shoulder. A whisper interrupted them.

"Al, have you ever met a celebrity..." Nick said into his Boss's ear. Alphonse followed Nick's finger to see Joe Pisciotto and his crew ambling confidently into the hall. "Fuckin' yellow suit? Is he serious?"

Nick was right. Pisciotto was wearing a yellow suit and his wife, a bright green dress and wide-brimmed hat, which she kept on all the way to their pew. Pisciotto's underboss and brother-in-law, Carmine Fiata, was just behind him, and Al recognized at least two others, Paulo "King Paul" Tomasi and Eddy Gargotta, against the back wall, mingling with the crowd. Don Pisciotto had come to St. Anthony's once before for Mass, but it had been many years. This was something else. Nerves bubbled as the Don watched them.

Jennie made the connection. "Daddy, don't talk to him, please. Let's just enjoy Mass."

"Don't instruct your Father," Cris snapped without looking up from her prayer book. Carrie's eyes went down the line to gauge her father's reaction. Bobby's and Johnny's followed. But Al steadied his outward expressions, turning his cane slowly in his hand, as the Pisciottos found their place.

"I'll talk to Tomasi," Nick said, standing to leave despite Sonia pulling him back toward the pew. He shrugged her away, moving briskly to the back of the church where he masked a conversation with Paul Tomasi by perusing a wall of church pamphlets. Johnny kept his eyes on the other Pisciotto enforcer, Eddy Gargotta, a hulking figure with jet-black hair streaked with gray on either side of his head. Carrie couldn't move her eyes from the figure of Pisciotto and his yellow suit, brazen enough to visit their church unannounced. She could not hear what he was saying, but he was talking energetically to his wife, his sister, and his brother-in-law, a smarmy smile on his face. His smiles were familiar now, as often as she'd seen them recently.

"He wants to talk," Nick whispered when he came back. Al nodded and stood. Jennie went back to pleading quietly. Cris kissed her husband softly on the cheek and moved to let him leave. Sonia covered her eyes with her hand and Carrie rubbed her back. Bobby looked to Johnny for direction, but he was glued to the seat, unsure of what his father wanted him to do. In the end, it was Nick who followed Al to the back of St. Anthony's, down the steps and along the deserted basement hallway to the men's room on the far end of the vestibule where they waited on either side of the door. Tomasi and Gargotta were close behind, preceding Don Pisciotto down the hall, their heels landing on half-lit marble. Nick held the door open, and the men filed in. Eddy checked the stalls (he convinced one man to leave rather quickly) and left them to make sure no one else approached the door.

"Don Giordano," Pisciotto said, shaking Al's right hand. "We're always happy to see you."

"Don Pisciotto," Al said. His voice sounded disinterested and bored despite his heart rate. "What brings you to St. Anthony's?"

"You're not tired of me already?" the younger Don asked, his white teeth bared through taut lips.

"Old men tire easily. You do not seem to." Giordano paused. "That can be a good thing…"

"I do not, this is true. St. Anthony's is quite beautiful, but the same things bring me here as always." Pisciotto grabbed a paper towel from the sink and dabbed at his shirt where no stain existed. Al moved only his eyes to follow the man.

"I do not know what brings you to a church."

"Our Savior, of course."

"He is everywhere. If you read that book upstairs and you'd know."

Pisciotto nodded slowly and looked to meet the Don's eyes. When he spoke, it was with a purposeful Italian drawl. "He is in *Sicilia*. In *Colombia*. In *Afghanistan*, Don Giordano. Just ask and I will lead you to Him."

Alphonse laughed. "You'll want to start with the first chapter of that holy book," he said, pointing upward, "or you'll miss something important."

"It should be run by Italians. We must be the stewards. You want the trade to take root in Harlem? Chinatown? It is irresponsible for honorable Italian men to let that happen."

"It will suck the life from us. What good is money when all the doors are barred?"

Don Pisciotto shrugged. "You have all the answers, I am sure."

"Just that one. I will not entertain that question."

"I had to offer. I will keep your men away from it, if I can," Pisciotto said, bowing. "A sign of my respect for you."

"Not just in this specific endeavor," Alphonse said, an edge seeping through his tone. "My men will have no contact with the product and no contact with your tainted crews. Half a life in the federal penitentiary will make songbirds of your men. You overplay your influence on them."

Pisciotto's smile evaporated quicker than the other men thought possible. "Don't threaten me, Alphonse."

Al looked at Tomasi, the steel-faced statue Joe brought as his second. He was a testament to Pisciotto's values, compliant and strong. "Be specific about these men," Al said, his eyes back on his counterpart.

"The apartment construction is what you want most?"

"Obviously. Not a single man. You can have your cut, but only if that work is kept at a respectful distance."

"Fine. Docks?"

"We'll make arrangements by the boat."

"My men on the docks will all be clean. That is key to limiting my risk."

Al turned to Nick, who shrugged. "We will check."

"Fine. If it becomes a habit, I may double-check your own men."

"Go ahead." Al hesitated before his more reckless instincts prevailed. "What about your weekly news bulletins? Does this business affect them?"

Pisciotto's smile came back. "I will do everything I can to advance the cause of Italian Americans."

"I'm sorry to be difficult for you, but 'advance' does not mean the same for me as you."

"Are you offended by my wardrobe or my words?"

"Both."

"I'll do my best, Alphonse."

"Fine." The moment hung silent in the air as the two Dons stared full face into each other. Al's patience broke first. "Enjoy the service, Don Pisciotto. Father Bennie is a different sort of Catholic."

When Nick and Al returned, Jennie watched them all the way into their seats with a disapproving frown. "You missed the first reading."

"Then it will have the same effect it did last time."

A weekday morning in spring of 1973
Tony Maceo's house in Brooklyn, NY
"Kids are tough. Fuckin' tough in every sense of the word."

Tony was not in the room when his son Carmine was pulled into the world, so his first experience with him was in a nurses' stall outside the delivery room. The nurse prepared a metal dish with warm water and lay the red-skinned infant there, naked and screaming. Tony rinsed his son's chest and hair of the afterbirth, which shone in the water even as Carmine mauled it with his clumsy rage. The nurse dried him as they watched, Tony and his brothers and Papa Vic. The boy was presented to Tony in a soft blue towel, perfumed and swaddled. When Tony held him, his eyes grew wide and round and the screaming stopped.

Ana was a teenage mother but suited for the role. Tony knew lesser women would have struggled with the transition. He remembered the weak state she was in when he handed Carmine to her for the first time. Her eyes were puffy, her cheeks pale, and sweat clung to her hair and forehead before Vic had dabbed her brow. Carmine gave her life as he nestled against her breast, and her eyes grew quicker, her smiles wider, her words louder, as each hour passed. She fell asleep that night with the boy on his back and against her chest to the dismay of the nurses. Tony waved their concerns away when they were reported to him.

Carmine was eight now and short for his age, a point of discomfort for Tony. Ana noticed, even accusing him of making excuses to avoid watching their son play sports. Tony had always been on the edge of small, too short for basketball, but of average height and build, so he attributed the disparity to Ana's family, not his. Unfortunately, there were no cousins for comparison. Vito's wife would not have kids, not *could not* but *would not*, for fear of its effect on her social freedom. Tony knew Vito secretly hoped for a bastard, but it was yet to happen. Even their drunk mother, attached as she was to her eldest, was unaware of that secret hope.

Tony read the sports section on weekdays over coffee and a cigarette. The real news bored him unless it worried him, so he left it alone. Ana made breakfast for him and Carmine, eggs and bacon and toast, and he enjoyed the smell and the quiet moments as the food finished crackling and sizzling in the hot pan. Carmine dropped his schoolbooks on the table across from his father and distracted himself with a comic book, splashed across the front with blue and red letters.

Ana slid a plate to each of them. "You got your homework done then?" Tony asked Carmine. The boy mumbled, yes between forkfuls of eggs. Tony spun the schoolbooks to read their spines. "What are you learnin' down there?" Their hardcovers were hidden by a paper bag, but History and Science were scrawled in garbled writing down their length.

"Nothin', Dad." Carmine did not look at Tony for the plate of eggs and his comic book.

"Then what are you doing all day?" Tony asked with more force behind the words.

"I'm goin' to my classes. They just don't teach us nothin' in 'em."

Tony hesitated to watch his son eat, then said, "I know I have an accent, but it sounds like English should be your priority."

"Leave him alone, Ton," Ana said, monitoring from the sink as she scrubbed a breakfast pan. "He showed me his homework last night."

"A father can ask a few questions over breakfast." It would not hurt his son to provide an update now and then. "I'm tryin' to do my part to make sure he's not an idiot. So far, I'm not convinced."

Carmine continued to read his comic book, oblivious it seemed to the discussion around him. Tony's temper flared, "Have you forgotten how to have a conversation, kid? Look at us when we're speaking to you."

"Sorry." Carmine laid his fork across the plate and stared at Tony. This was not what Tony intended. *Ana has sufficiently undermined the point anyway.* "Never mind. Finish your breakfast and get goin' so you don't miss anything."

Carmine finished hurriedly and set his plate in the sink before sprinting toward the door. "Hey," Tony called after him, "say goodbye to your mother and I." Carmine scooted back into the kitchen, begrudgingly kissing his mother and father, and sprinted for the door again.

Tony finished his food in silence and walked his plate to the sink. He said to Ana, "Do not speak over me when I am talking to my son."

"He showed me it last night, Tony. I was just telling you."

"You heard me. That's a father and his son, Airiana. I intend to learn what is going on in his life *from him.* I know what it looks like when boys grow up with piece-of-shit fathers."

"Jesus," she replied, shaking her head. She was not going to let him maneuver there. "That's not the point. If you want to know what he's doing, help him with his homework. Don't bitch at me about it."

"I'm not gonna do his homework for him. C'mon now," Tony said and kissed his wife on the forehead.

One afternoon in late May of 1973
Brooklyn, NY

The clouds covered any semblance of the sun and threatened rain, but the smell of cat urine was enough for Vito and Benjie to roll the windows down and tempt fresh air into their borrowed 1961 Chrysler New Yorker. It was ineffective. In desperation, Vito stained the back seat with an entire bottle of Coke, but this did nothing for the smell and compounded his irritability.

"Stop tappin' the door," Vito said without pulling his eyes from the still, blank road in front of him.

"I'm not tappin' the door," Benjie said.

"The fuckin' dashboard then. Stop tappin' the dashboard."

"He's late."

"I know he's late. The dashboard has nothing to do with it. Quit tappin' the fuckin' thing."

Benjie stopped his nervous assault and held the fingers of his left hand in his right to prevent a relapse. The tick moved to his heel, and that version was quiet enough to escape Vito's notice or at least his will to comment.

"What if he knows about us?" Benjie asked after a respectful pause.

"He does know about us. That's the beauty of it."

"You know what I mean. What if he doesn't want to go along?"

"I'm sure he doesn't *want* to go along," Vito said, his voice sharp. "He's a penny-pinchin', short-run trucker with, I assume, a wife, a mom, a grandma, a couple kids, and who knows what else. He doesn't need this type of hassle in his life, but he's a man. He does what he has to."

Benjie was curious and bored and pressed on. "Then why's he do it?"

Vito made a few dismissive waves. "He thinks he needs the money Stanley is payin' him on the side. It shouldn't be this hard for you to figure out. Men do what they think they need to, and they do it all the time."

Benjie allowed another respectful pause before asking, "What do you mean 'he thinks'? Are you sayin' he doesn't actually need the money?"

"I mean *he thinks*. He could not need the money and think he needs the money, or he could need the money and think he needs the money. Either way though, he *thinks* he needs the money, and that's what's important."

Benjie lit another cigarette. "So how long do we wait on this guy?"

"I don't know. A while longer."

"Can I get out and walk around?"

"Fuck, Benjie. What do I care?"

Benjie walked to the back of the car and leaned against the trunk with an eye on the gray clouds above. Tony had suggested the meeting place, but his scan of the area left him quite unimpressed. To either side were warehouses (or that's what they used to be) with dock doors, maybe twenty in all, appearing every so often for the entirety of the building's length. Chain-link fences, ten feet tall and topped with barb wire, guarded the deserted properties from the next generation of looters. It was an outdated purpose. The yards themselves, once beaten sterile by an unremitting line of trucks, were losing a battle to the steady pace of nature. Crevices developed day by day in their asphalt floors and red brick walls; grasses, weeds, and little trees wriggled their way toward the sun. Benjie smoked his cigarette and counted broken windows on the length of buildings without another car or a person in sight.

The Maceos had borrowed jumpsuits from Louie's Riverside Collision center along with the car to mimic their conception of a truck driver. The suits were blue, buttoned, and stained with grease, which seemed to add authenticity to the get-up, although it was all undermined by their hair products and Vito's sparkling gold watch. Benjie had brought the snub-nose .38 Tony had given him, jabbing it awkwardly into his back pocket. He tugged it from its place while he waited and followed the gun's lines down the barrel with the sensitive tip of his ring finger, then over the sight and along the bottom to the trigger guard, the triangular bumps on its grips. He popped the cylinder from its natural position and touched the ends of the six bullets inside. The metallic black body carried lustrous streaks, and he twisted them to see how they behaved at this angle or that. He plugged the barrel with his pinkie; it was lubricated with oil and smooth and clean.

He stowed the weapon when his brother stepped out to join Benjie on the trunk. Vito's chubby fingers struggled with the lighter in the breeze until Benjie used his stomach as a wind break.

"Maybe we should run up the street and call Stanley," Benjie said. "I don't like this place. It's deserted."

Vito laughed. "You're supposed to be a criminal. Deserted places are preferable."

"What time is it?"

"Twelve thirty. We'll give it another five...and then wait some more if it's up to me."

Benjie tossed the butt of his cigarette on the ground and watched it roll away, trailing orange embers, pushed by wind gusts. He made a move to extinguish the last of it when the dull rumble of a diesel engine reached their ears. "Fuckin' finally."

The sound echoed against the warehouses and back over the road as Benjie and Vito walked shoulder to shoulder to receive their guest. The truck was a simple box truck, and not an especially large one, with BENSONHURT TRUCKING written on the side in big green letters. The driver stopped fifty feet or so in front of their Chrysler, and Vito and Benjie could see him start rooting around in the cab of his truck. Vito moved forward with Benjie trailing just behind, his fingers curled over the triangle bump grips of his snub-nose .38.

The driver flung his door open and jumped down to the pavement. He wasn't old, maybe early thirties, shirtless and wearing shorts, brown leather boots, and a boyish grin from ear to ear. "Hey," he called over the engine, "are you Vito?"

"I am," Vito said without a hint of his former aggravation. "I guess this is our shipment here?"

"Yes, sir. Route Number 23 destined for Diller House in Manhattan. Or *was* destined…no longer destined I wouldn't think." The driver laughed shamelessly as he said it.

"We appreciate the donation," Vito said. "Just pop the back real quick and we'll have a look."

The driver opened the hatch to reveal four columns of garments, everything from business suits to fur coats. Vito climbed inside to sift through the merchandise. Benjie wasn't sure what he was looking for, so he waited on the ground with the driver.

"So, you pick these up at the docks or where?" Benjie asked politely.

"I show up at the docks," the driver said, "and they point at the truck I'm supposed to drive. Today they pointed at this one." He was calmer than Benjie expected, calmer even than he was himself.

"How did you know we were gonna be here?"

The driver looked him over, as though suspecting this was a test. "My boss told me," he said. "Mr. Hartel."

Benjie nodded as if he expected this answer. "Do you like Mr. Hartel?" he asked, remembering the nerdy-looking man and the rigor of his skull, the ache of his own knuckles. He wondered if this driver had seen him the day after they discovered the logbook.

"Oh yeah," the driver said, "he's a great guy. He always finds us extra work."

Benjie wondered if the driver thought they were friends of Stanley's, and then he wondered how Stanley would describe their relationship if pressed by the driver at some point in the future. "He finds you work like this work?"

The driver chuckled. "Not usually this, but he's a helpful guy. He looks out for us." Benjie was still curious, but he was afraid of sounding nosy or, worse, suspicious. He let the subject drop.

"Looks like we're good," Vito reported from inside the truck. He walked to the edge and hopped down in front of the driver. "You know the drill?"

"Yeah," the driver said, "can you drive me to a phone booth after? I'll need to call my wife to pick me up."

Vito motioned at Benjie. "He's driving the Chrysler, so you gotta ask him. I'm the guy who breaks your nose."

The driver looked at the ground but nodded his head in agreement. "All right," he said, straightening his back and balling his fists at his sides. "All right, I'm ready."

Vito gave him a countdown, 1…2…3 and cracked him across the face. The driver stumbled back a few feet, instinctively covering his nose. It had reddened quickly around the bridge, but there was no blood and appeared to still be intact. The driver's investigation seemed to reach the same conclusion.

"Please, sir," the driver said, and Benjie prayed he wouldn't finish the sentence, "Mr. Hartel said my nose should be broken so the managers will know I was attacked. Hospital record…it has to be convincing, he says."

Vito looked toward Benjie, who could not help averting his eyes…

Benjie and Vito carried the driver by his feet and arms to lay him across the back seat of the 1961 Chrysler that smelled like cat piss. A few shots to the stomach had forced lunch and breakfast back out the driver's mouth and onto his bare chest and stomach. His face was a crisscrossed network of lacerations and bruises sure to convince anyone of the driver's innocence and subsequent desire to see the criminals brought to justice. Vito folded Benjie's blue mechanics outfit into a pillow to catch what blood they could not smother with one of the expensive coats, but it was of little use. Some local cat owner was going to be very disappointed with the service at Louie's Riverside Collision Center, although the smell of cat urine had been mitigated by the time the brothers left the driver on a South Bronx sidewalk a few steps from a phone booth.

An afternoon in early June 1973
Jerry's Place in Brooklyn, NY
"We were tryin' to buy the neighborhood."

The proceeds from Stanley's truck of imported clothing were better than expected. Vito unloaded them to a mail order warehouse in Brooklyn after stashing the load for a few days in his dedicated garage at the Collision Center. The take was just north of $8,000 ($8,275 to be exact), and it was agreed to cut Benjie and Stanley in for 10 percent, Tony and Vito for 25 percent each, and another 30 percent for Vic and the Family Brass. When Benjie walked into Jerry's Place after the sale, the whole stack was sitting on the table in crisp $100, $20, and $5 bills. He watched silently as Vito whacked the bulky heap up; a chunk pushed here, another here, until Benjie's chunk was whittled free and slid across the table. Eight $100s, one $20, and a $5.

Benjie fanned the bills in his hand and counted them. It was more money than had ever been *his* before. He had held more for his brothers, more for Vic, even more for his mother once, but the money had never been just *his*. He did not have a wallet either. He would use the $5 for that.

"Hey," Vic said, with the bills in Benjie's hand, "this is good stuff, kid. We're gonna make you a good earner. I can smell good earners a mile away. It's the unselfish kids like you who really earn."

"I'm just tryin' to help. Tony and Vito did most of the work."

"Whatever, kid, there's no need for the humility right now. Everyone's a deep thinker in a submarine. Enjoy the scores while you got 'em, and always keep an eye out for another. There's gonna come a time when you'd smack a guy for any of those eight bills."

"All right, all right," Benjie said, giving Vic the wide smile he wanted, "obviously, I'm gonna enjoy it. I'm gonna use these trucks to get my own place."

"Yeah," Vic said, "that'd be a good place to start, I think. We'll get you outta there. I could even take you by some places and make sure you're set up right." Vic hesitated, searching the kid's face. "We're proud of you, Benj. You should know you did good on this."

Benjie went out with Vito and Tony to celebrate their windfall and caught the subway home, rather drunk, just after dinner. The route from the station to his mother's building dragged through a section of tenement buildings where he and his brothers played as kids. The building still stood, its metallic sign hanging by one last nail: *Bumbledom Apts.* A boy was playing where they had, alone on the empty sidewalk with his shirt off and no shoes on his feet. He was carrying a bucket of water and spilled more with each step until he disappeared around the side of the building, giggling as he did. Benjie jogged to reach the corner, curious about the fun, but the boy was gone when he got there, invisible in a crowd of peers. Benjie continued his walk.

He gently pressed the door open when he reached his mother's. The carpeting was short and luckily didn't hold the smells, although the stains were evident, black and brown and red at intervals across its entirety. He hung his jacket on the door and patted the retriever Gari when he greeted him. He found his mother at the kitchen table with the radio blaring and her head slumped into her chest, a half-finished bottle of vodka sitting inches from her right hand. Benjie opened the refrigerator as The Doors played, grabbed a piece of ham from the butcher's paper, and tossed another for Gari, who devoured it. He threw still another on the floor and fell into a chair across from his mother, watching her chest move beneath her limp mouth and chin. He pulled the vodka to himself and took a drink. It burned angrily in his gut. He took another and turned down the radio.

"I'm listening to that," his mother mumbled, her body lifeless if not for her protest.

"No, you're not, Ma."

She moved enough for her head to wobble upward. She would have seen him if she opened her eyes. "Turn it back up."

Benjie took another drink, the burn again, and set the bottle on the table. The clink of the glass was enough for Sandra Maceo to open her eyes. "Why are you here?" she breathed.

"I live here. For now."

"Move out. Live with Tony."

"I'm gonna move out. But not so I can live with Tony."

Sandra Maceo stirred enough to peak beneath her eyelids at the boy. "Why are you here?"

Benjie looked at the living room, at the carpet stains and his mother's dirty clothes. He pulled three of the hundreds from his pocket. "If I give you this, are you gonna lose it?"

Sandra moved away from the money slightly, as if wary of it. "No. What do you mean am I gonna lose it?"

"Here then. Don't fuckin' lose it. I worked hard for that."

His mother folded the bills into her bra, wiped drool from her mouth with the back of her hand, and brought her eyes to her son's. He saw the self-inflicted lines on her face. He took another drink.

"I'm sorry, Benjie."

"I know, Ma."

She brushed at her eyelashes, but the tears weren't there yet. "You're more of my boy than even Tony and Vito. We was all we had then, for a while."

"Stop, Ma."

"I'm serious. We're a part of each other, me and you, and we gotta be there for each other." Her words were slow and slurred.

"I'm here for ya. I get it."

"I'm sorry, Benjie."

"I know, Ma." He took another drink. "Why don't we get you to bed? We'll start it all again, bright and early."

"Yes, son, that might be best." Sandy made to stand but faltered on the edge of the table, almost spilling what was left in the bottle. Benjie caught it and moved it to the counter.

"C'mon," he said, dipping her frail body back into his arms to carry her, "let's go then. We'll talk tomorrow, Ma. Bright and early."

The night of June 8, 1973
The Blue Raven Social Club in Brooklyn, NY

Ricky leaned against the center bar with his eyes toward the blue lights of the main stage where four or five of his employees were helping the next band set up for their act. Sammie Palmissano's kid nephews were two of them, lugging drums and soundboards around with sour looks on their faces. Ricky already regretted hiring the entitled assholes and had told Petey as much. To the left of the stage, Nico stood guard by the cardroom door in his best suit and tie. He was hopelessly distracted by a woman with short blond hair and a plunging red neckline, but still technically manning his post.

Petey had wasted no time using his newfound club ownership to his advantage. He staked out a permanent table near the front with two women (club employees, no less) accompanying him and Markie stationed nearby to gopher his drinks. Petey's jacket was off and slung over his chair so the girls could rub his arms with faux affection or snuggle their heads against his shoulders. Ricky shook his head and drank the last of his scotch.

Behind the bar, a tall, muscular man was working carefully to serve a group of patrons in what would be a cramped space for anyone. Ricky watched him squeeze around the other bartenders to reach a bottle, add its contents to a glass or tin, and repeat a few times before getting the man's attention. "What's your name?" Ricky asked when the bartender walked over.

"Sean Whelan," the man answered, betraying a slight Irish accent. He was a full three or four inches taller than Ricky, who was not small himself. Sean lowered his eyes by leaning against the bar. Ricky appreciated the courtesy.

"You're too big to work behind this bar," Ricky said over the conversational din of the room. Sean looked over himself as if noticing his size for the first time. He pleaded, "No, sir. I'm fine here, I promise. This isn't too small. Honest, sir."

Ricky held his hand up. "No, don't worry about it. I want you to work the other bar. You see that one?" Ricky pointed to the satellite bar just a few feet from where Nico was semi-guarding the cardroom.

"Yes," Sean said.

"I want you to work at that bar. Come on this side real quick."

Sean walked obediently to where Ricky waited. "What do I tell the guy in there now?" Sean asked, straightening his Blue Raven uniform. It was missing half the fabric necessary to cover him comfortably.

Ricky shrugged. "Tell him to come over here, I don't really care. And you, when you're over there," he pointed his finger into Sean's sternum, "you keep a close eye on that door and make sure nobody goes through it without speaking to Mr. Catalanotte down there." He pointed to Nico and mentioned his habit of becoming distracted. "No pressure," Ricky finished.

181

Sean hurried to his post, and Ricky scanned the stage again. Buddy Roehner was standing stage left talking to the next band with his own Blue Raven uniform on: an oversize gold watch, shimmering rhinestones on his suit, white luminescent shoes, and his beady eyes hidden behind pastel green frames.

Rick observed the women serving his customers next: short black skirts, fishnet stockings, bare upper arms with black elbow-length gloves, and exposed cleavage whenever it was possible. He couldn't remember how many he hired, but the girls were darting purposefully between tables as the main lights dimmed and the new band began their set. The first song was punctuated by a sharp and wild saxophone riff, which convinced Ricky to toss a fresh cigarette in his mouth, grab a bottle of whiskey from behind the bar, and march to Petey's table with his jaw set in determination. He was expected to show his respect.

"Petey, how's the front row?" he asked with the bottle stretched out in greeting. Petey smiled vaguely, his eyes already glassy and unfocused, and cracked the unopened bottle to pour himself a drink. "This place is gonna be great," Petey said pointlessly. The alcohol injected drama in his mannerisms, and he looked over the forest of misting ashtrays with reverence. Rick poured the women a fresh drink and then one for himself before adjusting his chair to face the stage directly. The music was loud, but he enjoyed it, and the saxophone was pleasant after a few drinks. They listened to two songs there before Petey managed another word. "Have you talked to Nico or Vinnie yet tonight? You know that's what I'm counting on you for."

Rick held his expressions in check. "Not yet. I just wanted to listen to a few songs first, and then I was gonna make my rounds."

"Go check with 'em now," Petey said, jerking a thumb over his shoulder. Rick quashed his cigarette obediently, left his drink on the table, and crossed the front of the room to the door where Nico was still talking to his blond lady friend. "Ricky!" Nico said with the woman draped on his arm. "Go on in there." He motioned to the cardroom door. "See what we've done with the place."

Ricky hugged Nico and nodded even though he'd already seen the "renovations," which were no more than Vinnie setting up a TV. Five men were seated at the table when he entered and a few looked up, but none of them acknowledged him. Vinnie stood against the wall, watching both the card game and the TV in the corner. "How's it goin' in here?" Ricky asked him.

"Steady," Vinnie said with a tinge of disappointment. "Just regular numbers for this game. We'll get more as we go. Gamblers are always slow to come to a new place."

"Who are they?"

"Dr. Scheinberg," Vinnie began, pointing to each man in turn, "who used to play a weekend game I ran outtav a hotel, so I moved him over here. Just get to know his name or whatever, no big deal. The guy with all the chest hair sticking out is Leo Notoriano, Provenzano guy. The guy next to him is Gerry Pachino, also Provenzano, who I went to grade school with. They're both friends of mine, and one day, they'll be friends of yours, kid. Don't borrow money from either of those motherfuckers. And you know him, right?" Vinnie asked, moving to a man with gold rings, a purple tie, and checkered gray suit.

Ricky shook his head. "I've seen him around. Maybe he hung around my pops when I was younger."

"Nick Pisani. I'll give you the scouting report in case he starts comin' in here. He's a big deal in this thing of ours, one of," Vinnie tugged his ear, "his closest guys. If he gives you somethin', you do it with fuckin' bells on. And the guy next to him is Paulie Panzavechia. He's a good kid with shit for brains, but he's another guy you gotta listen to. If he's speakin', it's prolly for Nick. You remember what I was tellin' you about, uh…" he tugged his ear again, "well, some guys show the same respect for Nick. They'll flash six fingers for him on account of his nickname."

"Six?"

Vinnie chuckled. "Nicky Six, some call him. There's a bunch of stories. First one I heard was he put six bullets in the forehead of some guy when he was sixteen. I didn't need to hear any others, but they'll tell them."

"I think he used to meet up with my dad at Little League games. Used to drive a blue Chrysler and sit in the lot."

"Keep him happy. He's a problem nobody needs."

"I'll do my best." Ricky took a few drags from his latest cigarette. "You see Petey's dates out there?"

"Yeah, the fat fuck," Vinnie joked. "He's gonna be the most expensive piece of furniture in the whole city. Five hundred dollars a night in lost booze and non-money-makin' women."

"It's good to be king."

Vinnie laughed. "In this place, that's the king," he corrected Rick, nodding at Nicky Six. Nick looked like he was having the time of his life. Huge smile, full drink, and what looked like the chip lead.

"Vice president has its perks too then, I guess."

Ricky stayed in the cardroom awhile, and Vinnie introduced him to the players, including Nick and his man. When he did return to the main room, Petey was still at his post, front and center with his jacket off. At least the turnout had been what they expected. The tables were full, and the band was good.

Sean seemed at home on the satellite bar, and Ricky allowed himself to take a seat there and rub his forehead, one degree removed from the action. Sean had been watching for him and immediately brought him a drink with a few extra fingers. Ricky decided the fair-skinned Irish bulwark was nothing like Sammie Palmissano's asshole nephews.

"Ya know," Rick said to Sean, "I think I'm gonna put you on this bar permanently. Is that somethin' you'd like?"

"Yes, sir," the bartender answered, radiating pure joy. "If this is where you want me, I'll be right here."

"I want to give you some special responsibilities," Rick said, and Sean leaned on the bar again. "I want you to get to know the names of every person who goes in that room, like memorize who's in there and who's *allowed* in there. Who has special privileges, who's got girlfriends and wives who come here, all that shit." Rick pointed at the cardroom door. "Do you know what's behind that door?"

"No, sir."

Rick took the direct approach. "It is a cardroom. The owners of this club are running a sportsbook and card games back there for additional income."

"Okay, sir." Sean's face had not changed much, but Rick could sense silent gears whirring behind his eyes.

"Do you know why we are runnin' an illegal gamblin' room out of the back of this club?"

"Added income. Like you said."

Ricky chose to be direct again. "It's because this club is owned by members of the Italian Mafia. Nico, or Mr. Catalanotte, over there is a member, Vinnie back in the cardroom, Petey up front there—they're all members. Do you know what that means?"

Sean answered, "I've just seen *The Godfather*, sir."

Rick almost snorted scotch back into his glass. "Perfect," he said, composing himself. "Does that change anything about this job for you?"

Sean's grin had returned. The whirring gears seemed to have stopped. "No, sir. I understand."

"Good to hear. If that ever changes, I want you to tell me first, like a man," Rick said, extending his hand.

Sean shook it firmly, "Yes, sir. Not a problem."

Sean went back to his growing line of customers, and Ricky went to work on his overpoured scotch, swirling the rocks against its bottom. The sleeve of his suit caught against a sticky spill on the bar top, and he fetched a wet towel to wipe it. When he returned the blond waitress named Kay was waiting for him. He had been aware of her since the first interviews.

"Mr. Caruso?" she asked in her bubbly working voice.

"Ricky please," he said, leaning against the bar before realizing his sleeve was back against the sticky spot he was set to remove.

"Ricky," she corrected, "I've got a table of four over there, and I'm pretty sure the two guys are snorting cocaine in the bathrooms. I wanted you to be aware of it. I've worked in both kinds of places."

His face grew hot, but he hoped the dim lights would mask it. "Which table?" Kay pointed to one with two women and two open chairs.

"How much money have they spent?"

"Maybe twenty dollars."

"Are they young men?"

"Early twenties."

"Fuck 'em." Ricky began walking toward the table alone before he thought better of it. He came back to the satellite bar. "Sean," he said, "how are you at kicking guys out?"

"I imagine I'd be pretty good at it, sir."

"Come with me. Kay, can you cover the bar for him?" Ricky walked between the tables with his Irish ally, and when they reached the table, the two cocaine users were back at their seats. "Hello, everyone," Rick began, "how has your evening been thus far?"

One of the two men stared at the two, confused and suspicious of Sean's presence. "The service has been pretty average honestly. Is there a complaint box?" he asked, laughing and looking to his companions for support. The guy chuckled. The girls looked skittishly between the men.

"We do in fact have a complaint box, sir." Rick could see why Kay had been suspicious. The man's eyes were bloodshot, and his companion was continuously grinding his teeth. "If you'll come with me…perhaps you'd all like to fill one out?"

"No, fuck you," the teeth grinder said. "We're here to enjoy the show. Just bring us the fuckin' card and we'll drop it in the box when we leave."

Ricky turned his attention to the two women. "Ladies," he said calmly, "me and my friend here are about to kick these two fuckheads out on their asses for snorting cocaine in my goddamn bathroom. You're free to stay. In fact, I'll comp your drinks so hopefully you can consume enough alcohol to retroactively blackout and forget you ever had the misfortune of sittin' across from these two."

"We didn't do any fuckin—" but Sean stepped forward, grabbed the teeth grinder around the chest, and squeezed him in a breath-depriving bear hug. The teeth grinder struggled to break free, but Sean walked him, feet off the ground and kicking, to the front door. Ricky yanked the second man up by the collar and pushed him forward as he followed a few steps behind. Their dates trotted after them despite Ricky's offer, too embarrassed to make eye contact with anyone else.

When they stepped through the front doors and onto the crowded sidewalk outside, Ricky said, "Check his nose," to Sean.

"What?"

"His nose. Check it. I wanna know if he's a nervous motherfucker or a liar."

Sean pushed the teeth grinder to his knees and aimed his nostrils at a streetlight. He reached inside the man's nostril, and when he pulled his finger back, it was caked in moist white powder. "Oh yeah," Sean said, "that's not sugar."

"Liars are worse than bitches." Ricky slammed his right fist into the other man's jaw, and his knees crumpled. He did not fall to the ground but was too scared to fight back, instead choosing to scramble. Sean grabbed him by his shirt and dragged him next to his friend, on the sidewalk and now both on their knees. Pedestrians were beginning to react, stepping an extra stride toward the street to get around the scene. Ricky threw a knee into the other man's face. The pain doubled him, and he cupped the blood as it came from his nose. Ricky laughed. "That's your guy," he said to Sean, "go on." Sean threw a punch across the teeth grinder's face. From then on, his cries were slurred by fluid and swelling. "Fuckin' sick motherfuckin' asshole," Ricky said over another knee and another punch, "disrespecting...my goddamn club." Another swing, a kick, another kick.

The teeth grinder was unconscious after a few hits from Sean, and the other man was left moaning on the sidewalk.

One morning in June 1973
The Blue Raven Social Club in Brooklyn, NY
"Wayne knew enough to pretend to not know anything."

Ricky had never been an early riser. When his mother would wake him for school, he often ate breakfast and walked out the front door, only to climb in a window and crawl beneath his bed to nap with the blankets pulled down to hide him from view. The carpet was musty and stained even then, despite his mother's best efforts.

He could usually steal a few extra hours in his alcove before he'd hear his father clambering through the house, talking loudly on the phone or back and forth with his wife. Ricky Sr. would wear his robe loosely fastened around his waist with the upper portion of his gut exposed as he carried the phone around with him, the cord stretched out behind him. Ricky would find some way to escape and sometimes hop the school fence to join his classmates, but more often he went to the Boxing Club to watch guys in the ring. He did odd jobs for Mr. Honeysett, the club's trainer and manager, who never shooed him away when he needed someplace to be. Those days were mostly spent cleaning, but as he got older, Ricky ordered speed bags, heavy bags, gloves, ropes, stools, shoes, and trunks, stocked the vending machines and the club store, all from catalogues Honeysett had stockpiled in his office. At the age of fourteen, the roughly built kid was meeting with sporting good salesmen and selling ad space on bulletins at the club. This was the experience he drew on as he browsed half a stack of restaurant vendor catalogs from his office at The Blue Raven, community college be damned.

Ricky claimed the second-largest office for himself and set about organizing it in the week before their grand opening. There were four offices in total located up a tight staircase behind the main stage and through a curtained doorway. Petey had the biggest for himself, then Ricky, Buddy Roehner, and Wayne Foster (again, the *owner*) was given the last one, which amounted to little more than a broom cupboard. Ricky bought secondhand filing cabinets and a small desk with scroll work along the fringe like he thought he'd seen in the movies. His only window faced an alley, and so the room was always dark if not for a solitary yellow lamp he'd scavenged from home. He strained to read the catalogs for a while until it became too much. He tossed them aside and went to search for coffee.

The main room was deadly quiet and the floor peppered by napkins, splotches, and smears from the night before, a respectable Sunday showing. Ricky wondered what their sales had been although he had no idea how to define a "good" night. *We should make a chart.* He remembered drawing bar graphs and line graphs in school whenever they talked about making money. A graph of the weekends, he thought, back to back, but he could not remember which was better for money. He found a broom against the wall by the kitchen and instinctively started sweeping up food droppings from around a nearby table. He followed the crumbs to the next table when he finished and then again to the next and the next. The table Petey had commandeered as his own was by far the worst.—

"Why are you here?" a high-pitched voice said. Ricky turned to see Wayne Foster, the twitching ball of nerves, staring at him from across the room. Wayne was wearing a worn-out flannel, jeans, and Converse sneakers, a very different image from their opening night.

"I came to fix the damage to this place," Ricky said defensively. "Why are you here?"

"Because my name is on this club, and I don't intend to see it fail."

Ricky was surprised to hear the little man say that and stood there for moment with the broom in his hand and a stupid look on his face. He gathered himself. "That's good to hear. I don't want it to fail either." They stared awkwardly for several moments, making silent assessments of each other. In the end, they both seemed to shrug in answer.

"That's what typically happens to these places," Wayne said. "You and your crew use them, you get *irresponsible,* and you bail right after you soak them for all the credit you can squeeze. That is Petey Caltagirone's plan, I'm sure."

Ricky was forced to note the familiar warning. "No, it's not," he promised.

"What are you to him?" Wayne asked, his eyes darting up and down. "To Petey I mean?"

"He's a friend of my father. My father got locked up, so Petey is givin' me a shot to make some money." Ricky thought about the graphs. "Do you have the books for this weekend?"

"The books?" Wayne asked, a smile cracking his lips.

Ricky felt the hot pang of impatience. "Yeah, somebody has to keep the books around here, right? I...I want to see them."

"The 'books' are the records of the 'counts.' You have to do the *counts* first and then you write them in the *books.*"

"I get the idea. Who does the counts?"

"Usually, it's the owners who do the counts. What time do you think Petey will be in?" Wayne smiled at the Fat Man's expense. "That's why I'm here. If I don't protect my name, nobody will."

Ricky felt sympathy for the man. Petey was going to get his money either way; that ship had sailed. He wondered if Wayne knew exactly what else Petey was capable of. "I guess I should help you then…I'm not an owner, but if I'm Petey's guy…and he's not going to do it…"

Wayne was surprised at the offer. "Yes, Mr. Caruso," he said, recovering a degree of their previous formality, "I would appreciate that very much. First, we pull the drawers out of those cash registers." Ricky nodded. He went to the main bar and fiddled with the register before he could figure out how to wrench the drawer free, but eventually, he had it and was able to collect the others before carrying them up into Wayne's converted broom cupboard.

"Maybe we can get you in Buddy's office," Ricky said with another twinge of sympathy. "He should be traveling a lot, right? Looking for bands?"

"Don't worry about it. I've had worse." The little man pulled a ledger from one of the drawers (his desk was two filing cabinets pushed together with a piece of plywood on top) and lay it open to one of the first pages. Small, neat handwriting filled the first few columns of squares all up and down the page with totals waiting to be recorded at the bottom. Wayne took the first register drawer, removed the twenty-dollar bills and flicked through them quickly. Apparently satisfied, he set them aside and did the same with a few more drawers until the stack reached over a foot high. He took a ruler, cut the bills right at twelve inches and pushed the stack to Ricky. "Count these. I'll make us some coffee."

One afternoon in June 1973
234 Park Avenue site in Manhattan, NY
"Another tentacle on the kraken."

The rain was no small obstacle for any of them. It muddied the gray dirt and stuck to their shoes like glue with only Cal Roselli wearing anything resembling appropriate dress for a construction site. Adam held an umbrella over Alphonse and Carrie, while Johnny jogged ahead with Cal to the makeshift canvas shelter erected and spiked into the ground. Buildings rose from the asphalt all around their muddy plot, but the only signs of urban life on-site were several formations of right-angle trenches lined with rebar. A set of blueprints lay over a small wood table in the tent, and Cal wiped his hands on his neon vest and shirt to prevent soiling its details. Adam shook the umbrella when they reached the tent and leaned it against a dry pallet before joining the others around the drawings.

"We're running the trenches here," Cal began, tracing thick lines near the bottom of the prints, "that will mark the foundation of the building. That will extend, eventually extend anyway, some forty feet down into the Manhattan bedrock with about twenty-five of those feet being accessible for basement storage divided into two levels. That much of this plot should be dug out this week and poured and anchored within the next two. We'll need prolly one week of minor installations and adjustments before we begin moving upward. The design calls for eighteen columns, eight of which are considered central, which should be set and reinforced by roughly this time next month." Adam got Cal's attention and motioned impatiently for him to speed the appraisal up. "We've got two crews, so first shift and second, making the operation run for about twenty hours a day. And since our buddy Dalton saddled up on our loans, we're quite 'liquid' at the moment. Clearwater bought these," he kicked a stack of smooth white stones as large as park benches, "last week at twelve points over standard. They're gonna fortify the trenches one layer below ground level when we get there. Heavy motherfuckers," he said, before remembering Carrie and apologizing unnecessarily, "so we gotta work with our guys on setting them properly, but these are good guys, Mr. Al. I've known a lot of them since I was first startin' out, twenty-five years some of them."

"I'm not worried," Al said. "I know you'll get it taken care of." The Don lightly kicked one of the large white stones for himself as the rain pounded the tent above their heads. A rivulet made its way through a split in the fabric and meandered its way under the stack as Al watched. He stomped its progress into the dirt. "What's the end date for this project given where we are now? Either one of you know that?"

"We believe the building will be ready to open in April of '76," Adam said. "How does that sound?" It was the first time he mentioned this date to Alphonse, although the Clearwater Board had discussed it several times.

"Is that a normal timeline?" Carrie asked.

"It's a little aggressive," Adam admitted, "but the tight schedule will give us room on the back end for delays without stretching into another winter season. If you have a three-month delay in April, that's not the end of the world. If it happens in October, you've got bigger problems."

"So, that's a construction-bein'-done deadline…okay," Johnny said, his shoulders bowed stiffly against his wet clothes, "but the real question is, when do we start rentin' and sellin' these units?"

"April is the goal for the completion of the general construction with the interior stuff possibly extending a few months beyond that, but we'll be able to sell the units before any of that. By that time, the full-scale interior mock-ups will be completed and we will be able to move on the units, although renters will only be making deposits on the cash end. That means it's just a one-time cut until we open for real, but the first wave should hit dry land in the second half of 1975."

Al had moved to scratching a green discoloration on the massive blocks, unaware the other eyes were all trained on him. "And when's the next milestone? Our next step forward?"

Adam shrugged. Cal said, "The first stone on the lower level, I guess. That's when there will be something to look at again besides big holes in the ground."

"I wouldn't advise making it a habit to visit the site," Adam warned, "but I'll obviously bring you whenever you want."

"No," Al said, "you know I don't wanna come out here unless I have to. I have promised someone a vacation and I intend to go on it. And, Cal, you know this, but I'll say it in front of everyone for the benefit of my kids." Al turned from the stones to face Johnny and Carrie. "Cal and Adam are gonna run things on-site, without influence from others, and I mean *anyone* else. We need to stay away from this whole place. It's protection for both us and the site. 'You don't shit where you eat' is how my father would have said it."

"I already don't wanna be here," Johnny said, showing Al the gunk on his shoes, "so that shouldn't be a problem." Carrie nodded next to him.

"All right, then," Adam said, "if that's settled, we've got another issue to discuss. The skim. The reason we're all doing this—"

"Cal, we really appreciate it," Al said over Adam's last few words. Cal got the hint, shook the Don's hand, and jogged back into the rain, leaving Adam alone with the Giordanos. Carrie watched Cal through the tent flap until the rain was too thick to see.

Adam leaned against the small wooden table and faced the others. "So," he said, "the money that comes from this place is going to start clean. The loans are legitimate, Cal's business is legitimate, Clearwater's investments are legitimate, et cetera, et cetera. As such, we need to keep this money as far away from the shadier aspects of the overall *business portfolio* as possible. We can't be a year in, two years in, ten years into this project and have money seized or in limbo for legal reasons. That's the whole point of all of this, the one, huge advantage of money that is positively legitimate." He chortled. "Obviously, if our legit money is as vulnerable as the non-legit money, we might as well take the drug money and go home."

"We get it," Carrie said, shifting her heels over the soft ground. These men may be able to stand in the mud for hours, but her stilettos were sinking further into the earth with each passing second. "Let's get to your point."

Adam looked from Al to Johnny but did not voice whatever he was expecting to find there. "You need truly civilian agents to shield you. Unassociated, or at least significantly less associated, people who manage your shell companies. So, first step: create an unassociated company. I've done that. The Clearwater Board will hire a financial firm, Tulles Financial, to do the on-site accounting per my forthcoming suggestion. If the government investigates this company for any reason, they will see a financial firm based in France that has existed for twenty years because, until very recently, this is exactly what they were. The key is the re-emergence of a very small American branch headquartered in New York which was about to be shut down, until I came along and rescued it. They have a physical office somewhere in the city, I can't remember where, but those details are unimportant in the grand scheme of things. Perhaps we relocate it, perhaps not. We can discuss that all in time. What is important is the American branch will accept some very large, very legit payments from Clearwater when the major construction begins. Tulles Financial will become your bulletproof shield. Now, once you spend the money or accept salaries or whatever, you're back to risking asset seizure should the law focus on any one of you specifically. But any money left in the Tulles coffers will be safe as long as the *company* stays clean."

"Does it have to be a French name?" Johnny asked.

Adam chuckled. "Yes. The continuity is the point of using them."

"So, what's the discussion for? Sounds like you have everything figured out."

"The discussion is about who your representatives are going to be."

"What do they do?"

"They will be the *legal* gatekeepers of the Tulles money, the 'owners of record' and the legal claimants to anything and everything left under the Tulles umbrella. Anyone not listed will have no right to any of it in the eyes of the law. And these individuals *must be clean*. If Tulles is specifically implicated, boom on everything."

"Why not you?" Carrie asked.

"With me on the Clearwater Board, there would be a conflict of interest so obvious even this group of board members would tell me to get lost. We need someone else, but someone unequivocally trusted. They will make it much easier for me to hide especially with the financial context Tulles will give us as far as tax filings, court rulings, work histories, W2s, all that helps camouflage the 'shell' of this shell corporation. And with the involvement of the other Families, I strongly suggest choosing an Italian to hold the purse strings. I don't want to take a bullet over some anti-Semitic bullshit."

Al's knees began to stiffen. He found a stone to sit on and spun his cane into the dirt. "Options?"

"Uncle Oscar?" Johnny suggested.

"I think that's a good option," Adam said. "That was the first one I thought of."

Carrie searched her father's face for a reaction. It was quiet and still, which she knew was an answer in itself. "Oscar is a male Sicilian with criminals all around him," she said. "And he wouldn't do it. It should be Ma."

"I thought about her too. It's good. It's more about trust than anything else, and she could never be forced to testify against you, Al."

"I'm her liability," Al said quietly. "With the right circumstances, they could get to both pots of money in a single case. It would be harder to do that if Carrie and Jennie ran it for us."

Johnny made a noise. "How is Bobby any different than you, Pops?"

"I'm not married yet."

Al's eyes turned up to hers. They were a wonderful brown even in the rain battered tent. What was in them? Worry? Anger? Or was it pride? "You and Jennie, both," he said simply.

Johnny kicked a clump of tacky dirt under the canvas with his shoe. "All right then."

"Draw it up quickly, Adam 'cause my vacation starts right after."

A morning in June 1973
The Met Gallery in Manhattan, NY
"Johnny didn't do himself any favors, Al understood that."

Al stepped over the faded gray line and wiped his fingerprint across the painting's gilded frame. He watched the security guard as he did it, daring him to declare these mounts off-limits for him to wipe clean, but the man wisely remained where he was and distracted himself with a spare museum pamphlet. The other patrons did not notice Al at all. "What does Adam say about it?" he asked his son, stationed a few paces behind him.

Johnny pressed two knuckles into his brow. "Adam says he's not worried about it."

"I would not worry about it," Al parroted.

Johnny tapped the guilty papers in his hand. "Cal is worried about it. Do you trust Cal?"

Al was grateful his son was not apathetic or lazy. *Sincerity is rare…and often stupid.* "I would not worry about things Adam is not worried about."

Johnny shook his head. "I can't do that."

Al smiled. "I know you can't." He moved slowly to the next painting, his shoes and steel-tipped cane tapping together against the floor. Johnny sulked behind him. "Change the subject," Al commanded. This painting was tall, maybe six feet or more, and Al had to step back to see it all.

Johnny wrung his hands together. "Fine. Did you know Petey opened a new club?"

"Yeah, in the Bronx." Al was somehow less interested in this subject than the last.

"Brooklyn. He sent your first cut."

Al flicked his cane dismissively. "Give it to Carrie for the wedding."

"Fine. It's two grand, so you know." Johnny had expected the money to go to Carrie but thought his father should know how much it was. Her "wedding fund" was a war chest by now. Perhaps the Don was keeping mental tabs, perhaps not.

"Give it to Carrie," Al said, curtly this time.

"I got it, Pops. The wedding."

Al refocused on the painting, a huntress and her bearded centaur. She was powerful, shown with her sharp and sturdy halberd before the centaur and his wooden bow, but her eyes related pity, her delicate hand seemed ready to tousle his hair rather than pull it. She wore a white gown, which flowed lightly to her ankles, covered in gold ringlets, green vines, and blue jewels, in front of gray rocks and a dull sky. Al had seen it before, seen it with Johnny next to him even. "I always liked Botticelli," Al said. "He was a northerner, but he could paint. A singular talent."

"This one is his?" Johnny asked.

"You see the laurels on her head?"

"Yeah, if that's the crown of leaves."

"What do you think those mean?"

Johnny did his best to drag his thoughts away from the papers in his hand and stepped forward to squint at the corners of the canvas for clues. "That's like the Olympians, right? Fastest guy in the village gets a pointless wreath for his efforts. And this woman is prolly the best axe thrower or some shit."

"It's a tribute. The laurels are a tribute."

"To the centaur?"

"To the guy who bought the painting."

"I guess that's the right guy to tribute," Johnny chuckled, hoping Al would let the conversation drop. Al let the silence settle on them, and Johnny knew he was not going to move on. He relented. "What does it mean then?"

Al softly patted his chest. "It's a sign of respect. The artist's respect for this man of influence."

"I know what a tribute is."

"It's an acknowledgment of the artists submission…so to speak."

"He crowned the lady?"

"It's an acknowledgment he values the opinion of the other man, the buyer, over his own. Botticelli would not have painted this," Al said, pointing his finger into the heart of the painting, "without the buyer. He creates the beauty for those around him, not for himself. This beauty is his tribute to another."

"Or for money," Johnny said, shrugging. "Or Botticelli did it all for himself and the guy that likes laurels had the end goal in hand. And then this rich guy's poorer friends stood around the painting and told him how pretty the laurels were, and now *we* think laurels are pretty and Botticelli is shakin' his head at us."

Al had to laugh. "Or he did it all for money. How would we know? I think the laurels are pretty though."

"*Father*," Johnny said with a hopeful, almost desperate, use of his limited Sicilian vocabulary, "can we talk about this?" He tapped the papers again.

"Say your piece, son." Stall tactics were of no use against Johnny's stubborn will. Al had learned this lesson many times.

"The construction is already overbudget, and Cal says he is going to need another loan if it keeps up." Johnny said the words with a grim look.

Al let them float away into the dull hum of the gallery. The other patrons were parents with their little ones, teachers and tour groups, art students, and security guards. None suspected the reason this man and his son would visit on a weekday morning.

"How did it happen?"

"Cal says his invoices are comin' in heavy. The plan is $2,000 or something for these guys, and he's getting charged $3,000, $4,000 or more by companies that are supposed to be friendly to us." Johnny extended the physical examples, but the Don shook his head at them. "If anything, these should be coming in *low* until we start seeing checks. Upcharges can come later, during the actual construction. These guys, these 'friendly companies,' are getting impatient for a cut, and Cal says it's flippin' him upside down and he's askin' me what he's supposed to do. How they gonna fuck up these receipts when we're goin' so far out of our way to keep a clean paper trail? You want Cal's company runnin' with money trouble right out the gate? We've already dealt with that problem, or so we thought with that fuckin' banker. We still haven't seen much money from Clearwater. He's got Dalton's loan, but that's all we've seen so far."

"Go see these guys then. What are we talkin' about here?"

Johnny glanced around, but none of the others were within twenty feet of them. "Some of these contractors are friends of ours. The ones slippin' big bills on us, they're supposed to be at the table with us."

"Who?"

"One he mentioned is East Bay. That's the Cavalcante's, Provenzano's guys."

Al worked at a canker sore on the inside of his cheek with his tongue. He had been working on it all day, as one does. "Are they doin' this with his blessing?"

"Hard to tell," Johnny said, relieved to have the proper attention. "My guess is the Old Man is losing his grip and they're taking advantage of his wandering eye. But I don't know. That's why I wanted to come to you and ask you what you wanted to do."

"Why isn't Adam worried?"

"He thinks we can get around it. He talks about managing their dollar amounts in total, not the individual bills. He said we'll take it out on the back end, once things are running smoothly."

Al nodded. His son might be right this time. "If we push back early, they'll claim they're gettin' screwed. That's what he's thinking. I'll look into it. I'm gonna talk to Adam and then I'll look into it."

"That's all I've been askin' for." Johnny curled the papers and tucked them in his jacket. "I'm tellin' you, Cal is freakin' out about this shit. He's scared to talk to you about it. I know Dalton thinks he's doing *us* a favor, but it's Cal's name on all them loans. He's gonna be the first one to sink."

"Nobody's sinkin'. Just keep Cal calm. Last thing we need is him losing his head on this fuckin' thing."

June 13, 1973 at 4:30 p.m.
Concrete Union Headquarters in Manhattan, NY
"It doesn't matter how many votes you get if you're counting the ballots."

Detectives Clayburgh and Murdock parked across the street and down a hundred yards from the cement union headquarters in an unmarked car. It had been no small task to requisition a camera with enough zoom to allow this position to be practical, but the detectives convinced Captain Quinn their Mafia-Union assassination angle was worth (1) a proper investigation and (2) opening the checkbook for. The first was much easier than the second. Admittedly, they were not quite sure how best to pursue their theory. Organize sting operations of Mafia associates, either gamblers or drug dealers or racketeers, and try and get information from them? Without knowing anything about who wanted Benfield dead, it was hard to pick a target, and any misfires would send others into hiding. They could bug Mafia hangouts, but which ones? And what evidence did they have to get a warrant? A housewife's description of two men she was "pretty sure" were Italian? Berdan's description of two tawny-skinned men? No, the detectives decided the lowest-risk, lowest-dollar move was to closely monitor the results of the union election. So, there they sat on a dry, hot June afternoon with heat waves shimmering up from the asphalt and through their polyester seats.

Clayburgh focused the lens of the camera on the front door. Two men wearing overalls and cement-laden boots were passing out brochures to the union voters as they slowly trickled through in teams of three to five men at a time. The vote was set for 5:00 p.m., but many of the members had left the jobsite early to mill around the lobby where street-level windows offered the detectives a good view of the interior. Clayburgh managed to grab one of the candidate pamphlets the day before, and Murdock was reading it for the first time as they waited.

"Newman identified the favorite as this David Ehlert," Murdock said, mumbling key points aloud. "Twenty-five years in the union… high school diploma…father was a mason…*instrumental*, it says, in the strike…two sons." Murdock looked up. "They always say that at the end. Start talking about their family. It's a guilt thing. Single men are really at a disadvantage in this world." He continued, "The long-shot guy here…Harvey Kandel…pension this and that…war veteran. That's a good one there, Andy. Wartime veterans in these working-class unions. I guess they figure if he has the balls to fight in the war, he's not gonna back down to some corporate fat cats. Fair assumption I guess…aha! *No kids.* That's why he's the long shot. If he had a couple kids, he'd be neck and neck with Ehlert." Murdock kept reading. "There's a third guy on here too that Newman didn't mention. Peter Haythe. Union member six years…some college… two-sport athlete in high school, it says. That's a rare one. We're not paying enough attention to these people's athletic ability, Andy. The union would probably get more shit done if they played basketball against the stockholders. Or football. Football would be even better."

"You read the part about Newman?"

"Yeah, nice little send-off at the back." Murdock flipped the pamphlet over to where a smiling picture of Richard Newman held the middle. "Thanks for his service and all that. He calls himself a 'union man for life.' Nothing about Benfield. Too depressing, I guess. Or maybe they just don't want to linger on it. It's been almost four weeks already, and his head hasn't grown back."

Clayburgh scanned a side parking lot, which only had room for about five cars, through the camera lens and paused there. One car, a black Fiat, was parked at the far end of the mini-lot with a sideways angle at the front door. It was the second time Clayburgh hesitated over them, two well-dressed men smoking and talking in the car for almost ten minutes with no indication they were about to open their doors or leave. "What do you think of these two?" Clayburgh asked, handing the camera to Murdock and pointing his eyes toward the Fiat.

"They look relaxed."

"Yeah. You recognize either of them?"

"No. Hard to get a good picture of the driver from here."

"Me either, but dark hair and dark complexion. Are you *pretty sure* they're Italian?"

Murdock looked again. "I don't know if I'm pretty sure, but I could see Mrs. Newman being pretty sure."

"Take some extra shots of them."

The detectives stayed at their post as the voting members continued to trickle in. Even after the 5:00 p.m. start time, members continued to arrive and it wasn't until after 6:00 p.m. (the two men still waiting patiently in the Fiat) when a significant crowd began to file out of the headquarters. Clayburgh first eyed the members through the lens of the camera, snapping pictures every few seconds, before scanning the wider area and focusing on the mini-lot again. As he aimed the camera a fourth or fifth time, he watched as one individual, a worker in overalls, broke from the normal flow of traffic and made his way through the small lot to where the two men waited. "Brady, look at this," Clayburgh said, tapping his partner on the arm. Clayburgh focused the camera on the lone voting member and then on the two men in the car, snapping several shots in succession.

"You can't really see their face all that well," he complained as he fired off more pictures, "or the driver at all really." The voting member leaned on the car, talking into the driver-side window for about a minute before turning away and walking back into the stream of human traffic. As soon as he stepped away, the black Fiat started up and backed into the street before turning right in the direction of Murdock and Clayburgh's unmarked car.

"They're coming this way," Clayburgh whispered. "Fuck." He dropped the camera on the floor. He could turn his head and hoped they didn't notice him, like any other driver trying to check the traffic in the street. They were not so lucky. When the Fiat passed, the passenger looked directly at them, doffing an invisible hat with a faint smile on his face.

"*Shit*," Murdock breathed, "they made us. They had us made the whole time."

"We need to know who won that election."

"God damnit," Murdock said, "I'll ask." He got out of the car and crossed the street to where many of the members were still filing out. "Hi, gentlemen," he said with his Broadway smile, "I heard you were having an election today. Can I ask who won?"

All the concrete men eyed him suspiciously, but one seemed to take pity. He said, "Paul Downes won. Our former treasurer."

"Oh," Murdock said, betraying surprise. "Did you vote for him?"

"No," the worker answered, "but I can't argue. He got 70 percent of the vote. He was a bit of a late entry, but I know a couple fellas who were hard up for him. I don't usually follow this stuff."

Murdock thanked the man and turned back toward the unmarked car. As he walked, he replayed the events in his head, but he had to be honest with himself. He had no idea what he had learned. He just knew he learned something.

The evening of June 13, 1973
Manhattan, NY
"That was an absurdly careless mistake."

As soon as he put a few blocks between him and the concrete union headquarters, Johnny pulled his Fiat into a parking garage and stopped against the curb. "He is going to kill me."

Nick shook his head. "Blame me. It's my fault. I should've expected them to stake the fuckin' election out."

"We both should have known. Goddamn." Johnny opened his car door and turned to Nick. "You stay here." Nothing productive would come from his comments during this conversation. Johnny walked up to a pay phone bank and dropped a few coins in the metal slot. His father answered after a few rings. "Hello?"

"Pops, we have a time-sensitive problem."

Alphonse hesitated, thinking through the potential issues. One stood out. "With the thing this afternoon? Did somebody have a problem doing their civic duty?"

"Not quite…there were some guys there, some badges and cameras were there."

"So what? You're a concerned citizen who likes to stay informed. Don't worry about it."

"I had a friend with me. A friend who's been seen around town recently. And with the cameras there…" Johnny paused to let his father to catch up.

Al let out a blistering string of Sicilian curse words. "You shouldn't have brought him to that," Al said through gritted teeth and anger Johnny could feel inside the earpiece. "How the fuck could you be that stupid? I didn't tell you to bring your friend to that."

"I know, I know. He was with me before I left. What am I gonna tell him? No?"

"You tell him to lay fuckin' low! Like I fuckin' told you to! You're not attached at the motherfuckin' hip! You're not supposed to be the motherfuckers causin' me problems, and that's all you've done. I've had it with you and your stupid fuckin' friend."

"Well, it's done now," Johnny said, struggling between a son's rebellion and a soldier's obedience. "What do you want us to do?"

Al slammed the phone on the counter and circled his kitchen. His son would wait, Nick would wait. *Reckless idiots. Of course, the police want to know who the next union president is, if only to question him about the Benfield thing. This is exactly the sort of careless heat Phil has been preaching about. I complain about Provenzano and Pisciotto and their lack of control, and here I sit with my men getting their fucking pictures taken.* Al picked up the phone. "You're gonna have to solve it, that's all I'm interested in now. And you better solve it soon. Those pictures won't stay blank for long."

"Where?"

"Just do it. I don't care how, just get it done. And make your friend do it. This is all his mess."

"All right, we'll handle—" Johnny started, but his words were cut by the dial tone. He threw the phone at the receiver and walked back to where Nick was waiting against the car. "He says finish it," Johnny said. "And he says to have you do it."

Nick punched the car hood. "Then I'm ready. Fuck this prick. Fuckin' yammerin' about shit he don't know about. What kind of man is that? I'm happy to do his neighborhood a service. Where's he live then?"

"Calm down a minute. He says 'soon,' but they won't have time to develop the pictures and bring the guy in before tomorrow. We've gotta think about this."

"You can drive right up to his fuckin' work and I'll wet him on the sidewalk," Nick said, his face flushed and twisted. "I don't give a fuck."

"Absolutely not. Let me think." Johnny had trailed Berdan for a couple of days at his father's request but stopped when he heard the investigation stalled. Still, those few days were valuable, and he was sifting through them in his mind, looking for an opening. "We can get him before he goes to work," he said finally. "He parks on the street. I know his car. Same time almost every day."

"When?"

"We'll meet bright and early. Four thirty."

* * *

Johnny rolled his window down for the ride. He was rarely up this early and the drive powered a cool, morning breeze. Nick seemed to be enjoying the same coolness, the same stillness of the morning, and leaned against the airstream to tickle the hairs on his head. Even in this city, where the lights never faded, there was a therapeutic relief in the quiet of morning.

"What's he look like, this guy?" Nick asked, his head still pressed into the counterfeit wind.

"He's a skinny blond prick. Full of himself, you can see it from a hundred yards. Probably born into money, if I had to guess. He walks around like his shit don't stink."

Nick leaned back to the seat and rolled his window up. "The other guy had money too, the first guy. I'm not gettin' enough money from these guys after. I didn't get nothin' from the last guy, and I probably won't get shit from this prick either. Maybe if we whack him at his car, maybe I can run into the garage and grab somethin'. A nice toolset I could use around the house or a sturdy shovel. I'm always looking for a nice shovel." He checked his .38-caliber revolver one last time before pushing it into pocket.

"He doesn't have a garage. I told ya, he parks on the street." Johnny pointed to a black front door set into a white three-story unit with lace-lined curtains and well-trimmed shrubs lining its front. "Here's his house." It was all handsome enough for a magazine cover if a photographer ever strolled past. There were no open spots for blocks around the place, so Johnny double parked at an angle with his front end pressing into the street. It would be easy enough to engage Berdan with an innocuous question and be on him a few heartbeats later with nowhere for him to go. The nerves were present, but manageable as they sat. Johnny had hoped they would arrive earlier, but Berdan's car was still there, a copper-brown Cadillac El Dorado. So they waited. And waited.

"You know this is the gun I used on my first job?" Nick said. "I haven't used it every time, but it was there on the first one." Nick held the gun with both hands as though it were a museum piece. "It was this Irish enforcer. Some red-headed motherfucker who clubbed one of our guys over the head in their own bar. I think it was Gallina who got his ass beat."

Johnny nodded politely. He was accustomed to Nick's autobiographical monologues. It was like listening to the dull thud of a hammer and nail. "Yeah, I remember Pops tellin' me stories about Sandy," he said, remembering a few vague tales. "He ended up with a limp, didn't he?"

Nick laughed. "Yeah, but not from that beating. He got his ass kicked a lot for a wise guy. Some guys are just like that."

Johnny's anger bubbled as he listened, perhaps from lack of sleep, perhaps not. Nick continued, "Most military guys, even stateside, are tough motherfuckers. Sandy's shit didn't translate. He got away from his unit and went all soft. Or maybe he was already soft, we never ran into one another over there, so I guess I can't say for sure. I just know this Irish guy beat his goddamn ass with a pool cue. Huge dude, must've weighed three hundred pounds. I took this .38 right here and put one in him from twenty yards or so before he even knew the reason. Is that how you'd want it? Or would you want a minute with—Hey." Nick hit Johnny on the arm. "Is that him?"

Johnny followed Nick's finger to an alleyway where a well-dressed blond man was walking toward the front in a green suit with a small brown briefcase.

Johnny's nerves flared. "Yeah. That's him."

"All right then. Wish me luck." Nick exited the car and crossed the street quickly. Johnny's window was still down and Nick's steps echoed off the quiet houses. Johnny scanned the street. There were three or four people outside and within earshot, but it was as good a moment as they were likely to get.

"Excuse me, sir?" Nick called as he reached the sidewalk and Berdan reached his car. They were about twenty feet apart, close enough that Nick instinctually tilted his head down to avoid his target's direct gaze.

"Yes?" Mr. Berdan asked, confused and annoyed. Another couple steps. Ten feet now.

"Did you talk to the cops?" Nick asked, raising his head now to face the man, eye to eye. Berdan's face went white and he stumbled backward, but it was too late. Nick drew the .38 and fired 1-2-3-4 shots in measured cadence as he continued pressing forward, closer, tighter. Berdan fell backward to the pavement, still and motionless. Nick crouched over his body, grabbed him by the shirt collar and pulled him to a seated position. He placed the muzzle of his revolver to the dying man's right eye and squeezed. Mr. Berdan's blood sprayed the sidewalk, and concrete jumped into the air behind him. Nick reset his target and squeezed again into his left eye before releasing the collar and allowing his victim to fall. He straddled the body as it lay and yelled to the sparse pedestrians at the top of his voice, "THIS IS WHAT HAPPENS WHEN YOU TALK TO COPS!" He pushed the gun back into his pocket and jogged toward the car before stopping abruptly, searching Johnny's anxious face for just a moment, and turning back. He kneeled by Berdan again, slipped the gold watch from his wrist and the briefcase from his hand.

"Look, John, we're rich," Nick said when he reached the car. Johnny spun the tires as they drove away.

The morning of June 14, 1973
19ᵗʰ Precinct in Manhattan, NY
"It escalated much quicker than we ever imagined."

Detective Clayburgh was at his desk, aimlessly thumbing a stack of case files when Captain Quinn arrived at the precinct. He did not greet them but watched closely as he crossed the bullpen in his dress uniform with three decades' worth of accolades on his chest. The others in the room stared determinedly at their desks, unwilling to risk the captain's eye contact for even the briefest of moments. When Quinn reached his office, he immediately cinched his blinds shut, and the furtive law enforcers around him were free to resume their routines.

Murdock dug a fist into his dry red eyes. "When he asks us, what are we gonna suggest?"

Clayburgh chortled into his mustache. "I'm not sure we're going to get *asked* anything." He grabbed Murdock's mug along with his own and fetched two fresh cups of coffee. The crime scene adrenaline faded quickly after their 6:45 a.m., arrival and by now their bodies were running on fumes. Their minds stayed restless though. The image of Christopher Berdan sprawled across the pavement, his face and chest marred by black blood circles, was difficult to shake. So they drank coffee and stared at case files that might as well have been blank.

Patty Uhlhousen was the captain's secretary and the first NYPD employee to speak with him each morning, so when her light-brown beehive disappeared into the captain's office, Clayburgh knew their summons was imminent. Murdock straightened his notebooks and took a few final pulls of caffeine before Patty reappeared, pointed two silent fingers at the detectives, and motioned to the office door. They rose in unison and made their way to the room.

The captain had already unbuttoned the neck of his uniform and was standing at the back of the room with a glass of brown liquor in his hand. "Sit," he said. The men sat. "Before we start this, I want to say I trust the two of you. Maybe you are both assholes and I'm going to get burned for that, but let's just start there. As men and as detectives, I trust you."

The detectives nodded. "Thank you, sir."

The captain grabbed two more glasses and a bottle from underneath his desk, poured the detectives their own drinks, and fell back into his chair. "Go ahead then, gentlemen."

Clayburgh began, "Mr. Berdan was shot, once in each eye and four times in the abdomen, while walking to his car this morning around 6:00 a.m. We recovered .38-caliber rounds from the scene. We have one witness on the street who claims there were at least five other witnesses who did not stay to talk to us. She told us that she could not identify the man, but she made a point of mouthing the word *mafia* to us." Clayburgh looked up at this, but the captain did not react. "We canvased the houses nearby, and two neighbors," he held up his fingers for emphasis, "claim the gunmen yelled as he shot Mr. Berdan."

"Yelled?" the captain asked. "What…in pain? Anger?"

Clayburgh glanced at his notes but didn't need them. "He yelled 'Don't talk to cops,' sir." The captain took a drink and nodded for him to continue. "According to Mrs. Berdan, her husband left at about the same time every day. She did not notice any suspicious vehicles, but their bedroom is on the backside of the house and she says they could have driven away before she had a clear view of the street. The other witness reported a vehicle, which she could only identify as 'not a truck' and red, spun out its tires as it was leaving. We did find marks confirming that on the far side of the street. That was when Mrs. Berdan came downstairs and she confirms there were other witnesses on the street who, quote, 'were so scared they ran.'" He paused. "She believes, like the other witnesses, that the shooter yelled immediately after firing, although she says she could not confirm what was actually said." They sat in silence for a moment. "That is everything we know right now."

The captain took another drink and wriggled his collar an extra inch away from his neck. "I've got the facts. Opinions?"

Murdock said, "Obviously, our assumption is it's connected to his coming forward about Mr. Benfield's murder. This precinct specifically is clearly and directly implicated. Somebody follows him for a couple days and, boom, hits him in the morning on his way to work."

"He screams in the middle of the street and we can't get one description of this fuckin' guy?"

"Only the woman on the street actually saw the shooter, and I don't think she got a very good look. Like Andy says, she was mouthing the word *mafia*, but she was also yelling she didn't see his face at the top of her lungs. You know, for the benefit of any neighbors that might be watching…"

The captain walked over to his window. "Let's talk about people with knowledge of his visit."

"Honestly, sir, anyone in the bullpen could've figured it out," Clayburgh said. "Either overheard us talking about him, checked a logbook, seen him waiting in the room, or looking through the book, anything." He took a drink of what Quinn had given him. "I think they got it wrong though. Whoever it was thought Berdan was worth killing. He wasn't. He couldn't make the ID. He was no help at all. If we had a suspect, he might've been an asset, but as it stood, we had nothing yet."

"Unless the Benfield shooter is a person worth protecting," Murdock said. "A more important guy than just some hired gun. Maybe they just didn't want to take a chance with Berdan. This way, he's gone for good, no chances."

"So, we're at 100 percent the Italians are involved, right?" the captain asked. "'Cause up till this point, all I've heard is you have witnesses of tan men walking around."

"Yes, sir, 100 percent. We are absolutely convinced the two men we saw at the union headquarters rigged that election, or knew it was going to be rigged, and we are absolutely convinced Berdan was killed for coming forward as a witness in the Benfield murder. The witness, the union implications…it's not a conviction's worth of information, but we'd be stupid to ignore the smoke."

The captain opened his exterior blinds and gave the morning sun free access to the office. "And what's the union angle? It's the cement union?"

"Benfield was the president of the union," Murdock said, "and shortly after his death, and by shortly I mean like ten minutes, the vice president retired under suspicious circumstances. And that 'suspicious' label is from the man's own wife. And then at the election, some nobody gets elected from out of left field with three-fourths of the vote. They're racketeers, this is what they do."

"There were two men in a car, waiting on the results of the election," Quinn remembered from the briefing they gave him the day before. "That's the conclusion of your stakeout?"

"The men in the car were there to make sure the election was successful, successfully rigged. Brady said the winner was a nobody, but that doesn't do it justice. He wasn't on the ballot. All his votes were write ins. It was absolutely blatant election rigging, but the union members don't seem to care."

"And how do you want to move forward, Detectives?" They hesitated to answer, and the captain turned to look at them. He was still a foot or so from his office window with the light bouncing off his various medals and shaved head. "Surely you have discussed some ideas?"

Clayburgh said, "We have pictures of the two men we think were connected to the election. We think we should canvas a few of the businesses around the union headquarters or related to the union contracts or something along those lines and see what we get."

Murdock fiddled with his notebook. "We also have...Paul Downes, the new union president. I think we should talk to him."

The captain sat back at his desk and finished the last of his drink. He went about rebuttoning his collar and dabbing perspiration from his forehead as he talked. "Leave Downes alone for now. If the canvas doesn't turn anything up, he'll still be there. But I want an ID on these two men at the election first...fuckin' wop gangs."

"Yes, sir."

"And you will report directly to me," Quinn said, his green eyes boring into their foreheads. "How many Italians work here?"

Clayburgh smoothed his moustache. "Maybe fifteen, sir. Do you mean Italian last names or ethnically Italian?"

"You get the point. Officer Rigatoni's don't work this case. I don't trust this place right now."

"Yes, sir."

June 1973
An outdoor produce market in the Bronx, NY

Ricky had sent the kid back inside to change, but he had not expected this. "You can't wear a fuckin' suit to a job like this," he had said. "Nobody is gonna believe some two-bit hoodlum is wearin' a $300 suit to a fuckin' job. You gotta go change," and the kid had done as he was told. He was lucky it was Ricky working with him and not Nico or Vinnie or Petey. They would have let him go dressed in the suit and then never let him hear the end of it. They might have taken pictures and hung them up at The Blue Raven for all the guests to see…but the second outfit, a faded orange and blue button-down, wrinkled flat cap, jeans scuffed with black (asphalt?) and extending just past midshin, may have been worse.

"I have to ask," Ricky laughed, "who the fuck would wear this shit?" Ricky laughed. "Like, at the store, who paid money for it?"

"It was my brother's," Benjie said. "I got all his old clothes."

Ricky poked a finger through the thigh of the jeans, exposing the pocket liner and pale skin beneath it. "And your brother is eighty-seven now or what?"

Benjie chuckled, his cheeks reddened. "No, he's thirtysomething. C'mon, it's not that bad."

"Kid, it's horrible, but at least they'll be lookin' for someone with a fuckin' time machine. That might throw them off our trail."

"I don't wear it *obviously*. This way, it don't matter if I fuck it up, ya know, 'cause I don't wear it."

"Says the guy who came out in a suit the first time. Whatever, here we go."

* * *

Mr. Birkhelder was going about his solitary business, chopping and rolling a log of red meat, while Benjie and Ricky watched him from a parking lot fifty yards away, hidden among a few cars like the weeds. A small light bulb swung above his head in the stall, and a soft breeze kept it moving, throwing shadows over one side and then the other. His arms were thick from butchering stuff, and his movements were deft and certain even in the unstable light.

"What's Petey got against this guy?" Benjie asked. No one had explained anything to him. Vic had just told him somebody from Petey Caltagirone's crew was going to pick him up a little after 8:00 p.m.

"It's not this guy, really. Petey's got a grander plan."

Benjie was too uncomfortable in silence not to investigate further. "He didn't pick this guy?"

"Kind of. He told me either Birkhelder," Rick pointed at the cleaving butcher, "or another guy, Krakowski. He said to avoid the Jew if possible. That could be construed as a hate crime."

"What's the grander plan?"

"That's above your pay grade, kid."

Benjie did not have another question ready and went back to watching Birkhelder chop and roll and toss, so Ricky filled the conversational void. "You work for Vic Palmieri then?"

"Yeah."

"How long?"

"I've known him a long time. I started workin' for my brothers first, about a year ago. Vic, not as long."

"Not long enough to have been arrested though?"

"No...you?"

"No. Jail is a boring-ass place to sit from what I've seen though. I was just curious though, not pryin'."

"What you goin' to jail for without an arrest?"

"My dumbass father. He went in last December."

"How long is he in for?"

"Ten to fifteen years, they said. Should be longer if they ever ask my opinion."

Benjie was again without a question. He looked back at Birkhelder, his forearms, red meat, and swaying lightbulb. He pulled a cigarette from his pack and lit it. "I know how that is, I guess."

It took Ricky a moment to find his meaning. "You've got family locked up?"

Benjie shook his head no. "I got a shitty father. My ma raised me with my older brothers. They're in the Life too. They're not *capos* or anything like that, but they're respected guys."

"*Capos?*"

"Yeah, like the leaders of a *cosche?*" Ricky's eyes were blank, and Benjie shook his head. "Never mind. Some guys in the Life talk like that."

Watching Benjie puff his smoke into the car made Ricky want a cigarette, so he pulled his own and lit it. "You ever see your shitty father then?"

"I've only ever seen a picture of him. It's from Christmas when I was a kid."

"He dead?"

"I don't know." Benjie thought about the question a moment longer. "I think my brothers might know where he went. But if they do, there's a good chance he's dead. Vito would've killed him."

Ricky hit his cigarette and cracked the window to coax night air into the car. "Not havin' him around might be better in the end."

"I could see that," Benjie shrugged. "And I ain't got nothin' to complain about. My brothers were good to me."

"What about your ma?"

"She's got her problems, but I'm alive, right?"

"Yeah, my ma is the same way. She's got her issues, but there were days when we didn't make it easy. Pops was always on some bullshit errands and prolly fuckin' other women for all I know. Ma did enough to raise us, pushed us in some direction at least, even if we didn't listen."

"Yeah, she pushed me somewhere, did something at least...I'm not too mad at her for that shit. I can barely take care of myself. She had three of us and raised me entirely by herself—"

Ricky sat forward and dropped his cigarette out the window. "He's movin'..."

They watched Birkhelder pull the chain switch on the light-bulb and throw darkness over his butcher block. The moonlight was enough to see his silhouette removing his apron and tousling through compartments on the edges of his stall in preparation to leave. They discussed not knowing which side Birkhelder would exit to. Ricky said, "No way to tell. We'll have to cover both sides."

"Okay. You want me to use that path and come in from that side?"

"Yeah, go quick." The two quietly exited the car, closed their doors, and moved to flank the stall. Benjie hustled to crouch in between two units a few spaces down from Birkhelder's on the right. He checked back along the narrow gravel path to the parking lot where a few civilians were still milling around their vehicles and talking with others as they left. They were far enough away to not matter, Benjie thought, but still close enough to warrant attention. If Birkhelder yelled, they would hear. Benjie's nerves blossomed, adrenaline pouring into his arms, his chest, his head. He took a few breaths, deep purposeful breaths, to encourage the adrenaline he felt. He flexed the tips of his fingers into fists and leaned from his alcove to peek again at Birkhelder's booth. He could see his form, visible but vague in the nighttime, flicking from one task to the next until he shoved the butcher block back and padlocked it to the foundation of his booth. When he turned to leave, he made his way toward Benjie's flank. Ricky was lost to the darkness. Benjie squinted after him, hoping he was just steps behind their mark, but he was not. Another few steps and Birkhelder looked taller than he had behind the block. Benjie was crouching, could that be it? Another few steps and his arms were thicker and shining despite the dampened light. Another few steps and he'd draw even. *Where was Ricky?*

Benjie jumped from his hiding place, no more than a step in front of Birkhelder. He was shocked to find himself taller than the man, but the other's muscles were imposing from any angle.

"Are you named Birkhelder?" Benjie asked, aware of the high-pitched uncertainty in his voice.

Birkhelder's eyes flicked up and down Benjie's frame. "Who are you?" he growled.

Benjie's mouth searched for an answer, his lips moving soundlessly, and Birkhelder's expression turned suspicious. Benjie acted. He swung at the man's jaw and connected. Pain cloaked his hand and slowed its function. Birkhelder's head jerked with surprise more than pain, and his recovery was swift. Before Benjie's hand could aid in his defense, Birkhelder landed a punch to Benjie's mouth, another to his rib, another to his ear and cheek. Benjie stumbled back but kept his feet. Blood stained his teeth. He swung again; the butcher blocked it and kicked him in the leg. Benjie swung again, more desperate, more wild, and this was blocked again. He was punched in the jaw and again in the ear, and then he was on the gravel. The rough surface sliced his back through his button-down as he writhed away and kicked, desperate to be on his feet and mobile, but Birkhelder avoided the kicks and fell on top of him. His weight pushed Benjie into the ground. More wild swings and he caught Benjie's arms, holding them where he would. He leaned close to Benjie's face and growled, his gray teeth discernable even in the sparse moonlight. And then they were not. As impossible as Birkhelder's weight and strength had been, it was gone in a moment, chased away by a streak and a boot, which splintered the butcher's nose. Benjie felt the spray of blood as Birkhelder shook his head in anger and frustration, still instinctively holding Benjie's arms. A second kick fell flush again, and the butcher scrambled to avoid a third. Benjie rolled and pushed himself to his feet. Ricky had not allowed Birkhelder to recover and smothered him with hasty pressure. A shove put the disoriented man on the ground, a kick to the ribs, a punch to the face, an elbow, a jab, an elbow, a jab, a jab, a moment for collection and another swing, more violent, more recoiled, more powerful, and another that forced Birkhelder's head sharply into the hard rocks. The butcher's arms stiffened, his movements ceased in a hopeful position, a position of surrender. Ricky relaxed to pace, breathing heavily, and allowed the injured man's senses to return. He stood and scanned the area, but there was no one close to them and the few in the nearby lot were giving each other furtive glances, if any at all, and making for their cars.

"Great work," Ricky joked, his smile obvious even in the murky understanding of Benjie's senses. "God damnit, kid. Now I'm tired."

"Fuck you."

"Shhh…we'll talk about it. Birkhelder?" Ricky said. "C'mon, dumbass." He walked over to the butcher, who was prostrate on his back, and patted his cheeks. Blood covered the butcher's nose and eyebrow and poured to the ground in a dark stream. At least a few of his teeth were chipped and broken, but his eyes opened, moving unfocused across the clouded night sky. "Hey, buddy," Ricky said, "you know Petey Caltagirone?" Birkhelder nodded. "Tell him, we don't want him over here. Tell him, he don't got the weight to protect his people down here. You got that?" Birkhelder nodded again. "Good. I don't wanna come back and remind ya. You're a humble butcher, not a hero. And next time, I'll be carryin'. I'll put one in your fuckin' head and bury you right next to your goddamn stall. Don't forget to tell that bitch-ass Petey Fingers what I said."

At the car, Ricky hesitated to turn the key, but sat instead in the darkness with Benjie wiping the blood from his mouth and inspecting the developing bruises on his brow and cheeks. Ricky said, "We can fix that, you know?"

"What?"

"You gettin' your ass beat. That ain't safe."

"He was stronger than me. And older."

"We can fix one of those. The other should be your advantage, not his."

"Whatever."

"Just sayin'. Just sayin' it's not safe for you out here if you can't throw hands better than that."

June 1973
Wedding boutique in Manhattan, NY
"It was a bad idea. It was always a bad idea."

The lace edges of the wedding dress dug mercilessly into Carrie's skin. She gave up adjustments and curled her fingers inside the sweetheart neckline while her mother tugged on her skirt and train. Jennie's reflection bobbed and weaved in and out of the mirror as she hustled to the shelves and back with another and another dress for her sister to try on. Each time she dropped one, Carrie's friend Kitty inspected and sorted the piece into one of two piles, Kitty smiles or Kitty frowns. The system was remarkably ineffective.

Besides the lace edges, the dress was modern but desperately restrictive around her waist and chest beyond anyone's ability to fix. The sleeves, half-sleeves ending at the elbow, were lined by the same lace as the neck and caused bulges where the edge squeezed her skin. She pinched a fold with her finger. There was enough work ahead of her, too much to worry about the tightness of her sleeves. "I'm not getting this one, Ma. It itches and these sleeves are ugly."

Cris gave an accusatory frown. "You're spoiled."

"Am I supposed to wear itchy dresses just to prove to you I'm not spoiled? And if I am spoiled, you spoiled me. Don't try and turn that around on me."

Jennie walked in front of Carrie and tugged the skirt to its fullest diameter, eyeing her lines. "She's right, Ma. I don't like this one. Where's the other one, Kit?"

"Which one?" Kitty asked, suspicious that Jennie was referencing one of her strongest frowns. "Not the high necked? Can we get rid of that one?"

"Fine, bring her that one there," Jennie said, her eyes rolling lightly. "It doesn't have as much lace. At least not on the neckline where it's digging into her."

"Ugh," Cris said, bopping Carrie's chest with the back of her hand, "so now you want to throw away the lace entirely?"

"I didn't even say the word *lace*, Ma." Carrie tugged again at the dress, impatient to have it back on the rack. "All I said was *this dress itches.*"

Her mother raised her hands. "Get married in a sheet then, Carrie!"

"Deal," Carrie said, but her sister cut it off and said, "Shut up. Ma, calm down with the lace. Nobody is getting rid of the lace."

"Here's the low-cut," Kitty said, and Carrie flattened the fabric against her skin. It looked as slim as the last one, maybe more so. She said, "My boobs will fall out of this one."

"Bobby'd like it…not that you need to worry about him," Kitty said, giggling over Carrie's shoulder. "Feel your power, Car. Remember, it's your day."

Jennie searched for the zipper on the back of the current dress. "How the hell do we get this one off?"

"You're completely giving up on this dress then?"

"For the sake of ending this conversation, yes," Carrie said. "This one's done."

Jennie found the zipper and pulled the dress from her sister's shoulders. Carrie kicked out of the white linen to step into the next. It was nearly as slim as she'd thought, but sleeveless and with less lace. "Better."

"Bobby will love it."

"Kitty's right, not everything is about him."

"Well, he should probably have some influence on the thing, even if he's not here."

"He wouldn't notice if I wore a twenty-dollar thing."

"That's not true, but it is more your day than his. We have to find one that speaks to you, Car."

Carrie held a satirical hand to her ear. "They're telling me to wrap this up and get the wedding over so everybody can go back to their lives."

"They don't mean that," Cris snapped with a scowl and another weak swat. Her angst was redoubling as she supervised.

"I do mean that. The money is already a nightmare."

"Your Father would cringe to hear you say that," Cris said. She delicately pulled Carrie's recently manicured curls over the back of the new dress. "He has worked so much for you. More money than we had combined when we married or for years after."

"I didn't blame anyone. Certainly not him."

"He wants his girls to be happy, and he'd do anything for either of you."

"Ma, end this lecture. It's a nightmare *and* it's nobody's fault."

"What about this?" Jennie said, holding a fistful of dress in her hand to slim the front and distract. "Could we trim this? Well, not us, but someone around here?"

"I would think they could trim that layer, right? Mrs. Giordano, what do you think?"

"I don't know why you'd want to. It's fine."

"Ma, it's gonna sag if we don't."

"Don't get married in a mud pit and it should be fine."

"I still think the beach is ideal. Did you ever think about the beach?"

"Bobby's parents would stab me in the neck. Catholic everything or they'll flip."

"Priests are allowed near water. Why would that matter?"

"His mother would freak if it wasn't at a traditional church with an organ and everything."

"It's hard to find a family more concentrated on traditions than your Father, but the Guiffridas are it. Was his mother born in Sicily? I know his father was."

"Yeah."

"Our compatriots in language," Cris said, almost reverent. "And good people."

"What does that mean?"

Jennie laughed. "What part, Kit? Compatriots?"

"The Guiffridas speak Western Sicilian instead of one of the other dialects," Cris explained. "The dialects in the hills, the dialects on the eastern side, they're different than those in the west."

Jennie continued to tug her sister one way and then the next, her brow furrowed with concentration. "I couldn't understand any of them if Daddy didn't talk so slow."

"I thought it was Italian?"

"Oh god," Carrie said. "Don't bring this up. Stay ignorant, please."

"Sicily has a distinct culture, Kitty," Cris said. "Like Georgia from Massachusetts."

"Like Massachusetts and Mexico if Daddy answers that question."

Kitty pressed on innocently, "Well, you grew up there, Mrs. Giordano, didn't you?"

Carrie made another plea with her eyes, to no avail, but her mother's mood did seem to be improving with this talk. *It may be worth the sacrifice.*

"I lived there until I was seventeen. We were poor and smelled like fish, and then we climbed on a boat with all the money my Father saved in his life and came here. Some good, some bad since. In both places, my family, the Levocchios, were poor and smelled. When Alphonse came along, he told my Father, he says, 'Your daughter is gonna get everything she ever wanted.' My Father thought that was the American dream."

"Did you then…get what you wanted?" Kitty asked with a smile.

Cris turned to Jennie and Carrie. "Hardly. I wanted two sensible daughters. I got zero."

"You were happy," Carrie said.

Cris shrugged. "All lovers are happy for a time. You and Bobby should enjoy yours for as long as you can. And then you'll have children and all your happiness will go away."

"What was Mr. Giordano like when he was younger? It's hard for me to imagine, honestly."

"He was smart and thought he was smarter than he was. Tough and thought he was tougher than he was. But unpredictable. That was what brought me to him. He surprised me when so many men were boring. I knew what they were going to say before they did. Alphonse had a passion in him then...and now, I guess. Different forms of passion, some would call it anger, some ambition, some aggression, some love. It all depends on your lens."

Jennie smirked at her sister through the mirror. "Do you see those things in Bobby?"

Carrie glared at the hidden jab. "I *have* seen it, thank you. You have to look a little harder sometimes. But it's there."

"I want my man to be boring," Jennie said. "I want to be so bored by him that I fall asleep by our pool in the Hamptons next to our helipad."

"Money isn't everything. I've told you kids this so many times. He needs to respect you. It's about more than money."

"Daddy doesn't *respect* you," Jennie teased, "he *loves* you, but he doesn't ask—"

Carrie heard the *crack* but didn't see it. Her eyes hesitated to look for it. She knew what happened but hoped the next moment might be a step in another direction, back in time to the easy pace of their conversation. It was not. The look on Jennie's face explained it, anger mixed up with shame and embarrassment and fear. She had rouge on her cheek, but their mother's hand marked her as if it had been covered in red paint. Kitty's jaw was slack, Carrie's flexed. Cristiana Giordano leaned close to her youngest child's ear, grabbed the lobe, and pulled it to her lips. What she whispered, Carrie never knew.

One night in June 1973
The Blue Raven Social Club in the Bronx, NY
"It was all a part of the ruthless pursuit."

Ricky frowned at the blue light cast over the stage, the band, and their instruments. "Is that the only light filter we have around here?" he asked Sean the Irishman but changed his mind before he could answer. "Fuck it, never mind. That's not my problem." Ricky downed the rest of his whiskey and showed Benjie the empty glass. "Shit's not bad, is it?"

"Not at all," Benjie said, smiling over a swollen lip. His eyes were already glossed by alcohol and flickered with sexual deviance each time one of the Blue Raven girls passed him. "Who is that?" he asked after a particular brunette.

"Laura," Ricky said.

Kay Dedrick heard the name as she dropped a tray of empty pints for Sean and followed his eyes for its source. "She calls herself Duchess if anybody else asks. You should probably learn the names of your girls, Ricky."

"I know her name. It's Laura. Duchess is nobody's name..." Ricky turned to Benjie. "Call her Duchess or whatever the fuck else she tells you to call her. There, you happy, Beatrice?"

Kay fought a smile. "She's got a guy that drops her off."

"An Italian guy?"

Kay shrugged. "How do I know if he's Italian?"

"He look Italian?"

"He looks like he's been fuckin' her, Italian or otherwise."

"All right, we get the point then," Ricky said. "What do you gotta break his heart for? Let her know Benjie is with us. He's a hard worker, well-endowed, I assume...I don't fuckin' know, tell her some good stuff about him. His right jab aside, he's not a bad kid. And with the swollen face, it's harder to tell how ugly he is."

"So romantic, the two of you. I can't promise she'll sleep with you, Benjie, but I'll let her know how beautiful you think she is."

Ricky called for his Irishman. "Sean! Two drinks, bud."

An aggressive new song howled from the stage, and the up-jump in volume received a soft cheer and brought a few patrons up from their seats to dance. "Who's the band?" Benjie asked.

"I don't know," Ricky said. "I don't pick the bands."

"Who does?"

"One of Petey's guys, Buddy. He's got a set of glasses that would put a few satellites to shame. You can't miss him." Ricky scanned the area quickly, but Buddy was nowhere to be found. "Let's look in on the cardroom, kid."

"I don't play cards."

"That's by far the smartest thing you've said to me." Ricky led the way past a few more girls to the cardroom door, introducing Benjie and Nico as they entered. The green felt table sat as it had before, a few feet from Vinnie's watchful eye and covered in chips of every color. Ricky recognized the men by now. Dr. Scheinberg looked to have parleyed a run of luck into a new gold watch on his wrist. Joey Jugs Poletti sat next to him, the underworld twin of Petey: an overweight Giordano Family decision maker obsessed with cigars and money. Ricky recognized Capello soldier Bennie Ricasoli at the table, whose emotions were so manic only Vinnie would talk to him anymore. And then Nick Pisani, already a blossoming regular, and his second, Paulie. Ricky had little direct contact with Nick, but the respect afforded him by the others was worth mentioning.

"…and that's Nick Pisani, he's one of—"

"I know Nick," Benjie said.

"What do you mean you know him?"

"I mean I know him. He's eats lunch with Vic at Jerry Turnino's restaurant all the time—" but the explanation was unnecessary because Nick had seen them from across the room.

"What in the fuck! Benjie?" Nick called, rising from the table and greeting Benjie in his usual way. "You get in a scrap, kid? What the hell is this?"

"Uh, yeah…I was helpin' them out." Benjie looked and felt sheepish about the bruises and his fat lip, but Nick was delighted.

"Ricky," Nick said, beaming at Benjie with pride and disbelief, "is this your fault? How you gonna let this kid get his ass beat? I thought you was a fighter?"

"I...I came in eventually," Ricky said. "I had to see what he's got first." It sounded more defensive than he wanted; he was thrown by the familiarity between two people so disparate in his mind. He looked briefly at Vinnie, his eyes pleading for another body in the conversation. None came.

"Well, no matter what the other guy looks like, this is a good thing. Rick, bring him a girl or somethin'. Look at this guy, I'm fuckin' proud of this guy." Ricky walked to the door and yelled something indistinguishable into the main room. "Take a seat," Nick said to Benjie with his eyes moving between cuts and bruises. "Pull a chair up and let's talk about it. You get any good licks into him?"

"A few maybe. I hit him a couple times before he knocked me off my feet."

"You gotta make that first one count somehow. Weightlift or spar or somethin'. That first punch is gonna be the most accurate one you'll throw, and you gotta make it count. You gotta cause some damage to the other guy."

"Yeah, I'm gonna be workin' on it. I'll have to."

"Still, that's some good shit, kid," Nick said, clapping Benjie on the back. "Don't worry about the bruises, they'll heal. If you throw a couple of them scraps together, you'll get the idea. The average man spends his whole life avoidin' pain, avoidin' a fair scrap like that, so when he's in there, he's uncomfortable, he wants it to be over. Most guys, the average guys, were born to turn and run. If you can smother that instinct, you'll be six steps ahead of average."

When Ricky returned, he had the girl named Laura or Duchess on his arm and a shameless smile. Benjie's nerves prickled his insides. Her slender body was not too slender to press firmly against the Blue Raven's uniform in all the right places, tight and true around her curves. Her hair was brown and to her shoulders and shined despite the rough light in the cardroom. Benjie was still in his chair as she made herself at home on his lap.

Laura carried their conversation until Benjie drank enough to push his confidence past its threshold. Then his grabs became more aggressive and his thoughts less decent for an hour or more, lost in his daydreams. *She is interested all right. Look at how her eyes shudder and blink. Look how she drinks her drink. She sees how I am with Nick, with Ricky, and she knows they're important. She knows the money they make*—until the cardroom doors clapped sharply against the flanking walls from some swift push. Petey burst into the room, his tie tracing his protruding stomach and a taut white dress shirt, translucent with perspiration. "Guys, sorry," he said with clumsy, drunken words, "we need the fuckin' room. Sorry, Dr. Scheinberg, Bennie, Paulie, sorry guys. Emergency. Ricky, Benjie, you guys too, get out. Vinnie will count the chips and pay out with a bonus for the inconvenience. Ricky, tell your fuckin' Irishman to throw these guys some drinks."

The men rose slowly but obediently from the table and made their way back into the club area. Benjie patted Laura on the backside and bid her follow him with the others to the satellite bar where he collected a whiskey pour for himself and another for the lithe brunette who had taken such control of his attentions. She smiled playfully as he ran his finger along her jawline, rested it briefly on her chin, and then cupped her cheek with his thumb against her lips. She bit it briefly, her brown eyes in his, and rubbed his chest until she grabbed his tie and pulled him in close. She whispered, "The bruises make you look dangerous. Are you dangerous?"

"More dangerous every day," he said.

"Good. Dangerous is good." She pulled back and finished her drink with one aggressive swig before setting the glass back on the bar with a forceful rap. "Sean, another for us. One each."

Benjie smiled and forced his own down. Laura let him hold her around the waist, teasing him with playful banter and touches as the two ordered Sean to refill their glasses again and again…

"Benjie. Get the fuck up." Benjie heard the words but could not obey. "Hey, get the fuck up, man. Now. You're still at the fuckin' bar." The words disappointed him instinctually, but his conscious mind was slow to grasp their literal meaning. And then the bottom fell out below him and his weight teleported him to the ground. His shoulder hit the hard floor from a sheer drop, three to four feet in the air, causing him to cough the air from his lungs. "Told ya, motherfucker. Get up." Benjie wheezed and opened his eyes, an inch from the floor. A soft kick tapped his ribs. "C'mon, man. Let's go." Benjie rolled over and saw Ricky, his suit halfway disassembled, standing over him. "C'mon, you can sleep in my office."

Benjie pushed his palm into his forehead to ease the budding discomfort behind it. "What the fuck?"

"Get up. You passed out on my goddamn bar. I've got somethin' for ya."

Benjie sat up, another degree of shame finding him as he did. "What?"

"Here," Ricky said, tossing him a stack of money several inches high. "For you gettin' your head bashed in. Congratulations."

"What?"

"It's not charity. Vinny came here tonight, not my Vinnie, another Vinny…Vinny Cacase came here tonight and had to pay Petey some restitution. I guess one of Petey's friends got beat up down at this market Vinny runs. Vinny says he can't believe anyone would have the balls to attack someone under his protection." Benjie could see Ricky's grin plastered from ear to ear. "Yeah, so there's your cut, Petey says. For bein' a loyal guy, I guess, and not beatin' up his friends."

Benjie flipped quickly through the stack. "Where's Laura? Or Duchess?"

Ricky laughed. "She's gone. It's 4:00 a.m."

"Shit."

"Yeah, not your best work. I hope it's not anyway. Get up." Ricky tugged Benjie to his feet as the kid felt blindly for the bar with his useless limbs. "In my office. This way."

"Where's Laura?"

"She's gone."

"Call her back. You're her boss."

"She's not a prostitute. You want some girl, go find her on the corner. Tonight might not be the night though."

"God damnit. How long has she been gone?"

"Long enough. Don't worry about it until tomorrow." Ricky showed Benjie his office before hailing a cab and heading home. Benjie tried to finish himself in the men's restroom and fell asleep on the tile floor with his pants around his ankles. Ricky found him that way at noon the next day.

One night in June 1973
Queens, NY
"If we had tapes of that…man, if we had tapes of that meeting…"

Alphonse twirled his cane into the passenger-side floor of his blue-on-cream Chrysler as Phil drove him through Queens. "I'm not used to sittin' in the front seat," he said to Phil. "Only when I'm driving the wife. I feel like I have to pay attention when I'm up here." The streetlights caught their faces in brief glints of light and shadow as they moved past blocks of empty black windows and burned-out shops. They were looking for a Health Club.

Phil asked, "How did he get his hands on this place, ya think?"

"I don't know. He was always into that stuff when we were younger. He probably always wanted his own."

Phil weaved his way through a series of clumsy turns until he found the street he was looking for. "Where the fuck am I supposed to park around here?"

"What do you mean? Park right there," Al said, pointing to an untended lot surrounded by crumbling half walls marred by graffiti.

Phil stared at Al, incredulous. "In the open? They'll jack the car."

"Nobody's gonna jack the car. Park right there. Who's gonna jack the car?"

"Who do you think is spray paintin' that graffiti everywhere? You kiddin' me, park in that lot? Do you watch the news?"

"Park the damn car, Phil."

"Okay, but…there's fuckin' hoodlums runnin' around out here." Phil stopped the car with an askance eye in each direction and hustled to open the door for Al. "Eight-four-three-two is the address," he said. "There should be some sort of sign around here, right? A storefront or some kind of mail slot." Phil stared at the address he had written down as if it might become a helpful arrow. Al started off along the sidewalk, and Phil hurried to catch up to him. "It's this way?"

"North," Al said. "There's bigger numbers." He pointed to an address painted on the sidewalk.

It was oppressively hot during the day, but the night was fresh and comfortable as they walked to the Health Club. Al evaluated Phil's ensemble (a black suit with white pinstripes and a red tie) as they made their way. He was a veteran, an old-school, dark-humored veteran, but he was not above the Don's judgmental looks. *Discipline.*

The pair slowed as they came to a well-maintained building with floor-to-ceiling windows and a neon sign that read "Health Club" in bright white lights. Phil pressed his eyes against the black windows. He knocked. Immediately, the overhead lights inside began to whir, pinpricks on the other side of the glass, and two hazy figures appeared and grew as they crossed the room. Al knew them as they got closer, the familiar shapes of Don Frank Capello and his under-boss Charlie Guiffrida.

Charlie pushed the doors open. "Don Giordano," he said, hugging and kissing Al before greeting Phil the same way. Frank Capello was just behind, and Al shook his head as long-forgotten memories pushed their way back into his consciousness. "Old Friend," he said, hugging Don Capello and then holding him at arm's length for a better look. He was still a robust individual with black hair combed back tightly over his scalp until it ended in subtle curls over his neck. "Old Friend," Frank answered, smiling. "Come on in. I have quite the night planned."

The lights were still whirring their way on as they crossed the main room, their path scattered with half-illuminated dumb bells, jump ropes, weighted balls, and bench presses until they reached a door on the back wall. Through it was a locker room.

"We've got a swimsuit for you," Charlie said, pointing to a row of lockers fashioned with clean towels and trunks. "This place has a hot tub…and a steam room." Al and Phil grabbed suits from the lockers and changed. The two stood awkwardly, naked for a moment and then bare chested, each subtly aware of the other's sagging form and hock-kneed joints. They grabbed a pair of towels and followed their hosts into the adjoining room.

The second room was tiled from floor to ceiling, and the hot tub itself was sunk into the floor, jets already pumping. Al motioned Phil in first, and he dropped quickly into the roiling water and backed up against a jet. Al was more cautious, adapting gradually to the heat with the water at his navel, as Charlie and Frank collected two bottles of scotch, four glasses, and cigars. Each man claimed a drink, a cigar, and a jet for himself.

"How'd you end up with a piece of this place?" Phil asked. Al snickered at both his manifest curiosity and the way he was resting his drink on the paunch belly he usually took great lengths to conceal. It balanced precariously just above the water line with condensation fogging the glass.

"The original owner moved here from Cincinnati, and he was a big Reds fan. Bet on 'em big in the Series last year," Charlie said. "I haven't touched a weight out there, but you can't beat this tub."

Frank sat directly across from Alphonse, swirling his scotch and drinking it quickly. Al sensed his friend was impatient to get along with business. *A good start,* he thought, *for whatever this meeting ended up being about.* "Frank, you remember the little gym we used to go to with the Black trainer?"

Frank smiled. "Honeysett," he said before moving his eyes to Phil and Charlie. "Floyd Honeysett ran this gym called, uh, Saylor's, I think. The other guys used to have a hundred jokes about bears comin' after him and other shit to rag him with. They hid a beehive in the locker room once, fuckers stung everybody. Floyd was a tough motherfucker though. I heard they sprayed shit on his windows once, right after King got shot or some shit, and that motherfucker sat outside his gym with an Enfield and two pistols, daring motherfuckers to come up there and touch his windows again. He was this little shithead too. He was a lightweight when he boxed."

Phil made a noise of acknowledgment. "I know that guy too. Well, I know his kid anyhow…his kid is a boxing trainer. Floyd Honeysett Jr. Saylor's is still around too."

Charles laughed. "I don't know why that name is funny."

"He's a boxing trainer just like his old man," Phil said. "They're both cranky motherfuckers too. The younger Floyd was no joke when he fought. They used to drive him to Baltimore and stage bare knuckle shit in the streets, and Floyd used to take on some big moth-erfuckers. All comers. He'd fight there for hours till the locals were mad enough to pull a gun on him. Then he'd thank them for the effort and scram."

A face from the past popped into Al's head. "You remember that big guy with the rash on his arm?" he asked Frank. Al turned to Phil and Charlie. "The guy had this big rash on his arm, permanent for some reason we never knew, but he was a goddamn ox. Arms like boulders. He used to do deadlift with Volkswagens on the street."

"You know that guy had a problem not too long ago?" Frank said. "The rash guy? His cousin had a bad boyfriend or some shit. Your man Petey helped me fix it. I always liked Petey. He's an easy guy to understand."

Al bowed his head and raised his glass. "Glad we could help administer justice."

Charles shook his head. "There's so much of that shit these days, these whack-a-doodle boyfriends. You have daughters, Phil?"

"No, two sons." Phil was sure Charlie knew that.

"What do they do, your sons?"

"One is an electrician with a good wife and two kids, and one is in construction with a whore girlfriend who spends all the money he doesn't have."

Frank pointed to Al. "Do they work for him?"

"Nah, never got into it. I guess that's a good thing."

Charlie resumed his line of thought through the building haze of cigar smoke. "The daughters thing is different than boys. With Bobby, it was easy. I knew what he was gonna be, and he knew what he was gonna be. From the time he's five, he knew, I just had to teach him the rules. It was like Sunday school or somethin' up at Bertram's

Diner on the weekends with the other guys around, swappin' stories. You know, same thing as, 'Hey, you're Catholic, here's the Ten Commandments and some stories about Jesus and his friends.' But the daughters. They're different. I never knew what to teach them. Al knows what I'm talking about. He's got Carrie and Jennie."

Frank had two daughters of his own, Theresa and Celia. He offered, "You have to let their mothers handle them. Or you should anyway."

"Al couldn't do that. He's a family man to his core," Phil said, emphasizing the point by tapping his fist against his chest.

"My girls weren't easier. They weren't that," Al said, his words fighting over the jets, "but they pushed away from their Mother. My girls came to me more than Johnny ever did. I don't know what I'm teachin' them half the time, but the girls listened better."

Charlie puffed his cigar. "That's why when you hear about these domestic problems, it's terrible. And we've gotta be out there, settin' it right, the dads I mean. Like this rash man's cousin Frank is talkin' about, where is she gonna go? Police can't fuckin' help her unless he's leavin' bruises everywhere and all the time. It's all a fuckin' mess. I've seen the blue shirts get called to the same house, five, six, seven times and not a thing happens, nothin'. That type of shit though, sometimes a beating isn't good enough to stop it. Some of those motherfuckers don't learn, no matter what you do." Each man's accent became more pronounced during their hypothetical moral crusades.

They sat in the bubbles and pontificated, awash in their conception of power, and Al observed the Frank Capello before him with amusement. His friend had been poor, dirty, and scuffed by asphalt with a chip on his shoulder that was present in his tone, in his walk, in his eyes. The man in front of him was different in the natural ways: gray chest hair, creases from his eyes and mouth, loose skin on his arms, but in more important ways as well. Al saw a man softened by privilege. *The angry boy is dead or dying, his likeness now pruning in a hot tub.*

Charles had changed too, since Al first knew him, but *softened* was not the word. His face held a resolve in his jaw and eyes that was as present as it had ever been. His hair was still brown but stiffened by treatment and fading more each day. The two Sicilians were about to give their children over to each other, and they would be connected by a sacred vow, a bond of ancestral values. The Don thought there were worse places for Carrie to land.

Phil struck an unassuming figure even at his best, even decades ago. His wide frames magnified his eyes and pushed his ears outward, giving his face a cartoonish look. Al knew the physicality was an artifice. Phil was a dependable, honorable man with *Cosa Nostra* in his veins since before they met some thirty years ago in a run-down Buffalo doughnut shop. Still, he looked more a bookkeeper than gangster, hence one of his nicknames, Buffalo Books, a combination of his nerdy visage and his hometown. Especially now as fog filled his glasses at regular intervals and he struggled to keep them clear enough to see.

The four men talked without direction. The conversation ran from the past to women to combinations of the two and children and money. The first bottle of scotch was empty, tipped over on the tile floor, before Al found a moment wide enough to move their visit along. As the persistent laughter fell out and their voices went quiet, Al finally pushed. "So, Frank, I am curious, what brings us to the Health Club tonight? I know you well enough to know you have a purpose besides our pleasant company, risking a meeting like this." Frank finished his drink before answering, so Al finished his own and poured each of them another.

"I want to talk big picture with you. The future of this city, the future of Our Thing," Frank said, rolling his cigar in his fingers and then puffing it especially hard.

"I'm listening. What is our future?"

"You've brought us a thing here, the Park Avenue thing, that can be totally legitimate, and that's great in New York, but we're chasin' fresh opportunities all over with the same blueprint. Atlantic City, Kansas, New Orleans. We have proven that if you control the labor, everythin' else falls in line around it, boom, boom, boom." Frank gulped his fresh scotch and swirled it briefly in his mouth before swallowing. "These construction rackets should be easy for everyone, but we both know there's guys not playin' ball the way they're supposed to play ball."

Al understood Frank's gist but was not going to be the first to say it, not in a room he did not arrange himself, among people who were not his. "You'll have to help me out, Frank."

Frank talked through puffs of smoke. "Well, you know we got a celebrity in our midst…and his best friend is a crippled old man, about eighty years old, that's watchin' the world pass him by. They're not doing this thing right, Al."

"The construction? Or something else?"

"The construction, the rights after, the street level with these poppy seeds or whateva' they are, all this shit. It ain't us. And then we got this long-term money about to come in, like I says and it's not just here, Atlantic City and so on, and we've got to be dealin' with stable motherfuckers. And a guy cruisin' headlong into dementia and a TV star ain't stable enough for me. Old Man croaks, who knows what that Family does. And the TV star, he's got everybody lookin' at him." Frank motioned between Charlie and himself. "We don't wanna be associated with that. It's not right."

Al puffed a smoke ring and followed it across the room until it impacted the wall. Charlie was impatient to support his Boss and offered, "My thoughts exactly. That's all bad for business."

"It's a liability, his being on TV," Frank said, his palms tapping the water as he spoke, "you just don't do it. Not for a goddamn defamation league or church softball game or your grandma's baked cookies sale. That shit is incompatible. He's puttin' his own guys at risk too, the selfish motherfucker."

"I'm hearin' a lot about one guy. Why the Old Man?" Al asked, although he knew the arguments as well as Frank. Pisciotto and Provenzano balanced the Commission votes 2 vs. 2 with Salvatore Lucania in jail and abstaining. If they whacked Pisciotto without Provenzano's approval, he would be irreconcilable, and if they brought the matter to him, he'd double cross them and tell Pisciotto their plans. The Commission would crumble. The choice was two or none.

Frank shrugged and answered, "He made his fuckin' choice. Years ago, that Old Man made his fuckin' choice. Now he can fuckin' live with it." Al saw what was left of the angry street kid flash in Frank's eyes. "And the money," he continued, "my god, it's less risk and more money. Our way of life needs protecting, *Cosa Nostra*. If we don't take care of business, we're gonna be havin' this conversation in five years whether the Old Man is around or not. And I don't know if it's gonna be in this hot tub or outside the pearly gates, the two of us shootin' the shit with St. Peter."

"If you want more money, who are you gonna find who's willin' to take less than what's already been bargained for?"

A smile tugged the corners of Frank's lips. "You don't think friends will start popping up like daisies when we tell them they can be the new Boss? There'll be a line of 'em wantin' better than what they got and less than these incumbents."

"How're you gonna guarantee that? That they become the new Boss of their Family? That should be for those *borgatas* to decide. There should be a vote of their *capos*."

"Because if they don't listen to us, I'm gonna to shoot them," Frank said with more snap than he intended. "If we do this, everybody is gonna be lookin' to us for the right answers. Boss of Bosses type shit and we just tell them what to do. We keep the peace, keep the money movin', and they'll love us. We'll be Caesar, come back around."

Al had his answer but wanted the conversation to play out. He had a point to make. "I don't think you have that power, Frank. To crown Bosses. We have a Commission for a reason."

"I have Lucania's vote," Frank said, his eyes wide, as if he had magically pulled a rabbit from the bubbling water.

"So, it's a 3–2 vote to whack two Bosses? And the no votes are the whacked?" Al laughed at his friend's sham adherence to protocol. "You think Sal Lucania's thumbs-up from a cell is gonna be enough for their guys to look the other way?"

Frank didn't answer but sat casually to indicate his silent affirmative.

"The first motive shouldn't be money. Not for something like this." Al was coming to the point he hoped to make clear for Frank, Charlie, and Phil.

"It's not just money."

"I know it's not," Al said although he suspected, for Frank, it was. "You can't talk about money first with these things. It's too big to be about money. *We're* too big for it to be all about money. If guys hear we're not gettin' paid enough, they start to take hard looks at their own bank accounts. It's gotta be about Responsibility and Honor. It's gotta be about who we are as men, or we're just causin' problems for ourselves. If you want to stay on top, you don't upset the apple cart. You tell everyone how important apple carts are."

"So, what're you sayin'?"

"It's gotta be about *omerta*. Members do not bring attention to *Cosa Nostra*. Ever. That is a line in the sand, the TV interviews and the Hollywood shit, and there's no comin' back from it. That's gotta be what's out on the street, the message for all to see. This is about protectin' our institutions, Frank. And we," he motioned to each man, "are the institutions."

"So, the Old Man gets whacked by association...or for the Afghan shit?"

"Both. The TV, the Afghan shit, those are threats to *omerta*. Members of Our Thing don't get to play those games. We have a responsibility to shout '*omerta, omerta, omerta*' from the hilltops until each of us is dead and in the ground. This sort of behavior needs to be dealt with, or we're gonna lose control of the whole thing. We can't stand for it, I agree, but the story has to be clear."

Charlie and Phil nodded in agreement. Frank took a drink of his scotch.

"The drugs too, Frank. We've gotta give that up. You can make it the rules, but if we don't enforce it, we're gonna end up outtav commission. Pun fuckin' intended."

"I honestly don't know how much of our money is from drugs. If any," Frank said hopefully. "I tell my guys not to touch it. They know."

"They touch it anyway. You know that."

Frank looked at Charlie. "How many guys you think are sellin' drugs on the side?"

Charlie thought a moment. "Five maybe? But associates. Not made guys. They know better."

Al knew it was much more than that, and of a higher order than street thugs, but it would've been disrespectful to press the point. "And if those guys have to look at thirty years? Forty years in prison? What do you think they're gonna do?"

"I know," Frank said, impatient with the conversation's direction. "This wasn't meant to be an audit of my Family's finances."

"I know. I know. I'm just makin' a point. If we do this, it needs to be about our principles and our values as an organization. Protect our institutions. It can't be about money when word hits the street level. Control the story."

"Agreed."

Al hit his cigar for the first time in a while, and his ash fell into the swirling pool of water. He batted it with his hand and it dissipated into the waves. "So, how you wanna do it, Frank?"

A glimpse of the warrior clapped across Frank's face again. "We fuckin' light 'em up."

"Who you want?"

"I want the fuckin' movie star," Frank answered, beaming at the others, "but we should both have guys on-site for each of them. Show a united front and shit. And there will have to be some collateral damage to the loyalists around them. Can't have resentful motherfuckers out here."

"All right," Al said. "My guys will run point on the Old Man. Has to be the same day, right? Or they'll hit the mattresses."

"Like fuckin' D-day. Six a.m. or some shit. Synchro-*nized*." Frank sank back into the water and against the edge of the tub. His face was red and sweating from the humidity in the room. "Get ready, boys," he said to Phil and Charlie, "it's about to heat up around here."

PART THREE

MOLES LIVE IN DARKNESS

One afternoon in the spring of 1984
Office of Levi Wirth in Philadelphia, PA

The yellow envy of the past. Nine letters. V rubbed his tired eyes, let the puzzle rest on his knee, and conceded his mind did not work as efficiently as it once had. It was a sad confession for a man of barely fifty. He twirled the pen in his fingers and let his eyes wander to the handsome desk guarding Levi Wirth's office door. Wirth's secretary sat behind it, a woman picked for her looks to radiate power to the helpless writers who came to beg before him. She had blond hair that fell to her shoulders, a tightly cut business jacket thrown open to suggest her breasts, slim legs crossed at the ankles above her high heels, and painted purple toes. She bit across her pencil like a pirate bites a knife and shuffled the papers on her desk, seemingly engrossed in her work. V adjusted himself, resentful of the position he was in. Wirth was an ingrate; she was his pawn.

Better than the other. Eight letters and connected to the yellow-envy answer, should he ever find it. The oil from his fingers smudged the clues and transferred the black ink to his hands, the problem worse for each minute he waited in this god-forsaken room. He wiped his fingers on his slacks in frustration, but it made no difference to his fingers or the slacks.

"Mr. Usenko?" the secretary said with a plastic smile. "Mr. Wirth is ready for you."

V nodded and made his way silently through the office door.

Levi Wirth was an old man with the serious energy of experiences both good and bad. His hair was white and groomed, his nose long and thin with a bump to carry the weight of his glasses. When V came close enough, Levi hugged him like an old comrade. "V, it's good to see you. How's Helen doing?"

"She's good," V said, begrudgingly returning the smiles. "She's redesigning our house as always."

Wirth chortled and took a seat behind his desk as V fell into one of the leather guest chairs. "Of course, of course she is…as long as everyone is staying busy. And Brandon?"

"He's abandoned all of us for the Philippines."

"Oh...you know," Wirth said, remembering, "I heard he was working out there. He's with that nonprofit, right? I may have sent him a donation last year. Honestly, I can't remember."

"I'm not making a profit. I'm never sure about him."

Wirth shook his head. "Vyacheslav, you have always been a witty man. And, for the record, I see that in this manuscript as well."

V recognized the copy he had sent him on the desk, Wirth's fingers drumming its cover page. It was a thin attempt as manuscripts went, held together by brass fasteners, its pages curled from a recent reading.

"How do you feel about it so far?"

I don't know how to feel about it, any of it. I am frustrated, bored, ashamed, and hateful of every single word I write. I cannot bring myself to tell anyone how terrible it all is, and so I've taken to locking myself in my office and reading the sports page or listening to a handheld radio when I say I'm working. "I feel good about it honestly," V said. "It's the best I've felt about anything I've written since *The Conciliators*. And I'm enjoying it again. First time in a long time I've really felt good about what I'm writing, ya know? About the subject, the characters. It's not a perfect process, but it's enjoyable."

"Good." Wirth made a short note on his legal pad. "That's always the first step, to find the enjoyment."

"How did you feel about it?"

"Good," Levi said, his tone abrupt and cautious. "I think there are good elements. And potential. I see potential here for sure."

"Go ahead." V waved his hand to push him further. "*But...*"

"I see the potential," Wirth said again. He tried to keep his voice encouraging, but V saw the disappointment in his eyes. It was not what the publisher had hoped for. "It's obvious you have put time into this project. How many people have you visited in person?"

"Five in person."

"I can see that, V. I can see that."

"*But...*"

Wirth took his glasses off and set them on his desk as if he could not bear to see V's face any longer. "It's been six years already, V. If I'm being honest, with a person I consider a friend, I think you are procrastinating for your own purposes. There is good material in here," he held up the thin stack of paper, "but it is disjointed, disorganized…it lacks a sense of cohesion. It feels *stunted*, for lack of a better word. This is more like your old work than *The Conciliators*, and I don't know why. You know what that means though."

"It means you're going to buy it and bitch about the sales when it tanks."

"No," Wirth said patiently, "it means you're not doing work that fits your potential."

"I'm not a failing high school kid. You don't think I have enough adjectives in there? Fine, I'll add some. Make me an offer."

"Be serious for a minute. Jesus." He'd made Wirth mad, but not enough for him to lose his cool. The scolding would be professional. "You know that's not what I'm saying. I'm saying what is here is average work, and I've seen you do better. Take that comment for what you will."

"Not bad enough for you to take those off your shelf though," V said, waving at a few awards on Wirth's bookcase inscribed with both their names.

"And I never will. You did great work on *Conciliators*, and I expect you will again. It may even be with this manuscript." Wirth gave the cover a few successive pats.

V walked to the bookshelf at the back of the room to collect his thoughts, remind himself with the trophies. He knew Levi was right and it sat in him like a stone. "I'm wrapped up in these people," V said eventually. "That may be my problem. I'm more wrapped up in the people I meet than the characters I write. I know it's some kind of emotional rubber necking or whatever, but I can't take my eyes off them."

"Sometimes the research is more fun than the writing."

His most recent interview had been especially unnerving. To see the way a man's eyes could change… "It's hard to square them with what they're accused of. Or even admit to, in some cases. It's unsettling when you've just heard them talk about their kids…I want to capture that. I want to show you *that*."

"I can see that in the work. But its fuzzy. *We* can do better."
Wirth flipped the book open and showed V the pages were covered
by red pen strokes. "I've made notes. Read them and we can talk
about it."

V walked back to the edge of the desk and extended his hand.
"I'll read the notes. Thanks, Levi, seriously. I appreciate it." Levi nodded, handed V the thin, curled manuscript, and leaned back in his
chair with a curious expression on his face. V left, walking slowly past
the secretary in her tightly cut jacket.

When V got back to his house, his wife was nowhere to be
found. On the calendar hung in their kitchen, he found a bullet
point had been added since he left: *Missy's Bridal Shower.* His drive
back had been stalled by traffic and the clock read quarter after seven.
Helen had said she would be home for dinner. She would try and
convince him that she had not or tell him he should check the calendar more or maybe that he had seen the note and forgotten, but
he knew it had not been there when he left. He preferred to be alone
anyway.

V carried the manuscript to his desk and flipped through it.
Levi's notes were meticulous as always. V read a few pages' worth,
making his own comments as he went, and playing and replaying his
interviews on the tape player as he paced the floor. The work felt like
progress. He heard Helen come in but didn't feel the need to greet
her, so he reorganized his tapes, filed them into their little slots in the
drawer, and laid his manuscript neatly on top. The newspaper and
its failed crossword were nearby, so he shoveled those in as well. He
locked the drawer and replaced the key in the base of the dusty snow
globe when he paused and turned back to his desk. He only had
one lamp, an old one Helen had bought him a decade before, and
it sat on the corner of his desk. The smooth wooden surface looked
inviting in that moment. Something about the windows, dark with
night, the stillness of the house, his reluctance to see his wife after the
night he knew she had, all conspired to make him open the drawer
and pull the manuscript back out. But the manuscript was not his

first concern. First, with his pen in hand, he smoothed a blank sheet of paper and wrote: *Dear Brandon, my son...*

One afternoon in June 1973
New York City, New York
"They were no different than politicians to these
men. Promisers of a future dole."

Murdock held up a Snickers bar for his partner's inspection. "You want one of these?" This gas station had a wide selection of candy bars. And Yoo-Hoos in the glass bottle which were especially hard for Murdock to find.

"I can buy my own fucking candy bars," Clayburgh mumbled, eyeing a display of magazines by the register. George Foreman was staring back at him from the cover of *Sports Illustrated*, but he only allowed himself the swimsuit edition. Everything else was in the newspaper.

"I wasn't offering to buy it for you. I was asking if you wanted one." When Clayburgh didn't respond, Murdock added, "Snickers are my favorite candy bars."

"So, you're a salesman now? A Snickers plant?" One of the tabloids grabbed Clayburgh's attention with a headline about a woman impregnated by an alien baby. He went about finding the article.

"I'd be a Pay Day plant, if anything."

Clayburgh laughed against his better judgment. "How could you rep a candy bar that wasn't chocolate, you un-American asshole?"

"Chocolate is a saturated market. Every traditional candy bar has chocolate. There's no room for growth anymore," Murdock said, his lip twisting to fight off a smile.

"So, your plan would be to sell the nonconforming candy bars?"

"Yes."

"I can't even think of any other candy bars without chocolate."

"Twinkies."

"That's not a candy bar."

Murdock waved a teasing finger. "It's a *nonconforming* candy bar. Same general purpose as a candy bar. No one would turn down a Twinkie if they asked you for a candy bar."

"Then you can call anything a candy bar. Is a corn dog a candy bar?"

"Doesn't meet the sugar threshold."

"Popsicle?"

Murdock shook his head. "The temperature isolates frozen treats."

"You're an idiot," Clayburgh said. Murdock continued his perusal.

Clayburgh paid at the register (Murdock had left his wallet in the car), and they set off around the corner to their patrol car. Murdock fell into the passenger seat, ruffling on the floor for his notepad and chomping into his Snickers. "So," he said, "we've done the two sites in Bensonhurst," he said, "one in Borough Park, one in Midwood…we should head over to Bath Beach. They have three over there."

"Fuck that, find a closer one. We've wasted enough time on this today."

"Kensington? I think this one has a little dive bar next to it."

"Fine." Clayburgh set the address on the seat between his legs. "I honestly expected better results from this."

"It's only the third day. It can still happen."

"I know," Clayburgh said, waving about stack of pictures from the union election. "I just thought these two would be easier to find, is all. They made us and still sat at that election for over an hour."

"It would seem they're more behind the scenes than we thought."

"It makes for a boring day."

In Kensington, the detectives sifted through a maze of lights to locate an amoeba-shaped construction site on the far end of a strip mall. The main area included a few storefronts with scaffolding and a collection of paint cans, buckets, electric cords, and various other implements marked by incomplete towers, rebar skeletons, scattered tools, and roughly a dozen neon-clad workers. Dust coated the windows, doors, sidewalks, buckets, and cars around the site in layers of varying thickness. "I doubt this is the nerve center of the operation," Clayburgh said as he parked. The detectives approached the chain-link gate cautiously as one of the workers met them, identifying himself as JJ, the site manager.

"How can I help you, gentlemen?" JJ was distinguishable from the other neon vests by his salt-and-pepper hair (instead of a hard hat), his white smile, and the clipboard he carried in his left hand.

"We were hoping to show your crew a couple pictures," Murdock said. "Nothing big, just looking for somebody and we think they may know a little about construction. He may be involved with a jobsite or two around here."

JJ clinked open the gate to give the detectives access to the site proper. "How do you know he's in construction?"

"We found his diary," Clayburgh said with reflexive bite. *Damnit,* he thought, *I'm better off keeping my mouth shut and letting Murdock be our public face.*

The overseer's smile evaporated. "Was my name in that diary? This address?" Clayburgh let his silence answer. "Then I'm sure I don't have much to tell you. These are all good men out here."

"Look, you and your crew take a look," Murdock said, extending a few photos for JJ, "and if nobody knows them, we can move on. We've been doing it all day. Help us out."

JJ shuffled through the pictures quickly. He had big, expressive eyes, and Clayburgh thought he saw them shudder the instant he had them. It was a subtle flick of his eyelids and gone before the thought could fully register in Clayburgh's head. "Never seen them," the man said, handing the pictures back. "My guys haven't either."

Clayburgh's mustache twitched. "I would rather the men speak for themselves." When JJ's eyes narrowed, he forced what he hoped was a tactful grin across his lips.

JJ waved a reluctant hand toward the rest of his crew. "Ask away then."

The crewmembers were shrouded in white concrete particulates that hung around them like a fog. They were, by and large, younger, sweatier, slimmer, and tanner than JJ; and their jeans and boots were worn comfortably around whatever body part was most familiar. Murdock and Clayburgh walked into the area of their highest concentration and let their hammering, pouring, sloshing, shoveling, and leveling come to a gradual halt. Most seemed eager for any distraction, wiping sweat, sitting down, or leaning over where they could as the detectives approached.

"Hello, gentlemen," Murdock began, "I'm Detective Murdock and this is Detective Clayburgh. How's it going today?"

One of the older men, whose thick arms were powdered to the biceps, answered, "It's hot out here, Detective. But if you keep talkin', we'll get a break for a minute, so go on along and do the talkin' part."

That was as warm a reception as they could've hoped for. Murdock continued, "We just have a couple pictures for you to look at. Nothing serious. Just askin' for names. That's it."

"A name is a lot to give a cop," another of the workers said, using the break to spark a cigarette. "I wouldn't want anybody tellin' the cops my name if they only had a picture."

"It's anonymous, and they're not in trouble."

"It's doesn't sound anonymous for them guys," the second worker teased.

Murdock let the comment go unanswered. "Here they are," he said, dealing a set of pictures to the workers closest to him. Their hands were stained with grime, and Murdock could see it being shifted to the prints as they each looked, shuffled them, and passed to the next in turn. The images made their way through the group slowly, each inspecting them at his own pace. Murdock could not tell if they were making an honest effort or simply extending the time their tools rested on the ground.

"I don't see anyone here," the gray armed man said finally. He stepped toward the detectives, but as he went to hand the pictures back, another man snatched them roughly from his hand.

"Actually," the snatcher said, "I think I do recognize this one here."

"Which one?"

"This one here, with the chest hair," the man said, pointing to the photo. "Gary, isn't that your sister? I hardly recognize her from this angle. Usually, she's on her back...looking deep into my eyes."

Most of the men laughed. Gary pushed the man hard from behind. "You remind me of her too, Gary. She's a rough one."

Clayburgh shook his head, angry for allowing himself a moment of optimism. He should've known better. "All right. Give me those if you're not going to help."

"Hey, we know this one," a high-pitched voice said from behind the snatcher. He was one of the last to get a look because the others had queued up in front of him. "Right here," he said, pointing. Most of the men looked at him sideways, while a few shuffled next to him for another look at the picture he held.

"Who do you think that is, Peanut?" one asked.

"He comes around on Fridays and talks to JJ right before we all go home." Peanut's eyes were locked on the photo. He missed the sharp change in the men around him. "This guy."

"The gravel salesman?" another asked.

"No, the guy in the suit that comes on Friday afternoons. You've seen him." The witness continued to stare at the picture, oblivious to the looks of the men around him. *He is making them angry.*

"There isn't anyone that comes on Fridays," another man said to the Peanut, "except the gravel salesman. And you don't need to be scoutin' JJ's meetings anyway. If he needs your advice, he'll ask for it. And he won't." He plucked the picture away from the witness and shook his head. "This guy don't come around here."

"C'mon, you've seen that guy," Peanut said again, now searching his coworkers' faces for support. "He wears all those rings? How you gonna miss a guy wearing gold rings at a construction site?"

"Or you're making shit up to impress the cops," another snapped back. "You got a record we don't know about? JJ might wanna hear about that. Maybe it's time for *me* to have a meeting with JJ."

"Do you know his name?" Clayburgh asked Peanut directly. The others stopped talking to listen.

"No, he doesn't talk to us. He just talks to JJ."

One worker spun around and faced Peanut, just one step in front of him. "Sounds like a bunch of bullshit to me. Maybe nobody should be talkin' to you if you're willin' to make shit like this up in front of all these witnesses."

"I'm not," Peanut said, all confidence completely gone. He'd caught on to the group's hostility.

Clayburgh looked over each man. "So, does that mean nobody else has anything to say about either of those men?"

"None of us," the older man with thick arms said, calm and serious, "has ever seen those men before, including Peanut here. He's just a dumb kid with poor eyesight. We thank you for the break, Detectives, but we need to get back to work. Have a nice day."

Peanut sensed the game was up. He grabbed his shovel and walked over to the humble beginnings of a small trench to spike the dirt. Murdock stashed the pictures.

"You meet with this man on Fridays?" Clayburgh asked as they walked back to the overseer. He pointed to the man Peanut had tried to identify. "This man?"

"I meet with several men throughout the week," JJ said, "some on Fridays, some on other days. But I've never met *that* man."

"I think you can guess where we're going to go with this," Murdock said. "We will bring you in, we will disrupt this site, call your employers. Final time, have you ever met with either of these men?"

JJ's expressive eyes were now slits, his lips pressed thin. "I have never met with him. I have never *seen* him, as I explained to you earlier."

Clayburgh mustache bristled against his nose. "I think you're lying."

"You are free to think that."

Murdock clapped JJ on the chest. "Expect to see us again."

"Can't wait, Detectives."

June 1973
19ᵗʰ Precinct in Manhattan, NY

Clayburgh saw Patty Uhlhousen walking, nose upturned and hips whirling side to side, in his direction and knew instinctually she was coming for him. She wasn't an especially contemptible woman, but she possessed a near permanent frown and a fractious disdain for anyone without a captain's stripe that made both the detectives reluctant to ever speak with her. "Clayburgh, you have a call," she announced from a few yards away.

"From who?"

"I didn't ask him."

Clayburgh set his jaw to prevent any unfiltered words from spilling out. "You didn't ask who it was?" was all he said, acutely aware an angry Patty, as opposed to snobbish-condescending Patty, would make life unnecessarily difficult for him.

"A male caller said he had a tip for 'Detective Clayburgh,'" she said. "Not much for *me* to ask him after that."

"I'll take it," Clayburgh sighed, tossing the alien baby article he was reading back on his desk. There was a script of questions she was supposed to ask every tipster, but his complaints would be in vain. His desk phone rang a moment later. "This is Detective Clayburgh."

"Everybody knows who it is in those pictures," a male voice said.

"What pictures?" Clayburgh asked, but he knew already.

"The two guys."

"Okay then, who are they?"

"I can't be the one to tell you."

Clayburgh grabbed a manila folder from his drawer and began making notes on the caller's voice: younger male, probably Caucasian, baritone American accent, not originally from the city. "So, who can tell me then?"

"Thomas Luparelli."

Clayburgh scribbled the name on the tab. "All right, and where do I find Mr. Luparelli?"

The caller hesitated and Clayburgh was afraid he lost the connection before the caller's voice came over again, "You shouldn't have much trouble."

Clayburgh got the impression the caller was smiling on the other end. "What does that mean?"

"He got picked up a few weeks ago. He's in jail."

Clayburgh wrote *JAIL* in thick capital letters under his other notes. "How does he know these guys?"

"Ask him," the voice said, and Clayburgh heard the click and then the dial tone. Clayburgh hung up the phone and jogged across the room toward snobbish Patty and her desk.

One afternoon in June 1973
Jerry's Place in Brooklyn, NY
"It made for a stressful week."

Tony found Vic sitting at his usual table, but he was not alone. Next to him sat a balding man with wide-frame glasses, dressed down to a polo shirt under his sport coat like a vacationing retiree in Boca Raton. Tony knew this man was Phil Scozzari. It was rare for Tony to speak with Phil, almost as rare as with Al Giordano himself.

"Phil," Tony said, extending his hands and embracing the two men with the necessary formalities, "it's good to see you." Something about Vic's tone that morning alerted Tony this meeting was import-ant, and now he was glad Ana had time to iron his shirt. Phil could dress down and get away with it when the Don wasn't there; Tony could not.

"Tony, how ya been?" Phil asked in his distinct accented whine.

"I've been good. Plenty goin' on in our little crew, I think you know. We've gotta good thing goin' over here with the Skip," he nod-ded at Vic, "runnin' things for us. A lotta promisin' action recently."

"Tony's been a good kid, helpin' me out here," Vic said. Vic's unmitigated compliment was almost enough to make Tony blush. "Him and Vito are good kids, and they got a younger one now. They're doing a fine job, these Maceo boys."

"What's the youngest one's name?"

"Benjie," Tony said. "He's been workin' for Vic goin' about a month now, and he's been drivin' me and Vito around for almost a year. He's just as young and stupid as we all were."

"That's good to hear, Tony," Phil said, smiling. "And I know you guys have been running hot here recently. I see the money, the good work." Frank the Bartender dropped a bottle of wine at the table, and Tony poured each of them a drink. After a toast, Vic was the one to push the conversation along. "I can't wait anymore, Phil. Let's get this over. Jerry owes me another helping of braciola."

Phil looked at Vic and then Tony. "You're right," he said, setting his glass down firmly. "Tony, this Family," he tugged his ear, "is on the brink of some big things. We've got money about to come in, big money, legit money. More money than we ever used to imagine. Money you don't have to hide under the mattress, don't have to hide from our benevolent government. You understand? We think there's a way for you to be a part of all that." Tony nodded and took a drink. "And with as well as you're doin' here with Vic, we thought this was the time to give you a bigger role. A bigger chance to earn." Tony thanked him. Phil waved it away. "Now, there is another part to all this. A complicated and difficult problem." Tony took another drink of his wine. "And for anything worth doin', there are risks involved. We," he tugged his ear again, "think we can identify this problem rather specifically." The words hung heavy in the burgundy filtered light of the restaurant.

"Are they risks that I would know?"

"Yeah, you would. They're two of the biggest risks out there."

Tony's blood rose involuntarily to redden his face. He feared it would betray his thoughts to Phil and clenched his jaw in a vain attempt to stifle it. Another moment and he dared a glance at Vic, an acknowledgment of that man's quickly broken promise, but there was none. His mentor's face looked of wrinkled stone. Tony let his eyes fall, a good soldier, able to regroup. "How can I help?"

"The Old Man." The comment itself was simple. No one else in the restaurant knew what was happening. Civilians could have been sitting at the table and not understood. But Tony did.

"I see." There was no option to refuse. "If this is what the Family needs..." Tony said, raising his glass and drinking from it.

"It is. It absolutely is." And there it was, released out into the world like Pandora's Box. No negotiation, no alternative, no second-guessing. It was done as soon as those words were spoken.

"Then I will do it."

"It will be coordinated," Phil said. He scribbled the date on a piece of paper and showed Tony. After Tony nodded, Phil tore the pieces up and put them in his pocket. "The other risk will be dealt with on the same day. And it won't just be you. You'll have at least one man from Don C. with you as well. Somethin' about a unified front or some shit."

"I'll get it done," Tony said with more confidence than he felt. "I'd like the other man to be the Calabrese kid, if I can pick. I trust him."

"I'll pass it along. But you're running point," Phil said, his soft smile at odds with Tony's nervous edge. "If you want more guys on this, you bring 'em. Vito, whoever."

Tony took another drink. "I appreciate the trust." He forced his own smile and hoped it looked genuine. "This is a big thing."

"The biggest move in twenty years," Vic said, his pale eyes shadowed by the dim, red light. "Since before Lucania went to jail."

"You'll be set up, for good, when it's done," Phil promised.

"Thanks, Phil. And I'll take what you've got comin', don't get me wrong, but I don't care about me. I've always been taken good care of." He pulled himself forward to correct his posture. "Phil, I do wanna say…I'm only sayin' this 'cause it's you, and I trust you… and you know me and I ain't the type of guy askin' for all kinds of favors or nothin'. But with you here, I just wanna vouch for my little brother to you in person. He's already done some work," to which Papa Vic nodded his assent, "and I just want you to keep him in mind. If we can get him to earn, if he can make his bones, he'll have a little extra protection on the streets, a little extra money in his pocket. Just keep Benj in mind, if you could, movin' forward." Tony waved the thought into the air with his hand. "I would want that more than money."

Phil reached and patted Tony on the arm, met his eyes over his downturned frames. "We'll remember. I promise we'll remember the kid after." The men sat there in the booth for a long time to finish their bottle of wine and eat braciola. When Tony finally left, he pushed Don Provenzano from his mind. It would be better to consider it fresh in the morning.

June 24, 1973 at 9:30 a.m.
Wallkill Correctional Facility in Ulster County, NY
"Sometimes there's no going back, no matter what God you pray to."

Murdock used the mirrored surface of the two-way glass to reapply a side part to his hair, while Clayburgh reclined onto the back legs of his chair, familiarizing himself with Tommy Luparelli's yellow sheet, until his partner was too much to ignore.

"Why are you combing your hair for this?"

Murdock continued his task with some concentration. "Because the humidity makes it stand up in the back."

Clayburgh looked into the surface of the glass to see if his partner was joking. He was not. "We're at a prison. Meeting a male prisoner. What does it matter?"

Murdock locked eyes with his partner's stern reflection. "It annoys me. I know it's there whether I'm around women or not." He could not stop a smirk. "You should be more supportive of me, Andy."

"I feel like Barbara wouldn't like you being worried about it." Clayburgh returned to Luparelli's yellow sheet. It was sizeable, but not violent or worth extended jail time until the current charges were added. Clayburgh deemed him "small time" in every sense of the word.

"For the record, my wife hasn't mentioned it yet, but I'm sure the prison staff appreciate a well-kept detective. It gives us credibility."

"That's a very vain thought to have, to think people are noticing your hair. You think you occupy everyone's mind around you."

"Everybody looks at everybody's hair. You're just a jealous old man with a startling hair deficiency. Do not take your problems out—" Murdock dropped quickly into his seat as the door latch clicked. A corrections officer in a brown-on-darker-brown uniform led his prisoner to the far side of the table and attached his shackles to a semicircle clasp sunk through the middle and bolted to the floor. Both detectives were surprised by the youth of the inmate, not even old enough to outgrow the pimples that clustered around his mouth and high on his cheeks. Luparelli had tangled black hair and pale skin that tried to blend into the gray background as he fidgeted into his chair. He was skinny, even frail looking, with a crooked nose and pencil-thin eyebrows.

"Thomas Luparelli?" Clayburgh asked unnecessarily.

"Yes." The kid's voice seemed calm although his eyes flitted from one detective to another and his spider-leg fingers drummed the table incessantly.

Murdock set about shuffling his notes. Clayburgh went ahead with the questions they sketched out beforehand. "You told the officers before you had some information for us?" He found it best to give informers early control of the conversation.

"Earn it. Ask the questions."

Clayburgh's lip twisted. He paused. "All right, then can we talk about the circumstances of your arrest?"

"What do you wanna know?"

"If you have something to tell us, there's a chance we can help you."

"I stole a car. Some guy's Buick."

Clayburgh made a note and set the pen in the fold of his notebook. "A little more than that please."

"My boss comes to me and says he's got a job…"

"Who is your boss?" Murdock asked, his notes now shuffled.

"That's not part of this," Tommy answered. "This is about your pictures."

"It's about the truth, Mr. Luparelli, and whether you know it."

Clayburgh was not used to playing good cop. "Let him finish, Brady. Go on."

Tommy continued, "My boss tells me he's got a job for me. Address, blah blah blah, he says there will be a 1971 GSX in the driveway that belongs to us. He says, go get it back. So, me and my friend drive out there and grab it. I couldn't help going 110 mph in a car like that, cop pulls me over, and I'm here. Not a lot to unpack really."

"What about the drugs?" Clayburgh said, pointing to the most serious charge[2] on the yellow sheet.

"The drugs were in the car already. I never saw them," he said, shaking his head, "and that's assuming the cops didn't throw them in there themselves. I've seen those fuckin' troopers do that shit. You might not believe it, but I've seen those motherfuckers pull shit like that."

Clayburgh hated listening to arrest stories. "Is there anything you want to tell us besides the drugs were not yours?"

"I heard you've got pictures of some guys," Tommy said.

Murdock spread the stack of pictures across the table, and Luparelli leaned forward to get a better look, smiled immediately, and leaned back again. If his hands weren't secured, he would have thrown them behind his head and put his feet up on the table. Instead, the chains simply clinked against the tables metal surface. "I know both guys. Name and rank."

"Go on."

"These are dangerous guys," Tommy said, although the words didn't match his toothy grin. "I want my girlfriend somewhere safe."

"We don't really have that ability, Tommy," Clayburgh said in an unfamiliar, placatory tone. "We don't even know what you're going to say yet, so how can I promise you anything?"

The kid's eyes flashed defiantly at the refusal. His objectives, whatever they might be, were clearly molded by anger, not redemption, and hate clouded his eyes. "We can only promise we will do our best to help you," Murdock said after hesitating, "if the information you give us leads to demonstrable progress in our case."

Luparelli collected the photos and cycled through them, choosing one and holding it out for the detectives. "This one is Nick Pisani," he said, pointing to the man in the passenger seat. "He's the captain of a crew. Fuckin' crazy motherfucker, but he's a guy most of the other guys love. He's Mr. Al's right hand."

---

[2] Tommy was pulled over for going 114 mph on I-78 at 3:12 a.m. on May 10, 1973. Tommy was not found to be intoxicated, but eight grams of heroin were found in the glove box along with a Beretta M1934 handgun registered to Tommy's uncle, Samuzzo Luparelli.

Clayburgh guessed at the spelling of Pisani. "Mr. Al?"

"The Boss of Bosses," Tommy said, the first respectful words he'd spoken. When neither detective gave him much of a reaction, he laughed. "If you haven't heard of him, you are *waaaay* behind."

"And the other one?" Clayburgh asked.

Tommy picked another picture up, this one a hazy outline of the driver, and extended it to Murdock. "I know him too, but I ain't sayin' his name without some protection. I gave you a name to nose around with. Two in fact if you incompetents don't know who Mr. Al is."

"We have a witness who says the driver may have visited her husband and threatened him, forced him to resign."

"Then ask *her* his fuckin' name."

Clayburgh thought it best to move forward. "And why do you think these two men were interested in a local union election?"

Tommy chuckled. "No matter what your question is, the motive is money. And they all make it hand over fist."

"How do you know these guys?" Murdock asked, writing in the margin of each picture in turn. "I assume it's not the country club."

"Nick oversaw the operation. He gave my boss weekly, sometimes daily, instructions on how to go about our business on the streets. It doesn't matter though, everybody in our neighborhood knows both of them. They would never tell you that though."

"You said Al is the 'Boss of Bosses,'" Clayburgh said. "The obvious next question is, who are the other bosses?"

Tommy looked the detectives dead in the eye as he started to speak. His voice curdled with rage, enough for him to lose control of his lips as he talked, spewing spittle and raising his voice. "Look, Detective, I'm no rat. Not really. This is straight up retaliation. They fucked me, abandoned me, and now I'm here to fuck them. I don't have anythin' against anyone else. And you two don't understand what I just did either. If either of them knew my name, they'd fuckin' kill me. In jail, on the street, in Mexico, doesn't fuckin' matter. Nick has known me since I was five years old, runnin' around their neighborhoods, and he abandoned me to this hellhole. Didn't trust me over a cop and a lawyer he's never met. So, now I'm gonna take my shot and hope the government is enough to save me."

Clayburgh thought the anger looked authentic. A little anger on the side of the law could be helpful, but this meeting was not enough. "We can't help you with the name of this passenger and no other info," Clayburgh said. "There's nothing to go to a judge with. Did you commit crimes at the request of Nick Pisani? Earlier you said your boss ordered the robbery. Would Pisani have known about this beforehand?"

"Check him out and come back with an offer. I can give you them when my girlfriend is safe."

"There will be no offer with this," Clayburgh said, more ardently than before.

"Fine. How about what you *should* be looking for?" Tommy leaned on his elbows, the calm back in his voice. "The Families are not happy with each other. I've heard Al Giordano is at odds with two of the others. Watch the newspapers for the names Cesare Provenzano and Joe Pisciotto. If something happens to them, you can bet Mr. Al and Nick Pisani were behind it."

Clayburgh and Murdock looked at each other and shrugged. "We'll listen, Mr. Luparelli," Clayburgh said. "We'll be ready, but no promises."

The morning of June 25, 1973
Ricky Caruso's apartment in the Bronx, NY

Ricky woke up nervous. He wasn't sure why, at least immediately, but knots were turning over in his stomach. He felt like there was something he was forgetting, something big and important, an uneasy mist shrouding the edge of his consciousness.

And then he remembered. He pushed himself up slowly and looked at the pink form lying next to him. She was naked still, facedown with the sheets around her waist and her blond hair spread over her pillow to show the darker shades beneath. Her breasts were mashed into the mattress and spilling out sideways, her back naturally arched and smooth. Ricky remembered the feeling of her, the taut muscles in her back as he held her on top of him, the cool sweat of her thighs and his, her lips as they met and pressed firmly against each other. He wanted to wake her up and act it all again in the morning light even as he was rehearsing polite exits for the sake of his normal comforts and routine. The anxiety around the raw and new was its own test.

He lit a cigarette and sat by his window, opening it to the sunrise. He ignored the orange and yellow rays, however, preferring to watch the subtle up and back again of Kay's breathing as she lay there. The pressure of her pillow had slackened her cheek enough to permit a small wet circle to form just beneath her lips. Her (nearly) unconscious efforts against the drool were enough to make Ricky giggle between drags.

A drink would take the edge off and calm my tumbling insides. He was still half drunk anyway, so he grabbed a bottle of whiskey and poured. His body did everything to reject the first drink, sending the contents of his stomach to the very back of his mouth before he could push everything back down. He took another drink and sat there with his stomach now grumbling for a different reason. The build to their moment was quick and obvious, and still he tried to understand why the night before had been different. He and her had shut the club down together several times without an ending close to this. Something had been different last night. They were closer when they said goodbye, close enough to really feel the other person's presence, close enough to *know* what the other was thinking...

Ricky put out his cigarette on the windowsill and went to the bathroom to wash off. The mirror was harsh. His chest drooped, his fingers were wide and soft around the knuckles, his cheeks were swollen and round, and a small bit of flab hung loose between his waist and belly button. *Unacceptable. Embarrassing.*

He kept his shower short for fear Kay would wake up and scramble off, but she was still asleep as he toweled off, so he dressed and left her be. He found other ways to occupy himself. First, he read the book he owned by the open window, imagining that if she woke to find him reading, that would be quite a positive impression, but he could only manage this ruse for so long and ended up in the living room, watching TV. He started with the news *(if it could not be a book, the news was probably second best)* and stared at the flickering faces as they reported the day's failures. But soon the angry vocal hum was too much, and he resorted to push-ups in a pitiable attempt to firm up before she left. He did enough to feel inflated and stopped.

She kept him waiting. When she stirred, he was through a full pot of coffee and a couple breakfasts. She appeared a few minutes after he heard the first suspicious noises in something resembling her club uniform. Ricky's nerves reemerged, stronger than before.

"Hey," she said with a faint smile.

"Hey," he said, unsure of what she was going to expect from him. Does he kiss her? Hug her? He wanted to. "How do you feel?"

"Good," she said, sitting next to him on the couch and gently mussing the back of his hair with her fingers. "You?"

"Fine." He had been planning this conversation for hours now but had forgotten everything. Her eyes were so blue. "Are you hungry?"

"Uh, no, thank you. I appreciate it. I just think I should get going." Kay looked almost bashful as she said it, and Ricky wondered what aspects she was regretting.

"You know this doesn't change anything at the club," he said, the words tumbling faster than he hoped. "I don't want this to affect anything there. You've been doing great. Fantastic. And everybody seems to like you. I might've mentioned that last night…"

"I don't want anything to change either."

"Well," he hesitated, "you can report to Wayne from now on if that makes you more comfortable. He's a good guy and smart. If you think things will be awkward or anything."

"Um, whatever you think. It's your club, right?"

"I just want you to be comfortable." Ricky liked her hair tossed and ruffled and the amused tug at the corner of her lips when he sounded stupid. He was desperate to know what she was thinking. He said, "And I want to see you again. If you want to, that is. It's up to you, no pressure. And your job is safe no matter what. And I'll tell everyone else they can go fuck themselves."

Tug, tug, smile. She waited another moment to answer, a long moment. His heart stopped, his stomach dropped. Kay hated him. Then she said, "Yeah, I think I'd like that. I had fun with you. Unexpected fun."

Ricky turned her words into energy, more energy than he could control. She couldn't leave. He needed to see her longer, desperately needed it. "Let me make you breakfast. I'm terrible at it, but I don't want you to leave."

She laughed at him. "So confident…"

"Well, if you came here for the breakfast, it's best to get that part over with. It's gonna be terrible." He scooted closer to her, enough for their legs and sides to touch. It wasn't confidence that moved him forward, but a reckless flurry of his nerve. Her eyes were so alive, staring back into his. There was an energy around her, an energy that unbalanced him. He just wanted to be in it, to feel it on his skin and see it in front of him. And he prayed to God she would not leave, not now or later.

The morning of June 27, 1973
The office of Adam Landau in Manhattan, NY
"It was a rigged game from the first."

Carrie fished her best business attire from the back of her closet, a Brooks Brothers Executive Collection single-button A-line skirt suit, and then wondered if she was taking the whole thing too seriously. It was a farce, a sham, and yet she was excited to see it through. She'd been positive on the idea from the start, and as the days passed, she had a chance to ruminate and her enthusiasm grew exponentially. Tulles Financial would simplify several aspects of her personal accounting: tax filings, bank loans, car payments, etc., but the ancillary benefits were perhaps even more significant. She was going to have a business card, just like the one Adam had handed her father more than a decade ago. Kiara Giordano, President, Tulles Financial—her chance to influence the world on a higher order of magnitude, a weaponization of a few bright white cards and an honorary title.

She had only been to Adam's offices a few times. They were nothing to behold from the sidewalk; he took after her father in that way, and she respected him for it. Just simple brown brick and few tinted windows. The main doors opened into a small atrium with a communal building-wide secretary. Johnny met Carrie and Bobby at the woman's desk and led them to the elevator, past chipped floor tiles and a WET FLOOR sign sitting in a coffee spill.

Her father, Jennie, and Adam were waiting in front of Adam's unit when they arrived. Jennie had worn a blue summer dress and flats, but Carrie held her head up against any unspoken criticism of her expensive attire. "Father," she said, kissing him on both cheeks and hugging her sister and Adam in turn.

The office was less humble than the street front suggested. Its ceilings were high, detailed wood embellishments strung the room, and a small collection of professional art adorned the walls. A matching bookcase split the two windows and ran to the ceiling although the books themselves were disordered and frequently dropped or tossed when Adam finished using them. Visitor's eyes were also drawn to a chalkboard-on-wheels that was pushed to one corner, covered by a series of scribbled figures and dusted on the bottom with chalk leavings. A small round table stood next to his desk, and he had tucked a few chairs in there, each padded with black leather. The one orderly aspect of the office was here, a set of official-looking packets, squared and prepped for their arrival.

"So, how does this work, Adam?" Jennie asked, already impatient for the end.

"It should all be pretty simple. You sign a few lines and at the end you will be the proud new owners of Tulles Financial."

Jennie sat at the small round table. "Let's do it then."

"No, Jennie," Al said, a hand on his youngest's shoulder. "Adam needs to explain this situation fully. God forbid, there is ever a time when you have to discuss these relationships with the Clearwater Board or…other interested parties, you will need to have at least some understanding of how this is going to work. You will literally own this company and you'll be responsible for its actions. We can't have you flying blind."

Adam clapped the official-looking-packets together. "Right, so what I have done first is acquire the name and all the related legal documentation for a small French financial firm called Tulles Financial that is currently registered to do business in the United States, and they actually have done business here in the past and have tax filings going back to the 1950s. Why? It is important, or at least helpful, for both the Clearwater Board and any other potentially interested parties to see this company has financial context. That is, this company was not created yesterday and, therefore, not created simultaneously with the 234 Park Avenue project. Nothing about this," he tapped the packets with his finger, "is illegal. Your ownership will be absolutely legitimate. It's on record as having been facilitated by an overseas broker with the purchase happening in France. It was made with cash and like assets on June 1 in the name of Kiara and Gina Giordano with supplemental financing from a Swiss bank on the condition of anonymity, etc. etc., you get the idea. The Swiss loan has already been repaid in full, it's just a way to avoid any red flags. Buying a business entirely with personal cash raises eyebrows. You may also ask, why do we not simply let Al or Johnny run this company? The answer is first, we think it unlikely the courts will be so gung-ho about indicting two Italian women as they would be about two Italian men with criminal records. Should some, obviously false, charge be brought forward, we expect the proceeds from Tulles' investments will be safer from any predatory parties with you as the 'owners of record.' And two, Al thinks it more important now than ever, that his two daughters have financial security no matter what the future brings. This company will be that security for you, permanent financial security. In fact, you already have five employees at the newly established Manhattan branch, ready to restart the day-to-day operations for you. Carrie and Jennie, the two of you can have as much or as little involvement as you want. If you wish, I can continue to consult on the Tulles business, but after these papers are signed, I can no longer be connected with Tulles in any official capacity. The Clearwater Board would frown upon that, I think, although a few of the members are generally aware that I took part in the acquisition. Let me be clear though, for all *official* purposes, your father has absolutely nothing to do with 234 Park Avenue or Tulles Financial. You need to be aware of that in case you are ever asked to meet with any member of the Board, etc."

"You've already hired the five employees for us?" Carrie asked.

"Yes."

"How will they know what to do?"

"The first person I hired is a man named Gideon Hayes, and he will run the day-to-day of the company for you. He has been around Wall Street for a number of years and is generally aware, although not entirely aware, of our circumstances moving forward."

"And what if me and Jennie want to hire our own men?"

"You are right to test me, Carrie, but Gideon is known to the Clearwater Board as well. His presence gives Tulles legitimacy, with Clearwater, with other potential clients, with everyone. They will have less reason to do extensive background work with him in the fold, not that they would find anything untoward if they did. He is a necessary asset, plain and simple."

"And the others?"

"Three were hired directly from the would-have-been defunct Tulles branch in Chelsea. Again, this is in the interest of creating a continuation of the former business entity. And I hired a secretary. A woman named Rosabel, Sicilian even."

"I want to meet her."

"Jesus," Jennie said, "can we get through this first? I have stuff to do."

"Your hair appointment can wait."

"As if I need a hair appointment…"

Adam held his hands up. "Look, Gideon is a must. If you want another secretary, that's up to you." He flipped past the first couple of pages in the packet. "First signature is here," he said, pointing. "This agrees to the financials, which are detailed…here. Al, if you want to glance at them, it outlines what we discussed on the phone. This has already been executed, so you really don't have to worry about that part." Jennie signed quickly, a large and loose marking, and passed the pen to Carrie, who made a show of reading before eventually making her own mark, neat and small on the line. "Here is the lease on the office space. Pretty standard. Sign here. Here is Gideon's contract. Sign here."

"How much are we paying him?"

Adam's eyes flickered with amusement. He should have expected pushback from Carrie, but he hadn't. "One hundred twenty-five thousand dollars. Which is about 5 percent more than he was making."

"That was nice of us," Carrie said. "I just want to make sure we make more."

"You will make significantly more. Sign here." The sisters did and Adam flipped a few more pages. "This is the contract with Clearwater. You are charging them a percentage with a mechanism for fluctuation between 1–5 percent depending on a variety of financial circumstances. The table is here. By the project's conclusion, the Tulles earnings should total about $4 million. All other points of access, the ones not involving Tulles, will be directed through Roselli Construction and their subcontractors, but the majority of the Giordano family money, your actual family's money, will go through this company. Those other points of access will have to accept the legal and financial vulnerabilities of the Roselli company. Sign here."

Jennie did. Carrie perused the table.

"What is the FFR?"

"The Federal Funds Rate. It's a measure of interest rates determined by the Fed and useful for determining how much money is worth when it sits in a bank."

"And how much is it worth now?"

"Less than when it builds a skyscraper. Please sign, Car. I'm happy to meet with you any time you want to talk about it, after today."

"You have a hair appointment too?"

"I wish. I have meetings this afternoon. Getting this through Clearwater's middle management drones has been harder than I thought it would be. This afternoon will clear that up."

"It will," Al said, his silence finally broken with his rough growl, "and we will hurry of course." The comment was his specialty, a command obscured by its politeness. Carrie signed the final page and handed the packet back to Adam.

"Perfect," he said as he stood, smiling and shuffling the paperwork into his briefcase. "Congratulations, you two. You are the proud owners of a defunct French financial firm."

"Maybe we can make T-shirts," Bobby said. "Start a softball team."

"You and the old secretary."

"I like your enthusiasm, Bobby," Alphonse said. "Carrie is a pessimist. Don't let her break you."

Carrie frowned at their team-building attitude.

"All right, Daddy," Jennie said, kissing him on the cheek, "I have to go. Carrie," another kiss, "Bobby, Adam, thank you for hosting this wonderful party. If you need anything else, just let me know." Jennie pushed her way through the office doors and did not look back.

"It makes me sad," Al said, sighing.

"What?"

"I bet that secretary is a sweet ole lady and Jennie will never meet her."

The morning of June 28, 1973
Wallkill Correctional Facility in Ulster County, NY
"Luparelli, Thomas. Aged 19."

The smell of shit was oppressive in the small cell. A lack of ventilation made the porous bars of the fourth wall ineffective, and the air hung where it was, stagnant and warm. Clayburgh rubbed peppermint into his mustache. Murdock dropped three cinnamon lozenges into his mouth and breathed through cupped fingers around his nose. "I'm not sure we needed to see this scene when it was fresh," he said. "To be honest, I'd believe anything I read about this place as long as I was at my desk."

Clayburgh went to all fours and looked under Thomas Luparelli's bed. Through the delicate lattice of cobwebs, there was a book pressed against the back wall, an orange hardcover settled into the dust of the floor. "There's a book back there." Murdock knelt and reached blindly until he got it, read the title silently, and handed it to Clayburgh. *Les Miserables.*

"That's about prison, isn't it?" Murdock asked.

"I don't know. I wouldn't have thought our friend knew either." Clayburgh flipped through the thick set of pages to check for evidence of contraband and then tossed it on the bed.

Tommy lay faceup on the cold concrete of his six-by-nine in the dim morning light of Pod 2 on Cell Block A. The front of his uniform was covered in brown and red vomit, blood vessels had burst to color the whites of his eyes, his lips were purple from a lack of oxygen and had been darkening since his death sometime after 3:00 a.m. The smell was of Tommie's making, the stains evident down the backs of his legs when the detectives first arrived.

"Pardo!" Clayburgh called, his voice properly sharpened by the scene. The metallic clink of Officer Pardo's boots answered him until his face peeked into the cell. "Yes, sir?"

"Find somebody in charge of something at this place."

Pardo's doe-brown eyes made skittish contact as options cycled through his mind. "Warden? Or shift commander? They're, uh, both here, sir, if you want them."

"Both."

Pardo's heels clinked away at a jog.

"Is he Italian?" Murdock asked when the clinks faded.

"Pardo? No, I think he's Portuguese. Or Brazil or something. Why?"

Murdock shrugged. "Keepin' my eyes out for Italians, is all. Our witnesses have been turnin' up dead, remember? Make a note of that if you haven't already."

Clayburgh went back to the floor for a closer look at the needle resting in Luparelli's forearm. The body was glass and wider than most with black liquid still clinging to its sides. The needle mark was red and swollen, like he'd tried to lance a pimple, with the needle itself pushed an inch or more into his vein and the plunger down as far as it would go. He'd used his own sock for a tourniquet and it lay to his side, the foot it had covered now bare, its skin bluing along with his hands and face.

"There's no track marks," Clayburgh said to his partner. "How long was he in here?"

"May 10."

"That wouldn't be enough time for them to heal if he was a serious user beforehand." Clayburgh looked at the dead man's face, his tangled hair, his crooked nose, the bile crusted on his lips. "His story rang true to me when he told it. About gettin' fucked over by Pisani."

"He was certainly pissed off. You kind of forfeit the right to complain when you're stealin' Buicks for the mob though."

Clayburgh held the picture the guards had tweezed from Luparelli's open palm. "She might do the complaining for him," he said. He flipped the image over and read the inscription for the fourth time. They were thin letters, written in a flowing hand with pencil. *You or her.* At least the kid knew love before his time came.

"Detective Clayburgh," Pardo said when he returned, "this is Warden Baines, who is the, uh, warden, obviously, and Officer Vastolia, the shift commander for the morning guards."

"Thank you, Pardo. Mr. Vastolia, your guards have no idea how this picture got into his cell?"

"None at all," Vastolia said. He was distractingly fat in his brown-on-browner uniform with a billy club on his belt and what looked to be a refurbished .32-caliber CZ Yugo on his hip. It was a strange choice of handgun for a prison guard.

"You trust those men?" Murdock said. Judging by his overly furrowed brow, Vastolia was already at the top of his list of suspects.

"I will not do them the dishonor of saying I don't," Vastolia said, glancing briefly at Baines, "but I'm also not going to pretend this cell was impenetrable. It happens, Detective. We can't watch all eighty men all the time. If the kid asked for a picture, it could've happened."

"So, the question is, who is the woman?"

"It's his wife," the warden, with his gray suit and his gray pepper buzzcut, said. "They got married just a few days ago so, as Mr.

Luparelli put it, 'they were legal for taxes,' which basically meant he wanted her to inherit any money he had left, as far as I could tell."

"You did a ceremony here?"

"We had the justice of the peace come down for him. It's not as rare as you might think."

"Did he seem disturbed or angry during it?"

Baines looked to Vastolia, who said, "No, he looked happy. Like every groom before he's married."

"Did anyone else come with her?"

"A man came with her to drop her off. She said it was her father."

Murdock pulled one of the Pisani photos from his jacket. "Was it this man?"

"No. Not him, Detective. He was a tall man, over six foot. Brown hair, dark features. Less of a gut than this," Vastolia said, jiggling his immense stomach with his hand.

"Stop," Murdock snapped. "Less fat jokes." Clayburgh turned his laugh into a sniffle before Vastolia or the warden noticed and the guard let his stomach fall limp once again.

"And the needle?"

"It's one thing to bring a picture of an inmate's wife to him," Baines said, "but an entirely different thing to sneak in drugs. I would stake my reputation on it, none of our guards did *that*."

"Your reputation aside, Mr. Baines, I'd like you to make your staff available."

"If we must."

"You must." Clayburgh glanced around the room, his sights sticking on the book. "Did Mr. Luparelli ask for this book specifically?"

"Most likely. It is from our prison library. You can tell by the rebound orange cover."

"What's it about?"

The warden paused. "I'm surprised you haven't read it."

"I haven't"

"It's a novel about a former prisoner and his pursuit of revenge."

Murdock chuckled and shook his head. "If I were you, Warden, I wouldn't be lending that one out."

* * *

"Here," Patty Uhlhousen said as she tossed a scrap onto Clayburgh's desk.

"Thank you, Patty." Clayburgh flattened the paper and read the numbers off in his head. *I don't think the captain would care anyway, not really. Deep down he would know I'm doing the right thing. Either way, Patty will make sure I find out the answer.*

The phone rang a few times before a woman's voice came over the line. "Federal Bureau of Investigation, New York Office. How may I direct your call?"

"Ma'am, my name is Andrew Clayburgh. I'm a detective at the 19th Precinct here in New York City. I believe I have some information that may be of use to your Agents."

"Do you know the Agent's name?"

"No, sorry, I'm reaching out because I think I have information that may help them in a rather broad area. And I'd like to hear their opinion on my own case."

"What is that area, sir?"

"Organized crime. Organized crime in New York specifically."

"Hold please." Clayburgh opened Luparelli's file. A new file brought about a set of incompatible feelings. On the one hand, a new file was a reason for sadness, a reason to wonder why he'd ever wanted this job with its perpetual death. On the other, a new file meant an immediate and obvious flurry of activity, a relief from the still sadness of his previous failures. A few days later, you knew if you would either catch the perpetrator or not and the failure returned. But meeting Luparelli beforehand threw a wrench in his system. He was more angry than anything else. Angry at himself for not protecting the kid, angry at this unknown group of murderous men, angry at Warden Baines and his buzzcut and Officer Vastolia and his rippling fatness.

"Detective *Clayburn*?"

"Yes, ma'am?"

"The Agent in charge of organized crime in New York City is Special Agent Clerow Wilson, and he's in a meeting right now, but he'd like me to take a message for him and he'll get back to you."

"Do you know when his meeting is over?"

"He has a lot of meetings, sir."

Clayburgh shook his head. "Fine. I believe some very powerful criminals are about to be attacked by members of Al Giordano's Crime Family, specifically two men by the name of…"

June 30, 1973, at 4:30 p.m.
Italian Heritage Day parade on Columbus Circle, Manhattan, NY
"Power ain't meant for the patient."

"It's impressive how many of us he gets to show up to these things," Ricky said to Petey, who was shoveling lasagna from a paper plate into his mouth.

"It's more than I would've guessed. The food is shit though. And it's hot as fuck out here." Petey paused. "And don't say *us* yet…I know what you meant by that. Not yet." Ricky turned, nodded.

Petey was bursting through a light-brown sport coat and blue shirt, both doused inevitably and spotted by dark pools of sweat. His face was red to his collar, and his hair looked as if he had been dunked in one of the nearby fountains. His size made crowded areas uncomfortable, and he became especially ill-tempered at festivals, parades, and sporting events no matter their underlying purpose. Ricky was, to his constant frustration, Pete's favorite companion to these events. He suspected Petey saw lessons in his rants of the attendees, which he wanted to pass on or perhaps he was simply eager to preach about the crowd's overall malevolent nature and knew Ricky would listen quietly. Whatever Pete's thoughts on the food and heat, the festival had tens of thousands attendees, enough to make this one more impressive than most. People stood shoulder to shoulder for two blocks in either direction from the main stage in Columbus Circle, and most pressed even tighter as Joe Pisciotto's scheduled keynote grew close. Ricky could not see the current act from his vantage point, but the voice of an Italian language crooner was pumping from a set of nearby speakers.

"Who is this singer?" Ricky asked. "Do you know?"

"Some *Napolitano*. Fuck this Italian shit though. Give me Sinatra, in English." Petey scraped the last of his lasagna from the plate. "Why isn't Markie with ya?"

"There's an alcohol shipment today, and Markie does inventory after with Sean."

"That's the big motherfucker?" Petey held his hand above his head like a measuring stick.

"Yeah, he's like six five. Fuckin' big as an ox."

"Jesus." Petey dropped his empty plate on the ground. "All right, I need something easier to eat while we walk over to the stage. Pisciotto is gonna speak soon." He scanned the nearby food trucks. "You want some *spiedini*, Rick?"

"Yeah, I'll take a couple." The two walked to the side of the truck, around the line of customers, and bought five or six *spiedini* through the side door before making their way toward the stage. Rick simply fell in behind Petey and rode his wake through the masses.

"Can you see?" Petey asked as the stage became visible.

"Yeah, I'll be able to see." The two settled into an area on the right of the stage with an angled view. The music stopped minutes later, and the crooner and his band filed off, leaving a single microphone in the middle of the stage. A few people were milling around the sound equipment, but Ricky didn't see the media-loving Boss of the Pisciotto Family among them, so he focused on his *spiedini*.

"You know what any of Pisciotto's top guys look like?"

"Yeah," Ricky said, trying to think through all the new faces he'd encountered over the last few weeks. "I met, uh, Chuckie Esposito a few weeks ago at the club. He's a captain, I guess. I've met Paul Tomasi, a made guy. Jimmy Gazaria..."

Petey shook his head. "I'm not looking for them."

"Who you lookin' for?"

"Carmine Fiata." Petey squinted toward the backside of the stage. "Short, bald guy...always chewing on a cigar."

"What do you need him for?"

"I just want to know where the motherfucker is, that sneaky bastard. I don't want him leavin' too quickly." Ricky tried to follow Petey's eyes with his own, although he would not have any idea who Carmine was if he punched him in the gut. As they searched, a man addressed the microphone and it pulled Ricky's attention back to the center of the stage.

"Ladies and gentlemen," he said, "we thank you all for coming here today to celebrate with us!" The crowd let out a cheer. Some spectators had brought Italian flags or signs with short phrases, and they punched these into the air as he spoke. "We want to thank our sponsors for supporting this great event, our food trucks for the wonderful food, and of course, our entertainment. These singers have been just wonderful." The man clapped a few times and the crowd followed suit before he went on to list the most notable financial contributors. "But most of all," he said finally, "this event would not have been possible without our organizer, our benefactor, and as Italians, a beacon of our strength and unity even as immigrants or children of immigrants in this country. He has helped us restore respect for the Italian language, the Italian culture, and fought for us against the negative and unfair representations we have seen in recent years." The crowd cheered and applauded again. "A real force against discrimination in our judicial system, our economic system, our political system…it is my pleasure to introduce Mr. Joe Pisciotto!" The words reverberated through the microphone and off the tall, gray buildings that lined the square before falling back over the crowd. Their echoes mingled with cheers, screams, and claps as the Boss himself walked on stage and waved both hands to acknowledge his fans.

Pisciotto shook his announcer's hand as they passed before unbuttoning his collar and resuming his waves and smiles to the crowd. Ricky could tell the oppressive heat was getting to him even from his position some forty yards away. Both underarms were soaked, his hair was wet and pressed against his temples, and a V of moisture covered the front of his pale-yellow dress shirt.

Then Ricky heard static, radio static, close by and just beneath the cheers. He tried to keep his eyes on Joe but was distracted enough to scan the nearby patrons for the source. It came again, brief and close, a sharp *sssshhhhh* muddled in the din of the crowd. He looked over the patrons again, but they had not heard or else were better at ignoring it than Ricky. *Beep-beep, sssshhhhh,* the noise came again from the same source. Ricky knew it was in front of him, at the mid-riff of someone close by, and then he heard it again, *beep-beep sssssh-hhhh*—coming from the back of Petey's sport coat, a single step in front of him. He looked at Petey, puzzled as he had ever been. The Fat Man had not reacted. And then, in place of the beeps and the static, Ricky heard a shrill voice come from under the light-brown jacket. *"You see him, Pete?"* the voice asked before another loud beep. *Petey has a walkie-talkie.* He looked again at the patrons around them, but they appeared focused on Joe's onstage rhetoric and not the hidden walkie-talkie. Petey snapped the device from his belt and said, "No, I don't fuckin' see him. He should be right next to this motherfucker." Petey scanned the area desperately for his mark, even pushing a few people out of the way and edging farther right of the stage. Ricky followed. Pisciotto was still speaking, accepting applause for every few lines. Ricky followed Petey's search for a bald man with a cigar.

The two walked past the stage to the sparsely populated back-side, the home for a row of port-o-potties and the corresponding line. Petey shook his head in disgust and put the walkie-talkie back up to his mouth. "You see him, Vinnie?"

A pause and then the distorted response, *"No, and I've been all over this side of the stage."*

"Fuckin' hell," Pete said to nobody in particular. Ricky contin-ued to search and even jogged back toward the side of the stage to check again for any bald man with a cigar. He saw nothing before Pete appeared next to him, swears flowing from his lips and hurried communication with the others growing more frantic. His face was red, knuckles white against the plastic receiver...and then Ricky saw him. Across the yard, hidden at first by the thin metal skeleton of the stage, and then boldly walking alone with the late-afternoon sun on off his red scalp. There was no doubt. He was short and thick with an unlit cigar in his mouth as he was crossing the area on a line for the port-o-potties. Ricky tapped Pete on the shoulder, pointing to the figure. "Fuckin' Christ," Pete said before putting the walkie-talkie up to his mouth and laughing. "Vinnie, you're not gonna believe this. He's about to take a shit, back behind the stage."

"Fuck…I don't know if I can get over there. The speech is winding down. I'm comin' as fast as I can."

"Fuck this," Pete whispered, "I'll do this shit my fuckin' self." He pulled a silenced Beretta 70 from his jacket and took a step toward the cigar man, but Ricky grabbed his arm to stop him. He extended his hand instead. Petey followed the gesture from Ricky's hand up his arm to his face, eyes. "All right," he said. Petey dropped the gun into Ricky's palm.

"Fuck it, Vinnie," Petey said into the walkie-talkie, "we've got him. Tommie, do your part *now*." Rick scanned the area as he moved. Maybe twenty people could see him if they chose, but none had noticed this very serious exchange of a weapon between the Fat Man and himself. "Wait to hear the first shot," Pete said from a few steps behind before letting Ricky get ahead and fading into the background. The Beretta's grip slid ever so slightly in Ricky's hand as he walked, the soft rhythm of his steps enough to move it. There was no wind at all and hardly any sounds save the muffled speech running over the hidden crowd on the far side of the stage. He felt unseen despite those mingling around him. Their eyes were averted, their minds even further away.

When Ricky reached the door Fiata had disappeared behind, he put his hand on the latch to prevent the portable bathroom door from opening. He listened intently, silently, while a few people grumbled about the line without noticing the gun crudely concealed against Ricky's chest. He looked back at Petey. He tugged his ear and nodded a final ascent. Another second and Ricky wondered if this Tommie had heard Pete's command. Ricky heard a patron wonder, *"Does he think he can cut the line?"* Another second and he could hear the bald man moving around inside, finishing his business. Another second and his nerves were over him, his stomach roiling fast and angry, his mind anxious for escape. And it came. A loud report echoed through the circle and then another and then another. Screams and yells erupted from the hidden crowd, and the small contingent of line dwellers ran in all directions. Ricky felt the infectious chaos. He heard Fiata say, "What the fuck?" and stumble in his fear. Ricky allowed his mark to recover, leveled the gun at what he estimated was the man's chest or maybe a notch below, and squeezed the trigger. Bop—Bop-Bop—Bop, he fired and felt the man fall against the door. He moved his hand and let the body weight push open the door and spill onto the ground below. He looked down on Fiata's frame: four red pools had formed and were expanding on his chest, the unlit cigar drooped habitually from his lips, the skin slack around his neck and jaw. Ricky stowed the gun in his waistband and walked back to where Petey was standing. The Fat Man put an arm around him and patted his chest with an oversized, *spiedini*-stained fist.

June 30, 1973, at 6:35 p.m.
Arnold's Sbarro in Queens, NY
"It was like staring at the ocean with the goal of swimming across."

A few high-pitched beeps signaled for a newsbreak, and Tony turned the radio up in the 1956 Pontiac he borrowed from the Collision Center.

"Shots were fired today at the Italian Heritage Parade held at Columbus Circle in Manhattan. A crowd of some 15,000 had gathered to celebrate Italian history and culture when, as the featured speaker and well-known community organizer Joe Pisciotto stepped forward to address the crowd, shots echoed through the plaza. Panic ensued, but when order was finally restored, at least two men including Mr. Pisciotto lay dead. Police say hundreds of witnesses have volunteered information, but they have yet to make any arrests in connection with these events. Early indications are it will take several days for them to evaluate the credibility of their leads and narrow their search. Reaction has been swift and sympathetic to the victims of this heinous attack and their families..." the newsman said, his voice trailing away as Tony turned the volume back down. "I guess that's it," he said.

"I guess so."

Tony had requested Sammie Calabrese to represent the Capello *borgata* in the hit of Don Provenzano as a nod to his father, Guiseppe Calabrese, who was killed on bad information by Provenzano's men

275

when Sammie was still a child. Tony always liked Sammie, an over-weight kid when he first met him, who had any shred of arrogance beaten out of him by his classmates. He had been an outlier for his height, the uneasy way he stumbled over words, his soft gut and cheeks, but he'd left those insecurities behind. His gut was no longer soft, his speech had calmed, and he'd proven himself a loyal, capable man.

Sammie and Tony spent a week scouting Arnold's, a small Greek and Italian restaurant bar known for its antique look and feel. Inside, the decorations were museum pieces, the wood bar rubbed smooth by pints, and the floor so tread by shoe heels that the once-red floor was colored black except right against the walls. Tony imagined these were all things that drew Don Provenzano to the place three times a week. By now, the pair knew the regular staff, who would join the Don, what they'd order and when they would show up. Sammie had slipped the hostess a couple hundred bucks to make sure the crew was seated in a booth on the first floor, making it harder for Provenzano's bodyguards to draw their weapons. Tony and Sammie would each carry two semiautomatic Berettas loaded with twelve rounds through the narrow bar area, left into the first room of booths, they would fire on Provenzano's table, and make their escape through the side exit, over a small fence and back to their car.

"I hate being nervous," Sammie said as he finished cleaning his Beretta for the tenth time. "You still get nervous before this shit?"

"You're either nervous or you're stupid."

Sammie's hands were practiced on the gun's steel, and he locked the final pieces at a crisp pace, finalizing his work with a bump of the magazine and its satisfying *click*. "Well, I'm a genius then. What time you got?"

"Six fifty-six."

"The Old Man should be comin' 'round the corner then."

The minutes stretched themselves, so much so Tony sec-ond-guessed his watch more than once. A steady rain began to fall as they waited, thick drops from the twilight sky. Tony played scenarios over and over in his head…it was useless. Those figments obeyed him, and so his eyes wandered, anxiously, until they fell to his partner's Beretta, readied and held in his lap. Sammie's hand dwarfed the weapon like a squirt gun, one of the type his son Carmine carried in the neighborhood when he darted here and there with his friends. Tony's stomach rolled to think about it, to imagine. There was more to consider, he thought. His brothers for one, his honor another, but he hated the thoughts. He tried all he could to muffle them.

"There he is," Sammie said when a black Lincoln finally stopped at the curb. The driver jogged around the hood, the rain coming down in sheets now, to open the door for his passengers. Tony did not use the windshield wipers for fear of being noticed but cracked his window and strained to see. The first to exit was undoubtedly the bent form of Don Provenzano himself, the second looked like his son Michael, the third a man Tony could not recognize.

"It looks like there's only three of them. The Old Man, Michael, and some muscle."

"That's good then," Sammie said. They'd seen as many as five eat with the Don.

"Yeah, should be. I have no idea who that third guy is."

Sammie leaned closer to the foggy windshield. "I'm sure he brings different guys all the time. How long should we wait?"

"A few minutes at least. We need him to get settled. Fuck comin' into that barroom if they're standin' there. We'd end up with fifteen civilian bodies next to all the rest."

The rain escalated as they waited, splashing into ankle-deep puddles near the curb, and the two men did not say a word. They felt a weight in the air, a die had been cast, thrown by someone else, and there was no way back.

At 7:33 p.m., the pair of *mafioso* stepped from the car in dark suits and brown ankle-length trench coats to make their way across Farrington Street and into the restaurant. Sammie led Tony through the cramped bar to the hostess stand guarding the dining room full of booths.

"Where's our friend at?" Sammie asked the young hostess he paid earlier, pointing expectantly toward the room of booths. Tony leaned back against her stand and kept a wary eye on the crowd and doorways.

"I'm sorry," the hostess said in hushed tones, glancing left and right at her coworkers. "I was going to sit them in the booth like you asked, but he was meeting people."

Sammie's lips twitched with disbelief. "What do you mean they were meeting people? I told you, his son told *us* to surprise him here."

"A group of men came in, six of them, and asked for a room upstairs. We sat them over an hour ago, and they've just been waiting, drinking wine, and eating breadsticks. When Mr. Provenzano's party arrived, he said it was to meet *them*. He knew where they were sitting. I'm sorry, I can give you the money back."

Sammie looked at Tony. *We have not discussed upstairs.* Tony asked the hostess, "How many rooms are up there?"

"There's four. They're in the biggest one. I'm sorry, but I don't understand why it matters. You're still welcome to join them. I just couldn't put that many people in a booth."

Sammie ignored her, his large brow furrowed by deep lines. "What do we do, Ton?"

"Honestly...I don't fuckin' know." Tony turned to the hostess again. "Did the six men leave a name?"

"Yes," she said, scanning her notes. "Mr. Fish, reservation for nine. And he asked for one of the upstairs rooms."

"Jonny Fiscella, has to be," Tony whispered up to his partner. "That's more than just the brain trust. He's got soldiers with him. Nine guys? I don't know who all he'd bring with him."

"God damnit."

Tony tried to collect his thoughts over the babble of the room. "Pisciotto thing must have freaked him out," he said to himself more than Sammie. "They knew about it beforehand or heard right after... and he called a group of them to meet. They could be upstairs talkin' about," he tugged his ear, "or Phil. Or Vic. Or Don C." All his scenarios had been set ablaze.

"Nine of them? Jesus. That's a lotta guys in that room."

"They won't all be armed." Tony knew that was little consolation and possibly untrue. At least half would be, maybe more. Sammie was looking to him for answers, and Tony could not offer any good ones. A decision seemed to be there, still seemed to exist in front of them, but in reality, it had been made a week ago and remade this afternoon before they ever made it to the restaurant. There was no security in half measures. "We have to do it. Backing away will give them time to plan. We have no choice. Surprise is our only advantage," Tony said, pulling Sammie away to make the case he'd made internally. "Try to keep moving in there. Don't stand still. Don't quit firing. Find the Old Man, fire at him four or five times, and then we both get out of there. Don't worry about anybody else." Sammie nodded. Tony clapped his shoulder. "Let's do it then."

The staircase to the second floor climbed at a steep angle and ended in a deserted hallway with two doorways on either side. Tony paused to listen. Most of the noise was coming from the farthest room on the left. He pointed to it and Sammie nodded. They walked softly, calmly, to flank the final room. Garbled Italian floated from inside, confirming their targets. They drew their weapons. Tony dared a peek and saw the Don, seated right in the middle. His heart beat quickly, his brow wet, his guns cold. *Four or five at the Old Man and run.* He counted for Sammie...*one...two...three...*

The sound of gunfire reverberated off the walls, puncturing the air and deafening the men. The first few cracks were sharp, but by the end they were nothing more than dull thuds against their skulls. Provenzano's men reacted with amazing speed upon seeing the two gunmen spin free of the doorframe and forward into the room. The Old Man was tackled from his chair by one of his guards, and Tony saw two or three bullets rip through that protector's back. He saw others reach for their pockets, only to come up empty-handed and dying. Tony squeezed the trigger, he was not counting how many times, until his weapons clicked and clicked without a report. He turned and ran back down the hallway, down the stairs into the bar, and through the crowd of hungry patrons to the door and then the street. He ran to the Pontiac and fired the ignition. He looked back at the restaurant. Tony sat there for an instant, searching for Sammie's hulking frame, but the first figure to emerge was not his friend. The man was slight and covered in blood, a pistol in his hand. Tony did not wait. He slammed the gas and sped off as bullets shattered his window. He ducked his head until the street corner where he turned out of sight.

He drove another block before allowing himself to check the mirror. He could see the corner. He imagined Sammie chasing the car around the corner, could have hesitated with hope, but his instincts were truly in control. He opened his window to the rain and sucked in gulps and gulps of fresh, cool air to calm himself. *I have to hide the car.* Bystanders had certainly watched him speed away, and the back window was shot out. Jerry's? No, he could not park it where it would implicate his friends. He could not go to his house. And then there was the stiffness in his right arm, the subtle failure in its movements. He looked, regretted it, and looked again. His coat was stained red from his wrist to his elbow, and a small hole had pierced the fabric about halfway between the two. He had been shot.

An evening in the fall of 1984
Home of Vyacheslav Usenko

V cooed delicately into his granddaughter's spongy cheeks and brushed his fingertip against her light-brown skinfolds. He rocked her car seat on the kitchen table, and each brief swing split her mouth into a wide, irreproachable smile he did his best to match. He failed and felt awkward, but the baby girl did not seem to mind. Instead, her brown eyes twinkled in the light of the chandelier, and the room was filled with forceful fits of innocence and joy.

V glanced into the dining room where his son Brandon, his wife Helen, and Brandon's wife Luzviminda (mercifully shortened to Luzi by her family) were sitting. He was by now accustomed to his daughter-in-law, a short, energetic woman with the black hair and brown skin of her native Philippines. She was a decade younger than Brandon, still just twenty-six, and holding easily to the handsome qualities of youth. V had seen the pictures of their house together, a ramshackle building near Luzi's village held together with what amounted to construction by-products. Helen oohed and aahed at each snapshot and humble-brag her son put forth about their life without "material objects." V was happy to laugh with his grand-daughter and ponder the difficulty of the Knicks' upcoming road trip. *A road trip that for all of its "material objects" would be devoid of monsoon-driven floods or poisonous snakes. And we're the idiots.*

V let them carry on among themselves. He pulled the giggling baby Lilibeth from her seat and lay back in his recliner with her on his chest. He wiped spit from her lips and let her grab his thumb and chew it. She was teething by now, and V felt her hardening gums as she explored his Cheetos-stained fingers. *Smart girl.*

A flash and camera snap brought him back from his abstraction. "What the hell?" he said, looking up to catch Luzi with the camera in her hands, his son and wife over her shoulder and smiling. "You're going to blind this baby, you psychopath."

"It was too cute, *Lolo*," Luzi said, using the Filipino word she had taught him a half hour ago.

V pulled his sloppy thumb from Lili's mouth. "I don't want to be *Lolo*," he mumbled. "*Lolo* is for people living in the swamp jungles. Can't you give me some other name? I want to be Wise Turtle."

Brandon guffawed stupidly for the benefit of his mom and wife. "Shut up, Dad. You're *Lolo*. Parents get to choose what kids call their grandparents."

V took his finger and flipped Lili's pouty lips. "I vote she gets to choose when she starts talking. You'd pick something better, baby girl, wouldn't you? Something I can understand?"

"She's going to speak mainly Filipino," Brandon said. He tried to make his voice sound commanding, but it fell short and seemed to falter and stutter in the air.

"Tell your dad," V said in Grandpa-instinct baby-talk, "you need to know enough English to talk to your Wise Turtle about the Knicks. And the Dodgers if they ever start to win again."

"We don't have cable on the island," Brandon said. Helen smacked her son playfully for arguing and sat down on the arm of V's chair to tousle the baby's hair and smack her husband next if need be.

"By the time this kid shoots her first free throw, they'll have cable figured out."

"I doubt it." The girls were laughing at the two now.

"You're right, she'll probably be hitting free throws before she can walk...well, then she can live with us. She shouldn't be raised in a country that can't figure out malaria anyway. I have genuine concerns. You were a survivor weren't you, Luzi? Of course you were, real Mowgli type I bet." Helen smacked V this time, but Luzi was laughing.

"Dad," Brandon said cautiously, "I want us to go to dinner tonight."

"Why? We'll just order pizza here with the girls."

"Luzi and Mom are taking Lili to the Light Show downtown."

V shook his head no. "It'll be too loud for Lili, and she doesn't want to see the lights. They're communist lights."

Brandon did not care what communist lights were. "Me and you are going to dinner. We should catch up, just the two of us. I'm sure you have plenty of advice to give me."

"Fine. We're going to Traci's then."

"Fine."

* * *

V and his son left just before the sun disappeared completely and made their way through the middle of town to the small "restaurant district" in the older section, which was almost unchanged since Brandon left. They drove straight to a small, cozy bar named *Traci's* V had been attending regularly since the early 1960s. The air outside was cooling fast, but when they opened the door, *Traci's* seemed to breathe hot breath on them from deep inside. A few of the regulars tipped their glasses to the Usenkos from V's usual side of the bar, but Brandon passed them for a corner booth. The place was simple and plain with a few neon lights, a dartboard, and some words scrawled out in sharpie on the white wood walls. The barflies had their backs to them, but it was the same regulars, their wide, soft frames now as discernible to V as any other. The group of them had found the bar almost simultaneously and stayed for decades to work through their problems together.

"I recognize some of the faces still," Brandon said, "even if their guts are larger."

"They're the same in any way that counts." V passed a menu to his son and grabbed another for himself.

Brandon counted the flannels, beards, and old stories around him. "I do miss this part of civilization."

"The drunks? They're the only people I'd miss."

"I meant bars. Air-conditioning."

"There's no air-conditioning here," V said, bristling at the assumption. "On Saturdays during happy hour, Traci opens the big fridge in the back so the coils unfreeze. It's the most popular time of the week, so she figures that's when it'll do the most good. There's a thirty-eight-degree breeze in here for an hour or so though. Doesn't help us much tonight."

"That's a nice sentiment, I guess."

"Sentiment, what? That's a fact."

"Don't argue with me. I'm just saying…"

V perused the menu he knew by heart for a few minutes in silence—"I love my granddaughter," he said, the short phrase the result of a long internal discussion about how to broach the subject.

"I know. I can obviously see that." Brandon's voice carried a twinge of guilt. "Seriously, I am so happy for you to meet her. We didn't want to fly with her, is all…that's the only reason…" but the bartender, an attractive brunette in shorts and hiking boots, interrupted them with two Busch Lights and a toss of her hair.

"Thank you, Mixie," V said, eyeing her neon blue and red features as he always did. "Have you met my son Brandon?"

"Oh, nice to meet you, Brandon. Did I guess right on the Busch Light?"

"Yeah, thank you."

Mixie threw a playful swat at V. "You know, now that you say it, you guys do look a lot alike. The eyes are the same. And these cheekbones." She ran her red nails along Brandon's cheek.

"He got married despite that. And he has a little baby girl now."

"Oh my god," Mixie said, gasping politely. "V, you're a grandpa?"

"Yeah, I am a *grandpa*," V said, making deliberate eye contact with his son as he said it. "I'm just another old man now. No longer apart of the youngsters like you."

"That's incredible," Mixie said, smiling and giggling. "Oh, I am so happy for you. Both of you, that's just wonderful."

They both ordered burgers, and Mixie left them to their business. The conversation came slow between them, and by the time their food came, they had barely spoken a word. The beers helped, though, and by the fourth one they were talking about work. Work and sports were the easiest topics for V to discuss with his son.

"Mom says you're writing a new book," Brandon said, grease dripping through his fingers while he chewed. He caught it with a napkin before it fell to the table or onto his basket of fries.

V shrugged and took an awkward, three-finger swig from his bottle. "Work in progress."

"About?"

"Mafia. I've been interviewing some guys as research."

"That's sounds very interesting."

V took another awkward drink. "You know, honestly, it's the first time I've been scared in a long time," he admitted. "Some of these guys just have a scary way about them. It's weird when a guy tells you he killed someone and he's sitting at the same table as you. One told me he sawed a guy's legs in two. Or fuckin' tied somebody up and shoved a live rat in his mouth. How the fuck does anyone do that? But others, it's not as easy. Others, I don't know, you don't seem to mind no matter what stories they tell."

"Anybody I'd know?"

"You remember the name Giordano?" V already knew the answer though. Brandon had been visiting when the trials began and read as many articles as he could find. Whenever he came home, Brandon read news articles for days and days, but V remembered the Giordano binge was especially enthralling for his son.

"Yeah, I remember that name. They had the craziest turf war with this other Family. Goddamn shootouts on the street."

"Provenzano. That was the other Family."

A glimmer ran through Brandon's eyes. V could not help but smile. "Right," Brandon said. "And then...the construction thing? Apartments? They were in that too, right?"

"Yeah, they were in on the apartment thing."

"A lot of money. How many of these guys have you talked to?"

"I don't know, I think seven now. There's something real about them, you know? Something authentic about these guys. My publisher called it a 'Batman angle,' but I don't know if that's the right way to think about it. There is some kind of sincerity in it somewhere, but you just feel dirty after. And sad." V slopped down another bite of his burger and a drink of his beer. "I'm having trouble with the actual writing though."

"You always told me to read other authors when I get stuck."

"I've been reading other authors. 'The crisp, clean smell of salty air on her face...,'" V mocked, "you know how bad the fuckin' oceans smell? Nobody can call that clean, but I can't recreate what I'm feeling...the shit I feel interviewing them...I can't find it outside that one moment. I can't find it at my desk. The only thing I could ever write at that desk is how to hate everything I've ever written, but still sell enough of the shit so that you don't have to write as many shitty books in the future."

"You can write about a sea captain without being a sea captain."

"I read one say, 'He gave her a look of pure justice.' What the fuck? And they all talk about the 'smell of blood.' I've never smelled blood. What does blood smell like?"

"You haven't been around enough of it. As in the quantity. You can smell blood if there's enough of it."

"Those hospitals smell like blood over there? When Lili was born?" Brandon did not answer but took a swig of his beer. "You sure it isn't death?" V asked. "I know death has a smell. Especially if death has been around for a while."

"You're either making it too complicated or you're just making excuses. I can't tell which."

V shrugged. "You could be right."

Brandon brought the true subject back. "Is it nonfiction?"

"It's a real story...call it what you want." V went back to chewing on his burger and beer. "Have you been writing then?"

"Only for grants. Nothing creative."

"You should still write creative things even if it's only for you." V recited the lines from his early years as a father.

"I don't need a push," Brandon said. "I don't have time. I know you think I live in a hunter gatherer society with no schedule, but this shit is hard work. I'm on the move fifty to sixty hours per week for these villagers."

"How do you work that much and you haven't figured cable television out yet? I'd have that shit up in a week, or there wouldn't be any villagers left."

"There's a lot going on. We're helping these people."

"I understand the point of what you do," V said, his features coiling in an unfamiliar way. "I just don't understand why my son has to be so involved in a problem so far away."

"It's important."

V gulped the last dregs of his beer and allowed the empty bottle to wobble noisily when he set it down. "I want to see my granddaughter."

"I know. And you will. It's important to both of us."

"She's the first thing I've cared about in a while. So that brings me up to four people. Your dumb ass, I'd prefer Luzi survives the next monsoon season, Lilibeth, and your mom, as much as she pisses me off."

"I know, Dad. I love you too."

"Don't forget that when you're sitting in the jungle."

The evening of June 30, 1973
Brooklyn, NY

Tony's jaw was clenched as if the pain had kickstarted the rigor mortis his subconscious thought inevitable. Every inhale was sharp and shallow, every exhale forceful. The farther he drove, the less adrenaline lingered in his system and the more intense the bone reverberating agony became. Fear was all that pushed him on. Disorganized, relentless, angry, desperate fear. He checked his mirror frantically, amazed each time it was free of blue and red sirens. He kept going, through the East Side along the river, making turns and running lights while every thought was clouded with pain and dizziness. He moved forward anyway, his left arm steering as the other drained its contents. His blood was everywhere. Floor, dashboard, consul, pedals, steering wheel, and door handle were all smeared with red by the time he passed over Broadway. He needed to stop, he needed to call someone, but he just kept checking his mirror for sirens. He knew he couldn't go home. There were old places, safe places; they were everywhere if he could remember them. Places he stashed cars or hid out from beat cops or gambled or played hooky or fucked girls or fenced radios…he was mad and confused and his blood was everywhere, worse now than ever before.

He saw a video store he knew and passed it. He wanted to go back to it, but his limbs wouldn't turn the car around. *Forward.* His sight was blurred by a hateful mist, enveloping him. His right arm dragged at him like an anchor. The other cars passed him with confused looks on their faces. *Stop passing me you fucking assholes.* He was desperate to speed off or stop, but he couldn't.

There was a pull-off to his right covered with gravel and bordered by a freestanding house, a light-blue house. He wanted to hide in a house so blue and so light. The Pontiac skidded as he hit the brakes and drove across with his left hand to click the gearshift clumsily into place. He pulled the cloth belt from his trench coat and wrapped it around the bicep of his useless arm to stall the incessant flow of blood, but the mist was winning, and his eyes glazed with contempt. His tourniquet was snug, not tight, so he placed one end in his mouth and stretched his neck backward as far as it would reach and then further and harder until finally it was as unbearable as the wound. He looked at the mess he created, the puddles of blood in the car, but his vision was narrowing and the blackness pushed him. He let his eyes shut. Now it was only the blackness. *I want to see blackness forever. Not these other things, these colorful things. I want it to be calm and black and nothing, forever.* His arm would not hurt and he would never have to have to think about anything…

Knock-knock. Tony did not want to see anything. *Knock-knock.* He did not want to see a goddamn thing again as long as he lived. *Knock-knock-knock.* He was going to kill whoever was making noise. His eyes opened slowly. An elderly man with shock white hair sticking up at all angles was peering through his windshield. "Sir," the man said, his jowls flopping about as he talked, "are you all right?" Tony looked at his consul, dashboard, steering wheel, door handle, floor, and pedals. *Stupid asshole.* He opened his door and spilled out at the man's feet. "Oh, sir, let me help you," the man said, reaching his hands under Tony's arms and providing what feeble assistance he could. Tony wobbled there, left arm around the old man and right arm cinched shut with his belt, while he refocused. His arm was still in terrible pain, but the blood loss seemed to have slowed.

"Help me inside," Tony growled, his head still foggy and slow. Dried blood flaked from his hand when he flexed it, thick and dark beneath his fingernails.

"Of course. We'll call an ambulance."

"No ambulance. Just inside." The man looked at him skeptically, but the intensity of Tony's eyes silenced him. The pair hobbled up the front stairs, into the light-blue house and to a seat at the kitchen table where Tony dropped. "I need to use your phone." The man set a black dial in front of him before stepping away to watch with reluctant interest. Who knew what fantasies were swirling behind the old man's forehead? Tony ignored him, swung the dial, and heard rings on the other end of the line.

"Hello?"

"Vito?"

"Tony!" Vito said, his voice unnaturally shrill. "Where are you?"

"I'm off the street, Vito, but I'm in bad shape. I need somebody. I'm shot." He tried to keep his voice steady, but it was difficult. The pain was back in force.

"Fuck. Fuck," Vito said, smacking his phone against some nearby surface. "How bad?"

"I don't think it's gonna kill me."

"Where?"

"My forearm through the bone." Tony inspected the wound for the first time since he managed to wrap the belt around his arm. "It's broken. I need some fuckin' painkillers."

"All right. Fuck. Where are you?"

"What's your address?" Tony asked the old man. "Two-oh-two on Eighteenth in Brooklyn. That's Gowanus, he says."

"All right, stay put then," Vito said. "I'll be out there."

"Painkillers," Tony reminded him.

"All right, painkillers. I got it."

Tony hung up, put his head in his left hand, and held it. He needed a plan. Vito would come get him, but he needed to get away. He could not stay in the city. He had to get out fast.

"Should I call the hospital?" the old man asked. "You look like you've lost a lot of blood."

"No." Tony pulled the empty Beretta from his pocket and leveled it at the man. "I'm sorry, sir, but you don't get to move until I leave." The man's eyes popped with fear and flitted from the gun barrel to Tony and back again. He raised his hands in surrender, his lips twitching soundlessly up and down. "Sit down," Tony said. The old man obeyed. "Hands on the table." Tony walked over to the window, which faced toward the street. The gravel pull-off was short and narrow. Pedestrians were walking on the sidewalk, about ten yards from the front step. Tony pulled the shades closed in the kitchen and entryway and sat down again at the table. The fingertips on his right arm were numb and purpling, but he was still afraid to remove the belt from his upper arm. Instead he rubbed his thumb over each finger to test their function, raining dried blood on the table as he did. They moved at least.

"What's your name?"

"Terry," the man answered softly, as if excess volume might be what set his captor off.

"I'm sorry this is happening to you, Terry. You are safe. I just can't have you movin' around."

"Don't worry. I'll be right here. You tell me when and where." His voice was Brooklyn and more blue collar than the house itself.

"We're just waiting on my brother, that's all." Tony moved to the cabinets, rummaging through them for anything useful. "He's goin' to come get me." There were coffee grounds behind one door, and he made a pot in the old-style coffeemaker on the counter. All Terry had was some Eight O'Clock, but it was enough to pass the time and distract him from the hole in his arm. "You want a cup?" Tony asked.

"Sure, I'll take one."

Tony found a second mug after more rummaging and poured for his host. In the confusion of his arrival, Tony had not taken much stock of the man sitting in front of him. Terry appeared to be well-off from the furnishings. Everything was of an attractive craftmanship, the paint looked fresh and modern, the kitchen and adjoining rooms were well-maintained. Tony's visit was unannounced, and yet there were no dishes in the sink, the garbage was empty, no untoward smells in the air. "Where is your wife?" Tony asked when he was back at the table.

"She died," Terry answered over his mug. "Cancer."

"I'm sorry to hear that." A picture of a younger Terry with what must have been his wife and four kids hung close by on the wall. Tony leaned over for a closer look. They were all dressed in outdoorsman gear, boots and backpacks and the like, with a snow-capped mountain rising up into the bright blue sky behind them. "These are your kids?"

"Yes."

"And where are they?"

"Holden is our oldest, he works at a bank. A teller in Connecticut. He gave us three grandbabies," Terry said, a smile crossing his lips and eyes. The thoughts seemed to calm his nerves, and he even let himself sink back into his chair. Tony leaned to the picture so he could see the features of the eldest. He had jet-black hair, a svelte build, and held his two sisters close to him. Holden was clearly his father's son; their faces were mirror images of a differing age. Terry continued, "We had two girls in the middle, Josephine and Margaret. Josephine married a pharmacist and lives in Maryland with another grandbaby of ours all grown up and off at school. Margaret, she has the light-brown hair, died in a car crash soon after that picture was taken. She was seventeen years old, my little girl, fond of her bright sundresses and Gene Kelly, just a few short months from graduation. And then our youngest, Henry there, he died in the war. He was one of those paratroopers. The Army told us his communication failed on a drop, and he ended up cut off from his squad and pinned down with another young boy from New York. They never recovered his body." Tony was surprised to hear of so much death in the light-blue house and noticed the extent of Terry's frailty for the first time. The figure before him was not the man of years ago, about to lead his children up the mountain. Now his skin fell loosely on his face like a warped mask, and liver spots covered his hands and head. His fingers were gnarled and disfigured, turning awkwardly at his joints. Tony turned back to the family picture and the ghosts that lingered there.

The two men got along well enough as they waited, reminiscing about their best years and after and how they lived. Tony told him about Carmine and his frustrations, and Terry told him about Holden, Henry, and his own faults. Their wives were beautiful with energy and verve, they agreed, but stubborn and rigid and uncompromising.

By the time they heard Vito's car crackling gravel beneath his tires, the blood was caked dry on the pistol grips and liquified on the table by Tony's sweat. He tried to wipe it cleanly with his sleeves, but it only served to smear what was there. He frowned and left it be.

"That's my brother."

Terry nodded. "I would think so."

"Thank you for the coffee."

"I wish you happiness, Tony. I'm afraid I can't wish you success but happiness."

"That sounds wise, Mr. Terry." Tony walked to the door and tipped his gun in salute. "To your happiness as well."

June 30, 1973, at 9:15 p.m.
Arnold's Sbarro in Queens, NY

Murdock was disgusted by the group of men standing at the far end of the hallway. "Why do they all have to have sunglasses? What percentage of people do you think wear sunglasses in normal society?"

Clayburgh glanced at them, more to humor his partner than for any real interest. "I don't know. Maybe 15 percent? Twenty-five?"

"And look at these idiots." Murdock kept his voice low so only Clayburgh could hear. "Six for six. Some kind of sunglasses anomaly. And do they not know how stupid it looks to carry sunglasses at nine o'clock? The sun is not gonna sneak up on you."

Clayburgh wasn't much more impressed than his partner. The men were the FBI Agents leading the investigation into what the hell had happened in the last six hours. Clayburgh was returning from a matinee showing of *Live and Let Die* with a rather chesty evening companion when he heard about the Pisciotto shooting on the radio. He was discussing Roger Moore one minute and the cold-blooded public assassination of Joe Pisciotto the next, then thirty agonizing minutes to get back to his date's neighborhood. He called Murdock from a pay phone and the two met at the precinct shortly after, intending to drive to Columbus Circle and work with whatever officers caught the case. That was not to be. As they were gathering their notes on Nick Pisani, Tommie Luparelli, the Berdan and Benfield murders, Al Giordano, and the cement union, another call came in. This one claimed there were five dead, six wounded following a gangland-style shootout in an Italian restaurant. When they heard the surname Provenzano mentioned, the two detectives switched objectives and made their way to Queens. It had been disturbingly easy to gain entry, but the Agents shut them out on the stairs until Clayburgh dropped the name Clerow Wilson, a note he'd managed to scribble following his call. They summarized their case to a crime scene grunt with an FBI jacket who told them to wait in the corner before trotting off to inform someone with sunglasses. And now, they waited.

"Do you think if I yelled 'sun' and pointed at the ceiling in a really convincing way—"

"You would get tackled and handcuffed?" Clayburgh finished. "Yes. I think that." He scanned up and down the worn and narrow staircase again. "It was bold to do this upstairs, right? Tight staircase. Patrons at the bar and you would know you're going to have to make your way back through. That's a lot of eyes on you."

"Shooting the primary speaker at an event with fifteen thousand witnesses…also bold."

"Fair. Still this location is not ideal."

At last, around 10:00 p.m., the Agent in charge approached the detectives. He was fit for his age (maybe late fifties) with salt-and-pepper hair, red cheeks, bleach-white teeth (at least he was smiling), and a brown leather shoulder holster wrapped around his torso. "Special Agent Gregg Meriwether," he said, "and I've caught this tragic scene. Agent Grimauldi said you guys may have some information for us?"

Clayburgh nodded and offered what he hoped was a genial face. "I don't want to overstate our case, Agent Meriwether, but we had informants telling us something like this was going to happen. Not when or where, but people knew what happened today was in the works."

"This and the Columbus Square shooting you mean?"

"Yes," Murdock said, "we think there is at least a tenuous link between this scene and what happened there."

"Well, let's have it, Detectives. What do you have for us?"

Clayburgh laid out the murders of Berdan and Benfield, the fingerprints at the scene, the warning from Newman's wife, and the connection to the cement union, Tommie Luparelli's ID of Nick Pisani before his subsequent "suicide," the tip Clayburgh left with Agent Wilson's desk, and the street-level belief, now validated, that the Mafia Bosses were about to go to war. Two of those Bosses had now been attacked in the space of three hours.

Throughout the explanation Agent Meriwether nodded politely. "It's interesting," he said, flipping through the surveillance photos of the union election. "Not altogether unexpected though, I'll admit, with a shooting like this."

"We think this may represent some kind of shift in power," Murdock said. "Two Bosses, as our witness called them, in one day cannot be a coincidence. Our informant seemed to think these gangs had deep-seated issues at the highest levels."

"It's possible. That's not what you want to hear, though, with something like. It means there may be more." Meriwether handed the photos back to Clayburgh. "The shooter looks Italian too."

Clayburgh was surprised. "You already caught the shooter?"

"I wish we were that good," Meriwether chuckled, "but no. The shooter is one of the DOAs. Or at least one of the shooters is. Witnesses say there were two shooters, both white men in coats and suits. Both here a few days before according to the staff. They, the shooters I mean, tried to have this party seated downstairs, but that plan was thrown off when additional guests joined. The hostess said they discussed it briefly and decided to go upstairs anyway, pretending to be friends of the men already there."

"Makes sense."

"What's the shooter's name?" Murdock asked.

"We don't know. No ID on him. No anything on him." Agent Meriwether looked back at the doorway, thinking. "Look, I can give you guys fifteen minutes in there if you want. Before they move the bodies."

"Thank you, sir," Clayburgh said. Their wait was worth it.

The detectives followed Agent Meriwether into the room. It was smaller than they expected, especially with the large table that dominated the floor. It was still set for dinner, although sprayed with blood at several points. The back wall was close, only about eight to ten feet away. *Fish in a barrel.* Immediately to the left lay a hulking mass of a man, facedown with a pistol in each hand. Murdock kneeled next to him to count the exit wounds on his back, like little carnation boutonnière's darkening and wilting as they stiffened. Clayburgh went to the table, four more bodies, still where they fell. Three were on the near side, shot with their backs to the door or in the process of turning, and another lay on the far side facing the back wall.

"Who are the bodies?" Clayburgh asked.

Meriwether pulled his notes and pointed at the men in turn. "Like I said, shooter is a John Doe. Nearside left is Frank Rizzo, nearside middle is Nicola Gurreri, nearside right is Calgero Ardizzone, and far side DOA is Michael Provenzano. Ring any bells?"

"Just Provenzano," Murdock said. "Not Michael though. Cesare is the Provenzano we were expecting. Any relation?"

Meriwether checked his notes again. "Yeah…Cesare was here at the dinner. He's Michael's father. He took two bullets and cracked a rib, but last I heard he's still alive. Apparently, his son shielded him when the shooters entered. That's how Michael ended up with *seven* bullet holes."

"Jesus."

"At least one of the father's wounds was a through-and-through on Michael too, so the son definitely saved him. Shame though. The father's old and barely hanging on. It may all be in vain."

Clayburgh flipped over Gurreri. He was shot through the neck, his blood dousing the table where he sat. "So, am I hearing you right that at least eight shots were fired at the two Provenzanos?"

"Yes."

Clayburgh counted more than a dozen holes in the back wall. "How many shots were fired total?"

"Our preliminary count is thirty-three this way," Meriwether said, pointing toward the table, "and thirteen the other way."

"That's one hell of a percentage in a group of…how many?" Murdock scribbled what numbers he could. He was hoping to see the crime scene photos as well, but that was a matter for another time.

"Nine men in the room, plus the two shooters."

"What did the witnesses say about the guy who got away? The one who survived the shooting I mean," Clayburgh asked, now kneeling by Frank Rizzo. Frank had not been able to draw his gun.

"Well, that's the biggest reason why I'm partial to your Mafia theory," Meriwether said, chuckling. "Each witness, I mean witnesses in this room, claimed he could describe the shooters in great detail when they reached the hospital, so I sent a few guys over there to take their statements." Meriwether gave another chuckle and shook his head. "They all claimed they were shot at by middle-aged Black women. Including Cesare Provenzano."

Clayburgh could not believe it. "His son dies shielding him from a hail of bullets and he's not going to help catch who did it?"

"He seems to have a different solution in mind."

"Of course, he does."

"Fucking lunatics."

One night in July 1973
Benjie's apartment in the Bronx, NY

Vito took in what he could of Benjie's apartment by only the scant light of the streetlamps falling through the windows. It wasn't much, worse even than their mother's, but Vito knew it was about claiming independence more than anything else. He could tell the units were converted office space, partitioned and sold as a dozen or so one-bedroom living spaces, each with their own unique architecture. Benjie's featured a large water pipe, fed down one wall and through the floorboards with a two-inch gap around it. It was enough that you could study your neighbor's hairlines as they watched TV.

Vito heard them well before they entered and took a seat in the living room chair, holding Gari by the scruff to prevent him from charging the door. Benjie came first with the girl stumbling a step behind him, giggling as he flipped on the lights. Vito stayed still and quiet and the pair did not notice him, not surprising given their engagement with each other. Benjie kissed her in the doorway and his lips moved down from there, tugging her dress from her shoulders after he closed the door. Benjie felt her chest, and she threw her head back and moaned. He pushed her against the wall, roughing her brown hair and tugging her hips into his. Vito watched, petting the dog. He would've been amused ten years ago, proud even, but he was impatient now. Benjie went further then, pulling the girl's dress to her knees, and Vito was slugged by a flash of white-hot anger. He drew his pistol and fired two shots, *Bwap-bwap*, into the wall just below the window. The shots were answered by puffs of white brick dust and simultaneous screams from Benjie and his moll. Vito was satisfied to see his brother's eyes so wide.

"Jesus fuckin' Christ!" Benjie said as the girl scuttled behind him. "You scared me shitless."

"That happens when you enter a house with your face buried in a broad's chest. I waited patiently. You, girl," Vito said, his voice getting louder, "wait in the bedroom. This won't take long." The poor girl looked at Benjie for instruction, her face lined with even more confused terror than his. "Now!" Vito said, and she disappeared quickly, objects dropping on the hard floor as she did. "When was the last time you fed the dog?" Vito asked, his voice now soft and toneless.

"What?" Benjie stood up to full height and tried to bring his heart rate back to normal. Vito was clearly mad at him, but the panic was melting away.

"When was the last time you fed Gari? He's skinnier than a dog should be."

"I don't know." Benjie avoided Vito's eyes. "A couple hours ago."

"Bullshit. It's 3:00 a.m. When?"

"I don't know." The alcohol had frayed his system, and Benjie was struggling to control the course of his thoughts. "Noon?"

Vito leveled a hazardous stare and walked silently to the kitchen and opened the fridge. Inside was a fresh roll of lunch meat stored in an otherwise empty drawer. Vito dumped it out on the floor. Gari attacked the pile, and Vito walked back to the living room. "You enjoy yourself tonight?"

"Vito, just tell me what I need to do," Benjie pleaded. "Or what I did, whichever it is."

"I called. Over the last two days, I've called here nine times."

"I've been busy, sorry. What do we need?"

"Vic said you were workin'. That doesn't look true to me."

"I was. I had to run around yesterday for him..."

"And today?"

"Sorry, Vito. I...sorry." Benjie faced his brother, long enough to finally see his eyes, and changed tactics. "You can see what I did, Vito. I needed a day off, and I fucked around."

"You don't get days off. I think we mentioned that."

"I know, sorry. What's the plan? I can go right now. Whatever we need to do."

Vito went back to the chair, and Gari returned with his tongue lolling out to sit beside him. "We can't do anything about it right now…but Tony is gone."

"Gone?" Benjie asked. "What do you mean 'gone'?"

"Like he ran away."

"Why? He in trouble?"

"Somewhat, yeah. He's in a bit of trouble. Did you read the papers yesterday? Hear anything on the radio? Your girlfriend don't work for the *Times*, does she?"

"No, what do you mean? Wait…" Benjie thought about two guys talking earlier at the club. "The shootings?"

"You know their names?"

"Nah, I just heard two guys got popped on the Circle."

"Yeah, and a couple more got popped at a bar." Vito scanned his brother's face. He saw fear, confusion, alcohol, and little else. "Tony knew some of those guys. And now he's real sad about it." Benjie's understanding came slowly and in parts from what Vito could tell. "He's gonna go on vacation somewhere and think about how sad these events have made him."

"Can I see him? Can I help him?"

"He's the type of guy that don't need much help. You know that."

"How long?"

"However long it takes. And then he'll come back and we'll be a big, happy family all over again." Vito stood up and started walking toward the door. His steps creaked the boards below him, and they whined into the night like some unsettled soul. When he spoke again, a short step away from Benjie, the menacing edge in his voice had returned. Every word was serious, each pause accentuated. "I'm gonna tell you two things, little brother. One as the eldest Maceo family male and your rightful role model and another as a member of Our Thing. First, there's nothin' more pathetic than a man who don't take care of his dog. If I come back and see that dog ain't been fed on time, I'm gonna beat your ass. And the second thing is," he rested his hand softly on Benjie's shoulder, "if there is ever another time when a member of this Family needs you and you can't be found, I will put the bullets in you myself."

The morning of July 4, 1973
Tony Maceo's house in Brooklyn, NY

Papa Vic coasted his Ford Galaxie into an open parking space across the street from Tony and Ana's Brooklyn home. "God dammit," he muttered as he stopped the engine. The day was hot, but Vic was sweating for other reasons and tried to dry his hands on the blue vinyl seats. He could see Tony's little boy running back and forth through the front window, wearing an American flag hat and T-shirt. *Independence Day.* He had forgotten.

Vic found himself on the stoop with his finger against the doorbell, then stepping back to pinch his nose and survey the street, then again at the door. *Bring-brunnng.* It was hard to watch Ana's emotions flash so viscerally across her face as he stood there with little comfort to offer. First, she smiled to see him, then without words she understood and her lips curled, tears welled behind her eyes, her shoulders slumped, and her mouth fumbled for words. "Is he dead?" she asked.

"No. No. He's fine, Ana. I promise." The words were hollow and fell awkwardly on the ear. He wanted to hug her, but instead he just watched with his hands folded and useless until she swung the door open and stood aside. Vic heard Carmine's feet hammering against the hardwood floors as he stepped over the threshold.

"Papa!" the boy called as he ran into Vic's arms. "Are you coming to the fireworks?"

Vic squatted despite the resistance of his knees. "Would you like that?" he asked, resting a hand on this boy's shoulder. Carmine's energy proved impossible to match, but Vic summoned what he could, a soft smile. "You wouldn't be embarrassed to hang around with an old man like me?"

Carmine jumped. "No! Have you ever seen the ones in the park? Those are the ones we're going to. They're the *biggest ones*."

"I haven't seen them in many years, little buddy. But maybe we could see them tonight."

"Yeah, you can come with me and Mom," Carmine said, then he gasped, remembering something of the utmost importance. "You want to see my baseball glove? Dad bought me a new one."

Vic admired the child's delight. "Go get it for me," he said, and Carmine disappeared back into the house to find it.

When her son was out of earshot, Ana asked, "What happened?"

"He can't be in the city right now."

"Where?" she asked, covering her eyes with her hand.

"North."

"Why?"

"He's protecting us." Vic placed a cautious hand on her back. "He's protecting *you*."

Ana snapped to look directly into his worn and wrinkled eyes. "We're right here. Carmine is right fuckin' here. How is he protecting *us?*"

"Don't blame him. Hate me if you have to hate someone."

"He's protecting *himself*." Ana blinked to dam her tears. "Don't insult me with anything else."

Carmine came sprinting back with a catcher's mitt on his hand. "See, Papa. It's the model Thurman Munson wears."

"Wow," Vic said. He stuck a few fingers in the glove to test the stiffness. Carmine beamed. "You'll have to break it in, nice and soft. You and your dad will have to toss the ball around."

"Yeah," Carmine said, "Mom got me some new baseballs too, so we can toss in the street and not worry about scuffing them up. All my other ones are scuffed up." He put the glove back on his own hand and flexed it himself.

"That's good, very good. We've gotta make sure you're practicin'."

Carmine held the glove to his chest. "So, can you come to the fireworks with us?"

"It's up to your mommy."

"Please, Mom?"

Ana's eyes shot daggers into Vic's chest, and he knew she had every right to stab him. He would have been happy to melt into the floor or walk out and enjoy his evening at Jerry's with the other regulars, conveniently insulating himself from her anger, but he felt worse for the kid than for himself. She hesitated but nodded, and Carmine started hooting and Vic smiled his pale-yellow smile down on him. "All right, little buddy. We'll go to the fireworks, but you gotta be extra good for your mommy today."

"I will!"

* * *

That night, Vic drove Ana and Carmine to the fireworks at the park, which were always an event, but he did not remember them being as crowded when he was a kid. He remembered sitting near the entrance with his friends and waiting for the opportune moment to distract the ticket taker and snatch their drawer of coins. He remembered running ahead of what passed for security guards down a block or two and eventually into a candy store, a dice game, or the like. Two decades later, he remembered running protection himself at these events until the city assumed control to elbow out the "undesirables." The park was never rowdier than in those first years after the change, and Vic stopped coming to avoid the headaches.

It did Vic good to see the child's eyes reflecting the fireworks in amazement and wonder. Wonder was a rarity in life, he knew. Disappointment was a more likely emotion, even on a holiday, but the kid's spirit did rub off, and Vic began enjoying it all despite himself. Ana hid her tears from her son with sunglasses, which Carmine did not find weird enough to comment on, and for that, Vic was grateful. Every few moments a new color would burst above them, and they'd stand on a green walkway, or a purple, or a red, all lined with carts of food and drinks, Carmine prancing along between Vic and Ana. Vic knew Tony would be gone for a long time. Cesare Provenzano's crew would come for blood and would not care whose it was, but the shooter they'd want most of all. Carmine would be lonely without him.

"You want a snow cone, Car?" Ana asked.

The boy smiled. "Yeah, purple."

"Can you watch him?"

"Yeah, no problem. Sit here, kid, and let's wait for your mom."
Vic took a seat on an empty bench as Ana worked her way into the
crowd. "Did your dad take you to any ball games this year? I bet
that's where he got the glove, from the Yankees themselves, if it's
Munson's model."

"He took me to one, but they lost. They played the Red Sox
and lost."

Vic noted a few pedestrians as they passed. He felt his age difference with the crowd of people, especially with the child next to him.
The world was moving faster than he remembered it. "You know
your dad is a brave man, right? A lot of people *think* their dad is a
brave man, but your dad actually is. That's somethin' to be proud of,
ya know?"

"Is that why he's not here?"

Vic could tell the kid had been wondering and knew enough
not to ask. Vic leaned in close, his whisper serious, "Your father did
something very important, Carmine. He did somethin' to protect
his Family. There are bad men in this world, and your dad stopped
them. But the bad man has friends, and so we gotta take care of your
dad so he can come back."

"He's goin' away?"

"He has to go away for now, but he'll be back. He'd never leave
you and your mom. He'll be back when he's done protectin' you."

"Like a policeman?"

The word stung Vic, and he shook his head. "No, not like a
policeman. Like a soldier. And he'll come back like those soldiers
who are off fightin' overseas, except he's not in some jungle and he's
not killin' some Asian child. And when he's done, he'll come back
for you and your mom, and everythin' will go back to the way it's
supposed to be. But in the meantime, you gotta help your mom get
along. We gotta help your mom along. She's gonna be sad sometimes,
but you gotta listen to her and make sure you're helpin' as much as
you can. You've gotta protect her the way your dad's protectin' you."

Carmine kicked his feet back and forth under the bench where they could not reach the ground. His head was down, but his voice was curious, not scared. "Where did he go?"

"He's gotta go somewhere where the bad men won't be lookin' for him and draw up his plans. He's gotta plan everythin' out real smart so he can keep us safe. And we've gotta keep all that a secret to keep him safe. You understand?"

"Can I call him?"

"I'll make sure you get to talk to him. Don't worry. We're gonna all work together to help, so he can stay safe. We owe him for doin' these things, so *we* can stay safe. But we gotta trust you to help us out, so your daddy can come back. Can I trust you, Carmine?"

"Yeah. I wanna help."

"Good, 'cause we're gonna need you. To keep Daddy safe, we need you. And if you're gonna misbehave for your mom and he's gotta come back, that's not safe, is it? So that's how you gotta help us. Take care of your mom and protect her from the bad men."

"I will. I promise. I could even sell my glove to help us."

Vic laughed. "Maybe, but we don't need to do that yet. Just take care of your mom. And help Uncle Benjie and Uncle Vito. They'll need help until your dad comes back. And if you need any help from me, you just gotta call me. Could you use the phone book and call me if you had to?"

"Yes."

"Good. Oh, here comes your snow cone. Go get the snow cone, buddy, and let's finish watchin' these fireworks."

The morning of July 5, 1973
The Giordano family house in Brooklyn, NY

Alphonse always liked pinstripes. He didn't remember when he first started liking them, but it was before his first communion. Al begged his mother for pinstripes then, and when she said no, he ended up stealing a younger parishioner's bicycle to pay for it and told his mom he borrowed the clothes from a kid down the block. The inclination hadn't come from his father. Ettore Giordano never wore a suit that wasn't plain gray, and Al could hardly remember him wearing a suit at all. When he died, Al went through his father's worldly possessions and found nothing he wanted (suits, pants, or otherwise), except for an old pocket watch their grandfather carried around Sicily before any of them left for America. Al didn't know where it was today, lost to time and indifference.

His own closet was chockful of suits, and he rifled through them wearing only a worn-out pair of boxer shorts and a few cool beads of bathwater on his back. Cristiana organized his suits by color, from light on the left to dark on the right, each with a matching tie slung around the hanger so he would never wear something incompatible in public. He picked one after a brief search, a black suit with pinstripes and a solid red tie, and set about dressing himself in the middle of the bedroom. Al could hear Cris milling about the kitchen as he slipped into his elected regalia; he straightened his tie clip, adjusted his belt, folded his pocket square, tied his shoes, and dropped his wallet into his back pocket. The stairs announced him to his wife via creaks and moans when he finished, but she paid him no mind even when she sensed his presence in the doorway. He leaned against the frame with an arm above his head to watch her work. Her hair hung loose around her face, framing its features with a brown and silver that gamboled in step with her morning energy. Her dress was white, and she was barefoot as she padded this way and that across the floor.

"Would you like to pray before we leave?" she asked with a hesitant smile.

"I won't fight it." Her smile grew, and he wished he had more to say.

She turned back pressing their favorite snacks into baggies. The prospect of their trip had removed a weight from her shoulders if you knew where to look. "We should pray then," she said, "before we leave."

Al dutifully walked to the radio cabinet he had built for his children when Jennie was still in diapers. It took him a while to get the drawers to roll correctly, to smooth the action of the tracks, but he'd done it. These days those drawers were a catch-all, and Al stored an old prayer book in there among an assortment of pens, paper clips, and batteries, so he could follow along with the holiday blessings at Christmas and Easter. There was a list of prayers on the inside cover, but he couldn't remember any other than the Lord's Prayer, and that was not listed. He wiped dust from it with his palm and lay his soft fingertips along the crisp edges of the binding. The fragile pages were painted gold around their borders as if with divine filigree, chosen to match the script embossed on the red leather cover.

"I've got my cheat sheet," he said, ambling back into the kitchen. "Let's go outside for this. *In all His natural splendor.*"

The pair went to the bench beneath the dogwood trees. The leaves were green now, not the wonderful spring white, but the air was calm and the heat bearable in their shade. "What prayer should we say?" Cris asked.

"You're the one that knows all the prayers."

She squeezed his hand. "Give me a topic."

Al thought for a minute, but he only ever had one concern beneath the trees. "Our children," he said, kissing Cris on the forehead. She took the book from him and flipped through the first pages. She said in Sicilian, *"I always make them up off the top of my head, but maybe we can find a formal version in here…"*

He kissed her forehead again as she looked. *"You remember this stupid bench?"* he asked in their language, tapping the bench's light-brown slats.

She laughed. *"Yes. You mean bringing it home?"*

"Yes," he said. *"We dropped it twice carrying it in and left a dent in the floorboard in the hallway. And then Johnny stepped on the nail from the busted board, and we had to take him to the hospital. That was the first thing this damn bench ever did, injure our floorboards and our son."*

"This one," she said, pointing at a page. *"This one is about kids."*

Al pulled his glasses from the pocket of his suit. *"Let's see if I can read this shit."*

They said together:

Oh Lord and Father, I commend my children to Thy care,
and mercifully supply whatever is lacking in
me through frailty or negligence.
Strengthen them to overcome the corruptions of the
world, whether from within or without;
and deliver them from the secret snares of the enemy.
Pour Thy grace into their hearts, and strengthen and
multiply in them the gifts of thy Holy Spirit,
that they may daily grow in grace and in knowledge of their Father;
and so, faithfully serving here, may come to rejoice hereafter. Amen.

The two old lovers held each other in the shade of the dogwood trees. Midmorning shadows sheltered them from the sun, and a light breeze even managed to squeeze its way through the brick-lined alleyways. *"We've done all right for ourselves,"* Al said, enjoying the warm touch and sweet smell of his wife before what he knew would be a hectic day.

Cris led Al back to the house after their reverie and finished collecting their foodstuffs. The suitcases were overflowing by the time Cris was ready to leave. Al found his keys and placed the prayer book back in its hiding place before waiting at the door for Cris to join him.

"Is the car here?" Cris asked when she noticed him waiting.

"I'm driving us," he said, shaking the keys for her to see. "Jimmy's girlfriend is sick. Better for us to be alone with our thoughts anyway."

Cris hesitated. "We're going to have to pay for parking then..." she said, pulling a few dollars from the coffee jar. Al grabbed their suitcases, and Cris pecked him on the cheek before she led him to the car. By the time Al stowed the luggage and joined her, fat tears were rolling quietly down her cheeks despite efforts to brush them away.

"Hey...hey, what's the matter?" Al put his hand over hers and wrapped it gently in his fingers.

"I'm just nervous," she said. "Good nervous, but nervous. I haven't been home in forty years."

"Try sixty years."

"I want to smell the lemon trees. You're taking me to smell the lemon trees, and I'm so happy."

He kissed her. "Don't worry, hun. Lemon trees, here we come."

Al let go of her hand, allowing his fingers to brush against its back. He turned the keys with a swift tug. The car failed. It was a familiar failure, a confusing failure. The key clicked into place, the engine turned over, but everything ended in a clunk. A hollow, hateful clunk of some cold metal against itself. But Al knew it was more, like a voice he'd heard years before, come around again. But the voice was no voice at all, but a roar. A bellicose roar with hot breath that burned the morning peace with orange-red flames, thick steel bolts and clear glass shards, all ripping the lovers from underneath.

The afternoon of July 5, 1973
The Giordano family home in Brooklyn, NY
"An explosion on Mulberry Street."

The metal was twisted black and gray, reaching up in desperation like the flames that maimed it. Small glass shards sparkled on the asphalt, and wherever the original blue and cream colors of the Chrysler could be discerned, they were corrupted by brown burns and singed of all benefit. The air was hot and still, and the smell lingered above the wreckage as Agents and techs milled solemnly in its wake, gathering what evidence they could from the viscera.

Detective Clayburgh stood a few paces back from the scene as taped off by the Agents. He could see Agent Meriwether on the other side of the yellow line discussing whatever Agents discuss while their grunts collect evidence. The bomb had certainly been effective. Clayburgh knew it was a 1973 Chrysler Imperial from the sparse notes he received at the precinct, but on the scene it was unrecognizable. The roof was blown upward, both passenger-side doors were blown out, the B-pillar support beams crumpled, and the dashboard was crushed forward into the engine block, which was the only aspect of the vehicle that remained in place. The Giordano house had seen debris crack the front windows and charred shrapnel lay on the front steps and porch.

Clayburgh turned to Murdock, who had decided to wear sunglasses around the Agents from now on. "Not the worst way to go if your time is up, I guess."

"I've seen better ways. Some people have even died in their sleep with the television on."

"I've seen worse." Clayburgh walked around the perimeter, avoiding a news crew as he did, and made his way closer to where Meriwether was holding court. He would have stood patiently and waited for an opportunity, but Meriwether saw him meandering and made his way to them.

"Detectives," he said, his mouth in a taut frown, "not the way any of us wanted to spend today."

"No," Clayburgh said, "but there is something to learn from this, and it's not good for anybody. This is a damn war zone. Three blatant, public attempts in a week? That is insane."

"Yeah, we had already been given an expanded budget off the Provenzano and Pisciotto news. We'll have a blank check now. The Agency cannot believe what's going on. I'm the first to admit we've had a poor record convicting these guys and don't always know what's going on in their heads, but I have never been at such a loss for words as when I got that phone call today. Unbelievable. Honestly, unbelievable."

"Are they both dead?"

"Essentially. The wife's wounds are way too much. First responders walked right past her, thinking she was part of the dashboard. She landed in the grass over there."

"Terrible." Clayburgh shuffled his feet. "Where do we go from here?"

Meriwether scanned the scene over and around his question, clearly wondering how best to proceed with the detectives in light of recent events. He had been gracious once, but they knew better than to assume such leniency moving forward, especially with the uptick in scrutiny. He let the silent pause run its course until Meriwether pulled a silver bolt tarnished by the flames from his pocket and handed it to Clayburgh. "The bomb was loaded with these. That's a hex bolt, ten inches long and nearly half an inch thick. They were packed in close to the explosion point below the driver's seat and ripped upward and outward through the bodies of our victims. The driver, Mr. Giordano, was completely eviscerated. Mrs. Giordano was struck by several, the most obvious entry wounds were to her ribs and left leg. They've been found as far away as the back porch and living rooms of two neighbors."

Clayburgh handed the bolt to his partner who raised his sunglasses to examine it. "Jesus," Murdock said, testing its weight, "what did the bomb look like?"

Meriwether hesitated again. "It was small, triggered by the ignition. As soon as he started the car, *boom*."

"Obviously," Murdock said, handing the bolt back to Meriwether, "we would like to help. If there's any way for us to do that…"

"My hope is now we'll have everything we need. The higher-ups are motivated, more motivated than I've ever seen them. They're going to throw everything they have at this investigation. These guys are going to have nowhere to hide. Offices, clubs, restaurants, cars… we'll be everywhere. I will help you guys when I can. We don't want to shut the NYPD out. You know, I should tell you, there's a good chance we use your informant's information."

"Luparelli?"

"Yeah, your interview will get us bugs on Pisani. I've seen a draft of the request. And we've discussed grabbing Pisani ASAP and using a fingerprint to compare to what your team found at the concrete murder. There are several angles in the works for bringing him in."

"Glad something good can come from the poor kid."

"It's clear, to me at least, this was retaliation. Giordano goes after them, they swing back. Which means two things. One, Giordano guys are gonna hit them again. And two, the other Giordano guys are in danger. So, we're focusing on the group of individuals we've identified as 'leadership' in our previous investigations. They'll contact your precinct for information, but I can read their names to you now." Meriwether pulled a folded piece of paper from another pocket and began to read, looking at the detectives after each name. "You know Nicodemo Nicky Six Pisani, obviously, and then Giordano's son is listed here as John 'The Crown Prince' Giordano, presumptive nickname there, and then Al's close friend Phil Buffalo Books Scozzari, and then three what they call *caporegimes*, namely, Pietro 'Petey Fingers' Caltagirone, Vincenzo 'Papa Vic' Palmieri, and Giacomo 'Joey Jugs' Poletti. Any of those ringin' any bells?"

"Just Nick, and after Luparelli's statement we found out Giordano had a son. The others I can check on."

"Here," he said, extending the paper to Clayburgh. "I don't need this. You can have a few days head start before our office makes the formal requests. We should have the bugs in a week or less."

"Thanks. We appreciate this, we really do."

"You were the first to this. He was your informant anyway, God rest his soul."

The evening of July 5, 1973
Red Hook, Brooklyn, NY
"Gloves…he wore gloves."

Gloves took a drag of his cigarette, the exhale hitting the windshield and dashboard with a swirling ball of blue-gray smoke. He cracked his window to vent the air, but it was raining and a few cold droplets found their way inside to moisten his pant leg and jacket. His fingers were clumsy inside his gloves, and when he tried to dry the spots with his fingers, ash fell on his hands, stomach, and seat. He took another drag.

"You ever met him before, Frank?" Gloves asked the driver.

"Couple of times," Frank said with a faint but perceptible Irish slur. "He used to lay money with us, ya know, before he got connected with—," he tugged at his earlobe, hesitant to say the name.

Gloves snickered. "You don't gotta do *that*," tugged his earlobe, "anymore." One side of his Lucky Strike was outpacing the other. He licked his finger and wiped the moisture across its body to stall it.

"How's that gonna work? The next guy gonna pick another body part?"

"I don't know what the fuck is gonna happen. I've got hopes, but who knows." Gloves pulled a 1911 Remington Rand from the glove compartment and tested the action on the slide just to the point of expelling the chambered bullet before easing it back again. He could not remember the last time it had been fired, but it was imperative the gun was untraceable, and he knew the Remington was. He'd procured it himself, filed the serial number himself, manipulated the magazine size and barrel fingerprint himself. It was a lot of work for him to leave behind.

"What'd your father do?" Gloves asked. "Ya know, when you were a kid?"

"He was a roofer."

"Like replacin' shingles?"

"Yeah, I guess. I don't know. He used to always come home with pitch and shit on his clothes."

"What's *pitch*?"

"Black shit. It's like roofing glue for the shingles."

"You didn't wanna be a roofer then?"

Frank had fingers and hands that looked soft but were dotted by callouses, fresh cuts, and freckles. He drummed them steadily against the steering wheel. "I remember he'd take these long baths on the weekends, a real bitchuva process, but when he'd sit down for dinner, it didn't matter. He smelled of the shit no matter what he did. Could've taken six fuckin' baths. Still every fuckin' day he went, put in his time, and came home. I could've learned somethin' from that, to be honest. But I didn't."

"Mine was a plumber."

Frank laughed. "I don't have to ask many questions on that one. I couldn't be a plumber neither."

Gloves tossed his cigarette and let his eyes level again on the house in question. It was not run-down but, like many in the area, was small and tidy, cramped if you had kids. Little garden boxes ran along the windows with a few flowers here and there, their stems curved and probably wilting. A fence and a weed-blotched walkway decorated the front. Gloves pulled another cigarette from his pack and lit it.

"You get sunburned a lot?" he asked with his first drag.

"Yeah, all the Irish get sunburned. It's a curse from the devil himself we traded for our alcohol tolerance. That's what Neil says."

"So, do you just not go to the beach then?"

"I wear whole bottles of Coppertone and pray for clouds."

"Somebody told me it's worse when the clouds are out."

"That sounds like it's made up. Who told ya that...?" Frank looked sideways to his partner, but Gloves's eyes were drawn down the street in a way that made Frank's follow. "Is that him?"

"I can't tell." The figure in question closed his car door quietly while shooting glances up and down the street before jogging to the front door and disappearing soundlessly inside. A moment later a light turned on and the man's black shadow flitted across the width of the window. "Close enough," Gloves said. He stabbed the Remington into his waistband and clapped Frank on the shoulder, a faint smile on his lips. "Showtime."

They approached the front door, Gloves moving briskly ahead and glancing purposefully from one neighbor's door to the next. Frank knocked and they waited, listened. Steps rang out on the other side until the door pulled back, inch by inch from the doorjamb, and a face half covered in floppy black bangs peeked out.

"Oh, thank God," Jimmy the Driver said. "Thank God, come in."

"What are you all worried about, kid?" Gloves asked, stepping across the threshold with Frank close behind.

"Fuck you." Jimmy ran his hands through his hair and paced the hardwood floor. His eyes were red beneath his bangs. "I've been terrified all day. You said it would be quick. I couldn't stay in this house any longer, so I just drove around, waiting."

"This is what quick looks like. Do you think I have buses and planes and automobiles just layin' around? Calm down. We're here now. Take a load off."

"No. I did everything you said, and I want outta here. There were a hundred cops there, and it's gonna take Johnny about two minutes to realize what the fuck happened, and then I'm a dead man."

"You don't need to worry about Johnny. He's at the hospital with his mother and sisters."

"I want out. Now."

"All right," Gloves said, unable to shake the smile on his lips. "One drink and we'll go. Whattya got for us? What you like, Frank? Whiskey?"

Frank sat down on the couch and let his arms spread across the back cushions. "Whiskey's fine."

"Fuck that," Jimmy pleaded. "I wanna go."

Gloves erased his smile, quickly. "I said sit down. *Now.*" Jimmy obeyed. "Thanks," Gloves said, his smile returning. "Whiskey?"

"It's in the cabinet above the stove."

Gloves pulled a bottle down and held the label under the kitchen lights. "Jack Daniel's wasn't Irish, was he?"

"Sounds like a right shit Irishman if he was," Frank said, "but it's Jimmy's house. You should be pourin' his favorites."

"You're right. What's your favorite up here, Jimmy?"

Jimmy would have preferred to not be consulted. "Jameson."

"Ooh," Frank said, getting up from his seat to cross the room, "I'll not let you pour such a sweet thing as that. Gimme the bottle." Gloves let Frank pour a sizeable amount for each man before he returned to his cushioned perch. "Just smell it, boys," Frank said. "Isn't she grand?"

Gloves raised his glass. "Cheers. To Jimmy's new life!" They each took a drink. "So, where you gonna end up, Jim?"

"Oh, I don't know." Jimmy was afraid to make too much eye contact and instead stared at his glass when he spoke. "I thought about California. Maybe try and get on driving for some celebrities."

"A fine goal," Frank said, contempt for the idea poorly concealed.

Gloves tipped his glass and said, "How much would it cost for your own, uh, chauffeur company? What do ya need? Your own limo or somethin'?"

Jimmy shrugged. "Yeah, I guess that could do it. Just my own car so I didn't have to kick up to anybody."

Gloves chuckled. "Kick up? That's funny."

"You know what I mean," Jimmy said. "I could be on my own then. Me and my girlfriend could do what we want. Move if we had to."

"How much does a limo cost these days?"

"Oh, I don't know. Ten thousand? Maybe fifteen for a nice one."

"Maybe we can swing it for ya. You've done a big thing for us. Maybe we can swing some extra money, I don't know. I can ask."

"Really? I would appreciate it, believe me. What you're doing for her schooling is already enough, but that would be incredible to drive my own car."

Gloves shrugged. "Maybe. We'll see."

Jimmy nodded, and a smile twisted his lips as he took another drink. The whiskey burned in his mouth, but bit cold in his throat, and he choked it back up into his nose. Jimmy pulled the glass from his lips, wide eyed with confusion. His glass was splashed with red, then half filled with red and then red flooded the floor in front of him, misting, spattering the ground. Jimmy choked again, but it was not the whiskey that did it, and he slumped forward onto the hardwood floor.

Frank finished his Jameson. "Why didn't you shoot him?"

"I put a lot of work into this gun. I didn't want to waste it."

The morning of July 7, 1973
Burn unit of the hospital in Manhattan, NY

Carrie's eyes burned on their edges, and the room steamed in front of her. It was an unpleasant room with beige walls and the white tiles that seemed to reflect the distasteful color back up into the air. And there was no missing the hospital smells, the clean it attempted and the staleness it achieved. On the bed was a lump, a near-motionless tangle of tubes and wires, covered by white gauze and clear tape. It was identified with a tag clipped to the section of itself resembling an arm, its only sign of life the mechanical undulation of its chest. What skin there was, held frozen by the nurse's work, was red-pink and in constant jeopardy of sloughing off to decorate the floor.

"Do you want some time alone?" Nick asked from his seat next to her.

"If you don't mind," Carrie said, blinking back the steam. "Just a little while and then come back. And I'm sick of seeing the nurses, Nick. Keep 'em out."

"Yeah, no problem." Nick collected their lunch trays and made his exit. His footsteps were enough, their echoes in the small room, to break the dam of Carrie's tears. Her face grew red and then purple and red again, and her eyes overflowed to cover her face with warm, wet lines. She held the IV stand in one hand for support and her mother's gauze, stained black by her charred fingers, in the other.

"I would wait to go in there," Nick said when Bobby approached with a sack of food from the commissary. "I told her I'd give her a minute alone."

"All right," Bobby said. "That's probably a good idea."

"Is this the first time she's been in there?"

"Second. First time was a mess."

"Can't blame her." Nick leaned against the half-wall protecting a nurses' station to ensure no one could sneak by.

"I can't either," Bobby said, shaking his head. "Unbelievable this week. Unreal." He pulled an apple from the food sack and tossed the rest on top of the half-wall next to Nick. "I don't know what to do for her. I've never dealt with anything like this."

"Look, Bobby, I hate to say this…" Nick began, then cleared his throat, "but Don C would never…?"

"Absolutely not, no, not in a million years. My Father would've never allowed that. I would've never allowed that."

"I know, sorry." Nick waved his question away. "I know Al had a soft spot for you. Trusted you. He was rarely wrong about these things and…I shouldn't have asked that. Sorry, seriously, sorry."

"I get it. It's so goddamn confusing. What the fuck is goin' on? Women aren't supposed to get hurt in this, no matter what else happens. Al was a good man, but at least he knew the risks. Cris should've never been hurt, no matter what Al might have done, whatever grudges there were."

Bobby had a sincere way about him, always had. Nick clapped him on the shoulder and tried to smile. "We're gonna need you, Bobby. I can feel it. Somethin' will come across the wires on your side, and we'll need you to be there. Carrie is gonna need you."

"I'll be there if shit needs to happen, I swear it. You let me know, Nick, and I'll be there. I promise"

She wanted me to dance when I was young but left me free to choose. She wanted me to practice and fall and grow and learn, my Mother. It was lost on me then. I was her. I was always her. A blue tube poked its way through the gauze around her mother's lips and down her throat to deliver air and vitamin paste. The nurses would make a show of their inspections every hour or so, talking to the still lump as if it could hear, as if she had thoughts and dreams and feelings, but she did not and Carrie knew it. So, she held the black gauze and remembered.

"We all know how it's gonna be," Nick said. "It's a war now. Like in the thirties when Our Thing was still being built. Before there was order to these things, before our rules were written. Chaos."

"I know. What about Pisciotto's new brass? Are they gonna be on board with us now that Al's gone?"

Nick noticed the term, *us*, but did not to comment. "Esposito is a good guy. Problem is this drug stuff has everybody fucked up. Too much money on the one hand, too much hard time on the other. I don't know which way he'll break with Al gone."

Bobby threw his apple core away and reached for another. "How's your new Boss gonna break on it?"

"Depends on who takes the reins. I guess we're about to find out if anybody has been hidin' their true feelings."

"What do you think?" Bobby asked before realizing he might be overstepping his bounds. "Sorry if I'm pressin' you, just curious."

Nick shrugged. "Too dirty if you're the one doin' it. Gotta keep that shit at arm's length."

"Yeah, my Father'd say the same thing."

I could've been more like Jennie around you. Especially when we went to church. She would at least open the prayer books and pretend. The salve had matted the brown and gray hair around her mother's ears, where the warm air melted it until it oozed in both directions at once. Carrie pressed her finger there to scoop it away. Her mother would never allow her beautiful hair to streak with such a spiteful buildup. *I love you, Mother. I did love you, always. I'll protect what's left. I'll watch them for you. I will keep us safe. All of us…even you.* Carrie wiped the tears from her face and stood, leaning against the IV stand. She flicked its bag of fluid and watched the level bounce.

"He was my mentor," Nick said. "I've been around him as much as his own children since I was six years old."

"I couldn't believe the way he accepted me into his daughter's life. More acceptin' of some things than my own Father."

"And Cris…" Nick shook his head. "She was the rock of the Family."

"She's everything for Carrie, absolutely everything. I don't know how her and Jennie will go on."

"And Johnny. He is his father's man, but his mother's boy. We'll have to keep an eye on him. Sometimes, in a state of grievance, people get a little more reckless than they'd otherwise be. We've gotta protect him. From Provenzano, yeah, but also from himself." Nick dug around until he found a bag of Cheez-Its in the cafeteria sack. "If it's Phil, we'll make a lot of money. He's probably the safest choice. He'd let us avenge Al and rein in some of the crazier ideas for revenge and shit. Most likely anyway. You can never tell with these things."

"And Vic?"

"I gave up predicting what he's gonna do, but he's an old-school motherfucker. He doesn't bullshit, not when Al was askin' the questions or anybody else. There's a lot to be said for that. I'd follow him to hell and back."

"Do you want it? I didn't ask, but that has to have crossed your mind."

Nick tossed a cracker in his mouth and stared off down the hallway to his left. A nurse was approaching and he met her eyes, but she disappeared into a room a few doors away. "I'd take it," he said, "but only so nobody could tell me to stop torturing the motherfuckers who did this. Medieval fuckin' shit, where they scream loud enough that the next time somebody comes for us, they would still hear the echoes bouncin' off the walls."

Her mother's IV bag was nearly full and stamped MORPHINE in black letters across the label. Carrie pulled its twin from the jacket of her A-line skirt suit and hung it in place to watch the pair swing delicately in the bright light from the window. Her mother's blue tube rattled with air, upward and downward, ever so slightly with each contraction of the ventilator. Carrie stared at it with the second IV needle between her index finger and thumb, hesitant at the climax and then sure of herself. She punctured the blue plastic husk and counted the drops as they began to fall. One, two, three, four, five, six, seven, eight, they dropped before her mind relaxed. With a final sigh, she opened the regulator clamp for both IVs and fell back into the chair, her eyes calm, her heart beating to the sound of the ventilator.

Summer 1973
Saylor's Boxing Gym in the Bronx, NY
"You ever seen a newborn giraffe? Like that
but without as much coordination."

The canvas wasn't padded at all. It was an unforgiving slab of wood that clunked against its moorings when you moved across its surface. Benjie always thought it was padded; it made sense to pad it.

His saliva was thick with blood and clung to his lips and tongue as they struggled to move. He tried to spit it out and clear the stickiness from his mouth, but the gob didn't go anywhere and attached to his chin. He tried to wipe it with his glove and step forward again, just out of range. It did not work.

The lunge was surprisingly long and more than enough to bring Benjie's cheek close enough to punish. A right cross landed flush and sent his weight back to his heels. Short, quick backpedals caught the weight, but the distraction of staying upright left him open for another strike. He felt two, although he couldn't tell you which had landed first, and he brought his gloved hands up to cover his chin and forehead. He could not see, and the shot to his ribs came as a searing, painful surprise. It crumpled his right leg. He led with his shoulder into his opponent's chest and pushed him back, desperate for space and a few unharried bounces on his toes. He didn't get them. His arms were tired and fell when he pushed away, leaving his face vulnerable again. This lunge was as effective as the last and the strike was crisp and true, and Benjie's skin burned as the glove peeled away. The skin below his eye felt stiff and warm; his breathing was shallow, hampered by his barking ribs; his legs felt molten, unbalanced, and heavy. He stepped forward cautiously, mouth open and searching for air, tongue flopping lifelessly in his mouth. And then, he was backpedaling again, confused and trying to breathe, and the canvas raced upward to catch him...

When Benjie opened his eyes again, Ricky's face was directly above him with a giant smile. "It's not fun hittin' a motherfucker that hits back, is it?" Benjie hated him then but did not have the strength to hurt him. And then the old hands of Floyd the Trainer were on him, brushing Vaseline into his cuts and smelling salts under his nose.

"Don' bleed on my motherfuckin' canvas, lil boy. Get yo' ass up," Floyd said in his Georgia rhythm. He flicked the jelly from his fingers and forced his hands under Benjie with the strength to shovel him through the ropes. "No lazy-people blood on this canvas...get out." The periphery of Benjie's vision was vague and distorted, but the combination of Floyd and Ricky's assistance was enough to prop him up against the side of the ring. Two new fighters were sparring before Benjie gathered enough strength to wobble forward to a seat against the wall.

"Watch these two," Ricky said, pointing back to the ring when they sat down. Benjie could not look. He pulled his gloves off and poked his swelling orbital with a mix of curiosity and pride. *Deep breaths. Control the breathing, Floyd had said...and then I got my ass beat.* He poured a cup of water on himself and stood to shake the droplets to the ground. Ricky smacked him to demand his attention. "I said watch, motherfucker."

Benjie obeyed begrudgingly. The two boxers were clearly heavyweights. One was a Black man with chiseled arms and a coarse beard; the other a taller, more slender man, with olive skin and heavy calves. "Those guys are huge," Benjie said.

"And heavy. They can fight for about two minutes and they're toast."

"Good luck gettin' anywhere near two minutes."

Ricky smiled. "It can be done. E-Bo is a motherfucker though." He pointed at the Black man, who seemed to be winning. "You know why he's called E-Bo? 'Cause Floyd says 'Every-Body scared to fight him.'" Ricky laughed and Benjie laughed at him laughing while still inspecting his own damage. "Floyd trains a lot of tough guys," Ricky said. "There's a lot of boxing in that old Negro's head." The two heavyweights traded a few devastating punches. "You know the other guy?" Benjie shook his head, momentarily losing his vision afterward. "The other guy is Joe-Joe. He's a guy like you and me, a guy tryin' to make it. But he's got a leg up. He's already runnin' around with Johnny Giordano."

"Runnin' around how?" Benjie asked, cautiously. Ricky was more willing to talk about these things in the open than Vic would appreciate. He told Benjie people like Ricky "were always runnin' for imaginary offices."

"Right now, he mostly punches people. But Johnny's a good guy to be followin' around for obvious reasons." He wriggled his fingers together. "*Monetary reasons*, no matter what happened recently." In the ring, E-Bo put Joe-Joe against the ropes but could not score a true knockout before Joe-Joe threw an elbow in frustration, and soon the two men were on the ground wrestling through their boxing gloves. Floyd turned away shaking his head as the ring broke into chaos behind him. Ricky asked him, "Hey, Floyd, I thought you said Joe-Joe was getting better?"

"Dat's the sad part, boy. Dat *was* better," Floyd said through a glowing set of stark-white teeth. "He too stupid for his own self." The Trainer took his bony hand and pulled Benjie's chin up, so he was only a few inches away and Benjie could smell the minty tobacco hidden in his lip. "Dis is yo' stupid center," he said, touching Benjie's forehead, "and dat's where you keep all the stupid in yo' head locked up. Now, you start gettin' hit in the head and all that is gonna start to fall out. Now, my problem with yo' Mediterranean friend over there," he moved his finger from Benjie's forehead to point at Joe-Joe, "is he be smugglin' stupid into my ring in places I ain't never seen befo'. He got stupid in his hands, he got stupid in his shin, I bet he got stupid in his own asshole if anybody care to check. Now, how am I s'posed to help a boy who is so determined to get stupid inside my ring?"

"Keep him outta the ring?"

Floyd clapped Benjie softly on his swollen cheek. "Nah, he got too much heart to keep his dumb ass outta there. Stupid with heart, we can handle. The brain can only remember one way after a while, and if that way is the right way, you can make a fighter. It's the smart fighters you have trouble trainin'. Ricky here, he's a garbage fighter. His brain workin' too hard all day. Joe-Joe just gotta quit spillin' his thoughts into the ring. He gotta stay even."

"You'll work him out, Floyd. They all end up bein' your brand of stupid."

* * *

Benjie leaned against the shower wall for a long time, gently kneading his eyebrows, cuts, and bruises. His ribs shrieked as he dressed, but the spar had done him good. He felt alive; he felt resilient. The trips to the gym with Ricky were enough to mitigate his anxious moments, his doubts, his fear. Even his dreams were easier. Where once he'd fled from nighttime spiders or strained to lift gray dream objects, he now fended off assailants with obscured faces and shadowed eyes in the back alleys near his mother's house.

His steps tracked water behind him to where Ricky was lying on a bench with a small notebook held awkwardly above his face. "You want a job at the club, Benj?"

"I can't work at the club. I work for Vic."

"Vinnie and Nico work for Petey. Why can't you work for Vic and the club?"

"Petey owns the club. It's not hard to draw that line for Vin and Nico."

"Just sayin'. I could get you in there for some easy gig."

"I wouldn't mind some extra money, if that's what you're really talkin' about," Benjie said, avoiding Ricky's eyes as he did. "I've got some jewelry that I still gotta sell, but that's not gonna last. I need more ways to earn. A way to jumpstart us."

Ricky set his notebook on the bench and sat up. "Work at the club like I just told ya." When Benjie stayed silent, Ricky said, "No...I do not have another *appropriate* way for guys like us to make money."

"What are the inappropriate ways? Just to ask." Benjie remembered Vito's comments to him when they were waiting on the first Hartel shipment: *You're supposed to be a criminal,* and Vic's before that, *You can't be afraid in my world.*

Ricky's eyes narrowed. "We're supposed to have a code."

"Yeah...I've heard." Benjie fiddled in his locker, again wary of Ricky's eyes, and hoping the silence would push his point upon his friend.

"Are you bein' serious, kid?"

"Yeah. Kind of. I don't know. I wanna do this the right way," Benjie backtracked, "and I know I can't be goin' around Vic."

"Good answer...you wouldn't have to go around him though, not really, if you went for it in the short-term. You can feed him the same cut as with everythin' else. Just cover the source of it."

"You talk about anything like this with Petey?"

"No. Fuck that. Petey makes enough money...but I've thought about it, how'd I'd work it, if I did get into that."

"How would you do it?"

Ricky stood and walked back and forth before the row of lockers. "We could go through the girls, feed it all through them."

"At the club?"

"Yeah. Just the girls, a trusted few. Have them push it, sell it, we protect them and give them a cut."

"Any of them use?"

"I've got girls that use. You can't get away from it these days. But that's not the real concern. It's the handling. The money, the drugs, it can't be on us." Ricky smiled. "We've got a code."

"What would Petey say?"

Ricky shrugged. "He's seen the druggie motherfuckers in there. We tell him we didn't know."

"*We* didn't know?"

"Well, if they ever said our names or somethin'. Petey is gonna side with us over them. We'd just tell him they were sneakin' shit from some Black gang. He might as well be a Confederate when it comes to the Black gangs."

"Who would you get it from?"

"I wouldn't get shit," Ricky said with mock offense, "but there's a group of our guys, not *our guys*, but ya know…they are interested too. I meet them at the club, in the cardroom, by the satellite bar, bring them backstage. They say we can use that place, funnel in and funnel out. Hide the money in the drawers. I'm the one who counts it all now."

"Me and you?"

"Unless you got an invisible friend who's been listening to us."

"My brothers?"

Ricky shook his head and waved his hands definitively. "Whoa, whoa, fuck no. Hell no. Two more heads to whack it up for? And they've got some serious traditional genes? No chance. If you wanna pay for their vacation, pretend it's from somethin' else."

Benjie finished buttoning his shirt, one of the shirts Vic had bought him, and stuck his hand out for Ricky. "If you're serious, so am I." Ricky made a show of a deep breath, a brief scan of the locker room. It was all naked men, the smells were of sweat and mildew, but he nodded and shook Benjie's hand.

The morning of July 8, 1973
St. Anthony's Cemetery in Brooklyn, NY
"A boat without a captain is no boat to be on."

Bobby stood outside the bathroom with his knuckle hovering an inch from the door. The sounds were familiar by now. *Thoump-thoump thoump-thoump* was Carrie's battered fist against the wall, the piercing *rheeeekkk* and coughing fit was her dry-heaving red-faced over the toilet, the clanging echo was the impact of her whiskey bottle on the vanity doors, the screams were rage exorcised through the veins in her neck, the sobs were dampened pleas of grief and failure. He had tried to soothe her aches, but all had failed. So, instead he hovered on the other side, his knuckle an inch from the door.

At the funeral home, Bobby shielded her from the fickle sympathy of the other mourners, and she buried her tears in his chest; his arms stiffened against her head to fortify a delicate cocoon. They were close to the opulent black casket, its lid closed to hold the lifeless rags of Alphonse Giordano as his visitors filed past to perform their final duty. Most of the attendees gave Carrie and Bobby a wide berth, but a few came close enough for him to shoo them away with a flick of his hand and an apologetic head shake.

He could not shoo Jennie, and the first time Carrie stepped out of his arms was for her sister. Their eyeliner ran on their cheeks and they hugged each other, palm into palm, before approaching the casket for the first time, together. Bobby thanked Jennie for handling the preparations in Carrie's place. He told her, her father would have been proud, her parents loved her, he and Carrie would be there for her no matter what, and none of those things were hard for him to say. He twinged as they spoke, considering young Jennie's position for the first time. *A woman on paper, a sheltered girl at heart.*

The line of mourners ran near the far wall where it hugged pictures of Christ, maids, drunkards, a naked victim dragged before King Midas and the like of reproduced Renaissance art. Bobby knew many of the visitors by sight: he acknowledged his father and mother with a somber nod; Don Frank Capello and his consigliere Angelo Calderone with a small host of their captains and soldiers; Al's own captains Petey Caltagirone, Joe Poletti, and Papa Vic Palmieri with their men; the lawyer Adam Landau; a scattering of local politicians, judges, bankers; Neil Burke and his cadre of Irish gangsters; Phil Scozzari, his magnified eyes wet and running; and more and more and more through the doors at the back of the hall and down the steps to the sidewalk and on and on. The turnout spoke to Al's deferential handling of his business, his discreet presence. It was enough for the city to concede him an empire.

"At least all the Provenzano grunts had the sense to stay away," Nick said from Bobby's shoulder as Sonia went over to hug and comfort the sisters. "How they holdin' up?"

Bobby shook his head. "It comes and goes. Carrie is…struggling with it."

"She's one of the toughest people I know, but this would've fucked anyone up." Nick tugged his suit straight, scanning the mourners as Bobby had. "It hasn't set in yet honestly. It's like when Kennedy died."

"He seemed untouchable. It never crossed the girl's minds, I know that. And Johnny is lost. Regina has no idea how to handle him."

"Cris could've held the kids together. That's the worst part." Nick paused, turned to Bobby. "I know you meant what you said at the hospital. I know you're with us."

Bobby nodded. "Anything I can do to help."

"We'll be in touch," Nick said, patting the younger man softly on his back. "Count on it."

Nick left his wife with Carrie and Jennie and walked back into the main hallway where an assortment of finger foods was laid out beside rows of water and soft drinks. Petey Caltagirone had stuffed himself into a well-worn black suit and was munching on a three-inch stack of cheese slices with Papa Vic by his side, speaking softly into the big man's ear.

"Gentlemen," Nick said.

"Nick," Papa Vic said, pulling him in for a hug and two pecks on the cheek. "Sad day, kid. It's a sad fuckin' day."

"It's like when Kennedy died."

Petey shook his head, and his ruddy cheeks wobbled as he eyed the cheese plate again. "Kennedy earned it. Not that man in there." Petey took another stack in his paw and ate it, talking through his bites. "I can never remember not knowin' him. I must've been five when he started comin' over to our house. He would bring cans to my parents and my pops would give Al a haircut for 'em. Some of the best sauces I ever tasted were in those jars."

Vic's ice-gray eyes were as soft as they ever got. "I remember he used to deal blackjack for us when he was a kid at this little car wash, we used to play cards in the back. He might've been eight or nine years old. One of the guys he's dealin' to leaves after a game, fall down drunk, and thinks he has less money than he should, so he gets all riled up and comes stormin' back. He yells, 'Where's that fuckin' kid?' and Al comes outta the back casual as can be, and this guy picks him up by the neck and shoves him up against the wall. 'You steal from me?!' the guy says and Al says no, ya know, as much as he can with a hand on his throat. The guy spits in Al's face, this little kid and he spits right in his face. So, Al pulls a couple bucks out of his pocket and hands it to him, tries to bribe him away basically. The guy doesn't give a shit, smacks Al across the face once-twice-three times, beats him I mean, wails on him, and then storms back out with the kid curled up on the floor. Well, Al gets up with his face all red and bleedin' and his eye almost shut for the swelling and walks over, still calm as can be, and hands each of us still sittin' there a few bucks. I asked him, 'What's this for?' That little shithead looks up at me with his blood-red smile and says, 'That's so you don't tell that guy about the twenty dollars I still got,' then the little punk pulls up a chair on our side of the table and says, 'Deal me in.'"

The ground was ready for him by the time they reached the gravesite. The rain made sure of that. Alphonse Giordano was laid to rest under a tree at St. Anthony's Cristiana and he had planted years ago when they reserved the plot. It was mature by now, and its branches were full of green leaves and its roots curled under the rough stone path nearby. The mourners spread in a semicircle around the headstone as they lowered the man reverently nicknamed the

Boss of Bosses into the ground. Jennie fell into her uncle's arms, slamming her fist into Oscar Giordano's chest. Carrie stood at the grave's edge, shivering in the summer rain with Bobby by her side. Johnny hid his eyes with sunglasses, but the tears ran past to join the raindrops. Nick held Sonia tight and watched the cold black box disappear into the ground.

As Father Bennie dismissed the crowd, Vic grabbed Johnny by the arm. "Johnny, can I get a minute? Real quick."

"Sure, Vic." Johnny let Regina pass him, and the two men stepped away from the line of traffic. Johnny's shoulders sunk from the weight of the day, but he fought to recover what he could. "Is this about the Family?"

"Well…yeah." Vic pulled the collar of his coat up against the steady rain and wind. "You've earned your say in how we operate, how we move forward. Nobody wants to do this without your father, but we have to. We have guys to protect, families to earn for. And we've gotta show a united front before we go take care of…what it is we know we gotta take care of."

"I understand. Pops would want us to move on."

Vic searched Johnny's face, but the sunglasses kept him out. "He knew the risks, kid." Vic laid an open palm on Johnny's chest. "We'll get through. He's still here, your mother is still here. We'll get through."

"I know, Vic. I'm fine. I promise," Johnny said, staring back from behind his tinted shield. "What's first?"

"We gotta pick a Boss, kid."

Johnny took a deep breath. "You or Phil, right? Nick?"

"Not me, kid. I'm too old for that shit."

"What's Petey think? Joey?"

There was no one near them, but both men double-checked before Vic spoke. "Petey says Nick." His voice was low and strained by the day's events. "We're about to go to war. Total fuckin' reckless, scorched earth war, John. Petey thinks Nick will be better at that than Phil."

"What do you think?"

"I think Phil thinks it's owed to him. And he might have a point about that."

"Pops would've given it to Phil," Johnny said, sure of his conclusion. "Or Carrie."

Vic laughed. "He may have. But I wanted to keep you in the loop, kid. Take a few days to think on it. It's gonna be tricky gettin' us all into a room to put this to a vote, but we'll figure it out. We'll figure this out together."

An afternoon in July 1973
Highway 20 East in New York outside Buffalo
"We liked Ray and he liked pancakes."

Tony pressed his forehead against the RV window until it got too warm and he felt his skin turning red against its surface. He rubbed the mark away as he leaned back, unbuttoned his collar, and adjusted the air vents to hit him directly.

"You ever been to Canada?" his driver asked. He was an overweight man whose hands were already covered in black grease when he picked Tony up early that morning. His name was Ray, short for Raymond, he had said.

"I've never been out of New York."

"You won't like it," Ray said. "They have a slower pace about them, whether you're in a city or not, and where we're goin' is no city."

"I wasn't expecting a vacation."

"You ever been to prison?"

"It's been awhile."

"It's a step sideways from that. The people are nicer, but the level of excitement is less."

"I'm not lookin' for any trouble."

"The guy you'll be stayin' with is a good enough guy. He'll keep ya alive anyway."

"That's all I'm askin' for. Shouldn't be long until you'll have to smuggle back the other way."

"I hope you're right. If you're still there in three or four months, you're gonna be one cold motherfucker."

Ray piloted the RV, a bulky yellow and orange and brown thing with its insignia scraped off, east along Highway 20 until they were just a few minutes from the Canadian border. There Ray pulled off to show Tony how his toilet folded forward to expose a small metal cubicle about four feet by four feet suspended beneath the floor and above the road. It *was* a waste tank, or had been, before being replaced by fresh metal of similar dimensions.

"Don't worry, I like ya too much to shit on ya," Ray said as Tony folded himself into the toilet box. The nuts and bolts creaked with each bump as they drove, and Tony was sure he was meant die spilling out from underneath an RV to be smashed by a trailing vehicle.

His dark thoughts sent him back to Brooklyn, to Ana and Carmine. Vic had called to tell him he had checked in on them and all was well. They had gone to the fireworks, he had said, at Carmine's request. They would be taken care of until the heat blew over, Tony trusted that, and no sane man would test those sadistic waters with Provenzano loyalists wandering the streets. Flight was the only reasonable solution, a temporary relocation. *Everyone is asked to do their time eventually.*

When they were safely across the border and a few miles along, Ray parked at a truck stop, lifted the toilet, and helped Tony crawl forth. "There's a diner here and I like pancakes," Ray said. The Diner, that was the full name in yellow letters on its roof, was as orange and yellow and brown as the RV. Ray chose a booth, and when he let his weight land on the bench, a puff of stuffing shot from the cushion onto the table. "Whoops," he said, chuckling at his girth. "Might be I come here too much."

Their waitress was young, maybe nineteen or twenty, and brunette with a slim figure beneath her yellow and orange and brown uniform. She smiled at the men when she shoveled them their plates, and Ray's eyes were on her for every step as she walked back to the counter. "Leave her alone," Tony said. "I don't have the funds to bail you out."

"A guy like me has to take advantage of what he doesn't have to pay for."

"That's very chivalrous of you."

"Chivalrous? What's a chivalrous?"

"Like knights. Like in King Arthur. The Honor Code."

"Ah…honor." Ray waved his greasy hand. "I'm just watchin'. And if my wife and her daddy were both here, I'd be doin' the same thing."

Tony let it drop when the girl disappeared into the kitchen. "So, what do you do after this? You have a stop on this side of the line?"

"I drop you first. Then I pick up cases of maple syrup from this place in Canborough. Then I go home."

"How often do you bring people over?"

"A few times a year. Believe it or not, there's not a lot of people who want to be smuggled into Canada. A few draft dodgers, people in debt, a couple innocent men who been framed. Had a guy running from a cult once, another had a contract on his life put out by his *sister*. Can you believe that?"

"My mother has probably thought about it," Tony said, clearing his plate of eggs. "Your family know what you do?"

"My wife knows there's somethin' going on, but she doesn't ask. She just knows every once in a while, I take the RV for a drive and then come back and take her to dinner at some fancy restaurant. When it comes down to it, she's smart enough to know that she don't want to know. We got two grown kids, and they ain't around enough to wonder. They just know about my car shop, and if I die early, they'll just think Daddy wasn't as bad with money as they all thought." Ray shrugged. "Seems to work for all of us."

Tony considered Carmine's reaction to his disappearance and then decided he had considered it enough. Ana was the active parent, the one monitoring his schoolwork, his bedtime, his sports. Tony would have to check in, or Carmine might forget him altogether. He would have to send Benjie over there. He knew if he sent Vito, he would come home to a criminal with bad grades and an attitude problem. "I don't know how much anyone has paid you for this. You mind tellin' me what it costs to get into Canada?"

Ray hesitated as the slim waitress dropped fresh coffee for each man. When she left and Ray regained his focus, he told Tony, "Three thousand dollars minimum for a trip, $1,500 per head after the first. Your bill was two grand as a favor, but I've trucked as many as eight at a time. A trip like that will keep my woman eatin' at fancy restaurants for a long time."

"Same setup every time? How would they fit inside the shitter?"

"Nah. There's one under the bed that'll fit as many as six." Ray laughed at the change in Tony's face. "I didn't want to tell you about that one. A man should earn his salvation, know what I mean?"

Tony spoke through his frown. "If you went more often, would the border patrol get suspicious?"

"I cross the border once a week already. I don't have stowaways every time I visit. Sometimes I just want pancakes or to see a friend of mine."

"You ever get searched? Like a top-to-bottom search?"

Ray set his fork down and leaned back into the cushions. "You got a lot of questions, friend."

"It just seems like a useful skill for a man to have. You're able to cross an international border. That's unique."

Ray's eyes were inscrutable little beads set deep into his wide face, but he seemed to be doing a set of difficult calculations in his head. "If you have a pitch for me, Tony, I'm willin' to listen to it. No promises."

Tony smiled. "The only promise worth makin' is money."

The morning of July 11, 1973
St. Anthony's Cemetery in Brooklyn, NY
"Second place is a death sentence."

St. Anthony's had a small cemetery. It was a small cemetery centuries ago when its first souls were laid to rest, and it was a small, crowded cemetery shortly after. The answer had been depth at first. Families would pay gravediggers to dig as deeply as they could and fortify the holes with bricks and crossmembers of various heights, designs, and distances. Relatives were then stacked, one on top of the other from the water table to the crust, and then sealed at the level of the earth and neglected thereafter except by rot and lichen. It was a solution for a time, and whole generations would come and go without concern for their final resting place. But the living are louder than the dead. With each passing decade, the choked voices grew softer, and their heirs envied the comfort of their eternal seat.

The decision had been simple and inevitable given the urgency of the moment, if still delicate in its execution. Alphonse himself had been among the men who freed the silent bodies and again among those who burned the coffins on the beaches as the tides carried the bones and sand away. Father Bennie secured the Giordano plot not long after so the young couple could be at peace beside each other when the time came.

Funerals were an all too common feature of *Cosa Nostra*, but the advantages of these events were not to be wasted: members could gather without drawing outside attention. And so, the Giordano Family brass used Cristiana's funeral as cover; the timing was too good to miss.

"Al could've done us all a favor and taken care of this beforehand, God rest his soul," Phil said as the coffin was lowered into the ground.

Nick hushed him with a wave. "Keep it down." The sky was bright blue, and the whole scene would have been idyllic if the heat were not melting the mourners beneath their black clothes. Each man swiped at puddles on his brow as they stood a few paces back from the main throng and praying to deftly accomplish their business.

"We have to talk some," Vic answered, a hand on Nick's shoulder. "Now first, just for the record, I don't want the fuckin' job. I'm too damn old. But we need a solution outta this discussion. Anyone here is welcome to put themselves forward. And no fuckin' speeches or shit like that. We all know each other. Now go. Petey?"

"Don't want it."

"Phil?"

Phil leaned forward to look up and down the line. "I would be honored," he said.

"Nick?"

"I want Phil to have it," Nick said with an emphatic swipe of his brow. "God knows he's done as much for this Family as anyone, including—," he tugged his ear, "but I want a promise from you, Phil. I want a promise that you will give the assignment to me when it comes down to it, when we have our end in sight. Promise me that." The line turned to Phil. He allowed himself a moment, then nodded.

"Joey?"

"Nick's right. Phil should have it."

"Johnny?"

"It's not for me. I'm happy to accept whatever decision is reached."

"Okay," Vic said, his voice low, "before we make this official, let's briefly discuss some topics, as a matter of gettin' us on the same page. A Boss, Don Cesare Provenzano, ordered the murder of our leader. His other crimes are well documented and extensive, as we all know, and are an assault on everything we as Men of Honor hold dear. I assume everyone here is in favor of retaliation?" Each man nodded yes. "I figured. Then, the construction…cut out Provenzano is obvious. What about Pisciotto's men? Chuck Esposito in charge over there now. He played no part in our problems."

There was a pause, and the words of Father Bennie hit their ears for a brief moment. Phil spoke over it, "Keep him. The unions and city managers he'll bring are too important. Esposito is a chance to start fresh. We should move forward. We don't have the resources to start stacking enemies against us."

Nick stared across each man's face in the wall of suits. "Fuck 'em all. If we bring him in, it's only a matter of time before he comes with another hand outstretched for us. I'm not sayin' whack him. I'm sayin' keep him out the business."

"C'mon, Nick, you know Chuckie," Petey said. "He didn't have nothin' to do with it. He's been, uh, discontent for years with Pisciotto's dumb ass. C'mon, we can't afford that."

Nick shook his head. "Fuck. Them. All."

Vic stopped them. "All right, we get the point, Nick. Phil already answered the question."

"We gotta button our crews up," Phil said, his hand jabbing the air. "We gotta be tight with our discussion right now. We know the cops are gonna come hard for everyone. The publicity of all this stung them, scared them. They have egg on their faces, and if we're not careful, we might have two wars to fight here."

"More careful than ever," Nick said in agreement. "No tellin' who they're gonna squeeze off the streets. And keepin' people quiet means crackin' down on anyone questionin' their vows, their new vows to Phil. Erase that idea from their fuckin' heads—"

By the time they saw her, it was too late. She was already in front of them, their secret meeting discovered, and Carrie's eyes, tainted by red, were burning through each of them in turn. "YOU'RE GONNA TRY TO PULL THIS SHIT HERE! I WILL ABSOLUTELY—"

"Carrie," Nick begged with a glance over the stunned faces of the others, "please. We're sorry. *You're right about this, Carrie. Do not ruin the funeral because of our stupidity. This should be all about your mother.*"

Carrie took another step forward, and a few in the line leaned back for distance. *"No more, you ignorant assholes,"* she fumed, searching the men's eyes for the ones who understood, *"or there will be consequences. This woman deserves your respect, and I will not ask again."*

One evening in mid July 1973
HQ of Clearwater Investments in Manhattan, NY
"I made his life a living hell."

Adam sat with his hands folded while Mr. Abrams, the architect of the Park Avenue project, presented points of supposed interest on a scale model to him and the assembled members of the Clearwater Board. Despite the details (the model contained real glass windows, a rooftop American flag, window gardens, and two fire escapes) and a two-finger scotch, Adam's enthusiasm was failing him. He realized quickly Abrams's spiel would contain no useful information. The project was on track, the investment was safe, and this man's semi-public calendar reading was entirely unnecessary. Adam, as well as his colleagues, preferred their ignorance of such trivial matters. But they were now caged in the boardroom and resigned to endure this minutia.

Despite several hopeful adjustments in his chair, Adam's lower back began to ache and whatever interest remained left him. He looked to the others and saw their impatient faces, searching for any sign of relief above their black suits and colorful ties and squares. *They will blame me for this idiot. They will do it in silence, but they will blame me.* Adam sipped from his drink, meddled with the buttons of his suitcoat, his pen, and sparse notes, combed his black hair for flyaways, twirled his wedding ring on the table, and used his shoes to scratch an aggravating spot on his shin, all for the benefit of a few moments' distraction. Those attempts ultimately failed, so he allowed himself to stare out the windows at where the Manhattan skyscrapers hit the summer dusk and its thin red shadows. He could almost see his fledgling building against that sky; its path inevitable now, its prominence defined.

The ache in his back overcame his patience, and he rose from his seat (Abrams continued, unfazed) and walked across the dark hardwood to a side table covered by various decanters. He grabbed the twelve-year scotch, poured three fingers this time, and stood there, staring at the blank wall as the tiresome echoes kept on. He collected himself with a breath and a swig before retaking his seat.

Adam could sense the architect's next points were among his last: "The contractors arranged by this Board," he made a gesture of thanks, "to build 234 Park Avenue, which are sure to be the most luxurious apartments and penthouses available in this fine city, have achieved fine progress. The work has been hot, of course, always is, but they seem to be a very capable lot you've found, Mr. Landau. The skill and diligence of the craftsman will make or break this project, I have no doubt."

Adam seized this opportunity. "Then we have already won, Mr. Abrams. We only hire the absolute best. If we acted otherwise, I promise this group would not be quite so wealthy." The financiers chuckled, and Abrams smiled stiffly, perhaps sensing his time in the limelight was facing a mandated close. Adam skirted the table to shake the architect's hand and press his exit. "We appreciate the detailed update, sir. All our fears have been quashed. It's time to let the craftsman, as you say, finish their business." The room clapped Abrams offstage, and Adam steered him to the door with just enough politeness to make him feel appreciated. "I believe the Board has some brief matters to discuss in private," he said as they made for the door, "however, if you wish, help yourself to a drink in the Crescent Room at the end of the hall. Tell Charlie down there, he's the Black man in the white uniform behind the bar, that I sent you. Enjoy a drink and we will all join you momentarily."

"Thank you, Mr. Landau, and very many thanks to the Board for your time." Abrams waved to the board members, all ten of them, before Adam snapped the door shut behind him and spun back to face his colleagues. "If that man ever offers us a detailed account of anything again, for God's sake, we say no." A heartier laugh from the financiers this time.

"Yes, that is the last one of those," came Henry Dalton's voice from his rail-thin body.

"He honestly comes in here and thinks we want to talk about wind dampers?" Louis Ansel said, spilling his drink as he did. "Build the fuckin' thing. Just know, if it falls over, we'll sue your dumb ass."

"I get my information from Roselli," Adam said. "He says we're on track, ahead even."

Eddy Reuter stood and cut his own path to the decanters. Eddy was a robust man, the most senior board member, and his steps rang against the walls. "The more important concerns, Adam, are financial. I have not seen the projections you promised me."

"I explained the delay. It should not be more than a few weeks, getting organized as I said."

Eddy poured his drink during a short silence. The others seemed to have elected him to drive this discussion, Adam could feel it in their shifting eyes. "You did explain the delay," Eddy said, turning back toward the members. "You did not explain the need for this financial management company, Tulles. My lawyer says they were hemorrhaging money just a few months ago. You've thrown them quite a lifeline with this contract."

"They hired Gideon Hayes. He's earned a lifeline."

"Maybe, maybe not. I'm not questioning your decision per se." Eddy smiled broadly. "Just commenting, as I do when things interest me."

Adam kept his tone light, avoiding Dalton's stare in particular. "The projections will be completed, by Gideon himself, in the next few weeks. I will provide them to you all with my comments."

Eddy took a few steps forward, close enough to pat Adam's shoulder with a soft hand. "It's not a problem, stay loose. But save yourself the time. The comments aren't needed, just the data, my good friend." Adam nodded. Eddy continued with a raised glass, "To the success of 234 Park Avenue, luxury living near the heart of American commerce and culture. And yet we ask God, as we embark on this endeavor in earnest, how can we fail?" Then the men laughed together and drank their sweet brown drinks.

* * *

The doorman pulled a blue Bentley T1 to the curb in front of the Clearwater Headquarters, and Henry Dalton's driver took the keys and his place at the wheel. "What a fantastic car," Adam said. He and the banker were the last two left waiting.

"It is." Henry puffed a cigar and breathed smoke rings into the black air without any sign of leaving, despite the car. "It's been a rough few weeks in our dear city, huh? So much violence it makes you wonder what possesses some people to do what they do." He ashed on the sidewalk. "I've wondered, are *you* ever worried, Adam?"

"About what?"

"Don't play coy," Dalton said, scorn disfiguring his face. "You exist in a dangerous world and have just recently lost your benefactor. Your protector, as it were. And I know from experience, mountaintops are lonely, Adam."

"There are many interested in what I do, Henry. I still have friends. Don't doubt their interest or motivation."

Dalton puffed again. "You have fewer than before."

Adam chuckled. "It's more about the quality of my enemies. I believe they are a rather unimaginative lot."

Dalton dropped his cigar at his feet and watched the embers splash the sidewalk. "For your sake, I hope you are correct. I have seen great men shrivel and shiver, paralyzed by their fits of desperation. The other way as well though. I have seen them overreach and fall when they feel they are in positions of real power. I do not want to see you in either circumstance, of course. You are too talented for that."

Adam felt his anger flash, redoubled by the scotch in his veins. "I will not play games with you," he said, staring up into Dalton's eyes. "I still cloak a set of vested interests, and although a man is dead, a *great* man is dead, I am no less favored than I was before. You want to see the monsters I shield? Pull the cloak and see what eyes peer out."

"You are a dramatic soul, Adam."

Adam stamped Dalton's dying cigar with his Ferragamo shoes. "Test me and you'll get to judge the drama for yourself."

One night in July of 1973
Home of Brady Murdock in Staten Island, NY

Allison Murdock was six years old. Her favorite nighttime activity was coloring, and her mother, Barbara Murdock, bought her new, blank coloring books almost every time she went to the store. Allison's favorites were *Captain Kangaroo* coloring books and her favorite character to color was the Dancing Bear, but she never colored him brown like he was on the show. She colored him purple or red or blue and made his stomach yellow or orange or green, depending on her mood. And sometimes she would dress up to match the bear, going to the closet before she started and finding a shirt or dress that matched the vision in her head, before settling in to scribble across the rough white paper. She held the crayons between her middle and ring finger and squeezed the life from them, her knuckles turning yellow and white. Brady watched her from his chair by the door. She would finish a drawing and rip it from the book, sprint to his bony knees and smile up at Daddy as she explained her colors and what the characters were doing and why. Brady would tell her he was going to hang it up at his work (and he often did on the fridge in the breakroom). He would take her drawing, fold it up, and drop it in the front pocket of his dress shirt for safe keeping.

Allison kicked her feet as she colored, and Brady swirled the scotch in his glass while he watched. He ran his finger along the unbuttoned collar of his shirt, pulling it away from the sweat on his neck. The windows were open and the sun was down, but relief was nowhere.

The phone rang, and Brady was quick to react as its rattle echoed off the walls. "I got it," he called for his wife, wherever she was. "Hello," he said, "hey...yeah, no problem. ... Which one? ... Yeah, I know where that's at, I think. ... I don't know, I haven't been over there in years, but I should still be able to find it. ... Yeah, I know...no problem. All right, bye."

"Who was that?" Barbara asked from close behind her husband. He flinched. He had not heard her enter.

"Andy," Brady said, forcing confidence. "There's been a break in one of our cases. I've gotta go meet him."

"Right now?"

"Yes, hun. I'm a detective. These things are time-sensitive."

"Yeah, but on a Sunday night it doesn't mean I can't be frustrated. But fine, whatever. Gimme a kiss." She puckered for a quick peck, but Brady pulled her in close, her hips and chest against his. He ran his thumb over her lips, her head in his hand. "I love you," he said. "You and Ally are my world."

She laughed at him. "Okay, weirdo." She kissed him and felt his neck and chest with her hands before stepping back and patting his cheek. "Go do your job."

Brady turned back into the family room, hugged and kissed his daughter, and left.

* * *

It was a large warehouse and looked abandoned from the outside with a gravel driveway that twisted past the parking lot and around to the back of the building, invisible from the main street.

Brady parked his car next to the only other, a 1970 red-on-black Chevy Chevelle SS 454. He killed the engine and walked through a series of spotlights to the exterior door described to him on the phone and knocked a few times. He was startled by how loud his soft knocks rang out on the other side and stood stiff and exposed in the night air until he heard footsteps clicking across the warehouse floor and the door opened.

"Johnny," Brady said, hugging the half-lit figure of Johnny Giordano in the doorway. "I was so sorry to hear about it, man. I was shocked." They broke apart, and Johnny held him at arm's length, tears welling in his eyes.

"Thanks. Just…thanks. We're good though. We're good. C'mon in."

The two walked past a series of mattress machines, pallets of cotton stuffing, and forklifts to a small office at the back with a single orange lamp that threw long shadows across the floor and walls. Carrie was waiting for them, sitting behind the desk in a high-backed chair. Brady expected her, but his stomach rolled all the same. "I'm so sorry, Carrie," he said. "My condolences."

Carrie combed a few bangs from her eyes, rose, and walked to the front of the desk, leaning back into its front edge and smiling thinly at the detective. "We will do our best. Thank you for coming. I know face-to-face meetings can be nerve-racking."

"No problem. I wanted to, as quickly as possible, but I was afraid any earlier would be too soon. Your family has a lot of eyeballs on it."

"Everything is going to run exactly the same," she said. "Johnny will do almost all the communication. The only other person who knows about you is me. And we want to keep it that way."

"But who's in charge now? With your father gone…"

"We still—"

"Johnny," Carrie snapped, her eyes flashing dangerously between the two men, "there's no reason for him to know any of that."

Johnny shrugged. "She's right."

"No, sorry," Murdock said, waving the idea away. "I wasn't prying. I just…it was just a question."

Carrie continued, her tone sharp. "We do trust you, Brady, of course, but there is no need for you to have that information. You should keep doing everything as you have been. Don't stick your neck out. The most important thing is you stay available to us. Every move we make should proceed with absolute caution, no panic. You should be a good cop, solve cases, get promoted if you fuckin' can. If we can help, we will." Carrie paused, running a nail across the surface of the desk as she rounded its corner and sat again in the high-backed chair. "I would think, with all that's happened, you may have some things to tell us."

Murdock nodded. Her words, her tone, were familiar to the detective's ears. "Yes, I do. For one, they're closin' in on Nick Pisani for the Benfield job. The FBI is working on a warrant to at least bug Pisani's hangouts based on the information from the rat I gave you. I would not be surprised to see him arrested soon. The FBI knows your name too," Murdock pointed to Johnny, "but our witness never said it, thank God. He only ID'd Pisani, or you'd be on their warrant too. After that ID, I removed any stakeout pictures with your face in them."

"What rat?" Carrie asked.

"Luparelli."

"Oh," she said, "I see." She pressed forward slightly, her arms resting on the desk. "What do they know about the two shootings?"

"Not a lot, but obviously everyone is on high alert. Luparelli told us *Pisciotto and Provenzano* were about to get hit and my partner reached out to the Feds beforehand, although they didn't take him seriously. When those two names came across, they lit up the switchboard. NYPD, FBI, everybody. And then your dad's name was swirling around as a potential conspirator, and then *he* gets killed right after. Everyone is desperate for answers. That's why I'm so worried about this Pisani guy. They're gonna want to nail his ass to the wall for anything they can and press him for answers."

"Nick can do some time if he has to."

"Carrie," Johnny started, "we can't just hang him out there—"

"We won't. I didn't say we'd hang him out there. We'll take care of it, but if he has to sit in a cell for a while, so fuckin' be it. This isn't the time to be sticking our nose into any federal investigations, any of us here. He may be safer inside anyway."

"I know it's not my place," Murdock said, "but I'd warn you, I think the FBI knows more than they've said to us. I think you guys should be careful until I can find out more, if I can ever find out more. There are two agents, Clerow Wilson and Gregg Meriwether, and I'm not close enough to give you much on them yet. Maybe we can work the situation, but right now, I'm frozen out."

"You're right about us laying low," Johnny said, "but there's more at stake here than some heat from the cops. My Father's name. Our Father's name. This shit cannot go unanswered."

"How bad is it going to be?"

Johnny chuckled, nervously. "Bad, man, bad."

"You have a daughter, right?" Carrie asked, eyes cold and leveled on the detective.

"Yeah."

"I'd move," she said, calm in the orange glow of the office light, "'cause I'm going to kill whoever did this to my family, and they'll have to burn this whole fuckin' city down to stop me."

About the Author

JR Hazard currently lives in the Midwest, where he dutifully records the conversations of individuals who exist only in his mind. This is the all-consuming passion of his life, which would make him insane had someone not agreed to publish this book. He appreciates the cover this affords him.

Of Empire and Illusion is the first novel in a three-part arc about the Giordano Crime Family. Book Two is expected to be available by the end of 2022.

CPSIA information can be obtained
at www.ICGtesting.com
Printed in the USA
LVHW091529181121
703614LV00017B/106